NET
FORCE
DARK
WEB

NET
FORCE
DARK
WEB

A NOVEL

SERIES CREATED BY
TOM CLANCY and
STEVE PIECZENIK
WRITTEN BY
JEROME PREISLER

HANOVER
SQUARE
PRESS

**HANOVER
SQUARE
PRESS**

Recycling programs
for this product may
not exist in your area.

ISBN-13: 978-1-335-91784-3

Net Force: Dark Web

Copyright © 2019 by Netco Partners

Library of Congress Cataloging-in-Publication Data has been applied for.

HanoverSqPress.com
BookClubbish.com

Printed in U.S.A.

In memory of Martin H. Greenberg

NET
FORCE
DARK
WEB

"What unites us is far greater than what divides us."
—President John F. Kennedy

"Life is a balance between holding on and letting go."
—Rumi

"I think we should be very careful about artificial intelligence."
—Elon Musk

PROLOGUE

Outside Valletta, Malta
June 30, 2023

I

Kali Alcazar sat at her laptop, the LED monitor rinsing her thin, angular features with its bluish cast. Candles flickered, their soft light dancing over the room's centuries-old sandstone walls. The house was quiet tonight, and she could hear the whisper of the incoming tide in the distance. On the terrace outside, the tomcat belonging to the owners of the rooming house sat with its tail curled around its haunches, its ears perked, gazing watchfully down at the gently swaying palm trees and the shadows they cast in the moonlight.

Keying in her cloud password, Kali went to the blockchain-encrypted storage folder she shared with Lucien Navarro, deciding to give the cracked data files another look before she sent them on. She began to read them, wholly focused on the screen, but keeping the gentle beat of the Mediterranean surf at her center.

Always at her center.

She had returned to the island—her grandmother had simply called it that, The Island—once a year since childhood. There were two exceptions, bound by her seventeenth and eighteenth birthdays, but she preferred not to revisit that dark, painful time.

Kali carried her memories inside her but would not let them become burdens. The heavier ones could only weigh her down if she failed to accept them, and she would have changed very few of the choices she'd made in her twenty-six years on earth. Her victories, failures, good decisions, missteps…she was the sum total of her experiences. Reverse a path, undo this or that, and she would be a different person.

She knew who she was and felt easy in her skin.

Now she read the bank files, page after page, the documents cross-referenced and hyperlinked to her notes. The stain on Volke Bank went deeper than the vicious Koenig and his puppet board of directors at NORN Aeronautics. They had been exposed, yes. But the bank's web of money laundering operations was stunningly vast. She had traced its radials to politicians and financial institutions in Moscow, London, and the United States…and to narco-traffickers, arms smugglers, and even the treasuries of outlaw governments. Volke had been washing money and expanding its contacts for years. While international regulators looked the other way, the strands of its illicit transactions were deftly interwoven with its legitimate dealings.

Kali scrolled down the screen. She had plucked a thread leading to Bank Leonides out of the complex tangle. With its ties to the Russian oligarchs, and shadowy cryptocurrency dealings, Leonides was one of the most corrupt financial institutions on the planet…but she had done what she could to sort through the facts, and was leaving it to others to do the rest. The information mined from Koenig's records would make for enough red faces on both sides of the Atlantic. The criminal, the merely lax…they all shared in the guilt.

Reaching the bottom of the page, Kali opened another

browser window, logged on to an anonymous remailer, and started to attach the files.

She was interrupted by someone knocking on her door. Three raps in hurried succession. Suddenly alert, she realized the knocks were on its lower panel. *Guzzepi,* she thought. An instant later she heard his high, excited voice out on the landing.

"Ku-sister! Ku-sister!"

She rose from her chair, went to the door, unlatched it, and pulled it partially open.

The boy was out there in his pajamas, looking up at her, trying to catch his breath.

"Guzzepi…what's wrong?"

He kept staring at her, his brown eyes wide with concern. She flicked a glance past him and down the curved staircase, then returned her attention to his face.

"Hurry," she said. Opening the door the rest of the way, waving him into the apartment. "Come inside."

The nine year old entered, stopping just inside, standing barefoot on the wooden floor.

She knelt so their eyes were level. "Ku-bro," she said. "Tell me."

He swallowed. "Two men," he said, his voice trembling. "They asked *Omm* about you."

"Did you get a look at them?"

"I was in my room…watching television…"

His eyes suddenly glistened with tears. She reached out and touched her palm to his cheek.

"Easy. It's okay," she said, smiling at him. "Ku-bro…these men…you're sure there were only two? No others outside?"

"I don't know. I—I did not see them."

"But you heard their voices. The ones who spoke to your mother."

"Yes." He swallowed. "I think they were Americans. They told *Omm* they knew you were here."

"And what did she tell them?"

"That you were in the beach house," he said. "When they left, she came to my room. She said I was to hurry upstairs. And let you know."

"That they'd gone to find me in the beach house?"

"Yes."

She nodded, thinking. "Where's *Omm* now, ku-bro?"

"Downstairs. She watches the door. In case the men return."

Another nod. She held her hand against his cheek another moment, smiling a little. "Wait here," she said. "I need to take care of some things."

She stood and went to the terrace. When she stepped outside, the tomcat moved lithely over to her, purring as it brushed against her arm.

Kali scratched behind its ears, looking down into the inner garden one story below. There was no movement in the shadows—or none she could see. But she could picture them clearly in her mind. The Blond Man…he would be out there with them. He had led the hunt since the beginning.

She took a breath of night air, smelling the brine of the sea. The beach house was a good hundred yards across the dunes from the front entrance. If they were heading over that way, she might have enough time.

Turning inside, she went to the walk-in closet and got into a pair of black knee-high riding boots, lacing them up over her leggings. Then she grabbed her backpack off the floor. It held some clothing, and she could always buy more. She would leave everything else except the computer. None of it mattered to her. She wasn't attached to her belongings, not even the laptop, and kept all her vital data encrypted in cloud storage. But the computer was her way in. Her portal.

She hastened across the room to it, clicked Send, closed its lid, and slid the machine into her backpack. Then she shouldered the pack and returned to Guzzepi, crouching in front of him again.

"Where are you going?" he asked. His throat was clenched with sadness and fear. "Those men will hurt you."

"No." She shook her head. "They can't."

"Ku-sister... *Kali...*"

"Shh. Listen to me." She leaned close, took hold of his shoulders, and dropped her voice to a whisper. "What did I tell you when you were little...practically the size of your cat? About when I leave here for a time?"

He looked at her, swallowing hard. "That you aren't truly leaving."

"And where can you always find me?"

He touched his hand to the middle of his chest, the tears spilling from his eyes now.

"Here," he said, sniffling. His hand remained on his chest. "In my heart."

"There you go, brave one." Smiling then, she leaned closer still. "Take care of *Omm*. Send her my thanks for her kindness and generosity. I intend to repay it someday."

He stood there looking at her. "Will I see you again, Kali?"

She controlled her expression. "After I close the door behind me, count to fifteen," she said. "Then go back to your room, okay?"

He nodded.

Kali smiled, squeezed his shoulders, and kissed him, once, briefly, on his forehead. Closing her eyes as she breathed in the mingled scents of his skin and hair. *This I take with me*, she thought.

Then she got up, stepped to the door, and went racing downstairs.

II

At the foot of the stairs, Kali pushed through the door into the inner garden, glanced left and right, saw no one, and dashed across the flagstones to its low north wall. With her violet-streaked black hair, black clothes, and black boots, she was a shadow among shadows as she propped her hands on the bricks and then scuffled over the wall into the adjacent alley.

She took a deep breath, looked around again, peering into the moonlit gloom. She thought she knew why the two men had come for her—or at least knew who they represented. It was only a hunch, and she might be wrong, but she didn't believe so. Munich had been a close call.

What she couldn't know was how many more of them there were…or where they would be. Assuming there *were* others.

She felt no desire to stay here long enough to find out.

She sprinted up the village lane, turning onto another, and another, staying off the sidewalks, where the recessed doorways lining them would be convenient places for someone to hide. She was headed south, zigzagging toward the city of Valletta. If she continued in that direction, stayed more or less parallel to the main road leading from the coast to the Portes des Bombes—the double archways marking the capital's ancient defensive line— she might find a place to wait out the night and then lose herself amid its morning crowds.

Kali's tall, thin frame cut through the streets, avoiding the pale throw of the streetlamps. She breathed rhythmically, letting her body set its own pattern, nimble on her feet despite her boots and the weight of her backpack. Tiny Pietà was dark and silent, the shadows cloaking its alleys as black as indigo, its stores closed, no shoppers, no strolling pedestrians, no traffic—

She stopped cold. *No traffic.* No cars on the street, no buses running. Yet she could hear a moving vehicle. It was a short distance off, the twisting streets and gaping archways tossing the sound of its engine about in aimless ricochets, making it hard to tell where it was coming from.

She stood listening a second. Two. Her heart pounding in her chest. The noise was rapidly getting louder, closer…

Up ahead. It was coming from the cross street ahead of her. There was no mistaking it. She heard it approaching from her right, the vehicle's wheels rolling over the cobbled roadway.

She glanced over her left shoulder, where an alley ran between two columned, weathered structures—a bank and department store that had been administrative buildings once upon a time under Napoleon. Most of Pietà's oldest buildings were connected, but the colonial architecture was different. The Europeans had liked their footpaths and carriageways.

Kali could slip into the alley, wait there for the car to pass. It might have no connection to the men back at the rooming house. It might drive on through the intersection and keep going, the sound of its engine fading in the night. But instinct told her otherwise.

She turned to retrace her steps along the street, thinking she could take another route to the capital…and then drew in a sharp breath. *So much for that.* There were two men jogging toward her from that direction, silhouetted in the glow of the streetlamps. How had they found her? Guessed where she was heading? Known which *path* she would take?

She barely had time to ask herself those questions before the thrum of an accelerating engine turned her back around toward the corner. The jogging men weren't the only ones who had tracked her down. The vehicle she'd heard, a dark Audi Q7, was veering onto the street off the intersection, its high beams splashing the buildings nearest the corner, then swinging toward her.

Trapped between the running men and the Audi, she looked over at the bank again. Even the locals would find Pietà's network of alleyways confusing at night, but she had no choice. She would have to trust that she could find her way through them.

Turning on her heels, she ran into the alley's mouth.

III

As Kali took flight, she heard the car screech to a halt, heard its doors opening, heard passengers getting out. Then multiple sets of footsteps in the alley behind her. She thought there were at least four of them chasing her, but could not risk looking back.

They were breathing down her neck.

Running fast, she reached a bend, ran on for several feet, came up to a thigh-high wooden fence, and vaulted over it into a back alley, knocking down several trash cans. Refuse spilled everywhere as she tenuously kept her balance.

One, two, three, four, she heard her pursuers jump the fence behind her and land noisily amid the upended garbage cans, banging and rattling through the trash-strewn obstacle course, the clamor awakening people in the buildings on either side of the alley. Lights flickered on, windows flew open, and confused, alarmed tenants thrust their heads out into the night to see what was happening below.

The tumult had momentarily slowed the men down, and she took advantage of it. Sweating profusely in the humid air, salt stinging her eyes, Kali plunged into a narrow walkway between two buildings and ran. She could see that it opened to a side street a few yards ahead, and was thinking that if she just could just get clear of the knot of alleys, get out onto the street, she would be able to gain her bearings, decide where to go from there. Find a way to put some distance between herself and her pursuers.

Her chest heaving with exertion, long legs working, she pushed on toward the sidewalk…and had almost reached it when she felt a hand grasp at her backpack. She clenched her teeth, willing herself to run faster, managing to briefly pull away. But then she heard a loud grunt of effort, the sound almost in her ear. The hand shot out again, this time grabbing one of the backpack's shoulder straps, yanking hard.

She jerked backward, spinning around on her heels. As her pursuer's arms locked around her, Kali caught a glimpse of his broad, blunt features and smartglasses, and knew she'd seen him before. She had time enough to wonder if the other man was with him—the blond-haired man.

Then she suspended all thought, letting muscle memory take over, letting herself *react*. She would be unable to match this one's strength. Instead she relied on her momentum and the element of surprise. As he pulled her toward him, she shifted her weight slightly and slipped her left hand behind his back, then grabbed his arm with her right while pivoting on the ball of her foot. Thrusting out a hip, using it for leverage, Kali pulled him over it, *rolled* him over it, bringing her knee up between his legs, hard into his groin. He stumbled forward, groaning in pain, and then sank to the pavement.

She shot past him onto the street, her eyes searching for familiar landmarks. To her left, the street sloped steeply down toward a small plaza, the wide stone stairs at the far end descending to the waterfront. The alleys had taken her well north of her original route toward the capital.

She sprinted toward the plaza without a backward glance, her tank top clinging to her body. There were fewer footsteps behind her now, but she could still hear them, and was sure at least two men had stayed with her. Their nearness was practically a physical sensation, a spreading coldness under her skin that made her arms break into goose bumps.

She reached the plaza in seconds, darted past a circular fountain, and then half ran, half leaped down the stairs. She could see the water of the harbor inlet spreading out before her, its surface spangled with reflected light—moonlight, starlight, quay lights, lights from the cargo ships wending across the water and the yachts resting at anchor in the marina. At the foot of the stairs and across a blacktopped road were bastions carved out of the hillside by ancient Muslims to repel the Barbary pirates, a tall watchtower commanding the fortification's highest point. Beyond the parapets of the wall was a descending band of darkness she recognized as il-Ġnien tal-Milorda—Her Ladyship's Garden, built during a subsequent round of foreign occupation. There were palm trees, shrubs, circuitous paths leveling down to the shore…

The garden's main gate was locked now after dark, but once, during a solitary walk, she had found a way up the landward side of the wall into the garden. If she could reach it, get to the garden, she might be able to lose her pursuers, then continue down to the harbor and hide among the quays and warehouses.

It hadn't been her plan. But now she felt it was her best chance.

Taking the last two or three steps with a running bound, Kali made for the wall.

IV

She filled her lungs with air and ran, so close to the wall that she scraped her elbow against it, pushing on with a burst of re-newed speed, wanting to put more distance between herself and the figures at her rear. She was coming up to the niche in the fortification she had found that long-ago day, the entrance to the walkway leading up to its ramparts. And she meant to be as far ahead of them as possible when she reached it.

Hurry, she urged herself. *Hurry!*

She spotted it then. At last. Just a foot or two ahead, barely visible. In the tarry darkness, she didn't think they would see it, or even see her duck into it. Once they realized she had dis-appeared, they would double back along the wall to look for her, and only then might they find it. But she was praying that wouldn't be until after she climbed to the top of the wall and down the other side into the garden.

Finally reaching it, she turned sharply into the entryway, into the wall, and discerned the flight of worn stairs ascending to the walk.

With another silent prayer, Kali raced up them as fast as her legs would carry her.

V

She emerged from the passage onto the walkway, fifty feet above the road now, the deteriorated medieval battlements on the seaward side of the wall resembling a row of loose, chipped teeth. A few feet to her right, the walkway slanted down to the uppermost terrace of il-Ġnien tal-Milorda. On her left, it climbed farther upward to a *guardiola*—a watchtower meant for a lone sentry.

She started right, toward the garden descent...and then froze.

She had heard a barely audible buzz overhead. The sound reminded her of a radio-controlled airplane, only quieter.

Kali peered up into the night sky—and her eyes widened. The aircraft came gliding over the wall like a nocturnal bird of prey. There were no running lights on its tubular frame, no external moving parts.

Of course, she thought with sudden realization.

She lowered her gaze and sliced it toward the stairwell. The men had appeared atop the wall, three of them, blocking her path to the gardens. All wore smartglasses like their companion in the alley.

They had marked her position all along, the stealthy UAV streaming images to their glasses. An air cushion variant, the drone was likely amphibious. It would have launched from somewhere off the beach on a satellite command, tracking her through every twist and turn as far back as the cottage.

Kali stared at the men, her heart pounding. They moved toward her along the walkway, closing in on her with slow strides. They did not have to run, and they knew it.

She whirled around and broke for the watchtower.

VI

The crenellated watchtower was at the wall's northeast corner, and Kali scampered past the weeds sprouting on either side of the walkway to reach it, bits of crumbled mortar and stone gritting underfoot. She ran up to a tiny landing, mounted another two steps, and then was standing in its entry.

She hurried in, her eyes sweeping its circular walls. A calm, detached part of her mind clicked away like a camera shutter. She would remember the windows looking out in every direction, moonlight pouring through them, brushing the graffiti scratched onto the tower's bricks with its faint silver luminosity. She would remember having the vague thought that, in faded, braver times, a solitary knight would light a torch here to warn his fellow watchmen along the coastline of a siege.

As she tore her backpack off her shoulders, she would also remember seeing the drone fly past the tower, throwing its sleek shadow across its curved interior walls.

Rushing to one of the seaward windows, she flung her pack through it into the dark. They would surely recover it from the hillside. Their nightbird might even detect its presence, its precise location. But she would make nothing simple for these men.

She turned toward the entry, then, to face them.

"Hands up over your head," said the tall one in the lead. "Up!"

Kali stared at them in silence.

They were holding firearms at their sides—small, stubby semiautomatic pistols. As the lead man moved closer, walking up the stairs, her eyes rose to his face.

The Blond Man. No surprise.

"I said get those hands up!" he said from the entry. *"Up!"*

She made a hissing sound and snatched the wrist of his gun hand, digging her fingers into it. He countered immediately with his free hand, striking an openhanded blow to her cheek that sent her stumbling onto the tower floor.

"You are now in the custody of the United States government," he said, kneeling over her, holding the pistol between them. "And, lady, let me tell you, you should thank the sun, moon, and stars it isn't somebody else."

BOOK I

THE MAN IN THE MIDDLE

1

New York City, USA/Satu Mare, Romania
July 1–5, 2023

I

From the moment she got out of bed that morning, Stella Vasile had been compiling a mental list of the things she would miss about New York. Hamburgers came to mind at once—nothing back home rivaled a thick, juicy American burger washed down with a cold glass of beer. Chinese restaurants, Indian, Mexican, Japanese...she wouldn't see many of them, either. Stella had thought about her favorite boutiques; she would miss the window shopping, their wide selection of name brand clothing, accessories and cosmetics. She also found herself thinking about the movie theaters within walking distance of her Chelsea apartment, and the countless bars where she would join her coworkers and acquaintances—she had no true friends—for drinks after work.

The best part of this city was its variety, she mused. In Romania, the *technologie vampiri*, as the authorities called them—with a disdain that was at least 50 percent envy—possessed immeasurable fortunes, built luxurious homes, drove the most exotic cars. But they could not find an open convenience store after eight o'clock at night.

Stella would have to get used to that all over again, but it was an acceptable downside. She'd reached a point in life where her priorities had to be put in order.

Checking the time on her smartphone, she saw that it was almost ten in the morning and watched for her expected email notification. The badge appeared at ten on the dot, her brother Emil punctual as usual. She could picture him seated beside Drajan Petrovik, awaiting his nod of approval. The two of them together, inseparable since childhood.

Opening the message, she read her assigned username and password, both of which would only be valid for fifteen minutes. Then she scrolled to the bottom, thumbed an embedded hyperlink, waited as the login screen appeared, and entered the information from the email.

An instant later she was taken to the download page. On it was a single button that read:

HEKATE

She pressed the button, waited again. As the status bar appeared, a call came in on her desk phone and she picked up.

"Berne Financial."

"Stella, it's Chloe. Any fires?"

"Everything's quiet," Stella told her boss. "No worries."

"Good, good. Listen, I need you to call Adrían and confirm our appointment for next week."

Stella checked the calendar on her computer. "Tuesday, eleven o'clock?"

"Right. At the office. Then lunch on me. Come to think, would you also make reservations for two at Monello's? Tell them we'd like a garden table."

Stella returned her attention to her phone. The download was complete.

"I'll take care of it right away," she said.

After calling the restaurant, Stella snatched up the smartphone again and rose from behind the reception desk. Then she strode to the suite's main entrance and locked it. She turned toward an inner door near her desk and went through into Chloe Berne's office.

The computer was idling quietly, its screensaver showing animated mermaids. Stella had always been annoyed by the ridiculous scene—here, at last, was something she would not miss.

She leaned over the keyboard, tapped it, and the underwater fantasy vanished. Enabling her phone's Bluetooth connection, she paired it to the computer, transferred the Hekate bundle, dragged and dropped it into the computer's main system directory, and then installed its archive with a click of the mouse.

Done, she thought when her installation was complete. The original operating system soon would be replaced by a mimic—one that was a teeming nest of malware.

Back at her desk moments later, Stella opened its top drawer and looked over the few personal items she kept inside. There was a makeup kit, a hairbrush, a bottle of hand cream, her prescription allergy meds, a rain poncho in a clear plastic case... nothing indispensable. Still, she transferred the allergy pills and makeup to her handbag, then decided to include the brush. That was it.

Stella clasped the bag shut. When she left work at the end of the day, it would be for the final time.

Unexpectedly, she realized that she would miss her job a little too.

II

"I have the machine all set for you...don't know why it's making so much noise," Chloe Berne said, and motioned toward her desktop computer. The CPU fan had been humming away since she'd arrived. "Guess this dinosaur's just about seen its day."

Adrían Soto smiled a bit absently. Chloe had been his business attorney for two decades, a close friend much longer. Since before Baghdad, and Malika.

Soto moved behind the desk. He had waited an eternity to let himself believe—truly believe in his *bones*—that his Dream with a capital *D* was finally about to come true. Pragmatic to the extreme, he always digested the realities that affected him like a cow chewing its cud. That hard-nosed, methodical nature had proven his salvation after the violence that took Malika from him. But it was no sure thing after his final deployment with CECOM, the army's Communications-Electronics Command. Back in the States, consumed by grief and loss, Soto's thoughts had swung between suicide and retribution, the two sometimes merging into the darkest of visions.

Those feelings nearly ate him alive. But as time went by, his happy memories prevailed. He would recall Malika's voice, so reflective of her moods, low and husky when she was serious, girlishly high when accompanied by her laughter. He would remember her love of singing and music, her dreams of coming to America and teaching young kids…and of having children of her own as his wife.

Soto's business, his innovations—they satisfied a passion that had burned within him since childhood. But the Unity Project was conceived in her honor. A light that sprang from the deep chasm of darkness that had been her death.

Relax. Believe. Good things will come to you…

"Adrían."

He felt Chloe's hand touch his arm.

"She's watching somewhere," the attorney said gently. "I know it."

Soto was thoughtful. When he started Unity, his expectations had been modest—it was hard enough making it through a single day to look too far into the future. Despite the lightning success of Cognizant Systems, the comtech company he'd formed only a few years prior with two civilian members of his old C4ISR team, he was slow and methodical in advancing its growth.

Those cautious principles also applied to the foundation. Unity's first center of operations was a leased storefront on East 114th Street, its secondhand desks occupied by volunteers. Soto's mission statement of bringing together people of different religious, ethnic, and socioeconomic backgrounds through what he called "participative enlightenment"—a donor-friendly term for organizing group activities to benefit the community—had evolved even as he put it into tangible form. He held a steady course, moving forward one step at a time.

In a similarly restrained fashion, Soto had curbed his excitement on the hot August night that the foundation hit its financial benchmark for securing a new home. He kept his cool through the late autumn, even after finding the perfect piece of real estate in the same East Harlem neighborhood where he was raised. Only after closing the deal one snowy morning in late March had he acknowledged it was all real—and even then Soto tried to stay calm and levelheaded.

Today, though...

Today, it was difficult to control his emotions. Malika had spoken often of the nine heavens. He wasn't even sure about the existence of an afterlife, a single heaven from which she could look down on him. He didn't *know* if she was watching. But he could feel her presence. She was with him, today, somehow.

"Go on, Adrían," Chloe said, motioning to her desk. "Life gave you the lemons. Now it's time to make some lemonade."

Soto's eyes grew distant. Once upon a time, he might have gone for an ironic version of the adage involving a bottle of tequila and some salt. But not now. There was nothing sour about this most special benchmark in his life, this moment he had planned and executed to perfection.

Soto lowered himself into Chloe's chair, reached for his wallet, and produced his online banking smartcard, preparing to transfer fifty million dollars into the escrow account established for the center's construction. After a moment he took a deep breath. *"Amor mìo, hago esto por ti, y para ti."*

The attorney's eyes were question marks. He caught her silent look, offered her a faint, reflective smile.

"A private toast of sorts," he said. "The truth, Chloe, is that I'm drinking from the sweetest of cups this morning."

She smiled, asking no further explanation as Soto typed in his financial institution's web address.

Five thousand miles away, in Satu Mare, Romania, Drajan Petrovik moved in for the kill.

III

Waiting in front of his laptop, Petrovik had asked Carla to bring him his *cafea turceasca* with a shot of chilled raki to chase it down. His earphones in place, he was listening to the staccato thunder of Apocalyptica's "Betrayal/Forgiveness," with its furious electric cellos and thundering drums.

It was 11:15 a.m. in New York, 7:15 p.m. Bucharest time, when a screen notification alerted him that his mark, Adrían Soto, was online. Petrovik lifted the coffee from its tray, sniffing the strong, full aroma. After a moment he took a sip and then tossed back the raki chaser, savoring the collisions of heat and cold in his mouth, enjoying the way the anise-flavored spirit laced through the coffee's sweetness.

Drajan had two open browser windows in front of him, the larger one showing exactly what Soto saw on his screen—a spoof site to which the businessman had been redirected. The spoof displayed a security certificate from a hacked Certification Authority, so the HTTPS protocol used by legitimate financial institutions would appear in Soto's address bar. Drajan knew the nonsecure HTTP protocol—minus the *S* at the end—would reveal a fraudulent site to any observant target; Soto warranted the extra measure of deception.

Drajan shifted his attention to a smaller window on the left side of his screen. One of the first tool kits to unpack from Hekate was a Remote Access Trojan, and it had activated the distant computer's webcam. He could see Soto's face clearly in his new window.

The businessman had chosen to input the transfer information himself rather than delegate it to his attorney. Although it wasn't something Petrovik necessarily expected, it made him glad he had obtained the valid security certificate. Success was in the details.

He drank more of the coffee, thinking. When Stella installed Hekate on Chloe Berne's machine, it had burrowed deep into its registry, running its stealthy exploits, opening a back door for him to push in the rest of his tools.

As he toured the hard drive, Petrovik had found the attorney's life a well-ordered bore. She kept photo albums of her apartment, her summer home, her two cats, her travels, and her family…which included a teenage daughter who was recently accepted to Brown University, and an ex-husband with whom she made several unsuccessful attempts at reconciliation. Her romantic life was a void. She had recently subscribed to a dating service for upscale professionals.

Petrovik had soon accessed her clients' financial files, easily defeating the machine's basic, out-of-the-box encryption. Though Berne did not store Soto's banking passwords—Drajan would have been surprised to find them there—Hekate's probes were able to sniff out the financial institution for Cognizant Systems *and* the Unity Project, a commercial bank called H&L Trust. After identifying H&L's online banking platform, it injected a payload of sleeper malware into its system.

All this occurred while Petrovik was sifting through the computer's data files. Then, as Soto typed the web address for his bank, Hekate had split his connection, bouncing him away from the site to a command-and-control botnet, or zombie server, in Belgium. That in turn redirected him to the spoof website hosted by a North Korean zombie. The double redirects made it difficult for anyone to trace the host network's IP addresses, and thus its physical location.

Petrovik had now successfully hijacked Soto's transaction. It was automatic up to that point, Hekate obeying its programmed imperatives, going through its electronic life cycle. But he would take an active part in the next phase of his double-blind. It always made Petrovik's adrenaline flow and rescued him from the tedium of computer work.

He drained the remainder of his coffee, lowered the cup onto its saucer, and leaned forward to study the businessman's face in a smaller browser window. What was Soto called in the news stories? *La Piedra*. The Rock of East Harlem. His broad, strong jaw, his prominent cheekbones, his self-assured expression…the nickname suited him well.

The fee Petrovik had demanded for his services was a million up front, US dollars, with a generous slice of the larger pie on execution, and Koschei didn't balk. But the Russians wanted more than to hit Soto's pocket. They meant to personally wound him, and that made the operation more gratifying. There was pleasure in taking a chunk out of such a perfect stone.

He turned to Emil. "Are you ready?"

Emil nodded, staring at H&L Trust's authentic login screen on his computer. Seated at the workstation to Petrovik's right, concentration making his pale, narrow face look even more gaunt than usual, he absently fingered the tunnel plug in his left ear—a stylized Mayan skull with diamond chip eyes and a mouth made of small red rubies.

Petrovik shrugged inwardly. These moments always made Emil anxious. Only when the job was done would he let himself relax. Petrovik suspected he would then indulge in something far more potent than coffee and spirits. Biohacking's edgy cachet among the *technologie vampiri* had become the basis of a trend throughout Europe, and was quickly flashing over the Atlantic to the United States.

Drajan was hardly a stranger to the cybermod underground. He was a silent partner in a Bucharest stim club, and had been tempted by the radical sensory, perceptual, and cognitive en-

hancements delivered by a combination of neural filament implants and nootropic drug cocktails. But the burnout rate for
users of the latest nootropics was high—and all too noticeable
in their sunken eyes and drawn, colorless faces. The communal
altered states that were a backroom trend at the clubs accelerated
the process; a person could only sustain the prefrontal cortex and
central nervous system overload for so long. There was evidence
that it could lead to a complete breakdown of self-identity...an
induced somatoparaphrenia that, as it progressively worsened,
could make someone forget what his own face looked like in the
mirror, look at his arm or leg without knowing it was attached
to him, or even confuse someone else's body with his own.

Petrovik was not Emil's keeper. Whatever their bond, their
common history, Emil was responsible for Emil. His indulgences
would only become Petrovik's concern if they began to affect
Emil's performance. So far, they had not. But Petrovik always
kept a close eye on him.

Returning his attention to the spoof page, he saw that Soto
had entered the Unity Project's system, and was typing his personal ID and password into separate input fields. Although they
appeared as asterisks on Soto's duplicate screen—as they would
on the real one—Petrovik could clearly read the alphanumeric
characters on his own monitor.

He angled his laptop so that Emil could see the code words
and type them into their fields. An instant later, Emil's login
advanced to a second screen that read:

PLEASE INSERT CARD AND ENTER RANDOM
VERIFICATION NUMBER SENT TO READER

```

```

Petrovik typed on his keyboard. Soto's bank used an RVN
security layer, in which a one-time numerical code was spon-

taneously generated and sent to a card reader for authentication. He would reproduce the RVN request on his fraudulent login.

The fake RVN request appeared on the spoof, looking identical to the authentic request on Emil's screen. Petrovik sat back in his chair and watched through the hijacked webcam as Soto put his card into the reader, obtained his RVN, and typed it into the computer.

Repeating the number to Emil, Petrovik waited while he entered it into his input field. The screen changed to Adrían Soto's account transaction page. They were in, logged on as Soto.

"All right," Petrovik said. "Freeze him."

IV

The popup notification in front of Soto read:

WE ARE EXPERIENCING HIGH USAGE SYSTEM DELAYS, THANK YOU FOR YOUR PATIENCE

Below was a digital time counter.

APPROXIMATE WAIT 6:00 MINUTES

Soto looked at the screen. "Wouldn't you know," he said, frowning.

"The Fourth of July weekend's over." Chloe shrugged. "I guess we're back to business as usual."

V

Even as the false SYSTEM DELAY notice appeared in front of Soto, Petrovik opened a third window on his laptop and hastily dialogued with the Korean zombie. The zombie, in turn, established an immediate connection with H&L Trust's web server. Hekate's python scripts and sniffer applications had been working their way through the banking platform for three days, the pythons spreading their attack algorithms through its layers like egg clusters.

Now the eggs hatched on Petrovik's command, flooding the system with web bots.

He clicked his touchpad. One window shrank and a new one opened, showing a map of the dataflow through H&L's internal network. Green flow lines represented a normal volume of data moving through the portals, orange lines the portals experiencing heavier-than-usual flows, red lines those in critical overload. Rapidly changing numerical values alongside the colored lines revealed the specific type and volume of data entering each portal.

Petrovik saw the effects of his bot swarm within seconds. One after another, the vast majority of green lines turned orange, then bright red.

His eyes focused, lips compressed, he dipped his head in an almost imperceptible nod of satisfaction. Hekate was performing beautifully. The system was signaling it was under an all-out assault.

He hoped the alarm flares would be noticed by those who were supposed to guard against such things.

In fact, he was betting on it.

VI

Alex Michaels looked at his baby girl with pride and affection, thinking she seemed ready.

"*A'kou!*" he ordered, the nylon lead in his hand. He left plenty of slack, its uncoiled length in a straight line behind him.

A large *Koerklasse I* German shepherd, Julia briefly met his gaze with her intelligent brown eyes. Then she was off on the trail. Her body language showed motivation and confidence, but not too much excitement.

Just right, Alex thought. He could almost always tell which ones would make good service dogs and was convinced she had what it took—more than any of the rest he was training. There was a special quality about Julia. He'd sensed it when she was still a pup.

At nineteen months old, Julia had one month to go before she was judged for her SchH2 intermediate training certificate. The trial would have three distinct phases—obedience, protection, and tracking—and Alex figured she had the first two in the bag.

But the tracking phase had some singular aspects. It was the only Schutzhund—or "protection dog"—trial in which the dog's training ran contrary to instinct. Their genetic predisposition was not to keep their noses to the ground. As hunters, they were hard wired to sniff the ground *and* air for traces of their prey. When a dog sniffed a footprint while tracking, it was mostly smelling the disturbance the foot made in the soil or grass. Exposed soil, crushed insects, pollen, roots—none represented a future meal. A dog's natural urge would be to note them, and then sniff the air for the scent of a tasty rabbit. If Julia did that while tracking, prioritized the call of nature over her duty, she wouldn't make the grade.

Her nose deep in the grass, she was off to a good start. Alex allowed her to set their speed and rhythm, paying out his rope as she calmly followed the prints. Julia would have to maintain a constant energy level, show mental endurance, and carry out her task with absolute focus.

She found the first article with ease, pausing, sniffing the footprint, snatching it up from where Alex had buried it under a thin layer of topsoil. He halted in midstride, waiting as she turned to deliver it. When she reached him, Julia immediately sat at attention.

"*Tov kelev,*" Alex praised her. He took the leather from the dog's mouth and then shortened her lead, indicating that she was to return to her task.

Julia instantly obeyed. A short distance up ahead, she found the second article, repeated her show-and-deliver, waited for Alex's signal, and resumed leading the way.

He had laid the first corner, or curve, about halfway up the trail, exceeding the cert requirements. Julia was rounding it when he felt his smartphone vibrate in his jeans pocket.

Whoever it is can wait. Finish the drill.

Alex promptly ignored himself, reached into his pocket for the phone, and read the caller ID.

"Leo, what's up?"

"Hey, Professor. Whattaya doin'? You out walking the dog?"

"Sure," he said. "Like you're inside playing video games."

"Look, I'm not trying to bust your balls. We need an assist."

Alex was silent. It had occurred to him on multiple occasions that Leo Harris, his liaison with the Feds—formally the Special Agent in Charge of Cyber/Special Operations for the FBI's New York Division—had ballbusting encoded in his genes.

"Tell me what's happening," he said.

"We've got a DDoS attack in progress. Big-time financial institution. I thought maybe you could rustle together your wireheads."

Alex stopped walking and shortened Julia's lead. "I have no idea how many students are in town. We're just past the Fourth of July. This is a big vacation week—"

"I have a calendar," Harris said. "I called the Ferago kid myself. He's already on his way to the campus."

Alex grunted. His top postgrad student, Bryan Ferago, had been interning with Leo's task force. And he'd worked on banking hacks before.

He looked up the trail and crisply raised his forearm, giving Julia the sit-stay visual cue. She obeyed at once.

"The intrusion," he said. "Who picked it up?"

"The bank's in-house cybersecurity. This is a major hot potato."

"And they tossed it over to you?"

"Uh-huh. Through your friends at DSAC."

Alex stood there, thinking, his crop of thick red hair whipping in the gusts coming off Long Island Sound. As former chairman of the Domestic Security Alliance Council, he wasn't surprised they were the conduit. An FBI-created security and intelligence-sharing partnership with the private sector to guard the national infrastructure, its members included some of the biggest corporations and financial institutions in America. It was Alex's position on its original leadership board that had put him on tap to head President Fucillo's new Executive Department of Internet Security—if her Net Force initiative ever passed through the mire of congressional approval and security agency opposition.

"Who's the target?"

"H&L Trust," Harris said. "A highfalutin business bank. Word on the street is it's got ties to that Volke Bank scandal in Germany."

Alex had noticed the agent seemed even surlier than usual. Now he thought he understood the reason.

"Are you thinking it's Outlier?" he said.

Harris grunted. "She could have set it up before. Goddamn if her handprint isn't all over this thing."

She? Before what? There was more to what was happening than Alex had suspected. "How do you know...?"

"I know she's a 'she' because the Virginia Farmboys have her in custody."

Alex took a quick breath of air. "Where?"

"Malta. But that could've changed. There're a lot of different people in a lot of different places who want to talk to her. And all of a sudden none of them are interested in talking to me." Harris paused. "Prof, *we* have to talk. In person. Where the hell are you?"

"Westchester."

"The kennel?" Harris grunted. "So you *are* taking the dog out for a piss."

Alex straightened his shoulders. "Give me an hour," he said. "I'll meet you at my lab."

2

I

Yunes Abrika did not consider himself a dissident or an agitator. He understood why the media branded him as such, but he resisted easy labels in general, and those names bore little relevance to him. Rather, it was evidence of the problem eating away at his country's core. Though not quite state-controlled, Birhan's television and radio stations were operated by Prince Negassie's closest friends, relatives, and political allies. They conveniently spun the truth, calling those who spoke out against the prince's policies radical.

After all the blood that had been spilled to gain independence, all the promises of an open press and free elections, how did his country's leader lose his backbone? Birhan's government was becoming a reflection of the hated Sudanese autocracy... and, he feared, a pawn in the geopolitical machinations of foreigners a continent away.

Abrika checked himself. He, too, was being immoderate. Prince Negassie was no tyrant. Nor was he a coward. He had once stood up to the slaughterer al-Bashir and his National Congress. The political and economic currents that led him astray were complicated. Abrika refused to fall victim to oversimplification. To do so was to bite at the same dangerous lure as his critics.

Standing with his back to the screen doors of his veranda, Abrika looked around at the young men and women who had come to his spacious riverside home. Some were chatting as they waited. A few were quietly sipping his wife Sekura's chilled *karkadeyh*—her special blend of hibiscus tea and spices. His *followers*, they were called. Another misnomer. Most were Abrika's students at Zayar University, where he taught cultural history. Some were fellow educators, or people who had read his articles. There were fifteen arrivals so far, with three or four more participants yet to show up. They represented no single agenda, no one religious, racial or tribal group. Their skin was every shade of tan and brown. They were Beja, Copt, Shukria, Qahtani, Baqqara, representing a diverse range of ethnicities, and a fair cross-section of the Birhanese population.

Yunes Abrika took pride in that. It had required an unprecedented coalition of tribes and political interests to form their nation. Required the sacrifice of thousands of human lives. These colleagues and young people who came to his gatherings honored that sacrifice with their presence. What they were calling for with a single voice was only the implementation of their nation's most basic constitutional mandate—a free election.

He poured a second glass of chilled tea and sipped. *Delicious*, he thought. And relief from the summer heat and humidity.

Abrika was raising the glass to his lips for another drink when he heard voices outside. Male voices, loud excited ones, then the unmistakable burst of automatic gunfire. A moment later there was a frantic cry—a woman this time—and another ripple of fire. It cut the cry short.

Sekura, he thought. She had gone out to let some new arrivals through the gate.

His glass dropping from his hand, spilling ice and tea, he spun toward the veranda door.

II

Lieutenant Kadidu Tanzir glanced down at the bodies in the darkness—two young men who had been walking toward the courtyard, and the woman from the entrance, all of them sprawled in widening pools of blood. The black-clad trooper who opened fire was less than a yard away on the gravel path leading from the road to the house, his R6 assault rifle still angled down at them.

"*Stupid!*" Tanzir hissed. "What have you done here?"

The trooper, Uksem, turned to face him. Near Uksem at the top of the path, the half dozen other men in their squad were frozen as if in tableau.

"I thought they had guns," Uksem said. Perspiration streaked his cheeks. He motioned the snout of his rifle to the first one he'd shot, a tall man in a T-shirt with the words Zayar University emblazoned on its chest above the red-and-orange Birhanese flag. The shirt was now plastered to the man's body, saturated with blood. "I was *sure*—"

Lieutenant Tanzir jerked his 9mm pistol from its holster, grabbed the collar of Uksem's uniform shirt, and pulled him up close, pressing the gun into his middle.

"Stupid *and* a liar," he said, noting Uksem's dilated pupils. "You've been chewing. Do you realize what you've done?"

The trooper opened his mouth, then snapped it shut, his eyes wide with fear. The sour stink of khat was on his breath, on his skin, his clothes.

Tanzir cursed to himself. Mix the banned drug with adrenaline and you got a fool with a quick trigger finger. The men on the ground had been outside the courtyard's gate when the one in the school shirt noticed the squad approaching, coming up from where they left their Toyota 4x4s. He'd turned in surprise, telling his friend to warn the people in the house. Then Uksem's rifle had spit fire, cutting both of them down even as the gate swung open, the woman appearing from the courtyard, screaming...

His rifle spit again, ending her screams, and she crumpled to the ground beside the other two.

It only took a few seconds.

Lieutenant Tanzir was an experienced soldier. He'd seen many people die before the gun. When they fell, they rarely budged from where they stood, but went straight down, as these three went down. Like God's helpless puppets, their strings to heaven snipped.

He expelled a breath through gritted teeth. Abrika and his people would have heard the racket. Now what?

His mind raced. He had instructions to roust Abrika and his supporters. To disrupt their meeting and intimidate them. They weren't supposed to come to any harm or even be placed under arrest.

"I should kill you on the spot," he said, and gave Uksem a shove that sent him stumbling backward. He was close, so close, to venting his anger with a squeeze of his own trigger, letting his pistol roar against the private's stomach.

Instead he lowered the gun, holding it straight down against his thigh, peering through the gate in the moonless dark. He'd heard a sound that might have been a sliding door being flung open. Then voices from across the yard.

A stand of trees stood between him and the teacher's residence, partially obstructing his view. But he knew the layout of the property from intelligence photos. The large, single-story house was at the end of the footpath, its main entrance facing north—about ten meters straight ahead past the trees. The living room where Abrika held his meetings was around on the east side of the house, behind the veranda. He and his group would exit that way, come around toward the sound of Uksem's gunfire...

Lieutenant Tanzir knew there was no time for indecision. He barely had time to *think*.

He looked at Nabat, his first sergeant. "Hurry back to the cars. Take Uksem with you—I want the dog kept out of trouble. There's a sack in the rear compartment with pistols inside it. You know which ones."

Sergeant Nabat met his gaze, gave him a crisp affirmative nod. They were weapons confiscated in civil defense actions.

Lieutenant Tanzir glanced down at the young man with the school shirt. "Put a gun in his hand. Make sure it's clean of your fingerprints. Bring the rest of the guns with you."

Sergeant Nabat nodded again and hastened off into the night with Uksem. The lieutenant didn't waste a second turning to his men.

"Let's go," he ordered. "Do exactly as I say."

An instant later, he hastened through the gate.

III

Yunes Abrika plunged off the veranda into the wide, grassy courtyard, and then went on toward the front of the house. The men and women who had arrived for his discussion followed behind him.

Abrika rounded the corner of the house. He saw about a dozen shadowy forms coming toward him from the open front gate. And on the path beyond the gate...

His heart clenched. There were bodies lying on the path. He couldn't be certain how many in the darkness. He couldn't distinguish one from the other. But he had heard Sekura. Recognized the sound of her voice. He knew she was among them.

Abrika had little chance to react before the figures reached him, their assault guns raised into firing positions, stocks pressed against their shoulders. They were troopers wearing the gray-and-black night camouflage uniforms and berets of a Civil Defense Force squadron. The one closest to him, halting a step in front of the others, had a small red lieutenant's badge on the right side of his cap.

Abrika couldn't make his vocal cords work. He stared at the troopers in mute shock and horror. Then one of the students, a young woman named Layisa, came forward to stand beside him.

"You are *alqatala*," she said, her eyes on the man with the lieutenant's badge. Her voice shook with outrage. "Murderers."

The lieutenant did not respond. He stood looking at her, his men waiting with their guns trained, ready to fire, as the other members of the group began moving forward from where they had halted behind Abrika. One, two, then the rest of them, standing abreast of one another, facing the CDF troopers there in the blackness of the courtyard.

"*Alqatala*," they said in gaining unison. The word became a loud, rhythmic chant. "*Alqa-tala, alqa-tala…*"

The lieutenant swallowed hard. Raised his hand in the air for his firing command.

"*Alqa-tala, alqa-tala…*"

"How could you do this?"

Soft and calm, Abrika's words came as a strangely level counterpoint to the furious chanting around him.

A second passed. Another. The two men just looking at each other. Then the lieutenant frowned deeply.

"It wasn't my intent," he said. "We are all puppets on strings, I think."

Abrika studied his features. "No," he said. And added nothing more, leaving only the chants of his followers to break the silence.

"*Alqatala, alqatala…*"

The lieutenant inhaled, straightened his chin. Then he sharply lowered his arm to his side and the machine guns erupted, stopping the chants with their own metallic voices.

The sound went on for a long, long while.

IV

Deep in contemplation, Lieutenant Tanzir waited till after he was back in his pickup truck, bumping over rough off-road terrain toward the highway to Zayar City, before he radioed his commanding officer.

There was no ideal solution to the problem Uksem created, but he had done his best to control the damage, utilized what scant options were available. The guns were left with the bodies, and the bodies moved in ways that would support his story. The right team of investigators dispatched to the scene would confirm the version of events he included in his action report.

With a resigned sigh, Tanzir entered the frequency for headquarters, holding his hand over the radio earpiece to mute the rumble of the 4x4's engine.

"Yes?" Captain Massi answered himself. Tanzir wasn't surprised. He was pretty sure the captain would have waited up till dawn for his call. As the national minister's cousin, Massi would not have ordered tonight's raid without the blessing of the capital's highest authorities. "What's kept you?"

Tanzir took another breath. This was going to be difficult.

"We've had some unexpected developments," he said.

3

I

Alex Michaels got off the West Side Highway at the 125th Street exit and pulled his Jeep Grand Cherokee into the Columbia faculty garage. Then he walked briskly downtown under the shade trees of Riverside Park.

He would usually pause to touch the flowers on his way down to the campus, raising them to his sensitive nose and inhaling the sweet perfume. He was in too much of a rush for that today, yet he still registered the commingled scents of wildflowers and tree pollen drifting up from the tiered green slopes to his right. Sorting the smells, trying to separate and identify them, was something he'd done automatically as long as he could remember—maybe his entire life. It helped disentangle the wires in his head.

Alex hurried up Amsterdam Avenue to the campus entrance. He could see Harris waiting at the campus gate, pacing back and forth on the pavement out front.

"Leo," he said. "What are you doing here? Thought we were meeting at—"

"You *know* this is urgent, right?" The FBI man stopped pacing in front of him. "Security told me you still weren't around."

Alex looked at him. "Someday I'll fool you and use a different gate."

The agent shrugged. "Could be. Not today."

Alex smiled tightly. He turned toward the gate and started up College Walk, giving a brisk wave to the guard inside the booth.

Harris fell in beside him. Heavyset at five-foot-eight, his dark brown hair receding from a smooth, wide forehead, the fiftyish agent had on Ray-Ban sunglasses, a light blue Izod golf shirt, off-white Dockers, and loafers. Alex couldn't help but think he would have fit in perfectly with a team of midlevel sales managers at a corporate golf outing.

Going up the broad flagstone promenade, they turned up the steps to Low Plaza and continued past the big domed library. A short right, another, and they arrived at the Shapiro Center for Engineering and Physical Science Research, a blocky eleven-story structure built in the 1990s.

Alex went through the glass doors a half step ahead of Harris, hastening past the security desk to the elevators. There were two public elevators, and a third restricted-access car with an iris scanner on the wall next to the door. The camera clicked, and the scanner's computer ran its analysis of their irises, pupils, eyelids, and eyelashes. A moment later, the men heard two quick beeps and the elevator door opened.

The car had no floor buttons. The door whispered shut behind them, and they shot up ten stories to the only stop.

Once upon a time, the tenth floor had been occupied by staff offices and a large clean room for research and experimentation. That all changed two years back, when the entire eight-thousand-square-foot space was repurposed for Alex's cybercrime investigation/training facility.

Not everything underwent a complete transformation; behind its stainless-steel door, the clean room remained essentially intact, although it now served as a state-of-the-art technological forensics room, its air scrubbers humming constantly as the HEPA filters trapped dust and other particulate contaminants. But the rest of the floor was consumed by its Cyberlab and adjacent HIVE—or Holographic Immersive Virtual Environment.

Alex led the way out of the elevator, hooking left toward a plain wooden door at the far end of the corridor. At the door, he stopped to get checked out by another biometric scanner, this one with an infrared hand reader that identified capillary blood vessels along with fingerprints and overall hand topography.

"Ever wonder which of your body parts the scanners will ask for next?" Harris said behind him.

Alex laughed as the scanner beeped and the door unlocked. He ushered Harris in ahead of him.

At first glance, the lab could have been any other shared office space. There were two long rows of workstations on either side of the main aisle with computer monitors and rolling media drawer units, each workstation separated from the one to its left and right by a beige partition. A few flatscreen displays on the walls, nothing fancy. But fancy things got done here, and he was proud of that.

He led Harris inside. On a school day every workstation would have been occupied by one of his students. Today, Bryan Ferago was alone. Seated at the far end of the room, the twenty-seven-year-old postgrad was focused on the monitor in front of him, wearing a fitted T-shirt, sneakers, and jeans, his sandy blond hair pulled back in a high, tight bundle.

If he heard the two men approaching, he gave no indication. When Bryan first signed up for his undergrad courses, Alex had noticed the occasional disconnect, or lag, in his social interactions and simply thought him an extreme introvert. He wasn't altogether surprised, however, when Bryan's mandatory psych workup for an FBI security clearance revealed level 1 autism spectrum disorder, or Asperger's, a high-functioning syndrome that often went undiagnosed.

For Alex, it was merely useful knowledge, something to help him understand the kid a little better. But Bryan's reaction was different. He did not seem to handle the clinical findings well, and had withdrawn into his own world for months afterward.

"What's it look like, Bryan?" Alex said without preamble, moving up to study his screen. It showed a three-dimensional cubic visualization of port traffic over multiple axes—a firewall-monitoring cube.

Bryan stared at the screen. "A heavy attack," he said. "Like nothing I've ever seen before."

II

"Data saturation's reaching a peak," Emil said, motioning toward Drajan's computer screen. Nearly all the flow lines to the network ports were blazing red. The online banking platform would be paralyzed in minutes, spewing out denial-of-service messages. "It'll soon draw plenty of attention."

Drajan gave him a tight nod. "Okay, let's keep going. We have nothing to savor yet."

Emil nodded and typed. On accessing Soto's account, he had filled in the required fields for the transfer, making its recipient a corporate account in the Principality of Andorra. Now he clicked ENTER to complete the transaction, shifting the fifty million to that account.

This was all only part of it, though. What Koschei did with his share of the money was his own concern, but Petrovik would not leave his twenty-million-dollar cut sitting there. He would steer it a second time to Bank Leonides, then have it put through a third wash cycle in the cryptocurrency exchange.

"Contact Nicolas," he told Emil. "Tell him we're ready."

Emil's fingers moved rapidly over his keyboard. Nicolas had flown out to the Pyrenees to facilitate the second-hop transfer, and the message to him would appear as an SMS on his mobile phone.

Drajan returned his attention to his own screen, opening a new browser window. There were different rules and policies for private and business accounts. Because Soto's was a business escrow, H&L would, as a practice, deposit the money to Bank Andorra immediately without requiring that an officer sign off. The Andorrans, in turn, would refrain from reporting the transfer to banking authorities—offering financial secrecy to elite clients who wanted their flow of funds kept under the radar. But they would still normally hold the deposit as long as seventy-two hours to keep international oversight committees off their backs.

Petrovik didn't like having to wait. Even expedited, the second-hop transfer might take a full day to clear. It left him open to the remote possibility that the theft of Soto's funds would be discovered, and the Andorrans served with an order to hold them.

Which was where the diversion came in.

Since their insertion three days before, Hekate's sniffers had been plucking and analyzing data packets from H&L's internal network flow. There were a lot of tantalizing digital fish in that stream, but Petrovik's only interests were the passwords and override codes harvested from the computers of bank managers. The managerial codes would be used to create a large account containing several million dollars in phantom funds, to be deposited in over three dozen fraudulent checking accounts. When H&L's cybersecurity personnel detected the massive DDoS attack, they would ticket it up to law enforcement, which would in turn search for the suspicious transfers—and find them.

But those deposits would be smoke without fire. They were distractions, there to make sure all eyes were turned in the wrong directions while Petrovik took freely of Adrían Soto's wealth.

"I'm going to enjoy this, Emil," he said. "Enjoy putting the mules through their paces only to have them come up empty."

Emil looked at him. "We could let them succeed at their withdrawals. Add to our profits—"

"No. I want things kept clean."

Drajan left it at that. Emil's instability was impossible to ignore. He could not be trusted with longer-range plans.

Turning back toward his screen, Petrovik quickly opened the dummy payer's account, using names, addresses, and personal information he had prepared in advance. Next he authorized and executed the phantom transfers. And then he was done.

He folded his arms across his chest. He felt charged, as if his body was humming with voltage. Hekate's debut performance couldn't have been more successful. He had needed just minutes. Minutes to send people half a world away chasing after mirages. He wished he could see them scamper.

Petrovik leaned forward, opening his webcam viewer. He *would* be able to see Adrián Soto, for a short while anyway, and supposed that should satisfy him. He had bled the rock of a fortune…and unlike Moses in the biblical story, he much preferred that rich blood to water.

Or almost anything else.

III

"Done," Soto said, glancing up at Chloe. H&L Trust's website had hung for closer to ten minutes than six, but his payment to the construction company had finally gone through.

He took his cell out of his pocket, saw he'd received a new email, and checked to make sure it was the bank's preliminary transaction confirmation. A second would follow within two to three hours, after it was fully processed by the receiving bank.

Chloe was smiling as he logged out of his account page. "Ready to celebrate?"

Soto said nothing. He wasn't easily overwhelmed. But this was one of those rare instances when he couldn't have avoided it if he'd tried.

"Have you ever heard of *bamieh*?" he said, his lips slowly shaping the words. "It's a type of stew."

Chloe shook her head a little.

"It's old, old Mesopotamian. With some Persian influence. Okra, tomatoes, lamb…tamarinds if you're from southern Iran or Iraq. Not to mention plenty of fresh garlic."

Chloe looked at him. "And just how great was Malika's *bamieh*?"

"Beyond compare—and thank you for the setup." Soto felt a smile trace across his lips. "On this occasion, she'd have prepared a feast for us. Tzatziki and tabbouleh for appetizers, mountains of rice with the stew, baklava for dessert. Chai tea."

"I was already hungry," Chloe said. "You're making my stomach growl."

"I haven't even scratched the surface," Soto said. "Malika was proficient in Gelet and Qeltu, the two major Iraqi dialects. And Kurdish. She knew the language on the street, which is how she got hired by the intel boys at CECOM…but I've told you this a thousand times."

Chloe smiled. "What's a thousand and one among friends," she said. "She'd bring in dishes for everybody to try, yes?"

Soto nodded. "Eventually our commander asked if she'd consider preparing meals for visiting brass and dignitaries. It quieted their aggravated snarls after the long flights from Germany. And got our requests processed faster than any other department in the zone."

Chloe laughed. "Food aces protocol," she said. "No surprise."

Soto looked thoughtful. "I'd tell Malika that someday her family would join us at the dinner table…that her cooking had the magic to bring us together," he said. "She was never optimistic. She saw ISIS coming in one form or another before most of us recognized the threat."

Soto fell silent. He could still hear her words clearly in his mind: *As an American, you don't understand the power of ancient hatreds.*

Chloe squeezed his shoulder. "Come on, my friend. We've

got a lunch reservation at my favorite trattoria. And you sincerely *have* revved my appetite with all this food talk. Let's go stuff ourselves silly."

Soto nodded and stood up. As he moved from behind Chloe's desk, he noticed her computer had gone into sleep mode, its screen darkened. "What happened to your hideous mermaid screensaver?"

The attorney looked at her computer, her head tilted inquisitively. "I don't have the slightest clue…it *and* Stella have been AWOL since I came in today," she said with a shrug. "Who knows, Adrián. I might've accidentally disabled it. Could be it's an omen."

Soto grinned.

"Of good things, no doubt," he said, following her out the office door.

IV

The computers in the Cyberlab were virtual machines. That was one of the things a casual observer would not have noticed about them. Although their physical shells looked and performed like normal computers, these thin client devices weren't very smart and had almost no memory or onboard data storage capacity.

Like ants in a colony, or bees in a hive, the individual terminals were nearly devoid of separate intelligence and active only as part of a collective mind. Their puny brains couldn't even handle basic word processing applications, and their operating systems had not been loaded onto internal hard drives, but were software-generated versions of the systems that could be accessed via a high-security cloud server.

Virtual machines. Since they did not truly exist in a physical sense, one small CPU and a single monitor theoretically could be used to create and access two, three, thirty, three hundred, or three thousand of them, depending on network capacity.

Bryan typically had between two and four virtual computers

at his workstation. In the basic two-machine configuration, he used one of them to read his email, write his reports, and perform most ordinary office-related tasks. The second machine was his dirty computer—the one he used to troll phishing websites, snoop around known or suspected counterfeit sites, and probe networks believed to be infected by malware, crimeware, or otherwise compromised. When he signed out of the Cyberlab's communal network, the dirty computer, and whatever harmful algorithmic fleas it might have picked up from sleeping with digital dogs, was deleted, wiped from the system, zapped out of existence before the bugs could hop off to the rest of the network's machines. Its lifetime was brief, lasting only the length of a single session.

Alex knew this was the machine Bryan used to access H&L Trust's online banking platform. Harris, or a member of his task force, would have furnished him with the necessary passwords, which in turn would have been provided to them by the bank.

He leaned over Bryan's shoulder, studying the 3D graphic on his screen. The cube was floating against a solid black background. Within the blue lines forming it were dense clusters of tiny red dots that seemed almost countless in number.

"This is the network flow to the destination ports," Bryan said. "It's all random data. Junk in. I'd say you can tell from the patterns. Except, well, there are no patterns."

Alex expelled a breath. "They're getting hit with a bot storm."

"*Shitstorm*'s more like it," Harris said.

Bryan looked at him blankly. Alex picked up on his confusion. People with autism weren't good with metaphors.

"A figure of speech," he said.

"Oh," Bryan said. He shrugged. "Anyway, we're just looking at traffic inside the firewall. Give me a second—I'll show you the traffic being blocked on the outside."

He tapped his keyboard and the view drew back, the cube shrinking in the middle of the screen, the black space around its borders filling with red, as if swiped by a paintbrush. "There you go," he said. "The firewall might as well be underwater. But check out something else while we're at it…"

He tapped the keys some more. The 3D image grew to fill most of the screen again, and then was replaced by a simple two-dimensional square. It was, Alex knew, the virtual equivalent of a lab slide, a cross-section of the original cube, the concentrations of red now appearing as several broad bands spanning the square.

"Jesus," Harris said. "No wonder this all happened so quick. They just blasted through the firewall like it was nothing."

Alex stood there a moment. "Bryan…have you modeled the source ports? Gotten an IP address?"

Bryan looked confused.

"I thought we all knew it going in," he said, glancing at Harris again. "Sir…?"

"Haven't had a chance to tell him," Harris said. He sighed, looked at Alex. "The IP address turns out to be the same as the bank's. The attack's coming from its own servers. Somebody injected python scripts."

Alex regarded him with dawning realization. "You ran the scripts against your database…compared their signatures with what's on file."

"And lo and behold, it was Outlier's handwriting," he said.

V

True to her own suggestion, Chloe Berne stuffed herself and then some over lunch with Adrían—and he matched her bite for bite. The waiter had just brought their dessert of tiramisu and espressos when her phone rang on the checkered tablecloth.

Chloe glanced at the screen lazily, then read the caller's name and lowered her fork. It was her colleague Bill Klein.

"It's Bill," she told Soto. "He's probably calling to confirm receipt of the transfer."

Soto nodded. Klein was the attorney representing McEwan

Design, the architectural firm hired for Unity's interior construction.

"Good afternoon!" Chloe said into the phone. "Mutual congratulations are in order."

"That's actually why I'm calling," Klein said. "Figured I'd see if you still plan on depositing the startup payment to McEwan's account today."

"It's done, Bill." Chloe eyed her tiramisu longingly. "We made the transfer before noon—as discussed."

Klein hesitated a beat. "Hmm," he said. "That's funny…"

"What is?"

"I checked McEwan's account balance for the second time. The payment hasn't been credited."

"Are you sure?" Chloe frowned.

"Positive," Klein said. "Knowing you and Mr. Soto, I thought it was odd that you'd be late."

Chloe looked across the table at Soto, her frown deepening. "We *weren't* late, Bill. Maybe you should check again."

"Doing it now…give me two, three seconds."

Chloe waited, looking at Soto across the table. He'd listened to her end of the conversation with growing puzzlement.

"Could this have something to do with the bank's system hanging on us?" he asked.

"I don't see how," she said, holding the phone away from her lips. "You received an email confirmation that the transaction went throu—"

"Chloe?"

"I'm here, Billy."

"I just logged on to the account," he said. "It doesn't show the deposit."

Chloe suddenly felt uneasy. "You're *sure* this isn't a mistake?"

"Positive," Klein said. "I'm looking at the account page."

"Let me get right back to you, Billy," Chloe said, and disconnected. Then she looked at Soto. "We'd better give your bank a call," she said.

4

I

The Black Hawk MH-60S variant banked moderately, its five low-noise rotors carving through the night.

Kali believed they were heading west, but couldn't be sure. She had been blindfolded before being led out to the helicopter, just as she was when they swept her off The Island by motor-boat. But their first stop, three nights ago, was easier to glean. The town of Pozzallo on the Sicilian coast was only fifty kilo-meters from Valletta, an hour across the Malta Channel at high speed, and their trip took roughly that long.

Handcuffed and shackled to the fixed base of her stool, she sat in the chopper's rear cabin, seeing only blackness out the window to her left—boundless, seamless, undiluted blackness. Although the cabin was well lit, she felt as if the black had sent tendrils through the glass and worked its way inside her, rising up her chest, swamping her lungs, filling her throat and mouth like bile.

Kali could have gagged on its taste.

She turned her head a little and saw Blond Man approaching from the forward part of the cabin. His pistol in a hip holster, he was holding out a clear plastic cup.

She was his prisoner. The thought repelled her.

"Here," he said from the aisle. "Drink."

She was silent. Her captor was tall and strongly built, with features some might call handsome, but few would call distinctive—except for his eyes. One iris was brown, the other, his *ocelot's* eye, hazel, with faint brown lines radiating from the pupil.

She regarded him another long moment, feeling her center of gravity shift as the helicopter came out of its bank.

"Go on." He met her gaze. "It's cold and wet."

She reached for the cup, the links of her metal cuffs rattling faintly. Then she took a sip.

Her lips were swollen, and her throat felt as if it was lined with sandpaper. She washed the water around her mouth and swallowed.

"Better?" he asked.

She remained silent. Did he expect gratitude?

After a moment he shrugged. "You led us on quite a chase. England, the Azores, Germany…and Malta, of course."

Kali said nothing, her face impassive.

"You might want to think about a couple, three things," he said. "We'll be landing soon. Then we're going to take a ride somewhere. You'll be asked a lot of questions, and I suggest you answer them. We can help one another. Someone like you…it's better for everyone if you cooperate."

She took another sip from the cup. Then she extended her manacled hands and let it drop in front of him.

Water spilled from it, sloshing over his shoes.

He glanced down, then returned his attention to her face. She observed a nearly imperceptible twitch at the hinge of his jaw.

"You've been around the maggots too long," he said. "If you have any sense, you'll take my advice."

Turning away without another word, he joined the rest of her captors where they were gathered near the pilot's cabin.

Several moments passed. Kali sat watching the empty cup roll back and forth across the metal floor of the helicopter, then looked up, her eyes going to the window. She saw parallel strips of light below in the darkness. *An airfield.* They would be landing soon.

She shifted her attention toward the front of the cabin, where her captors were strapping themselves in for their descent. As her eyes went to Blond Man, he looked quickly over at her, a glance she wasn't meant to notice.

Kali stared at him icily, leaving no question that she did.

II

Alex was thinking the attack on H&L Trust made no sense.

He didn't exactly know why he felt that way. But it was not a stray bit of confusion or uncertainty. *Something* was tickling at his mind. A legitimate question...maybe questions, plural.

He stood behind Bryan Ferago, studying the monitoring cube on his computer screen. The bank firewall was still being pounded by wave after wave of e-babble at a rate that far exceeded anything in his experience.

"Leo," he said, glancing over at the agent. "We can't stand around here watching. We have to find out what's happening to the money in this bank."

Harris looked at him. "H&L's cybersecurity division is on it."

"And is there some holdup with your people?"

Harris absently pulled his sunglasses out of his breast pocket and began fiddling with their stems. "I've got somebody down at the federal courthouse waiting for emergency subpoenas. But you said it yourself—this is the ass end of a holiday weekend. How many judges you think stuck around town to bake in the heat?"

Alex expelled a sigh. Even with the Patriot Act's two-decades-old currency provisions, Harris's task force would need to obtain a subpoena, and possibly court orders, before they could gain legal entry to the system. Law enforcement couldn't just wade into customer records and bank accounts without evidence of a potential threat to national security.

But...

He motioned to the pulsing waves of red on Bryan's computer monitor. "Leo, does it strike you that what we're seeing here is total overkill?"

"Matter of fact, yeah," Harris said. "It's like some crazy person set off a mountain of fireworks, then started dancing on top of it, yelling, 'Look at me.'"

"Any idea why anyone might do that?"

"A DDoS attack is supposed to be a distraction, and I guess you'd say we're plenty distracted right now," Harris said. "The bad guys knock out a bank's website. It looks like a run-of-the-mill server problem. An accident. While the system operators are busy troubleshooting it, the cyber-scumbags tiptoe in the system's back door and loot a bunch of accounts."

Alex nodded. "That's how it usually works, right. But there's no mistaking this for an accidental crash. You said it yourself... it *screams* takedown."

"I'm thinking the same thing, sir," Bryan said. "This attack is too amped. Like whoever's behind the hit wants us to know it's deliberate. A hacker would count on the sysops bumping it up to law enforcement."

Alex frowned, his brow creasing in thought. "Damn near everything's wrong with this picture. We're being played. I don't have any idea why. Or how. But we need to find out."

"Which isn't happening till we get our subpoenas." Harris reached for his phone. "I'm putting in a call to the favor bank. Keep your fingers crossed it's open for business."

III

Apples? Check. Bananas? Check. Juice...in the cooler. What else? Scotch tape? A coloring book...?

Judge Charlotte R. Pemstein was at her dining room table packing some last-minute items into her eight-year-old's travel tote when she heard the ringtone.

She stared at her purse. It hung over the back of a chair, her phone blaring away inside it.

Pemstein's first inclination was to ignore the call. Her second thought was to go one better. Wait till the phone stopped making noise, get it out of the purse without looking at the missed call list, and then kill the ringtone until she was blissfully up at Mohonk. Her third was to just go ahead and answer the damn call.

Somehow, inexplicably, that impulse won out, though she had a strong hunch she'd live to regret it.

"Hello?"

"Chuck, hi. It's your Double-Mitzvah Man. Which reminds me…we ever figure out if a *goy* like me is entitled to divine rewards for his good deeds?"

Pemstein assembled a response. She'd screwed herself, and she instantly knew it. "I assume you're aces with the Guy Upstairs, Leo."

"How about with a certain judge pal with your initials?"

"As Heaven loves, so do I," she said. "Leo, your goddaughter and I are about to leave for upstate. Okay if I call you back once we're there?"

"I wish. This can't wait, Chuck. It's big."

She said nothing. Pemstein had known Leo Harris for well over a decade, since she had been a freshman US attorney for the Eastern District of New York.

"What is it?" she said now, sighing.

"We've got a major banking system attack in progress. I need warrants so we can look into client accounts."

"And I'm the only judge available," Pemstein said. "How'd you know?"

"I didn't. Just took a shot."

And hit a bull's-eye, Pemstein thought. "You've ruled out administrative subpoenas?"

"They get challenged all the time. Can't take that chance."

She frowned. "My suitcase is in the trunk. The lunch cooler's on the back seat. I was packing the kid's travel bag."

"I did say this was major, right?"

"And big, yes."

Pemstein glanced over at the entryway, where Rachel was back from the bathroom, straightening the waistband of her shorts around her blouse.

"Ready, Mom!" she exclaimed, and beamed her a smile.

Pemstein's chin sank.

"Okay, Leo. Send an agent out here to Riverdale pronto. Make sure the applications are perfect. T's crossed, I's dotted. If I'm sticking around the Bronx, I don't intend to waste my time."

IV

"Bernal, thank you again," Nicolas said. "I realize it's an imposition asking you to come out here at this hour. You should be home having dinner with the family."

The bank officer smiled from behind the desk in Nicolas's hotel room on the *Prat de la Creu*. It was the ingratiating smile of one who was very used to being imposed upon by high-net-worth clients in expensive rooms.

"I have three manic young boys," he said. "They are my pride and joy, to be sure. But at the end of a long work day, dinner with them can be a mixed blessing."

Nicolas laughed. It was the obligatory laugh of someone who'd had many similar, wearisome interactions with fawning bankers in a dozen different countries.

Bernal keyed a final entry into his laptop, then waited for his miniprinter to spit out several sheets of paper. Nicolas, meanwhile, sat in a chair, admiring his view of the *Església de Sant Esteve*, its ancient stone bell tower rising against the green alpine slopes in the near distance. This nation was an attractive little dot on the map—although he would have preferred making his trip during the winter, when he could enjoy the tremendous skiing.

He drew his gaze away from the window; Bernal seemed about through with the financial red tape. The banker closed his computer and returned it to a leather briefcase, putting the printer in after it. Then he divided the transaction records into two thin stacks, slipped them into manila envelopes, handed one to Nicolas, and added the other to the briefcase.

"You're set," the banker said, rising from the desk. "The funds will be transferred to Bank Leonides within twenty-four to thirty-six hours."

"As US currency?"

"Of course." Bernal paused. "I wish I could have cleared your deposit faster. But this was the best I could do in our present climate. The Council of Europe has been carping again. An international transfer this large normally takes three to five days. Had it been a lesser sum, we might have further expedited it without—"

"No need to explain," Nicolas said. "My employer understands the delicacy of your position."

"He is a true gentleman." Bernal sighed. "The rules are set by individuals who do not understand the complexities of monetary transactions in this day and age. Everyone's considered a dangerous fanatic until proven otherwise, alas."

Nicolas stood and shook hands with him. "Next time, we'll have dinner together. And you can tell me of your three terrors' adventures."

"Yes," Bernal said, laughing again. "Without fail. Stories worth sharing."

May both my ears go dead before that meal, Nicolas thought.

He watched the banker exit the room, waiting only a moment after the door closed behind him to place his call.

V

Petrovik heard the satellite phone ring and read the caller name on its display. *Nicolas.*

"Is the bird in flight?" he asked, using his headset. Although the satphone's encryption was on par with American NSA Type 1 ciphers, he was cautious with his words.

Nicolas answered briskly. "Yes. I've been promised it will take no longer than a day and a half to reach the nest. That's the best they could do."

Maybe, Petrovik thought. But he had wanted better. Still, he relied on his specialists. Nicolas's expertise was routing funds, as Emil's was breaking into systems.

"All right, then," he said at length. "And you? What's your plan?"

"To stay put. I want to be here in case anything goes wrong."

"Good," Petrovik said. "There's a stim club right in La Vella if you get bored. The upstairs room can be interesting after midnight."

"I'll try to get into trouble." Nicolas laughed. "And here I'd thought I might be sleeping in my own bed tonight. *Arriverà la fine, ma non sarà la fine.*"

Petrovik felt a spot of fluttery warmth on his neck, under his right earlobe, and unconsciously touched a finger to it. "Just don't get into more trouble than you can handle," he said, and disconnected.

VI

Drajan sat staring as if into the middle distance, his expression remote, his fingertip on the tingling skin under his ear. The tattoo there was a stylized Wheel of Hekate, what the ancients had called the *Strophalos*: a circular maze with a six-pointed star in the center, symbolizing the mysterious journey of the spirit toward its realization.

Arriverà la fine, ma non sarà la fine.

The end will come, but it will not be the end.

Petrovik had not listened to the song in years. Nicolas quoting it had caught him off guard.

For a moment, he could see her face. Her dark, deep-set eyes like polished chips of onyx. He'd seen through their cold sur-

faces to the sparks of mischief, the occasional impulsive flashes...
and the deeper fires.

Kali Alcazar would have cut him down at the knees for using
her scripts. Yet they shared much more than that, once. Was it
for her alone to decide the boundaries?

He blinked with reptilian slowness, keeping his eyelids lowered a long while. When he opened them her face was gone,
but his finger lingered where it had settled.

"We'll have to wait for the money transfer," he said, turning to Emil. "Meanwhile, let's give the Americans some game
for the wild hunt."

Emil nodded. "They'll have enough to keep them busy," he
said.

And started typing.

5

I

Turning into the Long Island City gas station, Cris Walek lowered his window, took a last hit off his cigarette, and flicked it into the street, quickly raising the window again to keep out the summer heat and gasoline stink. Then he drove past the pumps to the convenience store, pulled into a parking slot, and tapped his horn twice, leaving the engine on so he could run his AC while he waited for his brother.

Although the interior of the Subaru was colder than a refrigerator, Cris was sweating bullets, his brow beaded with moisture. The truth was he'd been sweaty and nervous when he got out of bed that morning, and would be as long as he needed to wait around. He had never been very patient. The combination of anticipation and uncertainty was the hardest part for him.

His brother was another story. To have seen him that morning, you wouldn't have noticed Tony was feeling any different from yesterday or the day before. He was in a cheerful mood when he got up, made himself eggs and toast for breakfast, and headed off to work whistling all the way.

Cris leaned forward over the steering wheel, looking for his brother through the convenience store's plate glass window. After a few seconds, he saw him talking to a female customer as he rang her up, a pretty brunette in shorts and a halter.

Cris tapped his horn again. His brother glanced his way, acknowledged him with a flap of his hand, and then went on talking to the woman.

Sighing, Cris fidgeted his smartphone out of the cup holder, glancing at the text message again as if to confirm he hadn't been dreaming when it appeared.

It consisted of a single word: EXIT

He returned the phone to the cup holder and reached for his cigarettes, wishing Tony would step it up. They'd done jobs for the Romanian crew before. Being of Romanian descent themselves, they knew guys from the streets. Guys who'd do them occasional favors, pass along opportunities, ways to make a little extra money.

Cris supposed he and Tony were what they called middlemen. They helped move goods the crew lifted out of warehouses at the Red Hook piers or JFK airport. Every so often they would sell a piece of hot iron, maybe some jewelry without asking where it came from. Stuff like that. Once or twice they'd moved some weed or crystal for cash, a taste, or both, but that sort of thing didn't come up too often, although they threw some wild parties after those deals.

He lit another cigarette. What they'd been put onto now, though—it *did* feel like a dream. Glancing over his shoulder at the three empty gym bags in the rear, he imagined them bulging with cash, all of them so full he would have trouble zipping them shut. In his mind's eye, he saw the sports company logos on their sides replaced with the single word: EXIT. EXIT. EXIT.

Shifting around to look out his windshield, he was right in

time to see Tony hand the brunette a pen and paper. She scribbled something on it, handed it back to him and left. Tony followed a couple of minutes later, locking the door behind him.

"It's about time," Cris said with a frown.

Tony reached for the cigarettes and bummed one without asking. "Ain't no rush." He gestured at the storefront. "Good riddance to that joint. Wish I could see my boss's face when he gets here, finds it closed up tight."

Cris was backing out of the spot. In his rearview mirror he saw the brunette get into her car and drive off.

"What was she writing?" he asked.

"Huh?"

"On that piece of paper. I saw her write something."

Tony's smile was so large you could see all his front teeth. "Her favorite city. I asked her to name it. She wrote Paris. Then I told her I'll take her there this weekend."

Cris looked at him. "Paris."

"Wherever, I don't give a shit." Tony held his hand up between them, spread his fingers. "You and me, bro. You know what we got ourselves from now on?"

"What?" Cris said.

"The world at our fingertips," Tony said, waggling them in the air.

Cris grinned despite his nervousness. Then they both exploded into laughter.

They were still laughing as Cris pulled from the station and drove to make their first withdrawal.

II

His arms loaded with over half a dozen takeout orders, Han Jingrui stepped out of the Golden Wok Chinese Restaurant on Coney Island Avenue, Brooklyn, strode to the e-bike chained to a lamppost, and neatly arranged the plastic delivery bags in its basket.

The lightweight nylon knapsack on his back was empty. He was hoping that was about to change.

Seventeen, Han had started his workday when the restaurant opened at eleven o'clock that morning, and would continue making his deliveries until its kitchen closed at ten that night. He, his parents, and three sisters shared a one-bedroom apartment in Bensonhurst under the elevated subway tracks. The second-story walkup was sweltering in the summer and bitter cold in the winter. The trains rattled and clanked throughout the night and made it hard to get any sleep. Han didn't think his mattress on the floor was too uncomfortable, though. And he was far better off than he was in China.

Han had been working at the Golden Wok for six months. One of his uncles, a cook, had a green card that he shared with all the employed males in Han's family. The uncle's name was Zhu, though he called himself Joe to anyone who wasn't Chinese. If you were a non-Chinese person, and asked Han's father or brothers *their* names, you could bet they'd be Joe to you too. All of them Joe to anyone who asked and wasn't from their native country...and who might decide to report them to ICE. This was because with the exception of Zhu—the *original* Joe—every member of the Jingrui clan had been smuggled into the United States by the *se tao,* or snakeheads, who made their livings off such shadowy transport operations.

Now Han unchained the e-bike from the lamppost and swung up onto its seat. The cashier had handed him eight deliveries, from which he stood to take in between sixteen and twenty dollars in tips. He earned no hourly wage and got to keep about twenty-five cents on the dollar from those tips. Of the two to three hundred dollars he averaged weekly, Han paid half to the snakeheads, throwing most of the rest into the household pool. It didn't leave much for himself.

Han rode two blocks up the avenue and turned onto a tree-lined side street. His first stop was a two-family walkup. He got off the e-bike, chained it up, found the right delivery bag, and started across the sidewalk toward the house.

That was when he heard the text tone. Han wouldn't have owned a phone if not for Zhu-Joe; his uncle had put him, his father, and his next-oldest brother on his extended plan. Han paid his share of the bill.

He was glad to have the phone, basic as it was. But he wanted more. He wanted expensive kicks, designer tees, and sunglasses. He wanted a VR headset, one of the high-end mobile models some of the neighborhood guys unlocked to download Romanian vampire tech. He wanted money in his wallet. And as he pulled the cell out of his pocket, Han was hoping he would soon have plenty of it, a greater sum than he or anyone else in his family had ever dreamed about.

Shifting the delivery bag into his right hand, he held the phone in his left and read his text. The message was a single word:

EXIT

Han stood in the middle of the street, his hand shaking around the phone.

"*Shang di ju fu ni,*" he muttered in his native Szechuanese dialect.

This is a blessing from God.

Dropping the delivery bag on the pavement, he dumped his seven remaining orders out of his basket, unchained his e-bike, rode toward the corner, and turned onto Coney Island Avenue at a fast clip, heading toward the bank two blocks away.

III

When she received the international SMS on her phone, Stella Vasile was at an outdoor table in Herald Square, eating a red velvet cupcake, and adding fancy American treats to her mental list of things she would miss.

She reached into her purse and read the message:

EXIT

Her mouth dried up as the reality of what she was about to do crashed over her awareness. This was it. There was no turning back. Although she realized the true dividing line had been when she uploaded Hekate onto her boss's—*ex*-boss's—computer.

She pushed the phone back into her bag and got up, grabbing the handle of her duffel, the half-eaten cupcake left behind in her haste.

"Mind bringing that over here?" said a derelict at a nearby table. He gestured at the cupcake.

Stella looked at him, briefly at a loss for words. Then she picked it up, walked over to his table, and deposited it in his hand.

"Enjoy," she said, wheeling her duffel out of the square and across Broadway to the bank.

IV

Alisha Middleton got her debit card after answering an online classified ad, then receiving an email link to the web page for an overseas shipping outfit. The agency claimed to be hiring financial managers to transfer money between its partners and their clients. It would snail mail her the ATM card, and she would withdraw the cash and send it along to different locations as wire transfers, receiving a 10 percent commission on each transfer.

Alisha was no dope. She knew the whole thing was sketchy. She'd had four years of prelaw and studied a money mule case in class. But two unpaid student loans made the decision easy for her.

She went for it.

V

Matt Froda heard about the financial manager gig from a customer at the pub where he bartended. After his fiancée booted him out of their apartment, Matt had slipped into a funk. When he got wind she was dating a big-time heart doctor, Matt had started feeling like a small-time loser.

He knew the whole financial manager thing was a sham. But he figured he might feel better with some extra cash in his pocket, and a percentage of a few ATM withdrawals sounded like an easy way to put it there.

The customer who had told him about the job mentioned some kind of website. Matt asked for its URL and went for it.

VI

Tess Hollins, Karen Kimora, and Jenna Zahn were friends since practically forever. Single and in their twenties, they hit the Manhattan hot spots together most weekends, and didn't shy away from fun times. One recent Saturday night, Karen had met a good-looking guy named Tony Walek who knew how to cut up the dance floor...and was no cheapskate. Tony told her he was in retail or fuel products. He wasn't too clear on it. After a couple of dates, Karen tried to set Tess up with his brother Cris, but she wasn't interested.

She *was* interested when Karen passed along a tip Cris gave her for making some ready cash. You got an ATM card from some European shipper, used it to withdraw money from a bank account, then wired the money overseas and got a commission for your trouble.

Karen had known right off that the deal was as unkosher as a pork butt, but that was part of its appeal for her and Tess... and for Jenna when they told her about it. It had sounded like something from a spy movie, and they all cracked up when Tess fantasized aloud about the insane shopping binges and vacations they could go on together. Bloomingdale's, Saks. Then a cruise to Punta Cana!

When Karen asked Cris about the three of them getting debit cards, he said, "Why not?" and they went for it.

VII

Joseph Mentasti, whose family medical coverage lapsed after he lost his job as a building superintendent, went for it when his wife went to the clinic to check on a rash and was diagnosed with acute systemic lupus.

Mark Stadelman, a Staten Island postal clerk, went for it because he wanted to make some long-overdue repairs to his roof.

Nancy Fiorina, a young mother who had lost her husband to a car accident, went for it after coming home to her Bronx apartment and finding an eviction notice slapped on her door.

Elsie Lunt, a substitute teacher, went for it to get startup capital for a knitting boutique.

Brad Quill, an aspiring actor, went for it to pay for the nose job and abdominal etching he felt would propel him to the Broadway stage.

Sonia and Denny Yalin went for it so they could afford a prosthetic leg for their teenaged daughter.

Sister Josephina Machado went for it thinking she would use the money to buy clothing and blankets for the orphans at a Guatemalan orphanage where she would be stationed next fall. Maria Hubel went for it because she needed airfare to visit her ailing grandmother in the Netherlands. George Statlender went for it to fulfill his dream of playing baccarat in a Macau casino. Tom O'Donnell went for it to pay for floor pan replacement on the 1965 Mustang convertible he was restoring...

In total, thirty-seven men and women in the New York area were recruited as cash mules, all seeking to bridge the gap between world and want by going for the quick 10 percent after receiving Emil's text notification.

Every one of them was in for a devastating surprise.

6

New York City
July 5, 2023

I

Two hours after getting off the phone with Leo, Charlotte Pemstein handed the signed, sealed warrants to his agent in her study. The law hadn't altogether caught up to technology about the need for paper versus paperless warrants, making it an uncertain issue in courtrooms. Although it cost him some time, the agent had picked up hard copies at the judge's home to be on the safe side, figuring it was better to deal with it now than risk future complications.

In the meantime, Pemstein emailed electronic copies to H&L Trust's top administrators for immediate execution. The bank officials were eager recipients; they merely wanted to cover themselves against invasion-of-privacy lawsuits from clients who might prefer being robbed blind to letting the Feds examine their accounts.

As it turned out—and as Harris, Alex, and Bryan Ferago

were hoping—the online bank platform's imbedded FLS, or fuzzy logic systems, had already done a lot of their grunt work. In an online banking platform, fuzzy logic would generate red flags particular to financial transactions. If an account showed an unusual movement of funds—whether it was a high number of deposits or withdrawals, a single very large transaction, or something else of an atypical nature—the system would create a suspicious activity report, known as an SAR, for its human anticybertheft guardians. So as to avoid unnecessarily tying up manpower, fuzzy logic allowed that different types of accounts behaved in different ways. A major corporate account could transfer a lot of money into other accounts without triggering alerts. But a large sum flowing into or out of a personal account bore greater scrutiny.

As Alex and Bryan probed H&L's punch-drunk system, their first step was to call up accounts tagged with SARs. Harris looked them over as they appeared onscreen, separating the payouts that seemed legitimate—such as a big check or cash transfer going to an auto mechanic or house painter—from the more questionable transactions.

One jumped out at him.

"PRT Payroll Services," he read aloud. "This account *says* it was opened a month ago. But there isn't a single payout until today—"

"When it's emptied out in five minutes," Alex said. "Five and a half million dollars…all of it direct-deposited into a list of accounts."

"Personal checking accounts, thirty-eight altogether," Harris said, scanning the log. "All opened at a different goddamn bank… Halifax Savings and Loan."

"And check out the deposits into *thirty-seven* of the accounts," Bryan said. "They're all for the exact same sum…"

Harris had noticed, his gaze fixed on the screen. The figure for each was:

$135,135.13

"I've heard of equal opportunity employers," Bryan said. "But thirty-seven paychecks for that amount is weird to me."

"And number thirty-eight's even weirder," Harris said. The payroll outfit's deposit into that account was $540,540.52, which was four times what had been deposited in the rest of the accounts. It wasn't a standard amount for a weekly or biweekly paycheck…and what were the odds of an employer escalating salaries in multiples of a hundred thirty-five thousand and change?

His scowl deepened. "Bring up PRT's full records for me," he said to Bryan. "The company address, the Social Security number of whatever company officer started the account…and where the original deposit was made. I want to know who those employee checking accounts belong to." He paused. "Something else. When an account's tagged with an SAR, the system usually slaps a hold on withdrawals until somebody from the bank decides if there's any funny business going on. See if that happened here…and if anybody's *tried* to take out the money."

Bryan nodded and clacked away, but Harris thought he knew what he would find. His own fuzzy logic told him the numbers were practically screaming for attention, like everything else about the H&L cyberattack.

Somebody was playing games…and *how*.

II

Alex and Bryan didn't have to dig too deeply into PRT's history to ascertain the outfit was a total charade.

Its payroll account had neither a company rep's name nor an SS number on file, and lacked any record of how or where the multimillion-dollar startup deposit was made. There was no online transaction number, no scanned deposit slip, no address for PRT…nothing to connect it to a real-world place or person.

So much for checking out the payer, Harris thought. The payee accounts would be next. But first he wanted to bounce some things off Alex and the whiz kid.

"Here's where we are," he said to them. "Somebody knocks out H&L Trust's online banking network, creeps in a back door, and then transfers five-and-a-half mil out of a bogus payroll company account."

Alex nodded. "I'd be willing to bet the money came out of thin air..."

"When the system went down today," Bryan said, snapping his fingers. "*Then* the money was paid out to the Halifax S&L employee checking accounts all at once. Every single dollar..."

"Five million deposited equally among thirty-seven accounts..."

"And the other half mil, give or take, deposited into a thirty-*eighth* account at the same bank... Halifax," Harris said. "What's the account holder's name again?"

"Karen Engel," Alex said. "Middle initial *R*."

Harris nodded. He would shoot the name over to HQ so his agents could run a high-priority background check, though he had a hunch account thirty-eight would prove to have been opened with forged or stolen ID—there was nothing new about that trick for hackers and identity thieves.

"Those Halifax accounts would have SAR holds on them," he said to Alex. "They would've gone into effect as soon as they received those big deposits. And even before the holds, they'd have withdrawal limits."

"Unless the holds and limits were stripped," Alex said. "That's the only way all this money gets taken out."

Harris grunted in acknowledgment. "We have their account and routing numbers from the PRT transfers," he said. "Can we find out if anybody's tried to withdraw money from them?"

"Probably," Alex said. "I'm guessing it would be done through cash machines, since that wouldn't require anyone to show identification. But the data has to be pulled and collated from different banks. They don't all log it into the general database at the same time. There could be a lot of tries that haven't been logged outside their internal systems."

"We better get on it fast." Harris said. "Either those limits were removed from the accounts or we've got thirty-seven pissed off people trying to draw money from ATMs all around town with useless debit cards. No matter how that shakes out, I think there's a lucky winner with Karen Engel's ID wearing an ear-to-ear smile."

Bryan and Alex were both nodding their heads.

Harris snatched his phone off the desk and dialed headquarters. "Whoever the hell she is, we need to get our hands on her," he growled, listening impatiently to the ringing in his earpiece.

III

"After you, Ms. Engel," said the bank manager, calling Stella by the name on her forged identification.

She entered the elevator, and he followed her inside. A tall, handsome man in his early thirties, he wore a tailored blue-gray blazer with an employee name tag on the lapel that read Steve Grasu.

"I'd like to thank you for your patience," he said, pressing the button to bring them upstairs from the cash vaults. "We have strict procedures for a withdrawal as large as yours…"

"No need to explain," she said. "I'm the one who's taken up too much of your time."

Grasu smiled, his eyes meeting hers. "I don't think it would be possible."

She smiled back at him. "Well, that's very nice of you to say…"

"I sincerely mean it."

The elevator door opened to the main banking floor. Stella got out, shouldering the bag Grasu helped her pack with banded thousands—five hundred of them to be exact.

"I assume you'll want a taxi?" Grasu asked. "There are plenty on Broadway. I would be happy to grab one for you."

"You don't have to go to the trouble…"

"It's none whatsoever," he said. Making eye contact with her again. "In fact, I enjoy stepping out of my tedious routine."

"Do you really?"

"Absolutely. Every chance I get. Life is too short to waste, you know?"

They both were smiling now.

"All right, then," she said. "I'd appreciate you calling a cab, yes."

They left the bank through its revolving door, the heat draping heavily over them as they emerged onto Herald Square. Walking slightly ahead of her, Grasu stepped to the curb, his hand in the air. A yellow cab pulled up in under a minute.

"Good luck, Ms. Engel," he said as Stella slid into the rear, dropping her bag on the seat next to her. He leaned his head through the door. *"Cand transferti bani, cere pentru Sebastian,"* he said quietly in Romanian.

When you go to exchange the money, ask for Sebastian.

She nodded. *"Multumiri. Voi face."*

Thank you. I will.

"He'll take care of everything." Grasu lowered his voice to a whisper. "I couldn't use the bank's computer for the cryptocurrency transfer, of course. But it's for the best. You'll want to keep enough hard cash with you for an emergency."

"Multumiri."

He smiled and spoke even more quietly. "Will I see you later?"

She looked at him. *"Noi nu ar trebui.* It isn't wise. I'm leaving for the airport first thing in the morning—"

"And I promise I'll wake you up with a smile," he said. "It will be a night to remember."

She shook her head. "I won't be sleeping at my apartment."

"Where, then?"

"The Sherry-Netherland."

Grasu blinked. *"Tu nu sunt un gospodar, văd.* You aren't skimping."

"You said it yourself—life is short," she said. "The truth is, it's a gift from Emil."

He chuckled. "Do we eat out, or order room service on your brother?"

She smiled. "I'll let you help me decide," she said, still speaking in their native language. "Meet me there at seven thirty. The room is booked under the name Marjorie Daniels."

"Emil is thorough."

"Always," she said. "Now I'd better go—the poor cabbie has to earn a living."

Grasu smiled and shut the taxi's door, lingering on the sidewalk, watching it join the traffic heading up Broadway. Finally, he returned to his desk, wondering how he was going to keep his mind on his work for rest of the afternoon.

7

I

Watching the night sky for the helicopter's arrival, Captain Farai Massi, Civil Defense Force, Birhan, could scarcely believe the tumultuous events of the past five or six hours, although he acknowledged having played a part setting them in motion. Demonstrators marching through the streets of Zayar City, angry throngs massing outside the royal palace. Then the Molotov cocktails, the bonfires, Prince Negassie's effigy hung from the flagpole in Haria Square. It did not take long for the protestors and security forces to collide.

Already twelve civilians had been confirmed dead as a result of the clashes. Hundreds more were wounded or filling the prisons and hospitals. And even now the violence continued, spilling beyond the downtown area into the towns and villages. There were eruptions everywhere once news of the killings at Yunes Abrika's home leaked on the internet.

Massi shook his head in disgust. *An anonymous Twitter account.* Whoever posted the photo of the bodies must have been on staff at police headquarters or the hospital, but that was something to deal with later. His immediate problem was the unrest sweeping across the country—and his CDF base was not impervious. Although the compound was on the city's outskirts, Massi had established armed checkpoints around its perimeter.

Outside his command building, he could see the aircraft's navigation lights against the fading stars, bearing in quickly toward the illuminated helipad from the southwest. Most men of his cousin's high government position would be fleeing the capital. Instead, Ansari Kem was heading *into* Zayar City to join the prince…after a brief stopover here at the compound.

This was a strange hour for such a call, and Massi could only guess at its purpose. But he supposed it shouldn't have been a surprise when Ansari requested the military 'copter. His hardline convictions were always laced with defiance, nor had he survived this long bowing to his enemies. As Prince Negassie's former Director of Intelligence, and now as National Minister, he had shown a strong and occasionally vindictive hand.

Massi rubbed his weary eyes. A strange time, yes. Surreal, even. But the captain realized he could not afford to feign ignorance of what had brought on the chaos. The plan to roust Abrika and his followers was his cousin's. But Massi had handpicked Lieutenant Tanzir for the assignment and then issued specific orders to disrupt the meeting at Abrika's home. There would be nothing but added trouble for him if he tried to distance himself.

The *thock* of helicopter blades close overhead abruptly pulled Massi from his reflections. He could see the Russian-built Kazan Mil-Mi-17 lowering its wheels in descent. He stood on the apron of the landing pad, waiting with a small cortege of soldiers at attention behind him. Three o'clock in the morning or not—and with the nation coming apart at the seams—Ansari would expect a full official reception.

The copter touched down, its doors sliding open, the foreign minister and his coterie ducking their heads beneath its slowing rotors as they disembarked. Massi greeted his cousin with a traditional kiss on the cheek.

"Welcome," he said over the noise of the aircraft's slowing motor. "I only wish the circumstances were better."

"Those circumstances are the reason I'm here," Kem said. "And I'm not at all pleased, cousin."

II

Massi's office at the compound was a Spartan affair that reflected his practical, even ascetic, nature. He was prone to neither pride and conceit nor humility. If passion had stirred in him, he might not have recognized it. Had he done so, he would have seen it as detrimental.

His family hailed from what was once the Sudanese territory of Birhan. The border region had been a hotbed of political opposition to the regime of President Omar al-Bashir in the early 2000s, and the abductions in his upscale neighborhood near Zayar University—the same school where Abrika had taught, ironically—were regular occurrences.

As a child, Massi had friends whose fathers disappeared from their homes in the night, driven off in jeeps, never to be seen again. As a young officer in al-Bashir's army long afterward, Massi would sometimes ride in the jeeps that bore away the fathers. He'd felt a measure of sympathy for the wives and children, but it never prevented him from knotting the gag and blindfold.

When the Birhani secessionist movement gathered momentum, he had fallen under the watchful eyes of his superiors. Eventually, he sensed their watchfulness edging into suspicion and, under the advice of his cousin, defected to Prince Negassie's Liberation Front.

The choice was typical of Massi, rooted in pragmatism rather than conviction. He had not wanted to become one of the vanished—and that remained his priority.

He stood quietly now in a corner of the office, having yielded
his steel-gray desk to Kem. Lieutenant Kadidu Tanzir, summoned from his quarters, sweated in the foreign minister's gaze.

"Tell me again what happened at Professor Abrika's country
home," Kem said. He sounded every bit the former intelligence
man. "Do not omit any details."

Tanzir nervously went through it for the second time: Uksem
triggering his rifle while wired on khat and the three dead bodies on the ground. Abrika and his students coming on across the
courtyard, their repeated cries of outrage, and then the lieutenant's own decision to cover up what happened by eliminating
all the witnesses.

Kem regarded him without expression, his fingers pressed
together on the desktop. "And you believed this the only rem-
edy? Saw no less drastic option?"

Tanzir moistened his lips with his tongue. "It was my thought
at the time that no other would have been effective. A single
witness among the dissidents was the same as twenty."

"Is this still your thought?"

"Yes, Excellency."

Kem gave a slow nod.

"The private—Uksem, is it?" the foreign minister said to
Tanzir. "How have you disciplined him?"

"He's in the guardhouse tonight. Respectfully, I've spent the
past several hours on my action report, and haven't yet determined his penalty."

"What if I ask you to decide? Right now?"

"He is young. I might lean toward mercy."

"You think him worthy of leniency despite the conflagration
his actions caused?"

Tanzir took a breath. "My assessment would hinge on the
circumstances. It was very dark. The people he saw could have
been guards. There was a reasonable presumption of danger."

Kem stared at him, keeping his fingers pressed together on
the desktop.

"Very well," he said at length. "I appreciate your candor. You'd best get back to your report."

Tanzir bowed his head, gave Massi a quick glance, and left the room in obvious haste.

Kem watched the door close behind him, then turned to the lieutenant.

"If you don't mind," he said. "I'd like you to walk me to the guardhouse."

III

Surrounded by chain link and barbed wire, the guardhouse was a long, low structure far across the dusty parade ground, with security grilles on the windows and a pair of sentries patrolling its cinder block outer walls.

His entourage left behind at the officer's compound, Kem had Massi lead him there by flashlight. As they passed the mess hall and kitchen on their right, there was a sudden clattering noise, then a shadow lunging from the metal waste bins between the two buildings. Massi brought his flash around and glimpsed the hyena's scruffy mane, large pointed ears, and eerily reflective eyes as it stopped at the margin of the yard. The creature was thin, its barrel ribs protruding more than they should have. A moment later it turned away and loped back off into the night.

"I've considered poisoned meat to control them," Massi said, lowering his beam. "They take over the base after sundown."

Kem stared into the dark. "They feed on your throwaways," he said. "I would consider that a service."

The men went on toward the guardhouse, passing quickly through the entry gate to the heavy front door.

"Private Uksem Kgosi," Massi said to the duty guard. "We want to see him.

"The last cell…only three are occupied."

"Then bring me over." Kem brought his gaze onto Massi. "Wait here. I won't be long."

Moments later, Kem strode up to the cell, his footsteps echoing flatly off the concrete floor. Massi again heard the cackle of hyenas outside and felt the back of his neck become wet with sweat.

He turned to the guard, exchanging a brief glance with him. Although he would not customarily allow himself such familiarity with a subordinate, there was something about his cousin's tone—and the mocking cries in the night—that pushed him toward the human connection.

But Captain Massi would allow himself only that brief flicker of eye contact before he broke it off, his features becoming stony. Key ring in hand, then, the guard hurried up the aisle on Kem's heels.

Watching them, his collar damp, Captain Massi felt grateful he had stayed behind.

IV

His stool bolted to the floor, Uksem Kgosi sat wearing the same sweaty black uniform he'd had on during the raid on Abrika's home. He was slouched forward, his chin drawn down to his chest as the guard slipped the key into the lock.

Then the cell door clanked open and Kem stepped through.

The noise seemed to startle Uksem. He raised his head.

Kem spoke from inside the entry. "Do you know who I am, trooper?"

His face dull, Uksem regarded him blearily. Then his eyes began to clear, recognition coming into them like a light behind clouded windows. The look on his face at seeing the minister was a variation of the duty guard's—full of astonishment.

"Yes I..."

"Come here."

Rising slowly from the metal stool, Uksem shuffled toward Kem. One step, two, then stopping when the minister raised his hand in the air.

Kem's nostrils twitched. The air was hot and stale and the soldier reeked of the leaf. "Show me your teeth," he said.

Uksem opened his mouth, his breath a rank gust.

"No," he said. "Front teeth."

The trooper's lips peeled back to reveal the greenish-brown stains of habitual khat use. Kem moved closer to him, slipping his hand into his right trouser pocket.

"You made a mistake," he said. "Yes?"

Uksem nodded tensely.

"And how do you feel about your mistake?"

The trooper looked at Kem in silence. Sweat rolled down his forehead.

"Tell me." Kem gripped his shoulder. "I want to hear it."

"I am sorry," Uksem said.

Kem nodded, his fingers tightening around the handle of the switchblade in his pocket. He had carried it with him since he was in Sudanese intelligence.

All in one motion, he pulled Uksem toward him by the shoulder and took a large step forward, bringing the knife out of his pocket, clicking open the scrupulously honed blade, thrusting it into Uksem's abdomen.

It sank in like a steel fang, then came up hard in Kem's fist, scoring bone above the diaphragm. Slicing the blade back down, Kem twisted it in deep and then felt Uksem's abdomen spill out around his wrist.

The trooper's body jerked and he produced a small, moist bleat of anguish. Kem gripped his shoulder to steady him.

"Sorrier now," he said disdainfully, and then let go of the shoulder.

Uksem looked down at himself, groaning, his hands over his middle. Then he dropped to his knees and went over sideways, curling into a fetal position.

Kem looked around at the guard. "I'll need a towel," he said, displaying his bloodied knife and hand.

The guard nodded. Kem noted his blanched features without expression, then motioned toward the trooper.

"Drag him out to the trash," he said.

V

Half an hour after leaving the military compound, the Kazan landed in the arid terrain outside Zayar City. The abundance of rocket-powered grenade launchers had made it too risky to attempt to come down on the palace grounds.

Instead, they would take one of the prince's secret tunnels. In the helo's cockpit, the pilot and copilot settled in to wait as Ansari Kem's chief security man led him and the rest of his escort to the entrance.

The desert night was chill. Scarves around their mouths and noses to shield them from the windblown dust, the group hiked to the edge of a *wadi* less than a kilometer south of the landing zone. A false boulder was moved aside and a steel door pulled open. They climbed down a ladder into the passage, their feet clattering on the rungs, the last man to enter pulling the door shut above him.

A flip of a switch at the bottom of the ladder turned on the fluorescents. The passage's steel-reinforced walls were white. Additional corridors extended to either side. Painted stripes on their floors, each a different color, coded their separate destinations within the vast network of underground tunnels spooling off from the capital.

A green stripe underfoot meant Kem's group was in the corridor running to the palace. They silently followed it past bunkers lined with computer stations and niches crowded with food and medical supplies. Overhead, an intricate system of pipes and ducts cooled and delivered water to the tunnels while evacuating sewage and stale air.

Kem had a closet in another corridor where he kept some of his Versace suits. It had nothing to do with vanity. He was a government minister. If exiled, he bore no desire to negotiate with international peers in his nightclothes.

The group walked the length of the passage, reached a bend and entered a shorter corridor. At its far end, a wide flight of concrete stairs led up to a featureless steel door. There was a biometric code box on the wall by the foot of the stairs, and Kem's security chief went straight up to it. Tapping in a series of numbers, he presented his fingers and palm to the IR reader.

A green light flashed on above the door, and it slid open, retracting silently into the wall.

Kem followed his head security man upstairs and through the door into a brick-arched chamber in the palace's basement, the others falling in around him. They were met by members of the royal guard, their formal uniform shirts adorned with epaulettes and insignias.

A crisp bow to the foreign minister from one of the guardsmen. "Welcome, Excellency," he said.

"I'll see him alone," Kem said. "Where is he?"

VI

The Royal Palace of Birhan was barely a decade old, and Prince Negassie, a secularist and Anglophile, had incorporated many classical European touches to its Islamic domes, arches, and arabesques. But the spiral minaret that dominated its heights was an appreciative nod to the eighteenth century Palace of Ishak Pasha, which he had visited on a youthful visit to Turkey.

The Ottoman general and Grand Vizier, whose marauders had stormed deep into Eastern Europe atop their warhorses, and who once governed all of Georgia, had nested his fortress on a high mountain platform near the Persian—now Iranian—border. Of Greek or Croat origin, Pasha was influenced by the meeting of cultures around him and in his blood, and his palace showed a mix of traditional touches.

Negassie felt himself a kindred spirit. His father a Sunni Arab descended from nomadic Awadia horsemen, his mother a Protestant Brit whose moment of spiritual epiphany came watching the Beatles perform at the Cavern Club, the prince related to both worlds.

When he blueprinted the palace minaret with his architects, Negassie had wanted it identical to the Pasha's in all but a single respect, allowing for Western modernity by complementing its stairs with a high-speed elevator that would rocket almost a hundred meters—over three hundred feet—from base to pointed roof in under thirty seconds.

On the circular balcony overlooking Haria Square now, Negassie heard the *whish* of the elevator opening behind him, and turned from the fires below to see his foreign minister emerge from an archway.

"*Salām*, Ansari," he said, his face sober.

"*Salām*." Kem bowed slightly and put his right hand to his heart, proffering the other to Negassie.

Negassie looked at him. "I'm glad you've arrived," he said. "I was informed you stopped at the military complex."

Kem nodded. "I wanted a full account of what occurred on Yunes Abrika's property," he said. "The lieutenant involved in the incident, Tanzir, was present. As was my cousin, his commanding officer."

"Captain Massi, is it?"

"Yes."

"Tell me the truth of what happened," he said. The prince normally had a fit, vigorous appearance. Tonight, he was clearly drained.

"In summary," Kem said, "my cousin sent Tanzir and his men to speak with the professor about reported firearms deliveries to his home. Abrika held weekly off-campus gatherings with his students, so they thought it would be an opportune time."

"And the meeting was in progress when they arrived."

"Correct," Kem said. "But two armed followers refused to allow them access to the property."

"Do you believe Abrika encouraged this insanity?"

"In a sense. He recklessly had them watch the gate." Kem's face was severe. "Most likely he expected they would send word to him at the house. But one got nervous and opened fire on the troopers. A private named Uksem Kgosi was killed on the spot."

"And then?"

"The troopers returned fire in self-defense. Both students

died from bullet wounds. Tragically the woman who was with them was also killed."

"Abrika's wife?"

"Sekura, yes. As it turned out."

Negassie looked thoughtful. The night wind coming off the desert flapped his shirt around his taut frame.

"Tanzir believes the professor and his group were drawn toward the entry gate by the exchange of gunfire," Kem resumed. "When they saw the bodies of Abrika's wife and students, they confronted the troopers with weapons. We know the outcome."

"Regrettably, yes." Negassie turned back toward the balcony rail, motioning Kem to his side. "Look. You see the protesters' fires below?"

Kem leaned forward, peering down at the square. From their lofty vantage, the flames might have been eddying sparks and embers.

"The United States envoy phoned to inform me of President Fucillo's concern," Negassie said. "I expect she'll be speaking with me personally within hours...and that many other friends and allies will be awaiting their turns. We stand to lose a great deal if this escalates."

Kem was silent, pressing his fingers against the rail. "What will you tell them?"

Negassie gave him a quick glance. "It strikes me, Ansari, that the fires appear one way from up here, another way on ground, and yet other ways from distant locations. But in the end, they are what they are...do you follow?"

Kem looked at him. "I am not certain."

"I will tell the world what you told me," Negassie said at last. "The truth."

Kem continued facing Prince Negassie for a long moment. Then, saying nothing, he again turned his eyes downward to watch the swirling flames in the square.

In his mind's eye, he could see them rising like a whirlwind around him.

8

I

It did not take Harris long to find out what he wanted to know.

A quick computer search of the Social Security Death Master file—or SSDM—revealed that a Karen Engel, twenty-nine, of Mamaroneck, New York, had died six months before account thirty-eight was opened at Halifax Savings and Loan in Herald Square. Follow-up searches of local hospital records and newspaper archives revealed that Engel, an independent real-estate broker, was involved in a three-vehicle collision on the eastbound Major Deegan Expressway, and perished from her injuries two nights later at Cornell Medical Center in Manhattan.

All of this confirmed Harris's suspicions that someone had used a classic form of identity theft to forge a driver's license or passport with Engel's name and another person's photo. It wasn't hard. Besides being a handy law-enforcement tool, the SSDM was itself a convenient reference for the scamming vultures.

Since the Freedom of Information Act had made it available to the public, anyone with a laptop and internet connection could find a deceased person's SS number...

"And match it up to an obit notice in the papers, or even a name on a piece of mail sitting in the lobby of Engel's apartment, to get a home address," Harris said. He paced the aisle behind Alex and Bryan, thinking aloud. "From there they just have to know a good counterfeiter."

Alex swiveled around to look at him. "Your subpoenas were only good for H&L Trust's records. Karen Engel's account is at Halifax. You'll need a whole new round of paperwork to get into it..."

"And in the meantime, her ghost could be walking off with the five hundred thou."

"What can we do?" Alex said. "It's how it is."

Harris glowered. "In case you didn't know, Prof, this isn't a run-through. It isn't a systems check. And that makes 'how it is' really fucking bad."

Alex stared back at him.

Bryan kept his attention fixed on the computer screen. The Cyberlab here at Columbia and Harris's task force office at 26 Fed were at opposite ends of Manhattan Island—and in a way that epitomized the differences between the two men. Since starting his internship with the FBI, Bryan had realized they were also divided in their outlooks toward technology—Professor Michaels fueled by his vision of its possibilities, Harris living in dread of its abuse.

Watching them work together, Bryan sometimes thought of an electric current flowing between positive and negative conducting rods. Together they formed a circuit. Lose one or the other and you had nothing but a whole lot of wasted energy.

Alex had let Harris's last comment ride as he returned to pacing and shaking his head.

"Just so we're straight," Leo said, "I'm thinking whoever's behind this stunt probably knows Halifax's checking accounts are gonna have the usual limits. I mean, under normal circumstances. We all agree on that?"

Alex and Bryan nodded.

Harris suddenly stopped wearing out the carpet. "*So,* unless he hacked into Halifax's system, same as with H&L...and if he *did,* I doubt he would have bothered stealing a real woman's identity for account thirty-eight..."

"Then he would need an insider to free up the money," Alex said.

"Insider as in..."

"Anybody at the bank with access to overrides. From a branch manager on up."

Harris was thoughtful. "I need you to print out a list of those employee accounts," he said.

Alex and Bryan both looked at him.

"I say something wrong?" he asked.

"It's better if I email it to you," Bryan said. "Check your phone in about three minutes."

Harris frowned. "All right. *Email* it. I'm on my way."

"Where?" Alex said.

Harris grunted impatiently. "To the bank," he answered. "Where the hell else?"

II

Han Jingrui hopped off his bicycle half a block from the bank, walking it over to the outdoor cash machine. Nothing he was about to do would look suspicious—unless someone watched him closely. If any eyes did fall on him, he would appear to be making an ordinary withdrawal.

Still, the two thousand dollars he was about to take out of the bank was over twice the allowable amount on most cards. Its limits had been removed, and he could, if he chose, empty the account of every last dollar. That would be very noticeable, and he wouldn't do it. But he knew it was in his power.

Coming up to the ATM, Han saw one person ahead of him,

an elderly gray-haired woman. He waited behind her, trying not to betray his eagerness. Once he took out the money, he would slip it in an envelope, then ride over to a second local bank and withdraw another two thousand from the account. In the next twelve hours or so, he would repeat this at different banks until his legs were too stiff and sore to pedal. Finally, he would wire the money—minus his 10 percent—to the European address he had been given.

Han watched as the old woman took her cash from the dispenser, counted it, and walked slowly off down the block. A moment later he went up to the machine, wheeling his e-bike along beside him. He slid his card into the reader, entered the password...

And frowned in confusion.

The readout screen said:

FUNDS UNAVAILABLE
SEE BANK OFFICER FOR ASSISTANCE

At first Han wondered if the ATM was broken. But how could that be? He'd just seen the old woman use it for a withdrawal. Surely he made a mistake entering his password.

He slotted in the card again. The same notification appeared in front of him:

FUNDS UNAVAILABLE
SEE BANK OFFICER FOR ASSISTANCE

Han took a deep breath to quiet his anxiety. Another bank. He would try another bank. There were dozens around Coney Island Avenue. He was sure the problem was with the cash machine, not his card. It *had* to be the machine. He'd made an unlucky first choice, that was all.

He walked the e-bike to the curb, jumped on, and rode off again. The machine was screwed up, for sure. He would ride to a different bank and start over.

Everything would be okay, he told himself. Absolutely. Everything would be okay.

III

Cris Walek did not get too jittery when the first withdrawal was denied. Figuring something might be wrong with the automatic teller machine, he waved Tony back into the car and drove him over to another bank, waiting as he ran into the lobby. But the look on Tony's face when he came out told a bad story.

"Let's go," Tony said, slamming the door behind him.

"Where?"

"Just get us out of here."

Cris pulled from the curb into lethal Queens Boulevard traffic, reached over for his smokes, shook one out of the pack, and pushed it into his mouth.

"What happened?" he asked.

"The card was rejected," Tony said. "Three different machines. The third time I put it in the machine, I could've sworn the bank cop was checking me out."

"Shit! What do we do?"

"First thing, you could fucking stop cursing. It makes me nervous."

Cris sighed, drove on. "Listen, I could drive you back to the gas station—"

"No way. I ain't going back there. Ever."

"I was just saying, if you want. Your boss won't know you walked out yet—"

"Forget it." Tony shook his head. "That joint's history, man. Like the pharaohs. You saw me lock the door on it. *Lock* the door and throw away the key."

Cris frowned, the unlit cigarette dangling from his lips. "Tony...you think maybe something's wrong with the card?"

"What do you mean 'wrong'?"

"Wrong, like...*wrong*."

Tony shifted around to stare at him. "You think we got a *de-fective* hot card?"

"I was just saying…"

"Jesus Christ, bro. You're full of negative shit. Something goes different from how we expect, you plant a seed in my head. Get me thinking we have a screwed-up fucking card."

Cris was quiet a second. "Tony, I got you upset. I'm sorry. But the way you came out of the bank, talking about that security guard…"

Tony took the card out of his wallet and held it over his lap. "It ain't like we got this thing from AmEx," he said. "You get an AmEx card in the mail, you figure it's gonna work. It *don't* work, you call the consumer hotline, order a replacement." He pressed his middle finger against the pad of his thumb and snapped it against the back of the plastic card—*tok*! "This piece of shit…what're we supposed to do? Bring it back to those hot-head Romanian boys you know in Astoria?"

Cris briefly glanced over at his brother. "Why not try the card one more time?" he said, slowing for a traffic light. "It don't work, we drive on over to Little Romania, talk to the boys, ask them what's up with it. Maybe they *do* give us another one like AmEx."

"And what if they don't?"

"We tell them we don't like having our chains yanked. Bro, you walked on your *job* for that card."

Tony slowly raised his eyes from the card, squinting into the sunlight outside the windshield. There was a bank about a block up ahead of them.

"Okay," he said. "Let's check it out."

Cris grinned at his brother as the light changed. Then he toed the accelerator, switching lanes to pull up to the bank.

IV

An old-time S&L dating back to the nineteenth century, Halifax was a large gray concrete structure clad in elaborate ar-chitectural trimmings near Herald Square.

His creds in his bureau car's windshield to ward off gung-ho tow drivers, Harris left the car at a No Standing Zone sign on West 35th and walked a half block to the bank. Entering through a brass-framed revolving door, he saw a long row of teller windows opposite him, and then a carpeted area to his left for the bank officers. There were two or three at their desks.

Harris paused a moment to savor the air-conditioning, took off his sunglasses, and was about to head toward the officers when he noticed a tall guy with a name tag on his blazer walking quickly in his general direction.

"Excuse me... Mr. Grasu," he said, reading the guy's tag as he stepped in front of him. "You a branch manager?"

"Yes, sir," the guy said with a faint Eastern European accent. "But I'm just lea—

"I have a few questions," Harris said. "If you don't mind."

The manager looked at him. "As I was about to say, sir, I've signed out of the system for the day." He tipped his chin toward the other officers. "Anyone there would be glad to help you. Ms. Udin, or Ms. Roth, or the gentleman at the last desk, Mister..."

"Spare me the roll call. I can read." Harris debated whether to flash his ID card and inform Grasu he was here on a criminal investigation. But then he decided to let him go on his way. One bank manager was as good as the next.

"All right," he said. "Thanks."

Grasu nodded and hurried on past him.

Harris turned to watch him blow through the revolving door, practically spinning it off its shaft. On a steamy day like this, he thought, the only appointment that could make any sane human being move that fast would be one with a hot woman or a cold shower.

Definitely either-or, he figured, turning toward the other officers.

V

Filip's could have been any one of several Romanian restaurants that Cris and Tony's parents had dragged them to on a weekly basis when they were fresh off the boat—ornamental tassels hanging from the light fixtures, embroidered rugs on the walls, red doilies on the bar top and tables, and, behind the counter, an obligatory framed photo of some long-buried relative of the owner in a waistcoat and saucer hat, looking ready to play the concertina while doing high leg kicks to impress the village women.

At four thirty in the afternoon, it was still an hour or two before the old farts started filing in for their *mamaliga*, leaving the restaurant tables empty as the brothers entered, Tony a step ahead of Cris. The bar stools were occupied by several drinkers, though. Cris saw three or four guys he knew being served by Marius, the bartender. Two were Lonel Ilescu and his first cousin Grigor who'd been the ones who hooked them up with the bank card.

"Dude," Marius said to Tony.

Cris approached the bar, hurrying to catch up to his brother. The air-conditioner was set too low, and he was already warm. Above the racks of bottles and glasses, a flatscreen TV was flashing news images of a civil disturbance in Africa or the Middle East, somewhere like that, people running around like maniacs and shouting with their fists in the air.

Wanting to take the lead before Tony shot off his mouth, Cris moved in to stand behind Lonel and Grigor, who were midway down the bar nursing a couple of beers. Lonel's smartglasses were super thin fiber lens A/R, the latest joint.

"Yo," Cris said. "We were hopin' to find you here."

He reached out an arm and they exchanged soul-handshakes.

"How you been?" Lonel said. "You all right?"

"Yeah, man." Cris sidled closer, motioned to his eyes. "Nice specs."

"Thanks. They're Japanese. Fucking cost an arm and a leg, lemme tell you."

"Look, man, we need to discuss something..."

"Mind if I drink my beer while you talk?"

"Okay with me," Cris said. "But, it's, you know, a delicate subject."

Lonel lifted his glass to his lips. "Delicate how?"

Cris cleared his throat. "It's the card," he said in a confidential tone. "Something's wrong with it."

Lonel's expression was still blank. "I got no clue what you're talkin' about."

"The bank card. *It don't work.* We—"

"I heard you the first two times. Why you keep repeatin' the same stupid shit?"

Cris pressed his hand on the bar counter. "Lonel, listen. You gave us the card right here."

"I don't remember that," Lonel said. "But say I passed somethin' along to you as a favor. Why you gonna talk like we got a problem?"

"I didn't say we got a problem. I just said the card don't—"

"I told you. I don't know nothin' about no goddamn card."

"Maybe you would if my brother said the *piece of shit* card, you jerkoff."

Cris felt his heart jolt. This was from Tony, who was standing at the corner of the bar nearest the door, not having budged from there since they entered.

"What did you say?" Lonel peered at him over his glass.

"That you're a jerkoff." Tony brought the card out of his wallet. "And this is a piece of shit."

Lonel's jaw hardened. "Put that thing away."

Tony raised the card up higher. "What thing? Since you didn't give us this piece of shit, I got nothing in my hand."

Lonel thumped his beer glass down to the bar top. "Put it away," he repeated. "You don't know who you're screwing with. This ain't got nothing to do with me."

Tony just stood there holding the card.

A moment passed. Cris nervously watched the bartender ease closer to his brother, standing behind the counter with his arms folded across his chest.

"You do what he tell you," he said in a baritone voice, nodding toward Lonel.

"Jesus Christ, you too? If I ain't mistaken, Marius, you were standing here when the jerkoff *gave* me the piece of shit card."

Marius stood in front of him like a menacing wall. "I don't see nobody give you nothing," he said. "Now do what he tell you."

Tony looked at him, shifted his eyes to Lonel, then turned them squarely back on the bartender. "I got another idea," he said. "The jerkoff wants this thing put away, he can do it himself."

Even as Cris realized what his brother was about to do, he knew it was too late to stop him. His eyes widening in helpless dismay, he saw Tony let the card fly at the bartender with a snap of his wrist. Bouncing off his chest, it took a hop off the edge of the counter, skittered a foot or two across the floor, and landed somewhere under one of the restaurant tables.

The rest seemed to happen all at once. With a bullish snort, Marius shot his arms across the counter and bunched the front of Tony's shirt into both fists, hauling him up off his feet and halfway over the bar.

"You little fart," he said. "I gonna break you neck."

"Not before I blow a new *hole* in his ass," Lonel screamed at the top of his lungs, a pistol suddenly appearing in his fist just below the level of the counter.

Cris gasped in shock, staring down at the weapon, a black semiautomatic. Then he heard Grigor trying to calm his cousin. "Yo, Lonel, you can't be shootin' somebody over this bullsh—"

"*Shoot?*" Marius dropped Tony to the floor in a heap and craned his head around toward Lonel, his eyes fixing on the gun. "You crazy, man? Put away that gun! Somebody walk in the door, we all gonna be…"

"*I don't give a shit!*" Lonel screamed. "None of you gonna tell me *what* to put away!"

Cris would never know where he found the courage for what he did next. Without thinking, he dove at Lonel, grabbing him around the middle like a football tackle, knocking him backward off his bar stool. He heard a loud *pop* as Lonel's finger reflexively squeezed the trigger and the gun went off, then the loud crash of shattering glass as his lunging momentum carried the two of them down to the floor. An instant later they were rolling around in the aisle between the bar counter and tables, Tony and the rest of the guys at the bar falling over them, trying to pull Cris and Lonel apart by whatever body part or piece of clothing offered a handhold—

"Oh shit look what you do to MY WINDOW!"

Marius's booming voice startled them all into momentary paralysis. Lying with his back to the floor, Cris propped himself up on his elbows, and saw with astonishment that the restaurant's front window was gone, dissolved into mounds of splintery, glittering glass. Beyond that gaping emptiness, a crowd of bystanders was forming outside the restaurant—ten or fifteen men and women, maybe more. They were shouting in confusion, a few holding cell phones up to their ears.

Cris didn't need a formal announcement to know what number they were calling—and neither did Marius.

"Get out!" the bartender hollered. "Before the *politie* come."

Cris started pushing to his feet. He saw Lonel dash out to the street, then felt somebody snatch his arm, pulling him the rest of the way up.

"Let's go!" Tony shouted into his face.

They took off without another word, racing past Marius, over the broken glass, out the door, and then through the confused mob outside toward the Subaru. Although neither looked back to check, Lonel's crew had scattered in different directions amid the howl of nearing police sirens.

Only later on would any of them think about the fraudulent ATM card that remained where it had fallen.

9

I

"These figures *are* interesting." The bank officer studied her computer screen. "But I don't know that I would necessarily say they're suspicious."

Harris looked at her, a slight young woman named Chaitra Udin with olive skin, dark eyes, black hair, and a soft, pleasant voice. She'd confirmed that morning's direct transfers into the thirty-eight checking accounts on his printout, as well as the automatic SAR holds placed on thirty-seven of them…nothing unexpected there. What she told him about Karen Engel's account, however, bore out Harris's concerns. Its limits and holds were overridden, and someone with Engel's identification had already withdrawn at least a chunk of the five hundred forty thousand dollars and change deposited by the payroll outfit.

"One question for you, Ms. Udin," Harris said. "Don't you think something smells rotten here? I mean, lucky numbers and birthdays for thirty-seven *payroll* accounts? Thirty-eight counting Karen Engel's?"

She looked at him. "I can understand you thinking it's odd. But you get used to this sort of thing working at a New York bank. The payroll service only manages the accounting. Who knows how the recipients' employer works out their salaries?"

Harris sat waggling his left foot over his right knee. Although Udin had been willing to tell him Engel's withdrawal was a large one, she stopped short of disclosing its exact amount. The transfer of funds into the account was technically bank-to-bank, she said, and within her discretion to discuss in detail. But a debit from a Halifax Savings & Loan account by the account *holder* had an expectation of confidentiality, putting it in a category of transactions Udin insisted she could not discuss without permission from her superiors.

Harris told himself he would see about that.

"You *don't* think over five hundred grand seems like a lot of cash?" he said. "This is a personal account. And it went in and out the same morning."

She shrugged. "We're a midtown bank. We have clients with major assets. I wouldn't think twice about overriding an SAR hold if I had an ongoing relationship with a customer."

Harris reached for the glass of cold water Ms. Udin had gotten him and drank. "Thanks again for this, by the way," he said. "It's murder outside."

She smiled. "I was born in New Delhi. Over there, this heat wave would be considered sweater weather."

He shook his head. "How do people stand it?"

"I wouldn't know," she said. "My parents moved here to escape poverty, not the heat."

Harris hoped he hadn't somehow insulted her. He didn't think so, but you never knew. People were touchy these days. Not that he had time to worry about it. He decided to give Ms. Udin something else to contemplate.

"I think you should know there is no Karen Engel," he said, leaning toward her. "Not anymore."

"What do you mean?"

"She died in a car accident last winter. Whoever opened that account and withdrew the money stole her identity."

The officer looked shocked. "My God, that's awful…"

"Now you see why I'm here," Harris said. "Besides having a glass of water."

Udin looked at him. "You should talk to Steve," she said.

"Who?"

"Steve Grasu. He's one of our other officers."

"Tall guy? Blond hair?"

"Yes. Have you already met him?"

"He sorta pointed me in your direction." Harris was nodding. "Why Grasu?"

She glanced at her computer monitor. "I've noticed that Steve's the one who opened the Karen Engel account a while back," she said. "I already knew he approved the withdrawal today…which makes sense. We're quicker to override limits or holds for a familiar face. And he would have no way to know her ID was falsified."

Harris looked at her without addressing that statement. "What about the other employee accounts? Who opened them?"

"I didn't check. But I can do it right now if you have a minute."

He nodded, waited. She typed with two carefully manicured fingers.

"Steve did them all," she said. "That really isn't so unusual. If their boss banks with us, for example, they might be encouraged to open their accounts here. Steve might have handled everything for the company."

"Seems like a busy guy."

"Clients tend to prefer sticking with the same bank officer when they need things done. In fact, I think Steve brought Ms. Engel…or whoever…down to the vault and assisted her with physically counting the cash. He and Tiffany."

"She another manager?"

"Our senior teller," said Ms. Udin. "I think she's here for an-other couple of hours."

The agent swung his foot down off his knee. "I'd like to ask her some questions," he said.

Ms. Udin rose from behind her desk. "Follow me," she said.

II

"You can leave them right on the dresser," Stella Vasile told the porter. She had just settled in to watch TV when he knocked. "Thank you."

She stepped aside to let him through the door with her order of flowers, a lush arrangement of lilies of the valley, the delicate white bells nodding from tall green stems. "Here you go," she said, handing him a tip.

The porter gave the bill a quick glance. "Have a wonderful evening," he said with a smile, and left.

Stella closed the door and admired the arrangement, stand-ing there in a short, sheer leopard robe and her bare feet after receiving a mani-pedi downstairs at the hotel salon.

It was now almost 5:30 p.m., and she was feeling magnificently decadent. Her unanticipated night with Steve would be a perfect, romantic, and, yes, oh so *sexy* adieu to New York. First, though, there would a long soak in an awaiting marble bathtub, the water splashed with rose petal bath oil from an apothecary on 5th Avenue.

Passing the television on the way to the tub, Stella saw that the talk show she was watching had been interrupted by images from the African country Birhan—people running through the streets and getting clubbed by soldiers. She reached for the remote and switched to a cool jazz music station, frowning, not wanting to focus on the violence. It was sad, what was happening in Africa, but the world would survive. After all the stress she'd been through lately, she deserved some uninterrupted pampering and comfort.

Here in this room, tonight's priority was what was happen-ing with Stella.

III

Steve Grasu got home to his Roosevelt Island apartment at six o'clock, giving him enough time to shower, dash on some cologne, and dress for his date.

He quickly looked himself over in the hallway mirror and smiled. He was over half an hour ahead of schedule but felt too primed to sit still. Rather than hang around his apartment, he would give Stella a call and tell her he'd be a little early.

First, though, Grasu went to get an undercover money belt out of a drawer. He folded it in half, pressing it down against his kitchen table so it would be perfectly flat. When he slipped it into his blazer's inside pocket, it didn't make the slightest bulge. Stella Vasile would have plenty of him to feast her eyes on, but the belt was one thing he didn't want her to see.

Grabbing his phone off the table, he headed out the door in a sensational mood.

His night had begun, and what a night it would be.

IV

Harris spoke to the head teller, Tiffany Norris, in the bank's employee lounge. She seemed nervous in the way most people were when somebody who introduced himself as an FBI agent came around asking questions.

He took it as a sign she was a solid citizen. The ones who *weren't* nervous made him suspicious. Most people simply weren't used to having federal law-enforcement investigators pop up in their lives.

"Okay," he said, reviewing what she'd told him in the first minutes of their conversation, "Grasu asks you to go downstairs to the vault with him and Karen Engel. Then the two of you count the money together. This is SOP?"

She nodded. "You always want a second set of eyes for an amount that large…"

"Five hundred forty thousand plus, right?"

"Five-forty, five-forty. Exactly. It's hard to forget that number."

In the chair beside Harris, Chaitra Udin shot the teller a look of irritation. He ignored it. She had acted within her prerogative refusing to confirm the withdrawal total. He'd never told her he wouldn't ask someone else.

"And what happened next?"

"We got in the elevator, and she left with the money."

"Just walked out onto the street? With that much cash?"

"Well, Steve went out to hail a cab for her."

"Were you with him?"

"No." She glanced down, then back up at him. "He took care of it himself."

Leo noticed the hesitation. "There something else you want to share?"

She took a breath. "Steve hasn't done anything wrong, has he?"

"So there is something else," he said, deliberately avoiding her question.

She sighed. "I promised I wouldn't tell anyone. It has nothing to do with work. As long as Steve didn't make an inappropriate come-on, there's no reason he can't see her outside the bank."

Harris took a moment to digest that. "They made plans for *afterward*?"

"Well…yes," she said.

"You mean a date?"

"Agent Harris, I don't want to embarrass Steve—"

"Listen, nobody's putting this on the internet."

The teller produced another long sigh. "Steve told me Ms. Engel has a room at the Sherry-Netherland. And that he was heading over there to be with her."

Harris felt his pulse race. He needed Grasu's address. But first…

"Tiffany, I'd like you to describe Karen Engel for me," he said.

V

Neck-deep in rose water, Stella heard her smartphone ring on the sill of the tub. She assumed it was Steve again—could he have gotten to the hotel already?

Languidly reaching for the phone, she noticed the name on the caller ID. *Emil.* That surprised her. What would make her brother call now?

"Alo," she said. "How are you?"

"Concerned," he said. "Have you already checked into the hotel?"

"I'm in my room, yes."

"And your flight, when is that?"

Stella paused. She could practically feel his tension humming through the phone "Nine o'clock tomorrow morning. What's bothering you?"

"You can't wait."

"What do you mean?"

"Just that. You can't stay in New York that long. It's too dangerous."

She rose up straighter in the tub. "Has something gone wrong—?"

"No. But I've decided you are to leave tonight."

"What?" She blinked. "You must be joking—"

"Ne-am furat milioane," he said in Romanian. "The bank withdrawals are deliberate flares. Meant to draw attention. This is no joke."

"Emil, it's *insane.* You reserve a room with a view of Central Park, and then say I can't sleep here." She sighed. "This is Drajan's doing. It has to be."

"No. He doesn't know or care."

"How flattering." She sighed again. "Emil, I have plans…"

"What sort? Do they involve that peon Grasu?"

"Now you *really* sound like Drajan."

"Never mind. I've booked your new flight. A private airline. It leaves from Westchester regional around midnight."

She shook her head. "How can you expect me to jump at the last minute?"

"The reservation set me back six thousand dollars. But you'll avoid a security check," Emil said, ignoring her question. "The bank withdrawal—have you made the exchange to crypto?"

"With a thief named Sebastian before coming to the hotel. And at a terrible conversion rate."

"Hustle comes with a price, and he's quick and reliable." He paused. "Listen closely. I'll text you the itinerary. Follow my instructions leaving your room and the hotel. Use the elevator I specify. The exit. Will you have luggage?"

"A carry-on bag. Why?"

"Once you're outside, find a café or restaurant. Someplace with a public restroom. Take what you need from the bag and put it in a different one. Or leave everything there except for your ID and passport. Your choice. Also, you'll have to change your clothes..."

"In a *public bathroom*?"

"You're to follow my instructions to the letter. I can't stress it enough."

She frowned. "Damn you, Emil. You're putting me in a terrible spot."

"Not as bad as the one you'll be in if you're caught," he said. "Enjoy the next few hours. Make the most of them. You'll thank me rather than damn me afterward. I love and protect you even while doing neither for myself, sister."

Stella ended the call. Despite her protestations, she trusted her older brother with her life. Emil knew what was best for her. He always knew.

But she didn't want to think about leaving, not quite yet. Her new flight was still hours off. No sense getting to the airport too early. Steve would arrive at any minute, and she hadn't primped up for nothing.

There was still time to salvage some part of the evening.

VI

Grasu stepped up to Stella's door, knocked, and waited. Minutes ago, when he had called her after reaching the lobby, she'd simply given him her room number, told him to hurry upstairs...

and now here he was waiting at her door. He felt warmer than even the hothouse weather could account for.

Hurry upstairs.

What was taking her so lon—?

"Steve? Is that you, baby?"

Her voice was soft as satin behind the door.

He took a deep breath. "Yes. I'm out here."

"Well, you should be in *here*. With me."

He felt a fresh wave of warmth. His throat tight, he reached for the door handle, pushed...

Stella was standing there stark naked inside the entryway. Hair dripping, beads of moisture on her cheeks, arms, and shoulders.

"I just got out of the bath," she said. "Hope you don't mind."

He barely had time to step inside the room when her lips found his, her body pressing against him, her leg suddenly around his thigh, hands slipping under his shirt...

Grasu pushed the door shut behind him, inhaling the sweet scent of flowers as they tumbled into bed.

VII

Leo almost never rolled with his bu-car's siren and lights. SWAT personnel aside, bureau agents were not emergency responders; they didn't chase after highway speeders or answer ten-codes to make arrests.

But now his Mazda 6 was wailing and flashing like a carnival in hell on its way uptown to the Sherry-Netherland. Somebody had made off with a half million dollars while pulling a sophisticated jerkaround with two major banks, the Domestic Security Alliance Council, and the FBI...and that was only as far as he knew.

Leo was almost at 59th Street when he heard a beep in his earpiece.

"Ki Marton," Ria announced. Its name an agency acronym for Realtime Integrated Assistant, the robotic female voice had told him what he already knew after glancing at his dash display. He guessed the built-in redundancy was a good thing, but it got on his nerves.

"What's up, Ki?" Harris blew through a stoplight, cars and trucks clearing out of the lane ahead of him as he cranked his siren.

"We just got something in from NYPD," the TacCom said.

"On the card alert?"

"Affirmative. There was an incident in Astoria. A bar shooting. Details are sketchy. But somebody took off and left behind a piece of white plastic."

Harris straightened. "Who's got the crime scene?"

"Queens cops, sir. Hundred-Fourteenth Precinct, CSU..."

"Screw that," Harris said. "We have somebody heading there?"

"Roger, sir. Fahey and Musil. Also, the evidence response team."

"Okay. This one's all ours. Make sure the blues know it."

"Yes, sir—"

"I mean let 'em know *before* that card gets anywhere near their evidence lab." Harris hit a knot of cars and jacked up the siren's volume again. "I want the jurisdictional bullshit settled before the ERT gets there."

"Understood, sir."

Harris grunted as he swung onto 60th toward Columbus Circle.

"All right," he said, veering onto 5th Avenue. "What about Grasu? You get an address for him?"

"Yes, sir. It's on Roosevelt Island... Riverside Court. That's the high-rise there by the ball fields."

"Who's on it?"

"Friedman, sir."

"Okay, keep me posted."

"Yes, s—"

Harris thumbed his steering wheel control and disconnected without another word. Marton held about five jobs in their budget-strapped unit without complaint. But the SAC had been *sirred* to his breaking point. With the hotel a block to his left, he was in too much of a rush to worry about politeness.

VIII

"I'm sorry, sir," the clerk at the reception desk said. "But I don't see a reservation for a Karen Engel in our system."

Harris frowned, looking at him through his shades. He'd figured the chances were fifty-fifty that the owner of account thirty-eight booked her room under the Engel identity. With the answer being no, it made things more complicated.

He stood thinking a moment. Beside him at the desk were Tara Carrizales and Jake Allred, the agents who met him at the scene. Though neither one technically belonged to Cyber, they *were* with the New York Field Office, and as such could be attached to his command on request.

"Did you try an alternate spelling?" Carrizales asked. "*E-n-g-l-e*, maybe? In case a couple of letters were accidentally transposed?"

The clerk nodded. "Actually, I tried every last name starting with *E*," he said. "There's nothing close."

"The woman we're looking for is about five-six, brunette, shoulder-length hair," Harris said. "Pretty. Could be she came in wearing a yellow-and-green dress. With flowers on it...well, not *real* flowers..."

"A floral print dress," Carrizales said, clarifying.

Harris pretended not to see her swap amused glances with Allred.

"I can ask around to see if that rings any bells," the clerk said. "And leave a memo for the other shifts. But that description is very general...it would be helpful if you had a photo."

A scowl crossed Harris's lips. He hunched over the counter and rapped it anxiously with his knuckles, his eyes scouring the lobby for a woman who might fit the very description the clerk had pooh-poohed.

"Listen," he said. "I need you to go through your records for everyone who checked in under a female name over the past seventy-two hours. Start with single guests. Can you do that?"

"Of course." The clerk looked perturbed. "I didn't mean to be discourteous—"

"We also need a flash drive with your surveillance video for the past day or so. The lobby, hallways, entrances...wherever you've got cameras," Harris said. "Make it quick and we'll be fine."

"No problem," the clerk said. "I have to call for approval..."

"Then get started. I don't have forever."

Carrizales looked quietly at Allred again and then turned to the clerk.

"We appreciate your help, sir," she said with a sunny smile.

IX

The large white FBI evidence collection vehicle came lumbering up to Filip's Romanian Bar & Steakhouse shortly after the police sealed off the entrance with yellow crime scene tape. By that time, Ki Marton had cut the usual interdepartmental *red tape* to shreds, ensuring that Agents Fahey and Musil could take control of the scene without obstruction.

Custody of the white plastic ATM card, which was actually a silver-gray color—"white plastic" being law-enforcement jargon for *all* fake ATM and credit cards—was immediately given to the Bureau responders, who bagged and stashed it safely aboard their vehicle. The police forensics personnel groused a bit as they retreated to their own van empty-handed.

As for what had transpired there, the only witnesses to have provided any substantive information to the agents were pedestrians on the street, mostly senior citizens and housewives.

Outside the restaurant now, the muscle-bound bartender, Marius Petre, was doing an estimable see-no-evil, hear-no-evil routine for Musil. Meanwhile, Fahey was taking statements from members of the kitchen staff, who were likewise swearing they'd seen and heard nothing from their vantage at the back of the joint.

The tall, bearded Musil, whose forename, Amanjot, roughly

translated into "radiating the light of peace" in Punjabi, had long considered the name a mission statement defining his responsibilities in his present corporeal incarnation. For all the talk about the "new" FBI, there weren't many turbaned recruits during his time at Quantico. He believed this meant he needed to *represent* as an agent of justice and seeker of truth.

It was obvious to Musil, however, that obtaining any truth from the bartender would take some gentle insistence.

"Mr. Petre...that's pronounced *Pay-tray*, yes?"

"Yes."

"As I understand it, sir, you're saying that the window collapsing is a common occurrence—"

"I do not say common. It happen sometimes. When the weather hot."

Musil nodded. "Thank you," he said, pointing at the restaurant with his eyes. "Mr. Petre...do you see those men and women in there with brushes, tweezers and other things? The ones with the words *FBI Evidence Response Team* on the backs of their shirts?"

The bartender gave a sullen nod.

"Just so you know, sir, these very experienced people have recovered a shell casing from a nine-millimeter round."

A shrug. "Maybe it fall out of somebody's pocket."

"I greatly doubt that," Musil said. "The casing is ejected when the bullet is fired from a gun, and there are fresh traces of gunpowder on it. And on one of the bar stools. So, you see, it does look as if a bullet was shot from there."

Petre folded his thick, hairy arms across his chest. Musil was thinking they looked like felled trees at a logging camp.

"I told you," the bartender said. "Don't know about no bullet."

Musil half nodded. "Well, again, the casing was found in your bar. From a ballistics point of view, that spot lines up with the probable trajectory of a bullet if someone in the restaurant had shot at the window. From a bar stool, that is."

Musil thought Petre's frown was roughly the shape of Manhattan Island, and not too much smaller.

"When you will let me sweep up glass?" the bartender asked, motioning to the shards littering the pavement outside the restaurant.

Musil ignored the question. "Mr. Petre," he said, "I extend my humble gratitude to you."

The bartender just kept frowning. Musil took it in stride. Enlightenment was a gradual process.

"A moment ago, you guessed the bullet casing fell out of someone's pocket," he said. "That isn't possible. But *you* have made me wonder about the card."

Petre said nothing. Manhattan grew in size and proportion on his face.

"You *do* know the card I mean, don't you?" Musil asked. "Gray plastic?"

"No."

"No?"

"No."

"Well, it was found under a table. And I think it *could have* slipped from a pocket," Musil said. "It resembles a credit or bank card. A chip in front, strip in back. No other markings. Does that jog your memory, sir?"

"I don't know about no card."

Musil sighed. Out of the corner of his eye, he saw Fahey approaching from where he'd shepherded the cooks and dishwashers. He stepped away from Petre to confer with him.

"How are you doing with the staff?" he said in a lowered voice.

"You'd think they're *all* blind and deaf," the agent replied. "Not to mention mute."

"And the passersby?"

"They're talking some," Fahey said. "Mostly I got that there was a big crash when the window came down, then a stampede out of the bar. A couple of guys took off in a car parked across the street. A Honda, Subaru...something like that."

"And the rest?"

"They hoofed it out of here."

"Did anyone see the car's license plate?"

"A few tell me it was local." Fahey shrugged. "That's it."

Musil stood thinking a moment.

"You have any luck with King Kong over there?" Fahey said, nodding at Petre.

Musil shook his head. "Not yet."

Fahey gave him a commiserative glance. "That's why I like talking to rubberneckers on the street. Something like this, it's a break in their routine. They have nothing to hide or lose."

Musil was silent. He turned back to the bartender, extracting a notepad from his pocket.

"Mr. Petre, would you mind giving me your phone number?" He took out a pen. "In case I need to talk to you later on."

Petre had kept his arms crossed. "I don't have no phone."

A moment passed. Musil shrugged.

"Well, okay," he said. "Come with me, then."

"Come...where?"

"To headquarters," Musil said. "If I can't reach you by phone, I'll have to talk to you there."

The bartender looked at him, scowling unhappily.

Musil looked back, smiling pleasantly.

At last Petre grunted. "I just remember," he said. "I have phone."

Musil lifted his pen to the pad, his smile broadening.

"I'm delighted that I could guide you toward that recollection," he said.

X

"My God, Stella, you don't know what you do to me," Grasu said. He was on his back beside her, naked, his body covered with sweat, his clothes scattered God-knew-where throughout the suite.

She smiled, her head propped on his arm. "You just gave me a pretty good idea."

"Is that so?"

"Don't pretend you couldn't tell."

"Give me a minute to catch my breath, and I'll be happy to show you again."

Stella ran a fingertip down the middle of his chest, thinking she had to get dressed and out of the hotel. Her goodbye to New York, and Steve, had been short but sweet—and perhaps that was how goodbyes were meant to be. "Better yet," she said, "I'll give you fifteen."

Grasu turned his head on the pillow to look at her. "What do you mean?"

"Fifteen minutes." Stella unexpectedly sat up. She had thought of an excuse. "I ordered a gift from the salon and want to get it before they close."

"The salon," he echoed.

"Right, downstairs," she said. "It's a body lotion. Their own special formula. I'll throw on some clothes."

"And you need to pick up this potion right now?"

"*Lotion.*" Stella winked like the devil's mistress as she jumped out of bed. "Trust me. It'll be part of our night to remember."

Grasu's eyes followed her as she went into the bathroom. He was admittedly curious, and wouldn't have argued with her anyway.

Fifteen minutes would be more than long enough to skim a few thousand dollars from her bag...and that was a gift that couldn't be topped.

XI

The first guest list that the clerk provided for the agents contained the names of twelve female singles who had checked in since Saturday. Two of them had left on Sunday morning, and three more on Monday, leaving a very manageable list of singles still occupying their rooms.

Harris took off his sunglasses and read the printout, studying the names of the five current guests:

Elena Lindgrin
Zena R. McLeod
Daliyah Antar
Jessica Richmand-Bruns
Marjorie Daniels

"The names are in the order of arrival," the clerk explained to him, leaning over the counter. "We don't get a lot of women traveling alone. Most are on business trips, and with the holiday weekend there weren't many of them."

Harris rubbed his chin. "Any check in today?"

"Give me a second." The clerk typed with alacrity. "Here we go. Marjorie Daniels. She arrived just this afternoon. An overnight stay."

"What room's she in?" Harris's shoulders straightened as he rattled the printout in his hands.

"It's a luxury suite. On the twenty-eighth floor. Room 2806."

"You see anything else about her in the system?"

"Actually, yes. There's a notation that she would be expecting a visitor. A Mr. Grasu—"

Harris glanced sharply around at his agents.

"Let's go," he said, and hurried toward the elevators.

XII

Wearing a black summer cardigan, matching black slacks and charcoal midheel pumps, her hair falling loosely over her shoulders, Stella looked around at the half-closed door to the bedroom, and then opened the suite's front door and pushed her wheeled luggage bag into the hall.

She followed it out a moment later, noting the absence of any desire to take a last peek inside through the entryway or say another word to Steve. In her mind and heart, she had already made her parting with him and the city where she'd lived for the past seven years.

Time now to move on.

XIII

Emil watched his sister leave her hotel room on the left half of his computer screen, while on the right side he saw the deceased Karen Engel simultaneously walk out the same door in Stella's clothes.

The image on the right was a counterfeit, a software-generated ghost. Engel from the neck up, Stella from the neck down.

Emil gnawed on his lower lip. This would be the real test of his deepfake hack. He'd been breaking into hotel security systems since his teens and found nearly all of them worthless—and the four-star luxury hotels were no better or worse than the rest. Their priority was protecting their guests' credit card information. But endpoints like key card and video surveillance systems were full of gaping holes.

He shook his head as if to dispel any lingering doubts. One of the first things he'd done after booking Stella's room two weeks earlier was infiltrate the Sherry-Netherland's networks with a multistage Trojan download. The malware took under twenty-four hours to compromise its defenses, opening a wide, clear path to its CCTV suite.

The system in his control, Emil then went about generating his counterfeit Karen Engel. With her LinkedIn profile photo as his initial reference, he deployed his deepfake facial recognition software to troll the internet for matches.

She had left behind a full web presence. Accounts on Facebook, Instagram, and ClickChat, among other social media sites. The Facebook account was memorialized and held a rich trove of public photos and videos of Engel. She was also tagged in images uploaded to her friends' timelines, providing additional data for the graphical encoding process.

Within minutes, Emil's software used the images scraped from the internet to construct a high-quality copy of Engel's face, while training itself to simulate her most nuanced expressions. Every camera angle and variation in lighting conditions helped refine the copy by revealing different attributes of her appearance, including subtleties of skin tone, hair color, and other features, many of them imperceptible to the naked eye.

After that, Emil made the swap, digitally grafting his AI-generated facial construct onto a high-definition video of Stella's face. It was a critical step in his work. He'd known that not all heads and faces merged seamlessly. There had to be enough contact points for a realistic synthesis. But using Karen Engel for his sister's banking alias was no random choice. The women were about the same age, height, and weight. Their body types were similar. They had seemed a very close fit.

Still, Emil produced an audible sigh of relief when he first saw the doppelgänger on his computer. He loved Stella more than anyone in the world, and had bet her freedom on the tech and his ability to use it.

That was about a week ago. He'd then carried out his hack into the Sherry's security system, patching the Karen Engel deepfake into every past and real-time image of his sister in the CCTV network.

It had looked like a total success to him. What mattered was how it worked, though. Not last week or even in the last hour. But right *now*.

His eyes locked on the monitor, his stomach tight, Emil saw Stella/Engel sweep down the hall to the elevator and push the call button. As the doors opened, he switched his camera feed to the downstairs reception area, where the man who had flashed his FBI credentials at the clerk was hurrying toward the elevator bank, followed closely by two companions.

Stella was almost out of the hotel. Almost. Emil only hoped she also wasn't out of time.

XIV

"Lobby, thanks," Stella told the operator when she got in.

The elevator slid down twenty-eight stories and opened to the carpeted alcove with its pair of antique chairs.

"Have a wonderful day, ma'am," the operator said, pressing the button to hold the door.

Stella started wheeling her bag out of the car, paused while still inside, and turned to look at him in his dapper uniform. *A tip—why not?* she thought. Let him live a little.

"Give me a minute," she said, reaching into her purse.

Behind her, Leo Harris, his two borrowed field agents, and the porter who had delivered Stella's flower arrangement passed her open car and turned into the one beside it. Never seeing them, she handed the operator a fifty. He looked surprised but grateful.

"Thank you," he said with a grin.

"You're very welcome," she said.

And stepped out into the lobby as the FBI agents slid up to the twenty-eighth floor in the other car.

XV

Steve Grasu could not for the life of him figure out where Stella put her carry-on bag.

The moment he heard her leave the suite to go pick up her mystery lotion—or did she call it a potion?—Grasu had sprung out of bed. Then he'd located his blazer where it was haphazardly tossed over a chair in the living room and taken the folded money belt out of its inside pocket.

Although Stella had said she would be gone fifteen minutes, he wanted to play it safe, and was working on the assumption that she would show up in five or ten, which was adequate to lift a few stacks of the hundred-dollar bills he had packed inside her carry-on at the bank.

Grasu's problem was that he could not find the bag anywhere...and he was sure he'd noticed it alongside the front door when he arrived. There wasn't the slightest doubt in his mind. He had seen it in the split second before Stella jumped him.

He looked around now, checking the walk-in closet in the dressing area outside the master bathroom, finding it completely vacant. Puzzled, he craned his head into the bathroom, thinking Stella might have brought it inside with her for some articles of clothing when she got ready to go downstairs. But the bag wasn't in there, either.

He stood outside the bathroom door a second, wondering where the thing could be. Then he went into the kitchen, opened the cabinets, and hastily looked through all of them. You never knew.

Like everything else, the cabinets were empty.

Tensing, he went back into the living room. Stella had been gone several minutes, and he couldn't afford to waste the few that were left. Could she have put the bag underneath one of the massive pieces of furniture? It seemed a long shot, but...

He got down on his knees and searched under the vanity, writing desk, dining table, chairs, and sofa. The bag wasn't under any of them.

Rising to his feet, Grasu craned his neck this way and that, his eyes moving over every inch of the room.

Still no bag. He could only conclude Stella had left with the carry-on. But why would she do it? What reason could she have for bringing her luggage along to the salon?

Unless...

He caught a glimpse of himself in the hallway mirror and saw understanding lace across his features.

Shit! he thought. *Unless* she walked out the door with no intention of coming back.

He cursed himself soundly. That had to be it. *Why*, he didn't know. But it couldn't mean anything good for him.

He had to get dressed, get the hell out of here.

Grasu rushed around the room, gathering his clothes. He found his polo shirt on top of a dresser and pulled it on. Saw his jeans on the floor outside the bedroom door, picked them up, and slung them over his arm. His boxers...where were his shorts? He looked around, couldn't find them.

Hell with underpants, he thought, tugging up his jeans outside the bedroom.

The sudden, startling knock on the front door almost tripped him off his feet. Grasu stood a moment, petrified, one leg slipped partway into the jeans.

There was another knock. Then a gruff voice:

"FBI! If anyone's in there, open up."

He whipped his head around toward the door.

"Step back. We're coming in!"

The door slammed open, crashing back against the wall before he could move a muscle. Naked from the waist down, his fingers still holding the waistband of his jeans, Grasu stared at the doorway as the agents poured through with their pistols held out in front of them.

"Hands up over your head!" one of them shouted, his gun never wavering from Grasu.

Steve obeyed, facing the door, his arms straight up in the air, his jeans slipping from his fingers, crumpling down around his feet—

Looking down at them, he saw a flash of green and opened his eyes wide. To his surprise, there were bills sticking out of the hip pocket. Crisp new hundred-dollar bills. Three, four, he wasn't sure how many.

Stuffed into his pocket.

"I told you to get your hands up NOW!"

Grasu recognized the face of the lead man with the gun without immediately being sure *where* he knew it from. Then it came to him.

He was the one from the bank. The one who came through the door as he was leaving and asked for a manager.

Their eyes met over the barrel of the outthrust pistol.

"Well, if it isn't Steve Grasu, asshole bank officer on the run." The agent looked him over and whistled. "Think you might've lost your name tag somewhere, big boy."

XVI

Emil shifted his attention from the security cam view of the hotel room doorway to a window showing the sidewalk outside its main entrance. Stella had left the Sherry-Netherland. She was on her own now; he only hoped she would follow his instructions to the letter.

He took one last look at the fool Grasu, who had yet to manage putting on his pants. How could Stella find him a desirable bed partner? He would never understand his sister's poor choices in men.

It suddenly occurred to him that Grasu could become a problem. He did not know much, but he could offer investigators some crumbs of information…and enough crumbs leading in one direction could form a trail.

Emil considered that a moment. Better he didn't raise Drajan's ire by mentioning the subject to him. He would only be critical of Stella for complicating things. And he would not be wrong.

No, Emil decided. He could handle it himself. Contact the Russian directly. He usually played the middleman anyway. Koschei would just assume his request originated with Drajan.

Emil toed his chair back toward the computer and began typing an encrypted email. There was nothing to gain from waiting.

XVII

"Ki, we get an image grab on Marjorie Daniels?"

"Yes, sir. I emailed you some high-qual captures."

Harris was presently southbound on the FDR, Carrizales and Allred about a car length behind him, Grasu flex-cuffed in their back seat on his way to federal detention.

"Daniels…or *whoever* she is…has a good jump on us. And maybe forged documents," he told Ki over the integrated. "You send those pictures out with the APB?"

"Yes, sir. And in separate alerts to transportation personnel at the major exit portals. Port Authority, NTSB… I've also shared the stills with regional airports and private carriers via A-ISAC."

"Shoot them over to NYPD Intel too. I'd rather they get them twice than take a chance somebody down below fucks up."

"Okay, sir. Anything else?"

"Not right now. Keep me posted, out."

Harris blew a stream of air out his lips. With traffic moving more or less smoothly as he cleared the perpetual midtown bottleneck, he asked Ria to open the video captures and checked them out on his dash screen.

The frames were all sharp and in color. Daniels was between twenty-five and thirty years old, and wearing a black shirt and slacks. A slender brunette, pretty, long, straight hair. She would be easily recognizable to anyone on the lookout.

It was something, and that was always better than nothing, Harris thought, dredging for optimism.

XVIII

Stella stepped from the air-conditioned Mercedes sedan into the stiflingly warm night, her driver holding open her door. He seemed untouched by the heat and humidity in his crisp black suit.

"One moment, please, and I'll show you to your flight," he said, and waved a hand at the idling jet aircraft.

He shut the door and led her toward it, walking politely beside her. She was surprised at how nervous she had started to feel. After everything she had done in the past few days, what she was doing now seemed, if not easy, then uncomplicated. She wouldn't have thought it would be so stressful.

Some of it—most of it, probably—had to do with her brother's urgent call. Everything before that had felt like a video game or spy movie. Now it was different. The reality had set in. She was leaving America for what would likely be the final time ever. And she hoped nothing happened to detain her.

Emil would have been pleased by her faithful adherence to his instructions. At a Starbucks near the hotel, she found the restroom, took a large Vera Bradley duffel from her rolling bag, and transferred most of its contents to the duffel. Then she removed her lightweight cardigan, revealing the floral print blouse underneath. Her pumps went next, replaced by flip-flops from inside the wheeled bag. As a final precaution, Stella quickly did her hair up in a tight French braid before she stuffed the sweater and pumps into the bag, zipped it shut, and left it behind in one of the stalls.

From the coffeehouse, Stella had taken an Uber out to West-chester regional, where the airline's escort met her in a lot for private flyers and then drove her out here to the departure area.

As she strode across the runway to the aircraft, a sleek new Citation X, she saw a sophisticated looking young couple board-ing ahead of her. The captain and copilot stood in front of the lowered steps.

"Good evening, Ms. Vasile," the captain said with a smile. He was holding a small tablet. "May I please see your passport?"

Stella pulled it from the duffel, her heart still racing. It was the first time in days that she had reached for anything but fraudu-lent identification, yet she was edgier than at the bank or hotel.

A glance at the captain's tablet exponentially increased her anxiousness. She only needed a second to recognize the video capture on its display.

It was her. Leaving the hotel room. She was sure of it. The sweater. The wallpaper behind her. It was *her*...

And yet it wasn't.

The face belonged to Karen Engel.

She waited, her eyes on the pilot, watching him as if through a mild haze. He seemed to take a long time scrutinizing her passport after examining the doctored image on his tablet— but surely it was just her imagination. Within a few hours she would be in Paris. There was nothing to worry about. Yet she couldn't seem to breathe.

Damn Emil, it was his fault. Six-thousand-dollar charter or not, things could go wrong. Things could always go wrong...

"Thank you, and welcome aboard," the pilot said at last, re-turning the passport. "Our attendant tonight is Camille, and she'll help you settle in for the flight."

Nodding, Stella hurried up the steps.

10

I

At 7:00 a.m. Wednesday morning, Leo Harris got out of bed feeling tired to the bone after a long, sleepless night—a night spent thinking about an unprecedented digital hack-slash-theft involving two major banks, a very sketchy bank *officer* and person of interest in the developing investigation, and the impossibly alive and hot-to-trot Karen Engel, aka Marjorie Daniels… which was itself an alias. None to Harris's surprise, his search of the New York State Department of Motor Vehicles' database had shown the driver's license she presented on check-in at the Sherry-Netherlands to be an expert forgery.

And, of course, there was the Outlier business. He didn't know whether she'd given herself the online handle, or if someone else tagged her with it. But she was a legend on the Dark Web. Now that she was in Langley's custody, he wondered what they planned to do with her.

Yawning, Harris shuffled to the kitchen of his Jersey City condo in his T-shirt and shorts, poured some coffee from his automatic brewer, and then went to the fridge for a few slightly browned apple slices, a handful of even softer, wrinkled grape tomatoes, and some red leaf lettuce.

"Breakfast of fucking champions," he muttered, ripping the lettuce into small bits. When he finished with that, he put everything onto a paper plate and carried it into the living room.

Harris crouched in the middle of the hardwood floor, looked under the couch and chairs, and then around the old army footlocker he used as a coffee table. Finally, he peered under the television stand and frowned. Mack's stubby tail and hindquarters were sticking out from underneath it.

The paper plate in one hand, Leo rose and went to get him, setting the plate down on the floor near the couch. He didn't like his pet box turtle crawling around in that space and would have to do something to close it up. It was too easy for him to become tangled in the electrical wiring and cables.

"Get your scaly green ass outta there, will ya?" He snorted, reaching under the stand.

Mack's head poked out of his shell and Harris scratched under his neck.

Harris carried the turtle to the plate and set him down in front of it. Then he poured himself another cup of coffee and brought it over to the couch.

"We should put our heads together here," he said, sipping. "We've got a hacker playing with accounts at one bank...how do we prove the same thing didn't happen at *Grasu's* bank?" Minus the DDoS attack, of course, he thought. "The guy's a slimebag, but I'm not seeing how we can charge him. We both know his lawyer's gonna claim somebody stole his login info to set up those accounts."

Mack sank his beak into a piece of apple and chewed.

Harris sighed, his hands wrapped around his coffee cup. Steve Grasu probably wouldn't be in custody longer than a day, maybe thirty-six hours. His sleazeball attorney did give him the nod to say a few things, though. Grasu had professed to have no recollection of opening the thirty-seven employee accounts. He didn't specifically *deny* it, but claimed he didn't remember, and wasn't exactly sure why it would be a problem if he *had* opened them. He also offered a plausible explanation for what he was doing in Daniels's luxury suite at the Sherry-Netherland...which included an admission that he did, in fact, open a personal savings account for her alter-ego, Karen Engel, seeing nothing odd or suspicious about her. Karen's identification had checked out. She was a likable client, a pleasant person to talk with.

And, yes, a very *hot* woman.

Which, one thing leading to another, and the two of them having developed a flirtatious relationship, was how Grasu insisted they wound up having sex a few hours after she made her large cash withdrawal. And while the bank officer conceded that might give a hint of impropriety, he'd pointed out that their little tryst really didn't violate any ethical rules. It wasn't as if they engaged in hanky panky in the bank vault. Instead, they decided to consummate things after business hours in a hotel room Karen legitimately booked and paid for, albeit under the name Marjorie Daniels...something Grasu claimed to know nothing about.

As for the five thousand dollars stuffed in his pants pocket...

"Agent Harris, we should all be so lucky," his lawyer had offered. And then added: "Or good."

The fact that Grasu had removed—or ignored—withdrawal limits in allowing the woman calling herself Karen Engel to take out such a large sum of money so soon after the transfer, well, that was interesting, and definitely a mark against lover man Steve. But it was more a violation of bank policy than anything Harris could use in court.

He sighed, turning his mind from Grasu to the puzzle that was Karen Engel, *the Ghost Who Walked*. It was with her that things went way off the rails.

The video captures from the hotel security cams closely

matched not one, but *multiple* photos and videos of Engel that Ki Marton found on the internet. But considering that public records verified Engel was killed in a three-car pileup several months ago, it made for a logical problem to say the least.

Harris sighed again, watching Mack go at his salad. "She's dead and gone, buddy," he said. "No question. Meaning what?"

The turtle ignored Harris, leaving him to mull his question in silence. He had asked Ki to send the video off to Alex Michaels's lab for forensic image analysis. But the Sherry's desk clerk had already told him that the woman who checked into room 2806 as Marjorie Daniels did not, except in the most general way, fit the description of Karen Engel...and several other hotel employees confirmed it. Assuming, then, that the woman in the video was some kind of Karen Engel imposter, who was Daniels? And how could an imposter look that real?

Sometime in the middle of the night, Harris had found himself wondering if somebody could have pulled off a convincing face/body swap on the hotel's CCTV security system. Deepfake shit had worried him for years. But it would have required that somebody hack into the system and install an AI packet sophisticated enough to create a perfect Engel-Daniels mashup in *real time*. That same person, furthermore, would have needed to know exactly which surveillance cameras Daniels would pass on her way into, out of, and around the hotel...

It seemed ridiculous, a crazy stretch. So far, though, it was no crazier than any other theory. Maybe Alex's lab would turn something up. In the meantime, Harris was leaning on the fact Ki had put checks at every possible route Marjorie Engel, or Karen Daniels, or whoever the hell she was, could take out of New York City.

He sipped some coffee. His biggest hope for progress right now was with the H&L Trust attack. But it would be a while before Alex and his wireheads were able to sift the fishy IPs from the legit ones in the flood of network traffic. And then isolate the signatures of whatever tool or set of tools the hacker had used to infect the system.

The one thing Leo did *not* intend to do was sit around waiting for them to do their work. That was especially true when it came to Outlier, he told himself, switching his thoughts to the other track they had gone speeding down all night. The DDoS had absolutely shown characteristics of her attacks. But there was no evidence she orchestrated it. And if she *was* in custody, the timing seemed wrong. Take away the guesswork, and all he *knew* was that the agency had thrown up a wall when it came to sharing information about her.

"Could be they just don't want to go halfsies with me," he said aloud, finishing his coffee. "And could be we'll see about that."

After a few minutes, he got up and carried his cup to the sink. Mack had devoured the apple slice and was chomping into one of the squishy little tomatoes.

Harris thought the turtle looked content. Running the shower, he decided to take a tip from him as far as Outlier. While Alex's lab was running its analyses of this, that and the other thing, he needed to look outside the box and have a certain, special somebody make nice to him.

II

Looking at Tanner Woodbridge from behind her desk in the Oval Office, President Annemarie Fucillo might have admitted she had some empathy, if not quite sympathy, for her Secretary of State this evening. Empathy because of his clear and profound exhaustion. She could see the wrinkles proliferating on his face, their growth surpassed only by the accelerated graying and thinning of his hair.

But *sympathy*?

The Birhan situation was a grave human tragedy, a messy geopolitical challenge, and a tripwire for global and domestic economic instability. It was for just such a potential tempest that she had chosen someone of Tanner's ability as her SoS.

"What's past is prologue, Tan," Fucillo said to him now, lifting Celia the First Cat off her blotter on the Resolute desk. She did not want to go down as the one whose spoiled Maine coon clawed Queen Victoria's gift to sawdust. "We need to jump on our good friend Prince Negassie. Give him notice that this thing can't be allowed to escalate."

Woodbridge sat with his legs neatly crossed and his arms folded over his chest, a textbook illustration of defensive body language. "I'm no expert, but isn't that Shakespeare play you quoted there about some folks with family feuds?" he asked. "Respectfully, Madam President, I believe that's the story of these internal disputes, and where we could be headed if we're too quick to react."

Fucillo sighed. Tanner's cadences were all North Carolina honeyed ham. But he had been Senate Minority Whip for a decade before his Cabinet appointment, and a member of the Armed Services Committee even longer. The folksy routine made Beltway insiders comfortable and charmed the pants off foreign leaders.

There was nothing stale or predictable about his intellect, though. Woodbridge was one of the sharpest men Fucillo knew, with an innate capacity to research, absorb, and process information on the fly. He was also a canny and relentless negotiator who had a feel for using influence and power to his fullest advantage.

Still, she thought, Tanner's inclinations about Birhan were off the mark.

"'Internal disputes' is a clean, sanitary catchphrase," she said. "I prefer looking at the dirty specifics. Hours ago, Yunes Abrika, his wife, and those students were killed under highly suspicious circumstances. *Hours*, Tan, and protesters are already being shot and tear-gassed in droves. Things went critical in a flash. We *can't* sit on it."

"Maybe you're right," Woodbridge said. "Except I earn my keep here by asking myself *why* this particular powder keg went up so fast. That involves looking at some specifics."

"Such as?"

"Abrika was a unifier. A champ at pulling together sectarian, tribal, and political factions. Some people are glue. You take them out of the equation…" He shrugged. "When you say Birhan's fractured, it assumes the country was a coherent whole at one time. But it wasn't. At the start, they all had something in common—they wanted out of Sudan. Now they're agitated, and the various factions are pulling in different directions. Which ones are we supposed to partner up with?"

"The ones who align with our national interest," Fucillo said.

Woodbridge sighed. "Honest to God," he said. "I'm not even sure who that is right now. Any one of those groups could be another goddamned ISIS."

Fucillo let a moment pass, thinking.

"Our relationships with foreign partners are all complex," she said. "It isn't like you to oversimplify them, Tanner."

"Meaning?"

"There's an undeniable humanitarian crisis in Birhan. One we shouldn't ignore. And we have reasonable cause for a quick intervention," Fucillo said. "Our country, and the Europeans, have too much to lose if the fuel refineries and pipelines on the coast are shut down in a civil war. Those resources need to be protected. And then there's the Russian bear in the room. It has to be eyeing the situation closely. Deciding which faction to snuggle up with."

The secretary took a long, deep breath, making a show of it. Fucillo admired his theatrical prowess.

"Okay," he said, his buildup completed. "What specifically do you propose we do? Keeping in mind the Russkies will take exception, and probably hang us up in the United Nations forever. Besides having so-called research bases in the north and east, they've invested significantly in the country's economic development."

"As have we," Fucillo said. "If you're looking for leverage with the prince, I can inform him we'll withdraw our own foreign aid package."

"What part of it, Madam President?"

"*All* of it. Every red cent of the one-and-a-half billion dollars in economic and military assistance the Negassie government receives from us every year," she said. "Our humanitarian assistance is under a separate umbrella as part of the EU package. That's how it was worked out and it'll continue."

He looked at her, his brows in a frown. "You are aware that the military aid package involves technology and weapons manufactured in our country. What if they pivot further toward the Russians for the hardware?"

"I don't think they will. Not if it means jeopardizing the rest."

"But *if* they do, it would mean losing jobs in states whose entire economies depend on it. And there are some very powerful members of Congress representing those states. People you're going to need for your Net Force push."

"These are separate issues."

Woodbridge sighed. "There are no separate issues in politics. It's all a gorgeous, sweeping tapestry. Or a huge, ugly clusterfuck, if you prefer."

"Tan—"

"I repeat, Madam…consider *Net Force*. The FBI, CIA, NSA… if you intend to move ahead with your plan, you need the law-enforcement and intelligence agencies on board, or at least need to mitigate their opposition. That means getting support from senators and congresspersons who have clout with those agencies' directors, and will explain why you want an independent organization—a new Cabinet-level agency—taking umbrella command of our country's cyber defense operations. Those *same* politicians must then go home to their constituents and persuade them that the Russian hacks and infowars happened, and will *not* be called fake news—"

"Tanner…"

He exhaled forcefully, and Fucillo knew he was just heating up. "I need you to hear me out. Millions of Americans don't know why you're making a fuss about cybersecurity. A percentage of them, possibly a full third, still think election meddling is all made up. If we're going to get bipartisan congressional support for Net Force, we can't go alienating our key allies *in* Congress." He paused. "Paul Gamin from Maryland, for example. He was the CIA director's college chum."

"I know, Tanner."

"I know you know. And I know you also know a huge arms manufacturer's based in his state. *And* that it's got millions upon millions of dollars invested in contracts with Birhan." He blew out his mouth again. "I promise you, I didn't make things this complicated. They kind of got that way all on their own."

Fucillo sat back in her chair. "I won't turn complexity into indecisiveness," she said.

"But what if all that matters to our friends in the House and Senate is what their potential voters think? Make them choose between reelection and the greater national good, which one you figure wins out?"

She frowned and sat quietly awhile. Midway across the rug, Celia lay down in the middle of the Presidential Seal, rolled over on her back, stretched out, and shut her eyes. Her devoted mom, Madam President, thought she looked as if she was flying upside down in her sleep.

Woodbridge's sizable chin jutted out at the cat. "You ever want to trade places with her?" he asked, breaking the silence.

Fucillo nodded slowly. "Just about always," she said. "Apart from when she pukes up hairballs in the executive bedroom."

III

Harris sometimes thought the greatest difference since being promoted from the rank of mere Special Agent to SAC was that his phone now rang more incessantly than ever. Dressing right out of the shower, he grabbed his cell to dial Carol in DC and noticed three consecutive missed calls from Ki Marton.

Leo thumbed the Call Back button, pulling on white linen slacks he'd carefully matched to a purple dress shirt with white vertical stripes, a white collar, and white cuffs on its rolled-up sleeves.

"Good morning, sir."

"Whatever." He went to his closet for a pair of canvas loafers to go with the pants. "How come you never leave messages?"

"Well, sir, never's kind of strong. But I assume you'll call back when you see my ID—"

"Don't assume," Harris said, peering into the closet. "Okay, let's have it."

"We were contacted by our NYPD liaison this morning... Detective Payne."

"What about?"

"Does the name Adrián Soto ring a bell?"

"The communications hotshot. Conscious Systems."

"Cognizant, sir," Ki said. "He's the one, though. Soto or his attorney—I'm not too clear on it—reported an apparent robbery to the police yesterday."

Harris grunted. "This cyber?"

"Yes. Bank account hack...looks like a proxy hijacking." Ki paused. "It involves a major transaction. With H&L Trust."

Harris scrunched his brow. The bank's name was the first he recognized in their conversation, and it didn't make him happy. "How major?"

"Fifty million dollars, sir."

Harris felt the hairs at the back of his neck quill. "Hold on," he said. "Fifty million was *stolen from* Soto's account?"

"Correct," Ki said. "The timing seems to coincide with yesterday's denial-of-service hit."

"And Soto calls the goddamn police instead of us?"

"Or his attorney did, I'm not sure," Ki said.

Harris reached into the closet and grabbed his loafers off the shoe rack.

"Where is Soto?" he said. "The guy's based in New York, right?"

"His corporate office is down on Water Street. But he operates a nonprofit in East Harlem—"

"Payne give you his contact info?"

"Yes."

"Fire it off to my phone when we hang up," Harris said. "I want to talk to him right away."

"Yes, sir."

Back in the living room now, Harris saw that Mack had dragged himself over by the window to bask in the morning sunlight. As he bent to pick up the turtle's leftovers, he happened to glance at his wristwatch.

Carol, he thought suddenly. It was almost 8:00 a.m. Her afternoons were usually full of meetings. If he didn't get her on the phone before breakfast, he might have to wait all day before she got back to him.

"Listen," he said, "I've got another call to make. There anything else?"

"I've been trying to get a jump start on the bank security videos...the ones that have arrived so far, obviously," Ki said. "A lot of the surveillance systems use outdated media. It makes things a mess—"

"You're the AVI expert. Get it done."

A beat of silence. "Yes, sir."

Leo frowned. No reason to club Ki over the head because he felt stressed about calling his ex.

"How's Mark?" he said.

"He's going in for a second series of scans today. That will give us a better idea of what's happening." He hesitated. "Thanks for asking, sir."

"Yeah, well, don't melt all over me." Harris hung up, tucking Mack's salad plate under a plant in the habitat.

Love. It was great until it went bad—and then one of you remarried to make things even worse, he thought as he dialed Carol's number.

IV

Ki Marton took off his headphones, raised his glasses to massage his eyelids, and went to the water cooler to wash down a couple of Tylenols.

On his desk were forty-six packages of ATM surveillance videos messengered from as many banking centers in New York, New Jersey, Connecticut, and Pennsylvania. A small percentage of the recordings, mostly from small suburban and rural bank branches, were stored on obsolete CDs. The number of discs per branch depended on its ATM hours, and the capacities of its camera equipment and storage media. Since virtually all banks offered twenty-four-hour cash machine service, Ki had received between two and eight discs for each location.

The remainder of the *physical* surveillance videos in the packages were on USB drives, but the vast majority of them had arrived in digital form—as email attachments, or hyperlinks to video sharing sites. Another twenty or so emails, sent from the larger financial institutions, contained passwords for secure websites that allowed direct streaming of the surveillance videos from cloud-based storage platforms. When all was said and done, Ki would be reviewing between four and five thousand hours' worth of raw footage from area banks.

Returning to his desk, he neatly arranged the CDs into small stacks, then carried them across the office to his miniloader and inserted them a stack at a time. It immediately began copying the discs onto his computer's hard drive. Although a combo flash memory–CD duplicator might save him hours, the only machine on premises was in Evidence and Forensics, and the techs on another case had called dibs. Rather than wait for it to free up, Ki had forwarded some of the work to Professor Michaels's lab along with the Karen Engel hotel video, knowing they would receive high-pri treatment there.

He sighed. It made no sense that FBI Cyber lacked a piece of equipment costing under two thousand dollars. The wasted man hours were ludicrous, and Ki was burned out from spending what seemed like every waking moment here at headquarters. For that reason he'd already put out feelers for a position with Net Force when hiring officially opened up. He knew how much SAC Harris relied on him, and Harris was the best...

a brick agent who'd made his way up the ranks through sheer will, stubbornness, and dedication. But President Fucillo's new agency would put a whole world of high-techery at his fingertips, and maybe even leave him with time for an actual life.

Ki frowned and glanced at his wristwatch, thinking about Mark, the person with whom he was supposed to be sharing that life. Right now he would be at the hospital getting prepped for a PET scan of his brain. Ki wanted to be with him, but as usual the job demanded otherwise, and his partner was at the hospital alone.

Expelling another audible breath, he pushed his eyeglasses back onto his nose and sat down to monitor the progress of his video uploads. For sure, more coffee and headache pills were on the menu today.

Hour one of four thousand beckoned.

V

"Leo, hi."

"Carol," he said, the phone to his ear.

"How are you doing?"

"Okay, I guess."

"You always say that, you know."

"Say what?"

"That you 'guess' you're all right."

"I guessed I was 'okay,' but why split hairs?" Harris took a breath. He heard high-pitched children's voices at the other end of the line and felt his heart bite. "How's everything with *you*?"

"Hectic," Carol said. "Jackson's nanny phoned in sick. So I'm bringing him to his aunt's on the way to dropping Tricia off at day camp."

"And Ron?"

"Fine," she said. "Thanks for asking."

He didn't say anything.

Asking about her husband made him too real.

"I was going to give you a ring," she said. "But then I decided you were probably busy and would be in touch."

"What've you heard?"

"That there was a major DDoS bank job yesterday."

"Maybe more major than anybody figured," he said. "You get this from your people inside the NYPD?"

"We don't have people inside the NYPD."

"Carol—"

"We don't have anybody within the New York police. A few agents on unpaid leave may have given the department advice once upon a time. Informally."

"Then who'd you get it from?"

"What would you say if I told you? On an open cell line, no less."

"That they need to find a new project manager at Langley."

Carol was quiet. Leo knew she was smiling.

"Look," he said. "The DDoS isn't exactly why I called."

"But there's a connection."

"Yeah." He paused, thinking. "You probably guessed the reason, huh?"

"No guessing for me, Leo. I said I *knew* you'd be in touch."

He sighed. "I'm getting boxed out," he said. "It's bullshit."

"I'm sorry."

"You asked for my files. I shared 'em," he said. "Don't be sorry. Help me. These pricks won't even return my messages."

"Leo, I'm having similar issues. If that's any consolation," she said. "Listen, I was thinking we could—"

He heard her stepdaughter say something in the background again. Carol held the phone away from her face a moment, talking to her. She didn't sound pleased.

"I'm back," she said after a few seconds. "Are you still there?"

"Yeah."

"Tricia made plans to go to the movies tonight after camp. Without bothering to tell me or her father..."

"Uh-huh."

"And just now wants money to pay for her and her *friend's* tickets..."

"Uh-huh."

She sighed into the phone.

"Kids," she said.

"Yeah," he said.

They were silent.

"Leo, I need to chat with the princess before she flees the car," Carol said after a moment. "This thing you called about—it's been turned over to a special unit. I'm their primary interface. And I think they may be ignoring operational guidance."

Harris wondered exactly what she meant.

"We need to talk," he said. "Do it from our offices. On secure landlines—"

"I'll be out of my office, Leo."

"All day?"

"Mostly. I'll be tied up through this afternoon. Then I'm flying into New York overnight—Ron's picking up the kids."

Harris lifted his eyebrows. *"New York?"*

"That's what I started to tell you a minute ago," she said. "It's about the President's Net Force initiative. I'll be staying at the Warwick as usual... If you like, we can meet for dinner."

He sat on his couch holding the phone to his ear.

"Everything okay, Leo?" Carol said.

"Yeah," he said. "I just wasn't planning on company."

"Oh," Carol said. "Well, then, *surprise*. See you later?"

His hand clenched the phone. "Later," he said.

And disconnected.

VI

By 9:00 a.m. Wednesday, Ki Marton had finished his second iced caramel macchiato of the morning and was eyeing a Chinese takeout menu. Actually, several menus sticking out of the zipper compartment of a young deliveryman's backpack.

The deliveryman was on his computer screen.

Ki thought he had a decent lead, and was partly chalking it up to beginner's luck: since the very first surveillance disc that he randomly picked from the stack on his desk was from a Brooklyn bank, he had decided to call up Alex Michaels's map of phony ATM card rejections, concentrating on that borough to see if any patterns emerged.

What he noticed immediately was that almost twenty withdrawals were attempted within a two-hour period along Coney Island Avenue, a stretch of slightly run-down shops and apartment buildings running for about five miles in a north-south line through Brooklyn. Whoever made the attempts moved consistently northward on that strip almost from end to end, with the average time between tries being seven minutes—although some occurred less than four minutes apart, and others more than ten.

Common sense told Ki that a single cardholder, or team of cardholders, was responsible for all the failed withdrawals at the Coney Island Avenue locations. The chip data would reveal the actual number of cards, since a unique transaction code was generated each time one was used. But the banks would have to provide the data, and getting it from them would take time, and probably subpoenas in some cases. The analysis was also way outside Ki's expertise, and best referred to Michaels's forensic lab.

Still, he thought the person—or persons—had covered too much ground, too quickly, to have moved on foot.

And so Ki cross-checked the bank locations along the avenue against the videos he'd received thus far, and found five that corresponded perfectly. All were on flash drives, which had been predictable—this was primarily a low-income immigrant neighborhood, where banks were slower to upgrade. From there he only needed to match the time stamps on the videos to the ATM logs, and then hope the image quality was good enough to be helpful.

The Asian kid showed up on all five videos. About eighteen years old, he had an e-bike that he would either walk or ride up to the machines, depending on the bank and whether the machines were indoor or outdoor.

The instant Ki saw the menus in his backpack, he knew the kid was a deliveryman. In New York City, when they brought their takeout orders to apartment buildings, they often went up and down the hallways slipping menus under doors to try and drum up new customers. And this kid had fifteen or twenty in his pack.

Four of the five videos hadn't enabled Ki to read the lettering on his menus. But watching him step up to an ATM for the fifth time now, he finally had a clear, unobstructed look at them. The problem, though, was the resolution…it was much too blurry for him to read the print.

He slurped down the last of his macchiato, then took the lid off the plastic cup, slung some crushed ice into his mouth and chewed on it. Freezing the image of the kid at the machine, Ki framed his takeout menus and then zoomed in on them, enhancing the contrast, reducing the digital noise. That would improve the image's clarity by eliminating the grain and random flecks of color that resulted from badly adjusted light settings.

He applied a few more filters, dragging and clicking, zooming in little more, then a *little more*, pulling back slightly when he started to lose definition…

Ki smiled with his mouth full of ice, peering at the menus through his glasses. He'd felt a sudden rush. There was no other word for it. Some people got it from drugs, bungee jumping, or race cars. He got it when the synthesis of different information and evidence streams yielded definitive results. It overtook him in a giddy, exhilarating wave.

"The Golden Wok Chinese Restaurant," he read aloud, opening a browser window to search for its phone number.

Ki found it in seconds. Then he reached over his shoulder and gave himself a pat on the back.

It was too early in the day for ordering dumplings and lo mein, but none too soon to get to the bottom of things.

VII

Leo arrived at 26 Fed at twenty past nine to find Adrián Soto waiting for him in the reception area, wearing a cream-colored linen suit, white French-cuff shirt, and black suede driving shoes with no socks.

"Pleasure to meet you, Mr. Soto," he said. And it wasn't just bullshit. The guy had done some impressive stuff. "You want a coffee or tea?"

"I've already filled my quota of caffeine," Soto said. "Thank you."

The SAC nodded. "Follow me," he said, motioning toward a corridor to his right.

They went down the hall to Harris's office, a midsized room with plain law enforcement trappings—a fake-wood-grain desk, computer, swivel chairs, a small conference table to one side in acknowledgment of his rank. On one corner of the desktop was a framed photo of his late mother, on the wall behind the desk some commendations, letters, and his two honorary service medals.

Leo pulled up a chair for Soto, then went around the desk and sat.

"Thanks for coming," he said. "I'm not sure how I'd react in your situation."

"Oh? How do you mean?"

"Fifty million dollars is a hell of a lot to have stolen from you."

Soto regarded him across the desk. "It is, yes. But I'm not thinking in terms of dollars. Do you know what the funds represented?"

"Maybe," Leo said. "Like I told you on the phone, we just got the information from the police department. The FBI usually takes the lead with this sort of thing…"

"Respectfully, Agent Harris," Soto said, "I reported the theft to the NYPD because I'm an active supporter of security partnerships with them." He paused. "I believe in information sharing. And I trusted the department would port the information I gave them to the right agency."

Harris grunted. "Back to your question," he said. "From what I know, you're building a new center for your Unity Project. The funds transfer was supposed to route from your lawyer's escrow account to a construction company. That right?"

"Exactly," Soto said. "Communications technology is how I make a living. But Unity is my life's work. I committed to it in my fiancée's name when she was killed in Iraq. Through Unity... I carry on our devotion."

Harris wasn't sure he knew what that meant, but the bleak look in Soto's eyes was a powerful hint. "I'm sorry," he said. "It must be pretty important to you."

"It's beyond important...and far, far beyond me." Soto smiled grimly. "I realize I must sound elliptical, Agent Harris. We don't need to discuss this further. Unless you think it's relevant to your investigation."

"Let's wait and see," Harris said, thinking he wanted to get the basic facts of the rip-off straight before going any deeper. "When you made the online transfer...did anything seem funny? The look of the website, the login...?"

"The system hung, if that's what you mean. And there was a usage delay notice."

Which Harris knew was par for the course during a DDoS attack. The screen would have appeared when Soto was hijacked and switched over to the hacker's clone banking site.

"How long did that last?"

"Only a short time... I think the digital meter said six minutes," Soto said. "Chloe can verify it for you."

"Chloe...that's your attorney?"

"Yes," Soto said. "Chloe Berne. She assumed the delay was because of the Fourth of July holiday. At the time, so did I. But I've thought about that moment a thousand times since, and obviously know better in hindsight."

Harris looked at him intently. "Three-day holidays are target dates for attacks on online finance sites. The hackers'll infect a whole system while everyone's not looking. When people get back from their weekend trips, there's a surge in banking transactions, so it looks like the network's crashed from being overloaded." His features grew thoughtful. "Mr. Soto, did you get any sketchy emails lately? Click on a suspicious link...?"

Soto shook his head no.

"And would anybody have had access to your computer over the weekend? Besides you, that is..."

Soto seemed puzzled by his question. "I don't know," he said. "Why do you ask?"

"Just the logical place to start," Harris said. "I should let you know, we'll need to take your machine for analysis. Our forensics people—"

"I wasn't using my computer," Soto said. "We were at Chloe's office when this happened...didn't you know?"

Leo shook his head. "We're still waiting for the NYPD case file, Mr. Soto. Welcome to my world."

Soto paused, taking that in. "Chloe normally handles all my large money transactions," he said. His eyes had that desolate look again. "This was to have been a special occasion."

Harris pulled a notepad and pen out of his top drawer. "Where's her office located?"

"Chelsea," Soto said. "West 16th Street."

"And her law firm?"

"Berne Financial Services. That's *B-e-r-n-e.*"

Harris grunted and wrote in his pad. "Does she share the office space with another company? Any employees?"

"No. Well, there's her receptionist. Stella," Soto said. "I don't know her last name. The police already tried contacting her."

Harris looked up from his pad. "Why's that?"

"She was in the office just before the long weekend, spoke to Chloe before leaving, but was absent from work yesterday. And today, so far."

"You're sure she's still MIA?"

Soto nodded. "Yes. I called Chloe's earlier this morning and she's concerned. In light of what's happened in the past twenty-four hours, it's understandable."

Harris felt a hunch sprouting inside him. "Can you describe Stella to me?"

Soto nodded. "I'd guess she's in her late twenties, maybe thirty. Brown hair, slim. Very attractive."

A moment passed. Leo was still thinking. "Can you get hold of Chloe for me? So I can ask her a question or two?"

Soto looked at him directly, nodding.

"I'll try her right now," he said, and reached into his pocket for his phone.

VIII

It was a few minutes shy of 11:00 a.m. when Musil and Fahey's bureau car pulled up to the Golden Wok Chinese Restaurant in Brooklyn.

As he exited, Agent Fahey was thinking they could always count on Ki Marton to send them running around the crappiest of neighborhoods far outside the bounds of modern civilization. This restaurant was about as big a dump as the Romanian joint they had visited in Queens the day before—different borough, different ethnic cuisine, same public health hazard.

He frowned. Why couldn't anyone who tried using one of those dud cash cards work for a decent lower Manhattan pasta joint?

The agents stepped through the restaurant's door, the little clutch of bells above it chiming over their heads.

The place looked as if it hadn't been redecorated since Nixon was president. There were red leatherette booths, red paper lanterns hanging from the ceiling, white ceramic Buddhas on the walls, and a red velveteen curtain in back separating the dining floor from the kitchen area. The two women behind the front counter looked like mother and daughter: the older one in her fifties or early sixties and thick around the middle, the younger one maybe eighteen and slender.

"Good morning," Musil said, taking the lead. He displayed his ID card, gave his name, and offered a bright smile. "Your food smells wondrous."

The women stared at their visitors in guarded silence, their eyes going to Musil's turban.

He was no stranger to that reaction.

"I have a few questions," he said, reaching into his sport jacket for a hard copy image of Marton's deliveryman. "We were wondering if you recognize this—"

"Oh my God!" The younger woman saw the picture and gasped, covering her mouth with one hand. She looked at the other cashier, spoke through her fingers. "Grandma…it's Han!"

Musil traded glances with Fahey, then turned back to the women. "Han? Is that his name?"

They were staring at him now. Musil thought they looked worried.

Worried and scared.

"Is something wrong?" he asked.

The younger woman looked at her grandmother as if seeking approval. She got it in the form of a nod and turned to Musil.

"His name is Han Jingrui," she said. Her voice was quivering. "He's been missing since yesterday."

IX

Minutes after Adrián Soto left headquarters, Harris dispatched an ERT to Chloe Berne's office, gave the attorney a heads-up that they would be coming for the likely infected computer, and arranged to meet with her about the here-and-gone Stella Vasile. Then the SAC went to Evidence and claimed the white plastic card recovered from the Queens eatery, having decided to drive it over to Alex and touch base with him in person.

He drove north on West Street now, the High Line greenway running overhead to his right, Jersey on the left across the Hudson. With traffic relatively light, and the sun shining down over the water from a cloudless sky, the drive wasn't too bad.

Glancing out at the boats on the river, Leo could not help but think of Carol. She loved being near the water; it was something he had learned about her almost from the first time they met. Whisk her off on a long weekend, just give her a water view. It didn't really matter where, though she definitely had her favorite places. Virginia Beach...talk about views. They had spent their honeymoon there in a cabin near Hampton Road, the front porch looking out across the dunes at water bluer than he ever saw anywhere else in his life.

Leo sighed. Passing the boat piers on 34th Street, he flipped down his visor to block the glare of the sun. He suddenly remembered something Adrián Soto said to him back at HQ. He was talking about his bride-to-be dying in Iraq...about his commitment to her, and the Unity Project...

I carry on our devotion.

He could still see the look in Soto's eyes as the words left his mouth. It wasn't pain, but something else. Maybe something worse. Whoever robbed him took millions, but his loss wasn't really about money. They had stolen everything that was left of his girl in Iraq, everything he carried of her, everything that was *theirs*. It all was torn right out of him.

Leo understood. From the moment Soto gave him that look, he had known he would make whoever was responsible for the hack pay a hundred times over. But why? Why the hell did he want it so much?

He swallowed dryly. Why bother pretending not to know? That was the real question.

"Carol," he muttered into the silence of the car. "I don't need to think about this. I really don't right now."

Approaching 42nd Street, slowing as traffic thickened around the entry ramp, he lifted his sunglasses, swiped some moisture from under them, and glanced up at the rearview. Staring into his own eyes, he took a long, horrified breath.

They could have been Adrián Soto's.

11

I

Han Jingrui had not been home all night. He was *afraid* to go home. When his forged bank card was rejected at bank after bank, he'd realized he was in trouble. But only now, with FBI agents coming to see his family, did he realize how serious it was.

Why did he throw away those takeout orders? What was he thinking?

Things wouldn't have been so bad if he had delivered the food and *then* tried to use the ATMs. But how could he explain the missing orders? What would he tell Uncle Zhu?

Confused and afraid after his last unsuccessful withdrawal attempt, Han had started off on his e-bike without any particular destination in mind, wanting to escape from it all.

A while later, he found himself on a bench on the Belt Parkway promenade, staring at the container ships as they sailed beneath the Verrazano-Narrows Bridge. Though only minutes from the apartment, it seemed a world away.

Han had remained on that bench until he fell into an exhausted sleep. When he awoke, and checked the time on his phone, it was almost eleven o'clock the next morning. On impulse, he phoned his youngest sister, Jen, at the apartment.

She was frantic. The family was sick with worry, she said, wanting to know where he was. Han assured her that he was fine and asked if their parents were home.

They weren't. Father was at the Chinatown bus line where he worked selling tickets, and their mother was out caring for an elderly relative. Jen explained that she had instructions to phone her if Han showed up...or if there was any word about him.

Then his sister's voice lowered. "Han, you're in trouble."

"No, Mouse." Using his pet name for her.

"Yes. They called from the restaurant. Two men were there asking questions. They said they were FBI. One showed a picture of you to the cashiers."

"No."

"Stop saying that, Han. In the picture, you were at a cash machine. Uncle Zhu feared you were robbed."

"I wasn't. I told you I'm okay. I—"

"What does the FBI want?"

Han took a deep breath. "Mouse, I need money. Can you meet me?"

"I'm watching the twins. They're asleep."

Han was thinking he could jump on his e-bike and be at the apartment in a hurry. Borrow the money, and a little food too. He didn't know where he would go, but couldn't look that far ahead. He was an illegal immigrant. He had tried to steal thousands with a counterfeit cash card. He couldn't let them find him.

"I'll come to you," he said, and ended the call.

Ten minutes afterward, he swung off the bike in front of his building, where the shopkeeper downstairs was busily putting his goods out onto the street.

"Ni hao!" the old man said, dragging his arm across his sweaty forehead. *"Dao lar?"*

Hello! What's your hurry today?

Han didn't answer. Leaning the bike against a streetlamp, not even bothering to chain it, he ran upstairs to his apartment.

If he had stopped for even a moment, he might have seen the Dodge Charger approaching under the elevated train tracks, a black-turbaned man in the passenger seat.

II

"Take a look, Jot," Fahey said, his voice raised over the clatter of the train passing overhead. "This is it."

Musil studied the yellow e-bike propped against the lamppost. It was the same one from the video caps.

Their car double-parked at the curb, the agents were on the sidewalk eyeing the bike, the old storekeeper checking them out in a curious, appraising way. After a moment, Musil turned toward the apartment building. It was a two-story walkup, the shop on the ground floor, the apartment directly above it. The entrance was next to the storefront.

Musil looked at the storekeeper, producing his FBI ID. "Han Jingrui—do you know if he's home?"

"No speak English," the man replied, reading the card badge.

Fahey read the sale signs on the sidewalk bins, all of them written in English. After a second he exchanged nods with Musil. *Writes it just fine, though.*

They hurried toward the building's entrance.

III

Han Jingrui was turning his key in the lock when the apartment's door flew open, his sister standing on the other side.

"Mouse," he said. "I—"

"Wo yizhi haipa," she said in Szechuanese, snuffling. "I've been scared."

"Don't worry." He hugged her. "*Yiqie duhui hio qilai.* Everything will be fine."

She tilted her head back to look at him. "Is it the *se tao*? Are you in trouble with them?"

"I have to go," Han said. He had no time to explain. "Do you have the money?"

"Yes." Jen put her hand in his, and he realized she was holding several bills. "Fifty dollars. It was for the rent."

He felt a fresh pang of remorse. "I'll pay you back," he said, taking the cash. "I have to pack..."

He fell silent at the sound of the street door opening downstairs—followed at once by ascending footsteps.

"Come in...quickly!" She clutched his sides, looking past him at the stairs. "I'll hide you!"

Han shook his head. They both knew there was no hiding anyone in their tiny apartment. He looked over his right shoulder at the short flight of stairs heading up to the rooftop. The buildings on the street were all two stories, joined by common walls. If he hurried, he might be able to jump over to one of the adjoining roofs. Distance himself from whoever was on the stairs, then make it down to the street—

It was his only way out.

He gripped Jen's shoulders, kissing her forehead. "I love you, Mouse," he said, and whirled toward the stairs.

IV

Musil and Fahey were halfway to the second floor when they heard a door close above them. Then the clicking of tumblers. Racing upstairs, they turned up the hall toward its single apartment.

The agents went quickly to the door, standing to its left and right, staying clear of the middle where bullets could come flying through from the other side. Fahey took the lead, rapping on it twice.

"FBI," he said. "We want to speak with Han Jingrui."

He let a second pass. Two. No one answered him. But both agents heard a faint sound from inside the apartment. The creaking of floorboards.

Someone was standing there behind the door.

Fahey knocked again, harder, pounding with his brawny fist. "Open up," he said. "This is your last warning." The agents did not need a warrant; a fleeing suspect was almost the definition of an exigent circumstance under the United States laws of criminal procedure.

They heard the lock turn on the other side of the door. Musil inhaled, ready to draw his service pistol.

It didn't prove necessary. The door opened partway, a slight, teenaged Asian girl in jeans and a tube top standing in the entry.

"Han isn't here," she said, peering out at them. "I... I don't know where he is..."

She was not a good liar. Fahey edged around the door frame, his palm flat on the door in case she tried to slam it shut. "We need to come in," he said. "Step aside, please."

His hand still hovering near his holster, Musil was braced to cover Fahey's entry into the apartment when he noticed something—a movement—at the upper edge of his vision. It was above them to the right, atop a short set of stairs.

His eyes broke from the girl's terrified face to look in that direction. The roof door was ajar. He must have seen it swinging ever so slightly in the breeze.

She was partly telling the truth, he thought. Han wasn't in the apartment. He had no doubt of it.

"Frank...this way!" he shouted.

Then he swiveled and ran off toward the roof entrance, exactly as the boy had done moments earlier.

V

Musil burst out the door and saw the boy at once. He'd already jumped the low parapet between his rooftop and the adjacent one, and was running toward the back of the other building.

The agent thought he could guess his intentions. In New York City tenements, the ladders descending from roofs to fire escapes were mostly situated over their rear windows. This was to discourage burglars from casing a place from the street out front, climbing the fire escape to the roof, then entering a building through the rooftop door.

The boy was probably trying to reach the ladder. Planning to scamper down into the backyard, hop a fence, and disappear. And he'd gotten enough of a head start to do it.

Musil took off after him, Fahey following close behind. Softened from days of ninety-something-degree heat, the sunbaked tar stuck tackily to their shoe bottoms as they sprinted to the thigh-high parapet, planted their hands on it, and boosted themselves over onto the other roof.

"Han Jingrui!" Musil shouted. "Stop! We're FBI!"

The boy ignored him. Musil saw the egress ladder's rusty iron handrails straight in line with his path, confirming his hunch. He took a deep breath and turned after him.

Not for a second did he consider reaching for his sidearm. This was a teenager barely older than his firstborn daughter. A boy who showed no signs of aggression. Musil was not going to use his gun, not unless something drastic happened to change his mind.

He ran on, closing the short distance between them, Fahey pounding the tar at his back. The boy had reached the ladder, grabbed the handrail, and was swinging himself down onto its upper rungs.

"*Stop!*" Musil yelled, grabbing at his arm with one hand, catching nothing but air. The boy took a step down the ladder and Musil reached out again, this time getting hold of him, clenching his fingers tightly around his right shoulder.

"We just want to talk," he said. His voice level. "No one's going to hurt you."

The kid tried to pull free of his grip, jerking his arm backward so violently it pulled Musil off balance. He stumbled closer to the parapet, not releasing the kid's shoulder, his fingers digging into the sleeve of his T-shirt.

Meanwhile, Fahey had caught up to them. Coming alongside Musil at the roof's edge, he brought his gun out of its holster and held it in a shooter's grip, his hands wrapped around the butt, arms extended straight out.

"Okay, that's enough," he said. "You better get back up here."

The boy just stared at him, sweat pouring down his cheeks, his face trembling and frantic. He squirmed, struggling to break Musil's grip.

Musil would always remember wanting to signal Fahey to holster the gun. Would recall taking his attention off the boy for a split second, turning his head toward his partner, thinking the gun wouldn't do any good…

Then a hot, terrible flare of pain through the back of his hand brought his eyes back to the boy. He was biting Musil's hand in a desperate frenzy, sinking his teeth into the flesh above his wrist.

Musil grimaced, his fingers involuntarily loosening their grip on the kid's shoulder. Han twisted around on the ladder, wrenched himself away from the agent with all his strength…

And slipped. One of his feet had dropped off the rung on which he'd planted it, the toe of his sneaker trying to find the ladder again and missing. Gaping in surprise and horror, he swayed backward, his other foot suddenly losing purchase too. He clung to the ladder with one hand now, barely hanging on to the rail.

Musil leaned across the parapet, his arms outstretched. "Reach," he told the kid. Doing his best to sound calm, to be calm inside. "Reach for me."

Han Jingrui tried, his fingers trembling with effort. For an instant they managed to find the agent's injured hand, but they couldn't gain traction. It was the blood streaming down between Musil's knuckles, the sweat slicking the boy's fingers. It was gravity pulling him away from the side of the building, dragging him toward the ground.

Beside him, Fahey dropped his gun, the weapon clattering to the rooftop. A full head taller than Musil, with longer arms, he was reaching over the wall too now, groping for the boy's wrist, his arm, anything. But he was unable to get hold of him, the kid was too far down the ladder.

And then, Han Jingrui finally relinquished his grip and went sailing downward through space.

For Musil, the rest seemed to unfold in slow motion. His arms flailing wildly, the boy plummeted to the pavement, hitting it with a thud the agent would never forget.

A moment passed. Musil sucked in a breath. Fahey beside him, he stared down over the edge of the roof, impaled by guilt and sorrow.

"My God," he croaked. "Frank, what have we done?"

Fahey tried to answer but couldn't.

Couldn't.

BOOK II

HEKATE'S WHEEL

12

I

"Take a look around us," Blond Man said. "It will tell you everything you need to know."

Kali was silent in her chair. She had come a long distance from The Island, the helicopter flight ending when her captors slipped a burlap sack over her head and hustled her into a motor vehicle. The heavy slam of its door had told her it was armored.

When it stopped after a long drive, Blond Man and the others brought her into this room, removed the sack, and left her alone.

Until now.

He stood quietly in front of her, waiting. Kali just stared at him. She had seen all she needed of her surroundings.

The room was small and boxy. White walls, a door to her right, dark shades drawn over the windows behind the man. Its furnishings consisted of the wooden chair where she was handcuffed and manacled, and a table and chairs where two of her captors sat with cups of coffee.

All of them except Blond Man came and went in shifts. He rarely left the room, and was the only one who spoke to her. Here or aboard the helicopter.

"Do you know where we are?" he asked.

Us. We. The inclusive phrasing did not escape her. He was skilled at more than pursuit.

The nondescript room could have been anywhere, Kali thought. That was likely intentional. They would want her disoriented. But she was certain they had brought her north along the Italian coast. The drive took perhaps two hours, most of it on a straight, fast road. Halfway through the trip, she felt her ears repeatedly pop from changes in altitude, which told her they were traveling over elevated terrain.

Blond Man stood motionless. Watching her. The pupil of his heterochromic right eye was dilated, a frozen black circle.

"Remember what I told you about mutual cooperation?" he said. "I hope you take my advice. Otherwise there are going to be more rooms like this. Eventually a max prison cell. And that would be a waste."

Kali said nothing. She had once gone hiking up the slopes of Monte Etna. During her climb, she decided to explore the rocky areas around the Alcantara river, north of the great volcano. The trek she charted out roughly followed the course of the river as it wound toward the Ionian Sea. She was able to feel its nearness the entire time, even deep in the valleys toward Giadinni with the hills blocking it from sight.

It was the same for her in the armored vehicle. The water was close by, its proximity tugging at something inside her. Then, toward the end of the drive there was a gradual turn west. As she was led from the vehicle into a building, she had smelled exhaust and heard city noises—cars, people, the thick buzzing of scooters.

Where?

"Messina," she said. "The Via Nino Bixio. Where the Vespas park between the office buildings."

Blond Man slipped his thumbs into the waist of his trousers. But his expression betrayed no surprise.

"Good to know you still have a voice," he said.

She didn't answer. Her jaw was tender on the left side, where he struck her back on The Island. There was a slight burning quality to her soreness—a bone bruise, she thought—and it made talking painful.

Several moments passed. Blond Man turned away, pulled a chair from the table, spun it around to face her, and straddled it.

"You're good at covering your tracks," he said. "Border hopping, encrypted VPNs. It isn't easy to stay under the radar these days, and my team specializes in the toughest cases. But you had us going for a while."

Across the room, the two men at the table tried to look uninvolved with the questioning. Kali thought them better hunters than actors.

Blond Man sat watching her for perhaps thirty seconds. Then he reached into his pocket for a pack of chewing gum, pulled out a stick, and held it out. When she didn't react, he peeled off the wrapper and slid the gum into his mouth.

"We aren't flying blind with you," he said. "You've shaken some powerful people to their cores. Bankers, politicos, businessmen. We know they were all dirty as hell, which isn't coincidental." He paused, his eyes seeking hers. "I retraced your steps as far as I could. When you knocked out that troll farm in St. Petersberg, you were, what, nineteen? Twenty?"

Kali said nothing. Her face pale and composed, her forehead smooth under her raven hair, she stared straight ahead as if gazing through him at an imaginary point on the wall.

"You probably know I saw you in action two months ago. That night on Ruppertstrasse," he said. "I'm not sure anyone else on earth could have pulled that motorcycle stunt. Under fire, no less."

He folded his arms and leaned forward, studying her face.

"What you might *not* know, what I want to tell you, is that we believe your malware's been borrowed…though I suppose a better word might be *cannibalized*," he said. "But before I go on, I should ask how you feel about someone using your sleeper scripts."

Kali remained outwardly detached, her face without expression. This man was not a note taker, she thought. He held a surgical knife to his subjects, dissected them with his mind.

She stretched her fingers imperceptibly. Her hands were cramped from the cuffs, and she concentrated on getting out the stiffness. *Flexor carpi radialis. Flexor pollicis longus. Flexor digitorum superficialis.* The circulation returned to them, one by one.

Blond Man studied her features. "The word on the hacker sites…those big, bad underground *Dark Web* forums…the word is the good guys should be worrying about a superbug called Hekate. Sound familiar?"

He kept staring at her, chewing his gum, his head tilted slightly.

Kali felt her stomach tighten. His scalpel had gone deep.

"Another question. On Malta I noticed a little tattoo behind your ear. Right about here." He tapped an area behind his own ear with two fingers. "Looks like some kind of disc. Or a wheel. And I'm curious about it. About whether it has some special meaning."

Hekate of the Three Forms. Worker from afar. Goddess of the crossroads, powerful in heaven and hell.

The piercing of Kali Alcazar's heart manifested outwardly as the slightest hitch in her breath. Blond Man picked up on it—she saw it in his expression. He was good at concealing it, better than good. But she could see.

She silently cursed herself.

Several long moments of silence passed. Then he finally nodded.

"We'll talk again," he said.

And getting up off the chair, he went to the door, opened it, and stepped through without another word.

II

His head no sooner hit the pillows than his mobile satphone rang. A half hour had passed since he left Outlier in the room to consider some things.

He grabbed the phone off the nightstand. It was Morse. Her call wasn't at all unexpected.

"What is it?" he answered.

"You sound thrilled to hear from me."

"I just turned in," he said. "And the mattress has lousy springs."

"Our budget isn't what it used to be," she said. "It's barely nine o'clock in your part of the world. An early bedtime."

Which was her way of telling him she knew he was playing with Outlier's biological clock. And, he thought, screwing up his own in the process.

"So," he said. "Why the call?"

"You were supposed to deliver the detainee today. What happened?"

He scratched behind his ear. "A traffic jam."

"I'm serious. The station was expecting you hours ago."

He took a breath. "She's one of a kind. We lock her away, lose her as a resource, we'll live to regret it."

"That isn't your decision," Morse said. "Fox Team has the widest possible latitude conducting its operations. I've bent over backward to assure your autonomy. But as far as you're concerned, this one wrapped in Malta. The plan was never to weaponize her."

"No one's doing that. We're bringing her in gift-wrapped. I just want a few extra days to see what I can get out of her."

"Stop. My bullshit meter's going crazy."

He inhaled. "Is it Rome that's got you in a twist? Or something else?"

"I don't understand the question."

"Now I'm calling bullshit. Your legendary ex has been on Outlier's tail longer than me."

"That's seriously out of line."

"No more than you telling me how to do my job," he said. "Listen, I need some sleep. It was a long trip here. If you don't mind, I'm hanging up."

"No. I don't have time for your stunts. In case you need to be reminded, we're tracking your movements half a dozen different ways—"

"Talk to you later," he said, thumbing the Disconnect button without another word.

Returning the phone to the nightstand, Carmody lowered his head back onto his pillow and shut his eyes. It was hard enough getting to sleep. But he had things under control.

He had swallowed something that would give him a good night's rest, and figured it would kick in before too long.

III

Harris peered through the clean room's observation window, watching Alex and his lab personnel work at their sophisticated instruments in caps, hoods, face masks, coveralls, gloves, and boots. For him, they conjured up chilling images of scientists in biohazard suits working to stamp out some horrible plague virus. And he supposed that was sort of what they did here, although the bugs these experts studied and tried to eradicate were the kind that infected computer systems, not human beings.

"What they're doing's pretty cool, sir," Bryan Ferago said, standing beside him at the window. "We've had mass spectrometry for over a hundred years. But ionization methods were imprecise, and the equipment wasn't available to most labs."

Leo looked him. "A hundred years?" he said. "I can just about remember back that far."

"Well, sir, using ionization as a forensic technique would've been out of the question in those days," Bryan said, seemingly oblivious to his sarcasm. "Applying stable isotope analyses to something like that card back then...just trying to efficiently vaporize the plastic into ionic plasma...forget it."

Harris heard his molars grind together. This was turning out to be one of those days. After being stuck in traffic on the West Side Highway, he'd shown up at the Cyberlab with the white plastic half an hour behind the prof's civilian analysts. Both had high-level Top Secret with Sensitive Compartmented Information, or TS/SCI, Bureau security clearances.

Harris was familiar with one of the civs, Travis Kinsman. A polymer maven and former student of Alex's, he had assisted the bureau with dozens of investigations and appeared in court as an expert witness. The other was a programming expert—and another of the prof's wirehead postgrads—named Felicia Cheng, who helped Cyber investigate a rash of cell phone hacks about a year ago. Harris recalled that she had diligently attended to her lab work without saying much, a quality he was presently wishing would rub off on the Ferago kid.

"It fascinates me that they're paying so much attention to the card itself," Bryan went on. "I thought all the really valuable information was in the chip."

Harris kept looking through the clean room window. The card had to come from somewhere. One piece of plastic wasn't the same as another. Some credit cards were ABS plastic, and some were BVC. You got batches from this place, and batches from that place. And maybe the batches from this place had telltale additives like sand, chalk, or clay, while the other batch of cards contained cheap filler like walnut shells.

On the other side of the glass, Kinsman sat down at a computer keyboard and typed with gloved hands, using a software interface to adjust the settings of a boxy gray mass spectrometer. A tiny slice of the card had been vaporized by a concentrated electron beam, magnets separating its charged ionic particles according to their mass and weight. At a workstation across from

Kinsman, meanwhile, Felicia Cheng was removing the card's EMV chip.

Harris motioned in her direction. "What you thought about the chips ain't wrong," he said…not that he wanted to start the kid babbling again. "They're little computers, and any computer can be hacked. And if you can hack 'em, you can clone the cards. Doesn't matter that banks like people to think something different."

"So we have to find out if that happened," Bryan said. "Or possibly if there was an inside man at the chip manufacturer."

"Right," Harris said. "But far as where the cards were made, most come from China, India, and lately the Russkies. And you can bet that if a company's gonna use an additive, it's using what's local. Otherwise why bother?"

Bryan's eyes lit up. "Once you pay to import them, you're right back to escalating costs," he said. "The *additives* can tell us where the cards came from. The state, the country, the manufacturer if we have samples for comparison."

Leo nodded. "If we stick with it, and get lucky, we might find out who ordered the cards."

"And that's when the fun stuff starts," Bryan said, breaking into a smile.

IV

Yunes Abrika had been of the ancient Beja people, a great-grandson of nomadic Ammar'ar camel breeders, and grandson of the first tribesmen to settle the Hagar Oasis, near the processing facilities and pipelines along the Birhanese coast—once a crescent-shaped slice of northeastern Sudan.

Among the longest oil and natural gas pipelines in North Africa, the Hagar refinery extended almost a thousand miles from the Nuba concession in South Sudan to the Gulf of Aden. Energy companies from Qatar, Egypt, France, Germany, Great Britain, the United States, and most recently Russia all leased blocks of the concession, which produced over two million barrels of oil a day for its stakeholders. Beja laborers maintained its infrastructure, managing the pipeline's six pumping stations from initial injection to final delivery, loading the barrels onto trucks for transport from the huge circular storage tanks at Port Birhan to the city's shipping piers on the Nile.

A few minutes before four o'clock in the morning, Husam and Rajiya Abrika left their apartment in the working-class Satair housing development on Hagar Oasis with large hand-written signs and blown up photos of their only son, Yunes, his wife, Sekura, and their three orphaned children. In his seventies, white-haired and stooped, Husam's face was sunken with grief. Rajiya had eyes so bloodshot from crying their whites were a flaming red.

As the pair descended the stairs leading into the central court-yard, other doors began opening around them—men and women exiting alone or in larger groups. They carried handmade plac-ards of their own to protest the killings of Yunes and his wife. They carried traditional hand drums, gourd *shekeres*, bells, and kalimbas for when the time came to declare their outrage. Like the Abrikas, some were retired seniors, but most were in their working prime, the men mostly employed at the refinery, and the women in the hotels, stores, and restaurants of the service industry.

At this hour, they normally would have been heading off to-ward their jobs. Instead, they filed down into the courtyard, gathering there until over three hundred residents stood together in the predawn twilight.

Yunes Abrika was a favorite son to the Beja community, the pride of the oil workers on whose backs and shoulders the Birha-nese economy had risen. United in their heartbreak and indig-nation, they marched with a single purpose.

Today the workers would refuse to work. In Yunes's name, they planned to make their voices heard.

Over the next several days, their numbers would multiply. From home after home, street after street, and neighborhood after neighborhood, the two hundred strikers would turn into a thousand, the thousand growing into a human deluge that would soon spread all across the great oasis, sweeping inexorably toward the fields, refineries, and pipelines of Port Birhan.

V

"This is incredible," Harris said.

"I told you," Carol replied. "Trust me, Leo. I knew."

He swallowed a mouthful of his New York strip steak, took a deep gulp of cabernet sauvignon, and then gestured toward her dish with his glass. "How's that hula-hula fish?"

Carol chuckled. "The mahi-mahi's perfect," she said. "And don't think the clueless routine fools me for a minute."

"Hey, what can I tell you?" he said with a shrug. "I love a willing audience."

She ate quietly.

The restaurant downstairs at the Warwick Hotel was busy, its lights softened, its servers fanning out efficiently among the red banquettes, leather chairs, and blond wooden tables. They had asked for a rear table against a wall decorated with a Cornwell mural—Sir Water Raleigh and Queen Elizabeth.

"Okay," he said. "You going to tell me why you're in New York, or do I have to ask you everything?"

Carol watched him gulp more wine with his food. She was a slim, attractive blonde in her midforties, wearing a black crepe blazer, black slacks, and a pale blue silk blouse that closely matched the color of her eyes.

"I'm multitasking," she said. "I have a scheduled conference with the governor about his Wall Street cryptocurrency project…how it integrates with President Fucillo's cyber initiative. A Cabinet-level organization like Net Force, charged with oversight over our entire nation's cybersecurity, will need major backing and cooperation at the state and city levels. There are also issues related to her upcoming trip to New York. This is a domestic event, your playground, but there are intelligence aspects in which Langley has a role." She picked up her knife and fork. "Finally, I plan to meet with Alex Michaels to discuss funding for Net Force."

"And how come I'm not invited?" Harris said, pulling a face.

Carol smiled. "I would have contacted you days ago. But I've been preoccupied with a major cybersecurity issue."

"Namely?"

"We've heard chatter about some new superbug. Friend-to-friend networks, peer-to-peers, EfNets...it's pervasive on the underground web," she said. "This isn't a case where the *maker's* hyping himself. Or even the core members of a gang. You know how it goes these days..."

"Been a long time since the crews were three maladjusted nerds sharing two laptops in a basement," Harris said. "Remember those Global Inferno busts? Must've been my first year with the bureau. What was their motto?"

"'Global Inferno burns, Global Inferno cannot be put out!'" she said, and grinned. "So poetic."

"Right," he said. "We probably prosecuted thirty or forty of 'em. But most were in diapers. They peed 'em in court and walked."

Carol was nodding.

"That's the thing," she said. "The thrill seekers got their kicks vandalizing or crashing websites and aged out. The elites found sponsor governments, hooked up with their spy services. North Korea, Iran, China..."

"And goddamn Russia," Leo grunted. "Listen, I hear you about the chest-pounding on the internet. But superbugs hardly ever come as advertised." He looked at her. "So what's the deal? You get wind this latest one was used in yesterday's bank attacks?"

Carol leaned forward and spoke in a confidential tone. "With Fucillo pushing for Net Force, we already have a tighter system in place for exchanging intel with NSA. Their monitoring of the international P2P channels is impressive, Leo. There are hundreds of thousands of secret group forums and private texts. That's on top of *countless* hidden data and file shares…and NSA's able to separate out the high-grade ore." She paused. "The name that kept popping up was Hekate. It's supposedly a mash-up. A highly adaptive hybrid that can morph—*evolve* is a better word—on command after infecting a system."

He finished his wine, reached for the bottle, and pointed a finger at Carol's half-drained glass. She waved a hand over it.

"I'm fine, thanks," she said, and watched him refill his wine-glass. "You're hitting it pretty hard and fast, aren't you?"

Harris shrugged and drank, ignoring her. "I didn't hear you say why you think this Hekate might be what infected H&L Trust," he said.

Carol's eyes tightened. "Just a hunch," she said.

"Not that it's got some things in common with Outlier's mal-ware? Based on what I told you. When I didn't have to, that is."

She was quiet.

"Crap," he said. "Look who isn't talking all of a sudden."

Carol's eyes went to his. "I came here to talk," she said. "Am I required to do it at your pace?"

"I didn't say—"

She put out her hand in a *stop* gesture. "Let's move on. Seri-ously, Leo."

Harris breathed, his chest and shoulders rising and falling. He lifted his glass off the table.

"Adrián Soto came to my office this morning," he said. "He's the goods. The man's got a foundation in East Harlem, and the fifty mil he lost was going toward a public center. There was a girl, his late fiancée—"

"Malika Jamin," Carol put in. "She was an Iraqi national, a Sunni interpreter at CECOM. Her family was educated and solid middle-class, her father a newspaper editor and secularist…but with strong anti-Western sentiments. Her brothers followed in his footsteps, and one was even doing early web-based support for ISIS—setting up social media accounts, posting propaganda, the works." She expelled a sigh. "Soto was expecting her at occupation headquarters one night. She never showed up. As an officer with some clout, he pushed for an immediate search and got one. The next morning, our soldiers found her handcuffed and clubbed to death on the city's outskirts."

Leo shook his head. He turned the glass in his hands, staring into it. "Soto didn't give me details," he said. "But the fifty mil getting ripped off...it must be like she died a second time."

Carol nodded thoughtfully. "Eyewitnesses saw someone whose description matched her oldest brother—the keyboard warrior—dumping the body out of a car trunk. But this was Baghdad. Her father was an influential man, and she was a woman. A second-class citizen. The crime went unpunished."

Harris looked up from his wineglass. "I want to know if Outlier's connected to the ripoff," he said. "And if your people have her in custody."

Silence. Carol waited for a server to pass out of earshot.

"Okay, Leo," she said. "I'll give it to you straight. Even though I know goddamn well I may live to regret it."

He waited.

"She was run down by one of our paramilitary operations/specialized skills officers. He heads up a tac unit within our cyberwarfare department...the whole thing falls under the Special Operations Group."

"Deeper than deep," Harris said.

She nodded, leaning forward, discreetly glancing around the table. "His team is small, stealthy, and efficient. It's assigned prime targets—the most elusive, dangerous, or otherwise highly wanted individuals in our sights. Once in the field, he operates with close to full autonomy...we basically set him loose and trust them to do the job."

Harris swished the remnants of his cabernet around his glass. "Must be nice," he said. "So, what's your boy done to piss you off?"

Whatsh.

Carol looked at him. "You're slurring your words," she said. "I thought you were driving back to Jersey."

"You want to be my designated?"

"I'm not kidding."

"Me neither," he said, and raised his eyes to hers again.

She looked back at him steadily. "What is it with you tonight? I've seen you in bad states before. Never like this."

"That mean you won't come home with me?" He shrugged, drained what was left in his glass. "Sorry, Car. Blame it on the wine."

She looked at him.

"All right, Leo. Answers. To your first question...my SpecOp caught Outlier," she said. "That's the part you already know."

"And the shit side?"

"He won't give her up," she said.

VI

In his official suite at the Royal Palace, Ansari Kem had spent hours watching the state news agency's television coverage of the labor strike at Port Birhan's Hagar refinery. For all his concern about the Haria Square protests, Kem saw the strike as a potentially graver problem. Far graver, in fact.

He simply needed to look out the palace windows to see what was happening in the square. The demonstrators were loud and disorderly. They had caused damage to public and private property, disrupted business, and given the Western media scads of dramatic images. But they could be managed. The police and military were already taking steps to suppress them and would use more definitive measures if they persisted.

Kem did not trouble himself over bad press. It was diffuse and impossible to control through the direct exercise of leverage and power. But in Zayar City, both fell to the Negassie regime. And Kem was its hammer of justice.

Still in his morning robe, Kem leaned back in his armchair and turned his eyes from his television monitor to the tablet on his lap, studying a photograph of Uksem Kgosi's lifeless body. Tanzir had forwarded several to him overnight per his request.

He sat deep in thought, studying them for several long minutes. The soldier received harsh but warranted justice. It would impart a necessary lesson to other uniformed men.

The protesters needed something similar.

Out in the square below, they held torches, Molotov cocktails, and stones, while the government troops used guns. Pit them against each other and guns always won. Kem would not be reluctant to order the use of lethal force if the demonstrations grew uncontrollable. Their fires could be stamped out easily, and with minimal repercussions.

But he knew Haria Square was a microcosm, and that its torches had ignited a wider, deeper blaze throughout the nation's populace. He was concerned about what might happen outside the capitol, in the towns and villages where the prince's power reached its outer limits. The fire could not be allowed to spread that far.

In Port Birhan, the agitators had something which made the situation far more dangerous...and that was the real, quantifiable, and immediate leverage they gained from staffing the oil production facilities.

In life, Yunes Abrika had been a heroic figure. His success was his kinsmen's triumph and inspiration, his vision a projection of their dreams. But his death made him a martyr...and martyrs were untouchable. There was no bargaining with them. They could not be budged by persuasiveness or intimidation.

In death, their power grew.

As chief of Sudanese intelligence, Kem had learned that the only way to be rid of a martyr was to eradicate his followers. Swiftly and completely. Only when *they* were purged would one be rid of the ghost as well.

He was a man of decision. Of strength. The prince might be willing to let the flames devour him, but he understood what needed to be done. There was no avoiding it. No backing off in fear. For him the question was not *whether* to act, but only when...

And how.

VII

"Prince Negassie... Sami. *Salām*," President Fucillo said over the phone. A secure line to the Birhanese capitol established, she was speaking from her tiny office off the Situation Room under the West Wing. "I appreciate your availability on short notice."

"*Wa alaikum*, Madam President. Our gratitude is mutual. I'm highly aware it is midnight in Washington...my wife is currently visiting her family in Maryland. I appreciate that you've gone out of your way to call at an optimal time for me."

Fucillo shrugged inwardly. Every head of state on the planet knew she was a chronic insomniac. But she'd thought lowering the boom on Negassie first thing in the morning *his* time might actually give her a psychological edge in their conversation.

"I know these are difficult days for you," she said. "And I want *you* to know the United States deeply values our relationship with Birhan as a political and economic partner. That's been true since your War of Liberation."

"Thank you," Negassie said. "I have not forgotten your support in the past."

Fucillo took a breath. "Sami, we've always communicated frankly," she said. "The losses of Yunes Abrika, his wife, and his students are deeply troubling to me. Both on a personal level, and in my role as President."

"And you do know I share that sentiment..."

"I would never think otherwise," Fucillo said sincerely. She still did not believe Negassie would have ordered the killings.

"Mr. Abrika was a good man," he said. "Having grown up in Sudan under the tyrant al-Bashir, I've always encouraged dialogue with my critics."

"I'm aware of that as well," Fucillo said. "And I feel confident you'll do everything possible to see that the circumstances of this tragedy are disclosed in a full and transparent manner. So that there are no questions about what happened in the eyes of your friends in the international community."

Translation: I'm going to want the facts, she thought. *Which means you'd better stamp down on all the snakes in your regime's grass.*

"Madam President," Negassie said, "I can assure you, I will pursue a full and thorough investigation…and share its results with your government in their entirety."

"That's a great encouragement." Fucillo pulled a pen out of its holder and thoughtfully tapped her desk blotter. "But, again, I must be candid. The response of your CDF troops to the Haria Square rallies has been excessive when held up against acceptable human rights standards."

"Respectfully, I ask that you have patience before making that judgment," Negassie said. "Our national police are coping with an unprecedented civil crisis. There has been a great deal of confusion. We need to calmly evaluate the information we receive from the ground before leaping to conclusions."

Fucillo tapped her pen on the desk. "Sami, I trust my eyes. I've seen the images coming out of the square. And I'm convinced the troops have been overly aggressive. Also—"

"Madam President…"

"Allow me to finish, Excellency," Fucillo said firmly. It was time to flex her muscle. "In light of their behavior in the capitol, I'm greatly concerned about the potential for reprisals against striking Beja refinery laborers in Port Birhan. They're rightfully outraged, and they're grieving. That situation needs to be handled with sensitivity."

"I am very conscious of their anguish, Madam," Negassie said. "Everything will be kept under tight control."

"Then I consider this a very successful conversation," Fucillo said, noting his clipped tone. Sami Negassie was royalty by heritage, and a male in a highly chauvinistic society. His beestung reticence meant he'd gotten her message—or the part she had delivered thus far. "Our US energy companies are heavily invested in the Hagar pipelines. As is your government, I know. It's a valued partnership that I would not want damaged. Just as I wouldn't want to see our foreign aid package to Birhan curtailed...or eliminated. These are consequences that would pain me, Sami."

He was quiet on the line. Fucillo would never get used to the quality of the silence over a satphone connection. There was a hollowness about it like the silence inside a deep tunnel.

"You may be confident, Madam President. Your directness is always valued," Negassie said at length.

"Thank you," Fucillo said. "I'm glad we had this exchange. And before I forget... I do hope the princess will contact me while she's in the States. I would love to have her over for tea in the Rose Garden."

"I am certain she would be honored," Negassie said.

"Magnificent. You have a great day, Sami."

"And a pleasant rest of the evening to you, Madam President."

Fucillo hung up thinking she would have no trouble converting his well-wishes into a reality.

The prince would have a harder time with hers.

VIII

Drajan Petrovik slept in a high, gabled bedroom in the main building of his estate in the foothills of the Transylvanian Alps. Patrolled day and night by his heavily armed guards, with nothing but farmer's cottages for neighbors, it stood behind a wall on an undivided country road, a grand architectural collage of European, Moorish, and modernistic influences. Its roof was tiled with terra-cotta, its balconies supported by narrow columns, the polarized windows of the estate house shielding Drajan from probing eyes and the morning sunlight he detested.

Normally he kept late hours and did not begin his day until almost noon, a *technologie vampiri* in all respects. Yet this morning he arose from bed before nine o'clock, eager to shake off a restless dream.

Kali. Istanbul. Hekate's Temple… The Sacred Road…

Dream or memory, he needed distance from it.

Shrugging into his robe, Drajan stepped groggily out into the hall, leaned back against the bedroom door, and pushed it shut with both hands as if to contain something dangerous. His head felt like it was packed with wool, and he called Carla on the hallway intercom to ask for a strong cup of coffee.

Downstairs in his den, he put on one of the American wall-to-wall news networks. He was eager for reports of the success-ful lifting of Adrián Soto's fifty million dollars and his ATM decoy operation.

Instead his feed was monopolized with images from Birhan. He was well aware of the killings and protests, and wondered when his old friend Ansari would enter the picture. But his theft—and trial run of the new-gen Hekate iteration—had been commanding his full attention.

Now the focus of the story shifted to Birhan's coast. A work strike at a petroleum refinery, thick crowds with picket signs, soldiers guarding the tower platforms above them. And then, as expected, an image of National Minister Ansari Kem. He was speaking with a backdrop of the Birhanese flag behind him.

Drajan sat forward in his chair. The fuzziness gone from his mind, he commanded his AI to up the volume, and listened to the English voiceover.

"…in a brief, prerecorded statement, Kem warned that the Beja laborers are in violation of the law and must return to their jobs at once. He also advised workers against causing any dam-age to the infrastructure of the vast Hagar refinery, citing that his nation's Civil Defense Force would, in his words, 'take swift steps to defuse any terrorist conduct.'

"Speaking on condition of anonymity, one Beja strike leader responded to Kem's remarks by insisting his use of the word ter-rorist was 'a deliberately calculated excuse to justify the use of military force.'

"In carefully scripted remarks on state television, Kem also warned the United States against what he termed 'kneejerk intervention' and 'exploiting Birhan's internal tensions...'"

Drajan lowered the sound on his set again. Ansari's rhetoric was distinct even when he taught at Oxford—in part for its bluster, and in part for the militant extremism that ultimately resulted in his dismissal from the staff. But it had been years since Drajan attended his lectures. He was now a powerful figure at the center of global attention.

Wide awake now, a thought was stirring in his mind, and he would later remember this as its moment of ferocious conception.

IX

It was one o'clock in the morning when Travis Kinsman found his perfect match.

Kinsman's first hint that he might be onto something was his spectrographic identification of a dolomitic filler in the counterfeit bank card's plastic.

Still in his clean room garb, stiff-necked from intensely staring at spectrographics all day, the thirty-year-old Kinsman had already missed lunch and blown off a woman named Teresa he'd been chatting up online for weeks. But he worked best when he was alone. With Alex and the others gone for the night, he was taking advantage of the solitude and plugging away.

At first blush his discovery seemed unremarkable. Dolomite was one of the more popular mineral fillers in modern plastics. Abundant and cheap, it was found in many different types of sedimentary rocks, usually mixed with clay, gypsum, or iron oxide. But dolostone from different regions had unique and identifiable characteristics, giving it a kind of geological fingerprint. Kinsman was both skilled and experienced at reading them; the big question in his mind was whether he would find the sample files required for comparison.

In this case, the dolostone flour, or crushed dolomite rock, used in the plastic was rich in magnesium and formed from organic carbonates—rock created when biological remains like shells, bones, and decaying plants were gradually replaced by minerals over millions of years. When held up against Kinsman's geological database, its composition marked it as originating from the Central Black Soil region of European Russia. The Dankov field about three hundred miles outside Moscow, to be more specific.

Which brought Kinsman to his second database: companies that mined dolostone, and produced dolomite flour, from the Dankov field. That yielded only LLC Kavdolmit in eastern Ukraine…leading Kinsman to a third and final database, or actually, *sub*-database, namely that of plastics manufacturers using dolomite manufactured by LLC Kavdolmit.

He found four on file—two in Ukraine, one in Western Russia, and one in Romania.

Of those, the Ukrainian firms were dedicated exclusively to PVC plastic plumbing supplies. The Russian outfit, meanwhile, specialized in medical technology. The company in Romania, BOPLASI International, manufactured sheet plastic for insulation materials and credit cards.

Massaging his sore neck, Kinsman read the name off the computer screen and smiled under his face mask.

BOPLASI International. There it was. His perfect match. At 1:00 a.m. on the dot, for the record.

Not *quite* like finding love in the wee hours.

But for a research scientist assisting law enforcement, it was almost as satisfying.

X

Kali was moved again. This time she wasn't sure where. Nor was she clear how long or how far they traveled. There was another drive, a short flight—perhaps an hour aboard a propeller plane. Then more distance covered by road. Instinct told her they crossed the strait to the Italian mainland; after bringing her northeast to Messina from the bottom of Sicily, no other general destination made sense.

So where *specifically* on the mainland? Calabria? Naples? Somewhere else?

She wasn't sure. Everything around her looked the same. The table, the dark window shades, the door leading out to her right.

And Blond Man. He sat in front of her again, the two of them alone in the room. He was straddling the chair in his usual manner, watching her carefully.

"I want to tell you something I probably shouldn't," he said. "Straight talk."

She held her silence. That hadn't changed either.

"I'm under pressure to turn you over to certain people," he said. "Let's call them the regulars. They have their rules and I understand them. But it doesn't mean they're always right or applicable. We probably agree that some situations dictate stepping outside them."

Kali offered no response. She was hungry, thirsty, and her body felt stiff. Her legs especially. She had been in a chair for days.

"Listen," Blond Man said. "I told you about the Hekate malware. So trust me here. The regulars see you as a criminal. Once you're in their hands, you'll face the full consequences of the law. But I might be able to convince them you're worth more working on our side than in a max security prison."

She looked at him, impassive.

"We don't have much time," Blond Man said to her. "I need the names of hackers who've gone dark and are communicating in ways we can't monitor. It's something I can use to show your cooperation."

Kali merely stared.

After a while, he got up and walked across the room to the door. His hand on the doorknob, he looked back over his shoulder. "I can help you," he said. "But you need to work with me."

As the door shut behind him, she resisted the urge to let her forehead sink. There would be cameras recording her every move. She refused to show weakness.

Some minutes passed. The door opened again. Blond Man reentered the room, a plastic tray in his hands.

The aroma of hot coffee filled Kali's nostrils as he came back around in front of her. On the tray was a steaming mug and a plate with some food.

"You haven't eaten," he said. "It's nothing fancy. Coffee, bread, some sliced cheese. But the bread's from a local bakery and the brew's fresh."

She said nothing, the hunger in her stomach so great it was painful.

"I hope you don't toss this back at me like on the chopper," he said. "Water's one thing. Hot coffee burns."

He pulled the little table over from across the room and set down the tray.

Kali looked into his face. Kept looking for a long moment. Then, her wrists still cuffed together, she slowly lifted the coffee mug to her mouth and took a sip. It was good and strong.

Blond Man nodded.

"Take your time," he said, turning to leave the room again.

She reached for the bread and ate.

XI

Shortly before leaving the lab at two fifteen in the morning of July 8, Kinsman sent Alex Michaels an email linking the Romanian polymer tech firm BOPLASI International to the manufacture of the white plastic card retrieved in Queens. Awakening at six in his Westchester home, Alex checked his inbox first thing, then promptly forwarded the email to Ki Marton and Leo Harris and went out to check on his dogs.

At seven thirty, Marton arrived at 26 Fed, checked his phone for the correct time in Bucharest, and saw that it was two in the afternoon there. He was thinking that if he hurried to knock out an email to BOPLASI, he might—*might*—be fortunate enough to get a response that same day.

Using a Romanian translation app, Ki wrote a hurried query

asking for information about the outfit's sale of plastic sheets used to produce credit cards, including a list of specific customers. He then wrote the same request in English and copied both versions of the email, with his official FBI signature, to appropriate contacts on BOPLASI's corporate website.

He finished the job by eight thirty. At eight thirty-seven, the phone rang, and he picked up to hear the agitated voice of Warren Pike, the bureau's Assistant Director in Charge of Public Affairs in Washington, DC. Pike wanted to talk to SAC Harris the instant he stepped through the door.

He did not tell Ki the reason for his urgency. But Ki had a hunch. The death of the unarmed seventeen-year-old Han Jingrui while being pursued by two FBI Cybercrime agents was all over the news. The story had spread nationally overnight and was primed to explode with a vengeance, joining the Birhan commotion in the headlines.

It was going to be a major problem for the Bureau.

13

I

Wearing the red berets of the National Defense Force facilities security detail, Privates Bira Jamalm and Radi Ikrab stood on a railed lookout platform midway up a thirty-foot-high crude oil storage tank—one of five in the Hagar refinery's Block D—and gazed edgily at the crowd below.

Ikrab detested the Beja. In his eyes, they weren't true Birhanese but low-class *halabi*—dark-skinned gypsy migrants whose ancestors had come swarming out of the coastal hills in past centuries. Still, the striking workers were smart enough to know they had to feed their families, and that meant eventually returning to their jobs.

Beginning with the second day of protests, however, Ikrab and Jamalm had noticed young toughs from the Hagar slums mixing with the strikers…and they were informed the same thing was happening throughout the facility. The youths wore the orange colors of Beja street gangs and seemed to arrive in Block D with no purpose but to instigate trouble.

Now, on the third day, that situation had worsened. Three bare-chested gang members with orange headscarves had made their way through the line of picketers to shout up at the troopers from directly beneath the platform.

Their vulgar taunts were grating on Ikrab's nerves.

"Cockroaches," he said to Jamalm. "I'd like to drown them in a river of piss."

"Ignore them," he replied. "Those hoodlums just want to stir up trouble."

"Stir?" Ikrab said. "We already have plenty. Or haven't you noticed they've multiplied—" he snapped his fingers "—just like that?"

Jamalm frowned. He could not argue it. By his rough head-count, there were over a hundred strikers—mostly workmen with a sprinkling of women—around the storage tank, waving signs in the air, denouncing the Negassie regime. Similar crowds had circled the four other tanks in Block D and other key areas throughout the refinery.

The NDF guards were struggling to maintain a semblance of order. They made their security sweeps and rounds on foot carrying Chinese Type 56 assault rifles, or drove Marauder off-road vehicles with swivel-mounted, heavy-caliber machine guns, patrolling the facility's furnaces, distillation towers, and four blocks of storage tanks. In the few days since the labor stoppage began, their regular detachment at Hagar had been twice bolstered by reinforcements from headquarters. But the strikers and gang members continued to flock to the refinery, their numbers growing many times faster than the ranks of troopers.

Ikrab looked down at the three hoodlums now. He was thinking the thugs were much too close.

Then, one of them pulled something out of a shoulder bag and flung it upward. Ikrab had no time to register what it was before it smacked him wetly on the cheek and dropped to the platform.

His hand went to his face and came away covered with thick black slime and a horrible stink. Looking down, he saw a partly decomposed rat at his feet, its scruffy fur matted with gore where its gaseous, swollen body had exploded against his cheek.

Ikrab's throat constricted with disgust. He almost triggered a burst from his rifle, but was stayed by his partner's cautionary look.

"No shooting," Jamalm said. "It isn't worth the consequences. What happened to Uksem Kgosi should be a lesson to us."

Ikrab seethed. The photos of Kgosi had chilled him to the bone—perhaps most of all because National Minister Kem was said to have visited the trooper's jail cell before his death.

A lesson, yes. Ikrab knew that if he opened fire, one of the workers might be shot, and that would start a riot. He did not wish to end up like Kgosi because of it...but he also could not bear the hoodlums' abuse. It was too much.

Furious, he reached for the zipper of his pants, yanked it open, and urinated over the platform's edge. *"Filthy roaches!"* he shouted. *"Shower in this!"*

He was still holding himself when he saw the machine pistol appear in the gangster's fist. Then the pistol cackled and he felt something cold slap the side of his neck.

Ikrab's mouth filled with blood as he sailed over the platform's handrail.

Private Jamalm's eyes followed his partner's descent. He saw the gangster with the machine pistol start firing rounds into the sprawled body, saw guns appear in the hands of the other two gangsters, and heard bullets speckle the side of the storage tank behind him. Left with no choice, he raised his assault weapon to return fire.

A round struck him in the chest before he could take aim. He sank to his knees on the platform, his finger spasming around his weapon's trigger, involuntarily spraying the crowd with successive three-round bursts.

As his thoughts dissolved into blackness, Jamalm thought he heard the high, piercing shriek of a woman. Then voices of the protesters merging into a roar that swallowed him up whole.

Quickly rising from Block D, it swept over the refinery like a storm tide.

II

"What kind of press, or lack of it, are we getting here?" fumed New York Governor Kevin Bender. "I mean…what the *hell* do you people do to earn your inflated salaries?"

The governor's Director of Public Affairs, David Stiles, and State Operations Director Celeste Dewey tried not to squirm in their chairs. Bender didn't appreciate the Wall Street crypto push, his crowning endeavor, getting short shrift by the local media, and he wanted to be sure his advisors heard about it.

Neither dared look at the other as they sat in his Park Avenue inner sanctum. At moments like this, the Governor's unspoken rule was that all eye contact be directed at him and him alone. They were to endure their misery together but separately.

"I don't mean to sound insensitive about that madness in Africa, or the poor kid in Brooklyn, or Adrián Soto getting fleeced of all that money…"

A wise thing in Soto's case, Dewey thought, since he was a major political supporter and campaign contributor.

"…but how do we find ourselves without as much as a *piece* of the available daily coverage? New York's a 24/7 news market, for Chrissakes!"

Stiles felt a tension headache coming on. He had, however, come up with a strategy.

"Governor," he said, "you are absolutely correct. The media's beyond fickle. There's no perspective. It's worm's eye when it needs to be bird's eye—"

Bender thumped his desktop with the heel of his palm. A

tall, fit sixty-year-old with meticulously coiffed silver hair, he glared at Stiles.

"I don't want to hear your shit about fickle birds and worms," he said. "Three years I've been working on Crypto Wall Street." He paused, thinking. It had in fact been three *long* years of persuading arrogant, self-important bankers and corporate officials to make significant investments in cryptocurrency-related startups—and use his own Bender Corporation's newly opened TradeHub data storage facility across the Hudson as their primary exchange. "I finally get the President on board by linking it to her Net Force bullshit, convince her to join us at the Stock Exchange to announce TradeHub's opening, and I'm bumped from the news. Now what? Do either of you have a strategy?"

Stiles cleared his throat. "Actually, sir, we do." He motioned to Dewey without taking his eyes off the governor. "Celeste and I have concluded that two of the three unfortunate events that have grabbed the headlines—Soto and the Jingrui tragedy—can be rolled into our story."

"So they become one and the *same* story," Dewey added. "If we play this right—"

"Naturally, we don't mean *play* in a crass, opportunistic sense..."

"If we play this right, crass or not, whenever they mention Soto or the fucking sham cash card affair, they'll mention us."

"Meaning *you*, Governor."

"In connection with Crypto Wall Street," Dewey said. "Being how CWS and Net Force will help prevent these cybercrimes."

Bender looked at them with a broad, satisfied smile. "Am I commenting about Soto and Jingrui to the media today?"

Stiles nodded.

"Yes, sir," he replied. "And we've prepared some wonderfully moving things for you to say."

III

The moment he arrived at the office, Harris knew he'd picked the wrong morning to come to work with a hangover.

He plunked down in front of his computer and read Ki Marton's digital sticky notes. The good news was that Kinsman hit paydirt at the prof's lab. The bad news was that the Public Affairs Chief in Washington was waiting for an immediate callback. The neutrals were a check-in call from Alex, and reminders that he was scheduled for a full task force meeting about the bank hacks later that morning.

Harris fought the urge to hold off phoning Pike. Public affairs types only got more obnoxious the longer you made them wait.

"Leo," Pike said, answering his call. "I'm glad it's you."

"Thanks," Harris said. "We oughtta hang up right here so you can ride that feeling all day."

Pike forced a chuckle. "Good one, Leo," he said. "The truth is, I haven't had much to laugh about in the past twenty-four hours."

"Join the club," Harris said. "We're deep in shit here. In case you haven't noticed."

"How could I not? The press saw to it. And civil rights activists and Asian advocacy groups. And New York, state, and federal politicians. They were all very serious when they contacted me." Pike was quiet a moment. "Leo, listen. We have a very significant public relations problem with Han Jingrui."

Harris straightened a little in his chair. "I thought we had the name of a dead kid," he said. "Far as I can tell, that isn't public relations. It's a goddamn shame."

"You won't hear me differ," Pike said after a moment. "I know you think I sit around with my ass nailed to a chair. But I have to deal with things you don't. Important people with fixed notions of our organization. We're either the big bad FBI, or the inept, stumbling Feebs. Depending on who you ask, we either bulled or bungled our way into this predicament."

Harris shook his head. "Have you read Musil and Fahey's AARs?" he asked, knowing his field office's Assistant Director would have forwarded the after-action reports to Washington right away.

"Yes. Twice."

"Then just tell those people what happened."

"How about you tell *me*, Leo? Did your agents try their best to save a seventeen-year-old who put himself in mortal danger hopping across rooftops? Or recklessly chase him onto that ladder so he fell in a blind panic?"

Harris's hand tightened around the phone. "You got steel balls, Pike. How in *hell* could you ask me that?"

"Because I wanted to see if you would hesitate. Feel a tiny speck of doubt," Pike said. "I'm not saying you did. But let's hypothetically say so. Magnify that doubt ten times, twenty, you get a sense of the concerns I hear from people outside the Bureau. Reasonable or not."

Harris swallowed dryly. "Bottom line, Pike. Give it to me."

"We aren't there, not yet, but I can see a scenario that would require you to place those agents on enforced leave until this matter's thoroughly investigated."

Silence. "I got a third the men I need to handle a major criminal investigation. You saying I might lose two of my best?"

"If it should come to that, I won't like it any more than you. And it won't be my call—"

"But you'll make a recommendation."

"A balanced one, yes," Pike said. "As someone who gets paid to be protective of the Bureau's image."

Harris whacked the receiver down on its cradle and sat there staring at it awhile. All at once, his stomach felt sour—and it had nothing to do with drinking too much the night before.

IV

Carol Morse had awakened in her hotel room feeling out of sorts. Her mood improved somewhat when she called home and spoke to Ron and the kids. But two hours later, showered, dressed, and ready to leave her room for a busy slate of meetings, she still wasn't herself. On a day she needed focus, her thoughts were all over the place.

It was Leo, of course. No mystery there. She had seen him

at his surly worst before. But he was as down as she could remember last night.

Carol sensed whatever was bothering Leo had something to do with her, maybe everything to do with her. She had felt it at the restaurant, watching him pour down most of a bottle of wine. She knew him inside out—how could she not? They'd gone from being high school sweethearts to being husband and wife. Just kids…and they fell in love.

She stood in front of the closet mirror, taking inventory of her appearance for the day's high-level meetings. Hair loose, clean and shiny over her shoulders, wearing an appropriately conservative gray jacket and skirt, she carried the gravitas of a CIA official as if she were born to it. But that wasn't the reality.

When she and Leo were married in her second year of college, she had been holding a job as a part-time usher at Madison Square Garden, and Leo was working as a night watchman and taking classes toward criminal law. They made the rent, bills, and tuition but there was nothing extra. They talked about the Knicks games and concerts she could get them into for free, but they were always too busy to go, and their schedules were forever out of synch. They were still growing up, and responsible for one another, and the responsibilities often felt like burdens.

Leo had always wanted a career in law enforcement, but Carol's plans were never that firm. She would wonder if she got married too soon and missed out on something in life. But she never spoke about it, never shared her uncertainties, or asked Leo if he harbored similar doubts. She was afraid asking would hurt him, and didn't realize it was better to be honest even when it hurt. And even if it meant finding out their marriage was a mistake.

Leo was too bottled up to admit that he sensed it, or felt they were growing apart.

These were things they both carried on their backs. But she bore the weight of having been the one to say it was over. And of knowing she came home to a family every night, and Leo to a damned turtle.

Turning from the mirror, Carol unplugged her phone from its nightstand charger to see if there were any missed calls. She had tried calling Carmody right after dinner the night before, and then again earlier that morning, leaving messages both times.

She got his voice mail again now.

"Fox...it's Duchess," she said, stepping to the window. Ten stories below, she could see the usual flow of taxis and buses moving up 6th Avenue. "Get back to me. We're talking soon whether you like it or not—that's a given."

And it would be, Carol thought. If she had to use all the Company's muscle to make it happen.

She disconnected, got her purse off a chair, put the phone in it, and went to the door.

Out in the hall, a man and woman were laughing as they waited for the elevator. They were in their thirties and seemed happy.

Ron was a fine man, she thought suddenly. Solid, levelheaded, a good husband and father. She was pleased with their life together and loved his children. But she missed the way Leo made her laugh. He never tried to be funny, or thought himself funny, and that would only make her more amused.

Now the elevator arrived and Carol let the couple step in ahead of her. They nodded and offered her a smile. She smiled back.

Leo's shirts, she thought out of nowhere. What did he think he looked like in those *shirts*?

As the car reached the lobby, she told herself to get it together. Then her phone vibrated in her purse.

She read the display as she stepped out ahead of the happy couple. *Carmody.*

She hit the Answer button and looked around for a quiet place to talk. This was going to be serious business.

V

Its four cylindrical distillation towers pushing eighty feet into the air, the Afzal benzene and kerosene production unit at the north end of the Hagar facility represented nearly a quarter of the refinery's total output.

The three men dressed as Port Birhan gangsters came stealing up to the unit after sunset, crouched low to the ground, ducking between rows of trucks in the parking area. Headscarves wrapped around the lower halves of their faces, they carried sound-suppressed Truvelo Raptor assault rifles, and wore military shoulder packs and full magazine pouches on their belts. In each of their packs were several spherical fragmentation grenades and two TNT satchel charges attached to short lengths of safety fuse and pencil detonators. The explosive bundles were powerful enough to do the job many times over.

Squatting behind the rear wheels of a tanker, one of them peered around at the entry gate. He could see two sentries outside the gatehouse, their firearms slung over their shoulders. A third sentry sat in the gatehouse itself, his rifle on the counter, talking to the others through its open door.

The gang leader turned to his companions, raised four fingers, and then lowered his index finger to start a silent countdown. When his little finger bent, all three of them sprang from behind the truck, their carbines spitting rounds.

Surprised, the pair of standing sentries were cut down at once. The gang leader sprinted toward the gatehouse as the man inside rose off his stool, his hands groping for his rifle. Before he could raise the weapon off the counter, the gangster poured a long volley into the entryway.

Motioning toward his fellows, the gang leader entered the guardhouse, crouched over the dead sentry, and got his key card out of his pocket. A swipe of the card and the electronic gate swung open. The three intruders ran through, reaching into their packs for their grenades. They knew that closed-circuit cameras mounted on the fence had likely alerted more sentries inside the unit to their presence—and that the security lights around the tower cluster would make them visible targets.

They hadn't gone far before they saw four troopers emerge

from a control station outside the towers, and a separate group jogging toward them from somewhere off to the right. They yanked the pins from their grenades and hurled them.

The grenades detonated with loud bangs, the concussive blasts knocking the sentries off their feet as shrapnel tore through them.

The intruders hurried on. It was a short run to the pipes that delivered the fluid distillates from the towers to the tank farms. They would be filled with refined fuel.

The gang leader squatted where one of the pipes connected to a tower. Producing a satchel charge from his pack, he taped it to the bottom of the pipe, close to the side of the tower. Then he thumbed the striking pin on its pencil detonator and went on to the next tower. In the shadows nearby, his companions were doing the same at the other two distillation plants. They had set charges at key pumping stations along the line, but the towers were their principal targets.

The men knew they had to move quickly. Although it took just three or four minutes to plant each charge, the detonators were on fifteen-minute delays. That gave them slightly more than five minutes to quit the area.

His task completed, the gang leader dashed over to the others. Time was running down.

"Hurry," he rasped.

The three raced toward the security fence, past the bodies of the sentries by the gatehouse. Soon after they left the parking lot, the first of the charges erupted with a loud roar. The second blew moments afterward.

Pausing to glance back, the gang leader saw flame engulfing two of the towers. The remaining pair would blow in minutes, with chain reactions ensuing as the combustible fluids within the lines ignited.

"*Anarchie*," the gangster said to his mates, using the French pronunciation favored by Birhanese gangs. It added a nice touch to the charade. One never knew when cameras were present.

With that, he pumped his fist and ran into the night.

14

I

"Where have you been?"

"Would you believe *out to lunch*?"

"I won't bother answering that."

Carmody sat on a sofa in the safehouse on Via Giuseppe Gatto in Salerno, looking out the window at some tenements across the narrow street.

"Listen," he said into his phone. "I don't want to pick a fight—"

"But you'll do it anyway," Morse said. "The problem is that I'm on your side. Making me the least of your concerns."

Carmody rubbed his eyes, feeling light-headed. It was the Coprox, without a doubt. He had popped two ten-mils to get some sleep the night before, probably half a dozen since his team flew into Malta.

How many days ago had that been? He couldn't recall.

He reached for a glass of water on the table in front of him.

Daylight was rapidly wearing down, engulfed in the odd shimmery gray tones that precede a storm in Southern Italy.

"I need more time," he said. "She's on the brink of coming around."

"You told me that three days ago." Morse's tone was blunt and no-nonsense, but there was no real anger in it.

Carmody took a long drink, but his mouth remained dry. "I was wrong three days ago," he said. "Today's different."

Silence. He didn't think she was amused.

"Question," she said after a moment. "How's the weather outside?"

He glanced at the window. "Looks like we're in for a rainstorm."

"Then you're in luck," Morse said. "Italian roads are treacherous in the best conditions, and we want you to take special care of your passenger. I'm guessing bad weather will delay the remainder of your trip a day or two...but that's all."

He expelled a breath. "I don't know if I can work with that sort of cutoff."

"Your gratitude overwhelms me," she said. "One way or another your long, slow road to Rome's coming to an end. The day after tomorrow at the latest, you're going to meet the liaison there and put your girl on a plane for the States. Clear enough?"

Carmody frowned. "Couldn't be clearer," he said, and disconnected, dropping his satphone onto the table.

He finished the water in his glass and watched the rain come down outside the building. The region's summer storms struck in sudden, pelting waves, and this afternoon's downpour was no exception. He could hear it hammer the windowpane and sluice along the street below.

Carmody was hoping it wasn't a sign that his plans were about to be washed down the sewer as well.

II

Ansari Kem was pleased and surprised when he opened the encrypted email with his private key. The message from his former student was altogether unexpected, yet its timing felt almost providential.

It had been many months since he last heard from Drajan Petrovik. They deliberately restricted their communications after the War of Liberation, when Drajan attacked the Sudanese business databases with a computer virus, causing ripples of economic disruption through Africa and the Middle East.

Kem was in no hurry to reveal his connection to that cyberstrike.

In this part of the world, extreme problems required extreme solutions. Outsiders did not, and could not, understand. Even Prince Negassie, his fortitude weakened by his ties to the West, refused to fully embrace that understanding.

Kem stared at his tablet, holding it above his lap with one hand, his other hand fingering the silver pendant on a chain around his neck—a curved scimitar, its blade engraved with the Italian phrase *Prima di ogni altra cosa, siate armati*.

Before all else, be armed.

Ready to depart Zayar City, he had donned his military uniform and sat waiting in his suite for his security team. While doing so, he decided to write his cousin Massi of his intention to helicopter back to NDF headquarters to meet with him for a conference—one so infinitely delicate he would only have it face-to-face.

Now however, his attention was focused on the two brief sentences in Petrovik's email.

The new ruler must determine all the injuries that he will need to inflict. He must inflict them once and for all.

The lines, like those imprinted on his pendant, were from Machiavelli's *The Prince*. Seeing them on the computer screen, Kem almost might have believed Drajan read his mind, gleaning how he intended to restore order to his nation...as when he and Drajan would discuss the Italian politician's manifesto—among many other things—in their conversations at Oxford cafés. Although from very different backgrounds, and years apart in age, they had much in common.

Kem reached for a cup of tea on the table beside his chair. The real question was why Drajan contacted him. He would only do so if he had something to offer. Something *powerful*.

He thought a moment and replied with another quote from *The Prince*: Where the willingness is great, the difficulties cannot be great. Pausing, he added, I will be in touch tonight.

Kem took another sip of tea and stood up. Tucking the sword medallion under his shirt, he carried the tablet over to his briefcase and packed it away. Instinct told him something central had now changed in the great scheme of things. He wondered what it might be.

III

Alex brushed his hand over the Arabian jasmine he was nursing in the strong light of the Cyberlab's east window. A kid had lost his life, a great man was robbed of a fortune...and now there was Felicia Cheng's surprising and highly unsettling discoveries from the recovered ATM card. It made him quietly angry, but anger wasn't a useful exploratory tool. As a scientific investigator, Alex knew the importance of disciplined, systematic research. Solutions to complicated problems took time, patience, and focus.

He inhaled the sweet fragrance on his knuckles, then moved closer to the workstation where Leo Harris and Bryan Ferago sat waiting for Cheng to explain her findings. She had removed her hooded coverall to reveal long, straight hair that blended from black to red to fiery sunset orange as it spilled down over her shoulders.

"A couple of things about the card immediately jumped out at me," Cheng said. "First, it has a chip and magnetic stripe like a legit ATM card. Nearly all banks have switched over to chip readers, and retail merchants and gas stations were supposed to migrate no later than two years ago. But the deadline's been extended several times here in the United States. Some mom-and-pop stores and gas stations haven't yet complied, so the magstripe's used for backup."

Harris made a winding gesture. "Okay," he said. "Give me the second thing."

She straightened her round Lacoste frames and looked directly into his eyes.

"Both the chip and stripe are fully functional," she said. "A fraudulent magstripe card can be cranked out in somebody's basement—but I'll get back to that in a second. The chip is the impressive piece of work."

Harris grunted. Alex thought he looked dour.

"Chip cards are only made by a handful of companies. That in itself is a kind of security control, although some of those companies have dozens of vulnerable manufacturing facilities around the world," Cheng said. "What really makes chip-enabled cards tough to counterfeit is the way they interact with terminals. Each chip is essentially a microcomputer. It contains a central processing unit, RAM, and fair amount of data storage—as many as twenty-five megs for preinstalled applications. Whenever someone makes a transaction with a chip card, it handshakes with the terminal to create a one-time encrypted code, or token, using instructions in the chip. If the token gets skimmed, it doesn't matter, because it won't work a second time for a thief trying to clock up purchases. A new code is generated for every transaction, and that's controlled by a dedicated app—"

"Look, dumb as I am, I get all this," Harris interrupted. "How about we cut to the chase?"

Cheng looked at him. "I used a reader to access a cloud test environment for the card. A dummy banking network that processes transactions exactly like a real one," she said. "Amounts, response codes, credentials... I was able to view the entire authentication process as a grid on my computer screen."

Bryan was watching her intently. "And how'd it go?"

"When I inserted the card, it appeared to handshake normally. It wasn't rejected as a fake and there was no error reading. Nothing that would automatically set off alarms. Instead, there was an insufficient funds response." She paused. "Out of curiosity, I tested the card in simulated online *and* offline modes…and in each instance got the same response."

"So, if it happens offline, it must be generated by the card," Bryan said.

"Exactly." Cheng was nodding. "By a dedicated app, as it turns out. Very sophisticated."

Harris shook his head. "Wait," he said. "Why would somebody hack a bank, transfer money into bogus accounts, and deliberately give his mules dud cards that can't draw the cash? What's the point?"

"To keep us focused on the movement of funds, while making sure nobody actually got *hold* of them," Alex said. "Stealing money from Halifax wasn't the objective. It's about the diversion."

Harris suddenly found himself thinking about the Brooklyn kid, Han Jingui. His death seemed like more of a pointless, stupid waste by the second. *Shit.*

"Prof…you telling us the mules were duped?"

Alex held his knuckles under his nose and softly inhaled. "Deducing motives is your field," he said. "But whoever's behind this easily could have had them withdraw the cash. There was nothing to stop them *except* the app's instructions."

"Man," Bryan said quietly. "These dudes are serious gamers."

Cheng nodded. "It gets even better…or worse," she said. "There's a second app on the chip, a malware injector. That's where the bug was hiding out."

"The same bug that got into Chloe Berne's hard drive," Alex said. "And Halifax's network."

"And the magstripe," Cheng said. "But we need to be careful about our conclusions. Yes, they're malware scripts. They clearly share certain components. But there are also some conspicuous variations."

Leo looked over at Alex. "The magstripe...you have any idea why somebody would bother writing the bug onto it?" he said. "I mean, it was already carried by the chip, so why even bother with the stripe?"

"Insurance, thoroughness, whatever you want to call it," he replied. "Each card was a *double* injector. In case a terminal couldn't read the chip for any reason. The people that designed the cards weren't taking any chances."

"Meaning you think every bank the mules tried hitting up was infected."

"And the systems those banks interact with," Alex said, nodding. "Yes, I think we have to assume that."

Harris felt horror seep through him. There were a grand total of two hundred thirty machines and seventy different banks or bank branches involved...and it did not stop there.

"The card was logged into evidence at headquarters," he said. "The techs would've scanned it before sending it over here with me. That means the Bureau's system could be contaminated."

Alex nodded again. "They've been alerted to the threat, and the hardware and software used to scan the card's been quarantined. But we don't know how quickly the bug spread. Every government and civilian system with which it's interfaced is a potential target."

"Jesus Christ," Harris said.

Alex stepped over from the window. "We can still hope whoever infected Chloe Berne's and H&L's systems had limited goals," he said. "The bug might stay dormant...or at least stay dormant outside the financial systems. These aren't good scenarios, but I'll take them over dealing with an across-the-board internet pandemic."

Harris rubbed the back of his neck. "You want to tell me what we're supposed to do till we know?"

"Our only logical course is to stick with what we've been

doing. Figure out what the bug does, how it does it...and hope-fully find who spawned the thing," Alex said. "Thanks to Travis, we have a lead."

Harris looked at him in surprise. "Really? How's that?"

Alex frowned.

"Leo," he said. "You really *should* check your email once in a while."

IV

Carmody heard the rain fall outside the safehouse in wind-driven waves, drumming hard on the rooftop. It sounded like a dam in the sky had burst.

The room where he'd brought his prisoner so she could get a few hours' sleep—handcuffing her to the bedpost—was pitch dark at nine o'clock at night. He entered quietly without turning on the lamp, leaving the door open a crack behind him.

"At dawn we're heading down the coast to Amalfi," he said after a while. "I figure you've heard of it."

He could see her lift her head, raising herself slightly up on her elbows.

"There's a private airfield just outside town where I'm putting you on a jet. I won't have any control of what happens to you afterward."

She said nothing, keeping her head off her pillow.

Carmody found himself wishing he could open a window. Even with the rain coming down outside, he would have relished letting a fresh breeze into the warm, stuffy room. But she could create problems by making enough noise to draw the locals.

"We're out of rope," he said. "You have to assess your situation and make some decisions."

She didn't speak or move. He looked at her in the thin radiance slipping through the door.

"I don't want you to rot in a cell," he said. "But I'm an old soldier. I took an oath of service to my country. And I'm going to honor it and bring you onto that plane."

The room was silent except for the sound of the rain. After a full minute, he turned, stepped out, and closed the door behind him.

He was finished talking. The rest was up to her.

V

Blackout guards over its headlights and tail lights, the NDF truck—a dun-colored eight-wheeler with a ribbed tarpaulin over its flatbed—came rolling up to the long, prefabricated steel structure shortly after ten o'clock at night, stopping yards from its rollup entrance. Three Marauders braked to a halt behind the truck, their lights also shielded from aerial reconnaissance.

Two men jumped from the truck's cab, a dozen others exiting the other vehicles. In the rear of the lead Marauder, two passengers remained seated, waiting quietly behind their driver.

The troopers leaving the Marauders wore coveralls with nylon hoods and rubber boots that went almost to their knees. As they stepped out into the darkness, they donned chem-bio gas masks with goggles and skullcap harnesses, pulling the hoods up over their heads and securely tying the drawstrings. Then, reaching into their duffels, they put on thick elbow-length latex gloves that matched their boots.

The truck crew was at the entrance before the rest finished getting into their protective gear. They could hear sounds inside the building—agitated clucks and squawks. The noises grew louder as one of the drivers turned a key in the control box beside the door, rolling it up on trolleys.

When all was ready, the troopers in gas masks approached the building, filing past the first Marauder. Staring out their windows, the two occupants of its back seat continued to watch them with interest.

"Take heed, cousin Farai." The man on the right leaned toward the other. "We must be sure these men don't speak of this night to their comrades and loving wives."

Massi glanced at him, cautious of the driver's attention. "It has been arranged," he said.

Ansari Kem nodded. "I want to observe the process," he said. "Will you come?"

"Only if I must."

Kem, already suited up in his hooded coveralls, produced his gas mask and gloves from a satchel on the seat between them, and opened his door. The mindless gibbering of the hens met him as he stepped outside.

His mask over his face, he walked toward the coop. The lights beneath its ceiling had been turned on, spilling into the night. Kem entered and looked around. Hundreds of chickens milled on the floor or perched on tubular rails, fluttering and cackling. At the far end of the building, a pair of troopers had uncoiled a heavy-duty industrial hose from a mounted wall reel. One of them turned the handle of a spigot while the other aimed the hose at the chickens massed around their feet. Water blasted from its nozzle in a roaring high-pressure stream to clear the birds from that section of the floor, sweeping them away. Broken-winged and flailing, they were washed toward the far side of the coop.

Kem strode toward the group of soldiers as they shut off the hose, wading through drowned hens and pooling water. The men had activated a sliding mechanical hatch in the floor; concrete stairs descended from the opening into the lighted space below. Kem watched the twelve soldiers enter the hatchway, then followed them down into it.

At the bottom of the stairs was a rectangular depot of bare concrete. The five metal barrels against one wall had the fluorescent biohazard symbol on their outward-facing sides. Standing in a similar row along the opposite wall were containers of isopropyl—ordinary rubbing alcohol.

Sarin in its fully mixed state is highly corrosive to metal, and one of the deadliest compounds known to man. Colorless and odorless, its vapor leads to spasms, paralysis, and death within seconds of inhalation. A microscopic liquid droplet against the skin causes muscle spasms in the exposed area.

Inside the barrels, the volatile nerve-agent's chemical precursors were safely stored in binary form.

Kem eyed them a moment, then strode between them to the wall opposite the stairs. In four large wooden crates on the floor were thirty 140mm Russian sarin rocket shells. Separated by a rupture disk, the two removable canisters in each shell were sized to hold exact, measured proportions of the agent's components. When the shells were launched, the g-forces acting on them would burst the disk's aluminum foil membrane even as their natural rotation mixed the ingredients in midair.

The new ruler must determine all the injuries that he will need to inflict. He must inflict them once and for all.

Crouching, Kem touched a gloved hand to one of the crates. Tonight, the truck parked outside the coop would transport the rockets to the outskirts of Port Birhan, where towed launchers were deployed for his top secret operation.

He turned to the troopers.

"Get it done," he said, his voice muffled by the gas mask's circular filter.

Then he rose from his crouch, stepped back from the wooden boxes, and watched as they silently went about their task.

15

New York/Washington, DC/Paris/Birhan
July 8, 2023

I

The taxi swung off West Street onto 50th, drove two blocks to 10th Avenue, and pulled up to the immense converted warehouse that unobtrusively housed the Department of Homeland Security's Lower Manhattan Field Office.

Stepping from the cab into the soupy heat, Carol called Leo on her cell.

"Hey," he answered. "How's it goin'?"

"Okay… I'm about to head into a conference," she replied. "Listen, I have an update on the situation we discussed."

"Your boy in Salerno?"

"Yes."

"And what'd he report 'bout my girl?"

"I'll tell you in person," Carol said. "Do you plan to be in your office later this afternoon?"

"Not sure," he said. "I'm in Alex Michaels's mad science lab right now."

"Up at Columbia?"

"That's the place."

Carol had reached the building's main entrance. Besides the uniformed guards inside, her eye discerned several plainclothes security personnel on the sidewalk out front.

"My meeting won't be long... I can head up right afterward," she said. "I want to personally connect with the professor anyway."

"Great." Harris paused. "You know how to get here?"

Carol turned in to the entrance. "Leo, I may live near the Potomac these days," she said, "but I grew up right across the Hudson, same as you."

II

It was nearly midnight when the truck reached its destination, a tabletop bluff bounding the Hagar Oasis, about a mile northwest of the petroleum refinery. Already onsite, perched near the stone ledge, were two Marauders with towed sixteen-tube rocket launchers.

Beside Captain Massi in the rear of his vehicle, Ansari Kem stared out his window as the crates of 140mm rockets were carefully offloaded from the truck by the soldiers who brought them aboard—their coveralls, hoods, and gas masks now exchanged for regular National Defense Force uniforms and flashlights. Though also wearing the garb of NDF troopers, the firing crews in the Marauders were members of Kem's elite personal guard. Men he trusted.

Kem was unsure about the rest of them. Under no imaginable circumstances could word of what was being done tonight—of his role in it—be leaked.

His eyes shifted to the burning distillation tanks in the distance. After a while, he turned toward Massi. "I trust you're prepared for when this delivery is completed."

"Yes," Massi said. "Fully."

Kem noted his reticence. "Did you expect only parades and brass-buttoned dress uniforms with your command, Farai? We do what is necessary. My advice would be to toughen your stomach."

Massi nodded, a taciturn expression on his face. "It will be done."

Kem turned to look outside again. His Marauder and truck crews were returning to their vehicles, their ammunition crates left on the ground near the cluster launchers. He watched as the group sergeant hurried around to his cousin's door.

Massi lowered his window, nodding his permission for the sergeant to address him.

"We're set here, Captain," he said. "What are your orders?"

"Return to base," Massi said. "His Excellency and I are going to stay and observe. We'll follow shortly."

The sergeant saluted and rejoined his men. Then the truck and Marauders roared to life, swung off the bluff, and trundled down into the pass leading between the low, hilly slopes below toward the Zayar Highway.

Massi waited till they vanished from sight and then leaned forward in his seat. "All right," he said to his driver. "Get this over with."

Nodding without a word, the driver reached for the phone on his dash, fingered its touchscreen, and opened the GPS map view of the convoy winding slowly through the ravine.

Massi spent a minute or two tracking their progress. Then he sank back in his seat as the driver tapped the detonation sequence into the phone's keypad display.

The plastique charges under the vehicles' gas tanks blew at once, igniting the fuel within them. The explosions made the ground shake like a powerful earth tremor and rocked Massi's vehicle on its struts. He saw flashes of orange light from the gravel road forty feet below, then a large, tailing fireball that rose up and up into the dark night sky.

Massi felt severed from himself. When he breathed, it was as if the air entered a body other than his own.

"It's done," he said, his voice a thin croak.

After a time he grew dimly aware of a hand clutching his shoulder and turned to his cousin.

Kem's eyes were drilling into him.

"Stomach," he said.

III

"...time for us to stop thinking of cybercrimes as bloodless acts, with nameless, faceless victims. Crimes that don't take a toll on real people's lives," Governor Bender was saying to the gathered press. He displayed a photograph of a young man— dark haired, Asian descent. "Han Jingrui was seventeen years old. With family and friends who loved him." Bender pushed the photo out toward the cameras. "He plunged from a Brooklyn rooftop after being conned by experienced computer criminals..."

Watching in her study off the Oval Office, President Annemarie Fucillo glanced from the flatscreen to her Chief of Staff. "The man's an opportunist and a blowhard," she said. "But you know what, Randy?"

Randolph Severin looked at her from his armchair. "The champ speaks the truth—even if he needs a teleprompter feeding it to him," he said. "If we want Net Force to be more than another red tape machine, it'll need funding and legislation. And for that we need the country behind it. People don't get why we need all this government integration—and their tax dollars—to fight enemies they can't see."

Fucillo turned back to the set, wanting to see where Bender was headed with his comments.

"...and while we await a full investigation into the circumstances of Han Jingrui's death, we must remember that he wasn't alone. Dozens more were lured into a fraudulent cash card scheme. But we're *all* vulnerable to cybercrime. If Han Jingrui has a legacy, it may be to awaken us New Yorkers to the nature of the cyber*beast* in society…"

Fucillo lowered the television's volume. "Bender's piggybacking on Net Force to gain the spotlight," she said after a moment.

Severin could practically read her thoughts. When the whippet-thin Southerner was Fucillo's campaign manager, they would often strategize from dawn to dusk. "I have no problem with it," he said. "I can separate the message from the messenger."

"Agreed," she said. "America's been lucky so far. Nobody's managed a successful digital takedown of our infrastructure. But it's going to happen unless we get our act together."

He nodded. "Bender may only want face time. But he's doing us a huge favor putting cybersecurity in the spotlight."

"We should make the most of it," Fucillo said. "Use the opening bell ceremony on Wall Street to introduce Alex Michaels to the public. Even before my rally afterward." She sat thoughtfully, late afternoon sunshine slanting in through the study's east windows. "Our friend the governor is making Han Jingrui the face of cybercrime's consequences," she said. "I want people to see Alex as the face of our solution."

Severin nodded.

After a second she turned off the television and stood up.

"Politics," she said. "We use a kid's death to advance our separate agendas."

Severin was also rising off his chair.

"Our agenda's righteous," he said. "It's what makes us different from someone like Bender."

The President paused before she turned to the entry, looking at him seriously.

"I'll let God be the judge of that," she said.

IV

"So the parent outfit's Eliska International," Harris said, reading the name off Alex Michaels's computer monitor.

"In Odessa, Ukraine," Alex said. "And that company begat Rasmus LLC in Bucharest, Romania..."

"And *that* owns Pida Group Inc., in Homyel, Belarus..."

"Which has a Romanian subsidiary called SC Tomis Industrial," Alex said.

Harris grunted. Across the lab from where he sat on a rolling office chair, Bryan Ferago was bringing Harris's recently arrived ex-wife up to speed on his virtual recreation of the bank hack.

"Just so I'm straight," Harris said, "you're telling me SC Tomis bought the plastic sheets used to manufacture the bogus cash cards."

Alex nodded. "It has headquarters in several Romanian cities... Bucharest, Constanta, Oradea and Satu Mare. The Bucharest location received the sheeting from its producer, BOPLASI."

"Anyone know where the sheets went after they reached Bucharest?"

"No," Alex said. "SC Tomis's website doesn't provide phone numbers or physical addresses—other than the cities where there are corporate branches." He rested his chin on his hand. "Satu Mare jumps out at me. The place is a hacker's paradise—the local university might as well crank out degrees in cybercrime. Over a decade ago, an army of e-frauders migrated there to join the rest of the high-tech gangsters. I think the whole stim club thing started with its nightlife."

Harris sighed. "Could be this is where my ex comes in." He rose off his chair. "Excuse me while I suck up to her."

Straightening his Hawaiian shirt around his waist—it was pale green with large pink hibiscus flowers—Harris went up the aisle to Bryan's workstation. Carol stood looking over the kid's shoulder at his virtual network monitors.

On the H&L TRUST screen simulation, multiple bright red flow lines almost obscured the graphic rendering of the institution's data portals—a reenactment of the DDoS attack at its peak. At the same time, the monitor stamped Berne/Soto showed a CANNOT ACCESS SITE notification.

That drew Harris's eye as he came up beside Carol.

"What's the deal here?" he said, poking his chin at the monitor. "Isn't all this junk supposed to show us the spoof page Soto got bounced onto?"

"It is," Bryan said. "But it has nothing to do with my virtual machine being junk."

"Then what's the problem?"

"Either the spoof site's gone offline, or the malware has started to deconstruct," Bryan said. "That happened years ago when a North Korean bug wiped itself off infected hard drives so it couldn't be analyzed." He shrugged. "It would explain why there were only partial scripts on the fake card's chip and magstripe."

Harris mulled that over. "It doesn't wash," he said. "If the bug's committing suicide, how's it causing the DDoS hit all over again in your junk computer?"

Bryan spun around in his chair. "That's the thing, sir. The sum of its parts don't quite mesh. The scripts don't have the consistency you would see if a single person wrote them. Or a *team* of scriptwriters. Not that all the parts aren't brilliant, because they are. And that's the *other* thing."

"*What's* the other thing?"

"You don't need super-special code for a spoof redirect. Or a DDoS attack…even a super intense attack meant as a distraction," Bryan said. "This bug does a whole lot of different stuff, some of it without needing outside command and control. And it has built-in encryption algorithms that make its codes hard to read. Almost like…"

Bryan let the sentence fall off.

"What is it?" Harris said.

The kid shook his head. "I don't want to sound too arch about this Frankenbug," he said. "But I wonder if the hacker threw in the works to see how certain features would perform."

Harris looked at him. "Wait," he said, "you mean like in a *test* run?"

Before Bryan could answer, Carol lifted her eyes to his face. "Leo," she said. "Let's step outside."

"I was just asking—"

"I know," she said. "Once again. We have something to talk about."

He turned to her and nodded.

"Sure," he said, stalking out of the lab.

She counted down to thirty, giving him a chance to wonder if she would join him.

Then she did.

V

"I saw the look in your eyes when Bryan mentioned the bug seemed cobbled together from different people's scripts," Carol said. "I know what you're thinking."

"Then you know it scares the hell out of me," Harris said. He frowned, leaning back against the wall outside Alex's lab, Carol in the corridor facing him.

"I don't like it either," she said. "Not at all. Which leads me to why I wanted to talk."

"Outlier?"

"Yes," Carol said. "From what we just heard, it's easy to infer her codes were swiped."

He nodded. "I put four years of sweat and blood into the case. Shared everything I had on her—"

"I'm not disputing it, Leo." She flicked her eyes back and forth, checking that they were alone. "Carmody might have bagged her, but he wouldn't have done it without your work. Which is why I'm going to tip you off to something. A lot sooner than I should."

He looked at her. "Let's have it."

"I told you he brought her to Italy. I didn't say *where*," she said. "Carmody had her in Salerno last night. A safehouse. Supposedly he was heading up to the Rome station...and taking too long to get there."

Leo waited. He was reading all her signals. "You brought the hammer down on the son of a bitch."

"I ordered him to Amalfi. There's a private airfield near the village...we've arranged for a ghost flight to the States. With special contracted personnel."

"Freelancers?"

She nodded. "They have their instructions. In case Carmody thinks he can keep disobeying orders."

A second or two passed. Harris resisted the urge to hug her.

"I have a little more for you," she said quietly. "The Geneva Convention, and the law of our land, expressly state that any individual brought to custody overseas is to be transferred to our country for interrogation. It's the norm for agencies chartered to operate on domestic soil to take the lead. That means the FBI. Therefore, I'm turning Outlier over to you on her arrival."

He swallowed hard. "Car...thanks," he said. "You're the best—"

She cut him off with quick shake of her head. "This is professional, not personal. It's about the Net Force initiative. About making it happen."

"How's 'making it happen' have anything to do with me?"

"You're a square peg in a round hole," she said. "You don't even like using a computer, but you're head of New York Cyber, with an unbeatable record of clearing cases. And there's a reason."

He shrugged. "I trust my instincts. And I do the legwork."

"Exactly. An old-school brick agent. That's what we need."

"What do you mean?"

"The President isn't screwing around, Leo," Carol said. "There *will* be a Cabinet-level cybersecurity force. Once it becomes a reality, some of us are going to migrate into the new organization."

He shook his head. "Sorry, Car. Ain't where I belong."

"We don't need to discuss it now," she said. "But we also don't have to wait for it in order to work cooperatively on a new level. And I want us to start with Outlier." She paused. "I prefer this entire conversation stays between us until she's delivered to your custody."

They were quiet. Then the lab door opened and Alex Michaels stepped out.

He paused, glancing from one to the other. "Sorry to interrupt," he said, then hesitated. "I was just heading over to the HIVE…"

She gave him a questioning glance.

"A fancy acronym that gets congressional funding committees excited," Alex said. "It stands for Holographic Immersive Virtual Environment." He showed them a USB stick. "I'm putting this in the archives—want to tag along?"

She nodded. "Sure."

He pointed his chin toward a set of double swing doors. "Leo, how about coming with us? You can translate my technobabble."

"Why not?" he said with a shrug. "I'm used to explaining everything to everybody anyway."

VI

"The flash drive is my equivalent of a specimen slide," Alex was saying. "This one has a sample of the malware script we've grappled with these past few days."

"The Frankenbug," Carol said.

Nodding, he stepped up to the immersive reality hub's entrance and input his biometrics.

"Cloud storage is out of the question for these malware specimens…the last thing we want is to risk spreading the infection," he said. "I prefer keeping key research data in an internal mininetwork. It gives me direct control of the security environment." The door retracted into the wall. "Say hello to HIVE."

They entered. The room was circular and lit by cool blue overhead ceiling panels. Except for the entryway and its adjacent wall areas—these were covered with banks of computer monitors, control boards, and a heavy-gauge steel data storage vault—the space was entirely composed of large, curved floor-to-ceiling LCD panels, with two rows of movie-theater-style chairs in the middle of the room.

"Good afternoon, Professor Michaels," said the AI assistant. The soft lilting feminine voice bore a hint of a European accent. "And welcome to our visitors."

Carol glanced over at him. The voice had a vaguely familiar ring.

"Audrey Hepburn?" she asked.

He smiled. "I used an audio sample from *Breakfast at Tiffany's* for Eve's voice." He shrugged. "I'm a fan of classic movies. What can I say?"

Carol smiled and looked around the room.

"HIVE uses over a hundred Ultra 32K HD three-dimensional panels," Alex said. "Surround sound, multicamera optical tracking...our virtual immersions have precisely the same clarity as real-world views to a person with twenty-twenty vision."

He turned to the storage vault, pressed a combination into the keypad, and held his hand to the palm scanner. When he opened its steel-plate door, Carol saw tiers of sliding racks filled with USB sticks, hard drives, and other digital media.

"Your version of a CDC plague vault."

"Great comparison," Alex said. "This is where we store samples of the most destructive digital pathogens ever created. But it's beyond that. We're close to where HIVE will be able to simulate a bug's *evolution*—project the route of infection it may take, and even the form of its later generations."

"Like monitoring the emergence of a new strain of disease," Carol said. "I'll bet it never gets boring."

Alex pulled out a shelf. "Never," he said.

"And how do the virtual simulations play into things?"

"It depends." He paused with the data stick in his hand. "Using the Frankenbug as an example, we can choose to examine its binary structure from within. Or we can put ourselves inside a dataflow graphic, and observe its attack vectors during the bank hit. If we have enough audiovisual references, we can have an exact 4D recreation of Chloe Berne's office when Adrián Soto was hijacked and spoofed…relive it as if we're in the room with them. HIVE will also generate multiperspective sims."

"Can you do that right *now*?"

"I'd need about an hour's preparation." He turned to her. "We're beginning alpha trials on an upgrade that will allow someone in the HIVE to interface with infected systems in real time. In other words, it would put you the middle of a cyberattack as it's happening—like one of those balloons they drop in the eye of a hurricane. Finally we've tested standalone HIVE units…wireless connected headsets that don't quite have Eve's computing power or immersive capabilities. But they allow people in different locations to share a single virtual experience."

"So someone in Washington could, say, link up with someone here at the lab?"

Alex nodded. "Washington, London, Tel Aviv…orbital, suborbital, and extraterrestrial sites…wherever there's an internet connection. In the event of a major cyberattack on the national infrastructure, HIVE could become a sort of emergency command center as long as we maintain backup power and intranet," he said. "If you have time, I can give you a demonstration of HIVE's basic capabilities using an actual bug from our library. A Trojan attack we intercepted a year ago. The sims are already programmed into memory."

Carol nodded.

Alex pulled a shelf out of the vault, clicked the memory stick into a slot, and then looked over the contents of the shelf until he found the stick he wanted.

Alex pushed in the shelf and shut the vault. Then he turned to a cabinet and produced three pairs of immersive virtual reality glasses that reminded Carol of the 3D glasses they handed out in movie theaters.

"These frames have built-in motion sensors that relay your positional data to the sim computer." He handed a pair to her, the other to Harris. "Visuals are completely interactive. There are motion sensors and cameras imbedded in the walls that will instantly generate virtual avatars for us. We'll look exactly like ourselves, and objects will have the same spatial relationships with you that they would in the physical world."

Alex slipped on his glasses. "Eve, cut the lights."

They dimmed until the room went black.

"It's normal to feel some motion sickness and mild disorientation. For most people it passes quickly," he said. "Eve. Give us Silverline four-seven-three-two. Sys-infect version. Interior mode."

"Loading," said the synthetic voice. "Initiating scenario."

And then the room was gone and they were in a railroad car, speeding along a gravel track bed, its ties spooling out up ahead, warehouses and rust-mottled pickup trucks visible to either side through large picture windows and a thin, bleary fog. Ahead of them, the metal framework of a bridge or trestle spanned a wide gray spread of water.

Carol swayed with the train's movement. In the aisle seat to her right, a man in an overcoat was dozing with an open magazine on his lap, a laptop computer and cardboard coffee cup on his lowered tray table.

Standing to her left, Harris caught her forearm and steadied her. The man with the magazine shifted obliviously, his eyes still shut. In the window seat next to him, a twentyish woman in jeans and a ski jacket was quietly enjoying her view. She wore headphones and was moving her shoulders to music.

Carol's eyes went past her to the window. Every detail of the scenery seemed real. Tufts of winter scrub clung, spindly and bare, to the frozen berm along the tracks. Ice coated the branches like sheaths of glass.

"We're in the second car of a Silverline high-speed train, directly behind the locomotive, or power car," she heard Alex say behind her. "Eve's given us free first-class accommodations."

"Sweet," Harris said. "Only way I can afford 'em."

Carol glanced in Alex's direction. As promised, his virtual

stand-in was indistinguishable from the flesh-and-blood version. "Where are we?" she asked. "Looks like the Northeast Corridor..."

"Connecticut," Alex said. "A hundred twenty miles into the New York–Boston run. The crossing up ahead is the Thames River Railroad bridge, which links Groton to New London."

The train sped through the fog, the warehouses falling away to its rear as it approached a curving dockside rail spur. The spur was partially covered with grimy, half-melted snow.

"Eighteen months ago there was a hack into the railroad's control-and-communications system," Alex said. "The IPs led to a group of Afghan terrorists."

She nodded. "I remember this. The intrusion was detected before anything happened—"

"In our world, yes," Alex said. "We're about to experience an alternate reality."

Carol stood gazing out the windows. The train was about two-thirds full, most of the men and women in business clothes. She could hear the rhythmic knocking of the tracks under its carriage. It was getting close to the bridge.

"There are a hundred thirty-four passengers, a crew of twelve...and now three stowaways," Alex said. "The seat occupancy is accurately represented. People are sitting where they sat. We used the railroad's ticketing information to assign correct ages and genders. Eve's capable of extrapolating some highly realistic touches from the available data."

Carol nodded and faced forward. She had felt the train decelerate as it neared the bridge.

"It's four minutes past nine," Alex said. "The event clock's at under a minute. Speed is down to fifty-point-three miles per hour...but this will be jarring."

Feeling her stomach tighten, she looked at the bridge and abruptly saw a freight train coming over from New London on the southbound track—a diesel locomotive and four boxcars.

"That's the one from Groton's naval submarine base, isn't it?" she said, remembering the case briefing.

Alex nodded. "It's bringing canisters of spent—and highly radioactive—nuclear fuel from the subs to Idaho for disposal," he said. "Ten seconds...get set."

Carol inhaled as the Silverline nosed onto the bridge—and then felt a hard jolt. Their car bucked and she staggered forward. She heard the hiss of airbrakes, heard people cry out in shock as objects started crashing from chairs, trays, and overhead bins. The entire terrible cacophony seemed as real as her own heartbeat.

The Silverline bumped a second time, lurching to an abrupt halt. Even as Carol struggled to maintain her balance, the dozy businessman whiplashed into his lowered tray, overturning his cup, splashing hot coffee over his sport jacket and trousers. At the same instant, the young woman with headphones went flying over her armrest to smash into the window.

A briefcase skidded toward Carol. Then the businessman's laptop computer went clattering down the aisle. There was a tumbling cascade of other items—eyeglasses, magazines, phones, tablets, even a loose shoe. She had to consciously stop herself from sidestepping them.

More screams. Raising her eyes to the windows, Carol realized the front of the Silverline had derailed and stopped diagonally across the tracks. The freight train was still chugging toward it from the opposite direction, its locomotive nearing the bridge tower.

Alex just stared out the window as the train got nearer, clattering to a gradual halt. It had been moving at a moderate speed and stopped well before it would have crashed into the passenger train.

"This is a movable span...a drawbridge owned and operated by Silverline Railways," Alex said. "The hackers easily gained access to its lift controls."

Carol turned to him. The passengers' cries subsided as they saw the freight train halt before it got too near the Silverline. But she knew their relief was premature.

"The freight train's the primary target," she said. "A collision isn't in the plan...the people aboard our train are incidental."

"If you can use that word to describe the loss of almost a hundred fifty lives," Alex said. "It—"

Carol suddenly heard loud clanking noises outside the train, then felt something heave underneath her. She knew at once what was happening. The vertical-lift span was rising with the Silverline stalled across its tracks.

She sucked in a breath. Screams erupted throughout the car again as the train's nose tilted down into the gap. People were flung across seats, sprawled in the aisle, everywhere.

Carol rationally understood she *was* in fact on a kind of thrill ride, a what-if world, but that didn't change how it looked, sounded, and felt to her senses.

It *felt* real.

Eyes agape, she saw the freight train across the bridge slide into the gap, its cars piling together like children's blocks as it was finally seized by gravity. It fell end-over-end toward the river, its radioactive cargo hitting the water's surface with a horrific splash. The impact raised a column of spray and foam high into the air, water from the top of the column drenching the Silverline's windows.

Suddenly Carol felt the walls of the car shudder around her. There was a second jolt, another, and then the metallic squeal of couplings twisting and snapping as the Silverline tilted downward, its first few cars teetering over the edge of the span.

Carol knew it would be next to plunge into the river.

She turned to Alex. "Okay. I've seen enough."

He heard the tremor in her voice.

"Eve," he said, "terminate."

The room went pitch dark, then slowly brightened as the lights came up. Carol took a deep, slow breath, a hand on her stomach.

"Are you all right?" Alex asked.

"Yes," she said. "I just... It was very realistic."

He nodded.

"But thankfully not real," he said. "Months before the hack, I recommended a list of industry-wide cybersecurity practices to the National Transportation and Safety Board," he said. "The rail industry fought it tooth and nail. Congress finally imposed a fraction of what we wanted—but it included firewall software upgrades that sniffed out and prevented the attack."

"We got lucky," she said.

Alex nodded. "Luck is where preparation meets opportunity...isn't that the expression? The automatic train protection system warns conductors about problems on the rails. Without our upgrades, the hack would have disabled the ATP on both trains. But it remained active. The Silverline stopped before it reached the switched track. Its derailment was prevented and the freight train was never delayed on the bridge."

"And the public never learned about a near nuclear disaster in Groton–New London."

Alex nodded again. "Our safety net did what it's supposed to do," he said. "It ran in the background and caught the threat."

Like my people in the Company, Carol thought.

They stood regarding each other thoughtfully. Then Alex heard a triple beep tone in his headset.

"Sir," Bryan said on the com channel, "there's a call for you on the landline. I should've let it route..."

"It's okay. Take a message, please. Or transfer the call to my voice m—"

"Sir?"

"Yes."

"It's, ah, the President. Of the United States."

Alex looked at Leo and Carol, then pulled off his IVR glasses. "Got it," he said, and turned to leave the room.

VII

"Annemarie," he said out in the corridor. "What's going on?"

"I'm outside the West Wing literally smelling the roses," she said. "Are you in the middle of something important?"

"Actually, I just finished showing off my facility to our friend Carol Morse from Langley."

"Carol? I didn't know she was in New York."

"I believe she's here to consult with Homeland about the upcoming Net Force festivities. Her visit to my lab seemed a little spur-of-the-moment."

Fucillo paused. "You've handed me a segue," she said. "I'd like you at the Stock Exchange next week. When I ring the bell."

Alex watched Harris and Morse stride from the HIVE back to the lab.

"I appreciate the invitation," he said. "But I'm not comfortable with the spotlight. Net Force... I think of it as an invisible watchdog."

"Which conjures images of anonymous agents monitoring our online activities. The whole men-in-black perception of cybersecurity," she said. "We need to change that right off."

Alex pondered that a moment. She made a good case. Wasn't a Cabinet post public almost by definition?

And she *was* POTUS.

"Annemarie, when I accepted your appointment, I accepted everything that goes along with it," he replied. "If that includes helping to sell this thing to the public, you can count on me."

"Appreciated, Alex." Fucillo sounded like she had expected his answer all along. "That being settled, I have an idea. A way to really help people see you as a person. If you're open to it. And assuming it doesn't violate any laws or statutes."

In for a penny, Alex thought. "Okay, I'm game."

"Good," she said. "Since you used the word *watchdog*, I've been thinking about you and Julia..."

VIII

Troubled for more reasons than one, Lucien Navarro entered the library in his powered wheelchair, seeking calmness and clarity of mind amid the books he loved.

He rolled over to its balcony stairs, eased onto its lift platform, and pressed the Wi-Fi-enabled control on his armrest's touch-screen display. The sides of the platform came up and he began rising on the track. Rachmaninov played softly from discreet speakers in the red oak wainscoting—Navarro had programmed in the somber and portentous *Rhapsody on a Theme by Paganini*, Variation 18, Opus 43, to suit his brooding mood.

When he reached the balcony, he lowered one of the side panels to make a ramp and then rolled toward the glass-fronted bookcase holding his rarest editions, including the first printing of *Candide, ou l'Optimisme*. One of only a dozen true firsts of the biting satirical masterpiece, it dated back to 1759 and had been identified by its repeat of the title page's flower, fruit, and leaf ornament.

From a desk beside the bookcase, he took a pair of white cotton gloves, slipped his long, thin pianist's fingers into them, and opened the case to remove the book. He was careful not to handle it too often, but instead would frequently reread the novel in digital form. In his mind, it was hugely misunderstood. While it was said to be about the death of optimism, he viewed that interpretation as so much hot air.

To him, Voltaire saw knowledge as a tool for exposing the world's evils and hypocrisies, and for tempering optimism with reasoned pragmatism. At the end of the story, Candide spoke of cultivating his own garden. Why if not for the hope that it would thrive? Man needed to keep his knuckles in the dirt, turn the soil, mind his crops. He was given his memory of Eden not to lament its loss, but to strive for a new garden paradise. If he wanted it to bear sweet fruit, he would have to rub the sleep out of his eyes and get to work.

A thought for difficult times, Navarro mused as he set the book on his lap, ran his gloved finger over its calf leather front board, and opened it to the title page. Voltaire's writings had frequently inspired him when he collaborated on the Cybernation Manifesto, and tonight he felt the rare edition's beauty and weight would be a tangible source of comfort. Something to settle his mind and give him some peace, as holding a beautifully tooled copy of the Holy Scriptures might be for a person of faith.

It had been a terrible week for humanity. The killing of Yunes Abrika and his students in Birhan, the riots, the horrific video of the national police striking down workers. And, for Navarro... there was the shadow of Kali's disappearance.

He had not heard from her in over a week—not a word since she uploaded the Scepter of London files to Access Mundi, their shared cloud vault. Normally, after a few days, she would send a prearranged signal to let him know she was safe and well. At the very least, he would find digital stamps, indicating she had been inside the vault.

But there had been nothing from her. Nothing at all. In the past several days, his thoughts had assumed a decidedly worried edge.

Kali Alcazar could take care of herself. She had learned well from her family—the grandfather imprisoned for his democratic ideals, the grandmother who chose to live in exile rather than renounce them, the parents who had sought justice for the oppressed around the world...and suffered terribly for it.

She learned well, yes. And carrying on their legacy with a special kind of courage, she had created many powerful enemies.

Navarro expelled a breath. With his hollow cheeks, large, straight nose, dark-framed eyeglasses, and reserved demeanor, he presented a somber appearance to those who didn't know him intimately. Even before the accident, he was undemonstrative with his emotions. Their expression, if not the feelings themselves, were further dampened afterward. Left paralyzed below the waist, with minimal use of his left arm and hand, Navarro had learned to connect to stillness.

But in reality he was at peace. He tended his garden with diligence, and took pride in his work.

The questions he had pondered of late fundamentally related to that work. The Space was without borders or physical dimensions, yet those who entered it existed in two distinct worlds.

When the physical world threatened to impinge on the digital, to assert authority over it, was there a right to self-defense? And what of acting proactively against hostile terrestrial governments? Abuses such as those occurring in Birhan were an unthinkable assault on the foundations of civilization. If armies and economic might were legitimate deterrents—why not digital treasuries and cyberweapons?

Again, Navarro thought of Kali. He was helpless at certain types of decisions, prone to second-guessing himself. Not she. Kali kept a cool head. But when she acted, she never wavered...

He only wished he would hear from her. While she would tell him worrying was a waste of time, he could not help but feel something was very wrong.

Navarro studied the page for several minutes, closed the book cover, and sat quietly for a while. The Rachmaninov was approaching one of its crescendos, a piano glissando leading his hidden heart toward the melancholy grandeur of the strings.

Setting his book down on the reading desk, he raised his good hand to the touchscreen on his armrest, and typed in his password for Access Mundi.

It was possible she was all right. But he did not think so, and her silence left his mind filled with questions.

In the Space, he would seek to find the answers.

IX

It was 2:00 a.m. in Birhan when the rockets launched with their sarin payloads.

Peering through their tripod-mounted laser/GPS range finders, Ansari Kem's guardsmen zeroed-in on three separate locations per his orders.

One was the Satair community on Hagar Oasis, where, on a quiet morning only days earlier, Husam and Rajiya Abrika had left their apartment to march on the refinery.

Another rocket salvo was directed at the densely populated village of Tau on the outskirts of Port Birhan, a slum town where anarchist Beja gangs ruled the streets, sowing antigovernment sentiment and selling illicit firearms.

The third target was the area around the refinery's storage tank blocks, where the beleaguered NDF troopers, Ikrab and Jamalm, incited a crowd of picketers before they themselves were killed in the turmoil, causing riots that spread throughout the facility. The storage blocks had since become occupied by hundreds of protesting Beja strikers.

All told, there were between five and six thousand living souls within range of the bombardments.

In the Marauder, Kem and Massi heard the pop of unleashed propellants as the rockets jumped out of their firing tubes into the gloom. Traveling in parabolic arcs at speeds exceeding 700 knots, they would reach their destinations bare minutes apart.

Kem turned to Massi and saw him staring out the window. His face was as dour as it had been an hour before, when the convoy was eliminated.

This time Kem said nothing to him, but leaned over the front seat to address the driver.

"It's late and I'm tired," he said. "Take us from here so I can get some sleep."

X

Kem's favorite residence was an hour's drive northeast of the bluffs—a twin-level penthouse apartment on the Red Sea coast, with a terrace on which he could stand facing distant Mecca across the water.

He stood there above the shore after his return, dressed in a robe and slippers, smelling the fresh salt breeze from the east. The capital was far to his west, and the fires of Hagar burned to the south, unseen from his vantage. Only when the breeze shifted did he smell the smoke.

As he had told his driver, he was worn out from a long day and night. But before he went to bed, Kem wanted to contact

Drajan. This would be the first of several very important conversations with his former student.

He dialed a number on his satphone and waited.

"Yes?"

"Good evening—I'm calling as promised," Kem said. "How are you?"

"You know what's said about princes and governments."

"They are dangerous elements."

"And is that how you view yourself tonight?"

Kem smiled thinly. "Yes," he said into the phone. "Dangerous."

16

I

Leaving Salerno in the rainswept twilight before sunrise, the pair of black Range Rover Sports swung right off the Via Cilento Adolfo to Strada Statale 18, then made two quick turns onto the twisty corniche road to Amalfi.

Carmody drove the tailing vehicle, his detainee belted into the front passenger seat, her hands cuffed in front of her. He had deliberately removed her blindfold and leg shackles and arranged for them to be alone. The village was about twenty-five kilometers southwest on the Tyrrhenian Sea, the airfield just outside it.

There was some time, but not much.

The fog set in west of Vietri sul Mare, coming down from the bluffs to the right. It folded in around the Rover, bending the glare of its headlights back into Carmody's eyes.

"You'd think the downpour was enough of a hitch," he said. "This doesn't make things easier."

Kali stared out into the billowing whiteness and said nothing.

"I've talked a lot since Malta—maybe too much," he said. "But I know you paid attention."

She appeared to stare straight ahead, watching him peripherally.

Carmody drove on, his wipers laboring. He tried to fix his gaze on the road, but the mist had rolled across it like a blanket.

Not for the first time that morning. He thought of Morse's last call. It came after midnight, unexpectedly, as he was preparing to leave the safehouse.

She was unusually clipped, her orders given without preamble.

"Fox Team will head to Bucharest after the transfer of custody. I've arranged a separate flight for you."

"What's this in connection with?"

"We're ramping up operations at Janus. The site C/O will brief you on arrival."

"Bullshit. I don't like him. Or the way he runs his show."

"That's old news—it's time you both learned to play nice."

"Don't patronize me. I should head back to the States with Outlier. I've made progress with her..."

"We have people who are qualified to take over."

"She won't cooperate with them."

"I'll handle that. You only need to be concerned with your next mission..."

The Rover hugged the face of the slope as Carmody steered sharply into a curve. Morse was right. He *didn't* have to like Colonel Howard. She had risked her neck to keep America's global cyber operations from being totally gutted, black-budgeting them with discretionary funds, and routing the money through a puzzle box of real and nonexistent classified projects.

If Janus was where Morse wanted him, she was boss.

His hand on the gearshift lever, Carmody swore under his breath. The GPS told him he was close to Minori, halfway to his destination. His men had pulled ahead in the fog and radioed that they would wait at the nearest turnaround, five or six klicks up the road.

He gripped the wheel, flicking a glance at Outlier. She sat very still in the passenger seat.

"You need to make your decision," he said. "Tomorrow or the next day, you'll be in a different place…"

Carmody let the sentence fade. He focused on the road in the pulsing rain and mist. His eyes felt tired, and he regretted not sitting tight in Salermo.

It was craziness driving in this mess, he thought.

II

The blacktop wove on between the Monte Lattari and the sea. In the passenger seat, Kali sat looking at Blond Man without looking at him.

She was more convinced than ever the Americans were CIA. They had hunted her across multiple sovereign nations using resources only the clandestine service possessed. But the Agency's Italian Station was at the US Embassy in Rome, on the Via Vittorio Veneto. If she were in official detention, they would have taken her directly there rather than leapfrog from safehouse to safehouse.

Kali knew United States' law, and Blond Man was pushing its boundaries, if not violating it outright, by withholding her delivery to Rome.

She continued to regard him closely as he steered through the fog, noting the outline of a key ring in his right trouser pocket. She had seen him pull it out to lock the door when they left the safehouse.

She flexed her wrists, acutely aware of the steel cuffs around them.

The Rover bore on along the edge of the cliff. She had recognized that they were on the Amalfi Coast road, a hazardous stretch under the best conditions. If Blond Man opted to drive it in this weather, it could only mean one thing…

The waiting game was nearing its end. For both of them.

III

The mist parted to reveal twinkling harbor lights beyond the sheer, craggy drop to the left. Then the shroud of whiteness once again closed around the vehicle.

Carmody took a hand off the wheel and rubbed his eyes. The wind had picked up over the sea, blowing in an easterly direction toward the hilltops. Mingled rain and fog flapped across the Range Rover's windshield, the mist taking on amorphous shapes in front of him.

He leaned forward, downshifting with the left steering wheel paddle as he guided the Range Rover through a sudden S-turn. His palms were moist, the wheel slick in his grip—

The bright circles of headlights appeared midway through the second curve. Coming toward them, in their lane, on their side of the road.

Carmody blinked twice. The lights were dazzling. Blinding. He couldn't see anything else.

Adrenaline rushed through his bloodstream. The vehicle was coming toward them, fast, going to hit them head-on. He turned the wheel sharply right to avoid it.

"Hang on!" he exclaimed.

Kali whipped sideways, a gasp escaping her lips.

Carmody felt the wheel trying to wrench free of his grip as they scraped against the retaining wall that separated the road from the cliff. *Right, right, right,* he thought, steering hard in that direction, toeing the gas, wanting to pull his rear wheels away from the brink.

He shot his passenger a quick glance. *"Hang on!"*

Kali braced her feet hard against the floorboards. The SUV surged forward, the mountain suddenly appearing out of the mist, swelling in the windshield. They were barreling toward the slope, going to crash head on.

He angled off at the last instant, but the Range Rover's front end collided with the slope, its right headlight crunching up against it and shattering, fracture lines spreading across the windshield. Carmody's airbag deployed, cushioning him from the impact, but the whiplash sent pain spiking through the back of his neck. He reached for the shift lever, but the world went dark before he knew whether his hand closed around it.

IV .

Kali felt the whump of the airbag in her face, smelled the acrid propellant gas generated when it opened. Pebbles and dirt spilled down on the vehicle's hood. Stunned, she sat there belted in for several seconds, the deflated nylon bag sagging between her and the dash. Then she realized the Range Rover had jarred to a halt.

She looked around, assaying her situation. They had sideswiped the mountain, their vehicle spinning across the road, its front end in the southbound lane, its rear jutting into the north lane at a forty-five-degree angle. The vehicle's ABS system had likely saved it from skidding over the edge of the cliff.

Blond Man was slumped forward over the deflated airbag, groaning semiconsciously, his right hand hanging loosely atop the shifter knob.

Kali knew she could not stay where she was, stopped between two lanes, with almost no visibility in the mist. It was only a matter of time before a vehicle barreled into them from one direction or the other.

She either had to move the SUV or get out of it. Quickly. But first...

Opening her seat belt with her cuffed hands, she turned toward Blond Man. He remained drooped over the airbag, his body limp. She couldn't wait long. Not with the SUV stalled in the middle of the road. She needed the key ring.

Edging closer to him, she reached her hands out toward his trouser pocket...and stopped.

He was stirring a little. She sat watching him closely, and after a second he grew still again. Without hesitation, knowing this was her chance, she slipped a thumb and second finger into his pocket and carefully pulled out the key ring. The larger key—that was for the safehouse door. The other key's small size and cylindrical shape easily differentiated it. Watching him again for any sign of awareness, she pushed back into her seat, fumbled the second key into the lockhole of her handcuffs, and turned it.

Click.

Her cuffs sprang open.

Kali shook them off. But a vehicle was bound to come plowing into the SUV at any moment. She could not stay on the road.

She looked at Blond Man, ordering her thoughts. The outline of his pistol's concealment holster was plain under the back of his shirt. Her best chance would be to take the gun, drag him onto the roadside, and drive off in the vehicle. He could fend for himself afterward. Why not? It was more than he deserved. He had offered nothing but vague promises.

We can help one another...what puzzles us is that someone has been stealing millions, maybe billions of dollars outright...with your soft tech. The word is that this superworm is called Hekate. And we wondered if the name might mean anything to you.

Hekate. That wasn't vague at all. It was a gift to her, even if presented for his own ends.

Her face set. Time was running down. The Range Rover had been sitting across the middle of the road far too long, and she needed to hurry. Turning toward the passenger door, she pushed out into the swirling rain and mist.

V

Kali was soaked the instant she left the Range Rover. She hurried around to the driver's side, water sloshing around her boots, the road inundated, the fog cascading down the face of the mountain in woolly sheets. Reaching for the door handle, she became suddenly, acutely aware of her own ability to move without restriction. It was a powerful realization, but she immediately pushed it to the back of her mind. She could not afford a nonessential thought.

She opened the door and bent into it. Blond Man was rousing again.

"Can you hear me?" she asked.

He turned his head slightly, still half resting it on the flattened airbag, looking at her with unfocused eyes. There was a large red welt on the left side of his forehead, but no blood that she could see.

"You have to get into the passenger seat," she said. "We can't stay here."

He kept looking at her dimly and croaked something unintelligible.

Kali stood with the rain falling around her. She didn't know how badly he was hurt. Nor could she deal with it at the moment.

Leaning farther into the SUV, she undid his seat belt and pulled him toward her, backing up into the rain. She pulled, pulled, and he finally spilled sideways out the door, his shoulder hitting the slick, wet road.

The rain shocked him into semialertness. Shaking his head, he managed to push himself partly off the blacktop, rising to his knees.

Kali crouched beside him. "Are you able to walk?" she asked.

He looked at her, his eyes coming into focus.

"Can you walk?" she repeated sharply. "We have to get out of the middle of the road."

He stared at her through the rain another second. Then he slowly nodded.

"Think… I can…get my legs under me," he said in a low croak. "Gonna need…a boost."

She slid his arm over her shoulders, gave him a moment to steady his balance.

"Ready?" she said.

"Yeah."

He pushed up with his knees, leaning some of his weight on

her, but rising mostly on his own, staying on his legs as they moved around the back of the Range Rover to the passenger side.

Finally, he half slid, half fell through the open door into the seat.

Kali hurried back to the other side. Climbing behind the wheel, she pressed the Start/Stop button and hoped the engine would turn over.

It did, and smoothly. She straightened her front end, moved into the right lane, and expelled a small sigh of relief. The right headlight was out, and she could feel the vehicle pulling toward that side…but she knew she could handle it.

Her decision made, Kali bore south along the cliff wall toward Amalfi.

VI

"So my Rover's one hell of a bulldog."

Kali glanced imperceptibly at Blond Man. He lifted himself up in the passenger seat.

"Sorry, bad pun," he said, his voice rough. He touched his fingertips to his brow and winced. The bruise was swelling up. "How long was I out?"

She drove on. Although rain was streaming heavily down over the windshield, the fog cover had lightened a bit.

"Not long," she said. "We've gone about four kilometers since you nearly killed us."

"Those headlights were coming at us head-on."

Kali flicked him a glance. "There were no headlights," she said flatly.

"What are you talking about?"

"There were no headlights on the road," she said. "Besides yours."

He opened his mouth, closed it. Then tried again. "Are you saying I imagined them?"

She didn't answer.

Carmody rode in contemplative silence. He *was* getting fuzzy before the accident, and remembered thinking it might be the Coprox. Could he believe her...?

The truth was that he didn't know what to believe. And that greatly concerned him.

He sat without speaking for a while, listening to the rain splash up around the Rover's tires. His head was throbbing as he looked at the GPS.

"We're headed south," he said.

"Yes."

"Same direction I was going in when we spun out."

"Yes."

Carmody leaned back in his seat, closed his eyes. He was nauseous and dizzy and thought he might have sustained a mild concussion.

"Two things," he said. "First, I don't know why you took me with you. But I do know you probably saved my life."

She kept driving in silence.

"Second," he said, "my name's Mike."

A moment passed before she glanced over at him.

"Thank you," she said, and drove on through the pouring rain.

17

Amalfi Coast, Italy
July 11, 2023

I

Its runway parallel to the beach, the airstrip had been established at sea level in a wedge-shaped coastal inlet between Amalfi and the tiny village of Furare to the southwest.

Carmody stood smoking a cigarette in the light, warm evening drizzle outside the office terminal. A single Range Rover Sport was parked to his right. Off to the left, a sleek Gulfstream IV twin jet was refueling on the tarmac, lines running to it from a tank back near the hangar. Two of his men, Wheeler and Long, were standing at the tarmac's edge.

Behind the Gulfstream, a small group of mechanics were doing some last-minute maintenance checks on a second Company-issue plane—a Hawker Beechcraft turboprop designed for shorter hauls. That was the one he was expected to board after his handoff of the detainee.

He blew a stream of smoke from his nostrils. The headache

he'd been nursing since the incident on the road wasn't helping him think straight. But he needed to clear his mind.

The door to the aluminum-sided terminal swung open. De-Battista, the aviation outfit's wrinkled, white-haired owner, emerged from his office and strode over to him in the waning daylight.

"Your people can get onboard," the old man said in English, motioning toward the Gulfstream. "It will be ready for take-off in minutes."

Carmody nodded. Smoke trickling from his nostrils, he flicked his cigarette butt to the rain-dampened ground and crushed it out with his foot. Then he bent and picked it up.

"You're a neat one, *amico mio*," the old man said.

A shrug. "I clean up my own messes," Carmody replied.

DeBattista grinned as they reentered the terminal together. A small waiting area and hallway ran back to the left of an unattended reception desk and some metal folding chairs. Carmody dropped the extinguished stub into a trash receptacle and followed DeBattista up the hall.

The other two members of Carmody's team—Dixon and Schultz—stood guard outside a door midway along its length. Schultz turned the knob to open it.

The room beyond was square, lit with overhead fluorescent fixtures, and furnished only with some more folding chairs. Outlier sat without restraints on one of them. The trio of contractors who arrived with the Gulfstream a half hour earlier stood facing the entryway. They were all male, brawny, and in their twenties or early thirties. The one in the middle had long brown hair, a thick beard, and gold studs in his right nostril. He wore a loose black polo shirt over green military khakis. His upper arms bulged under his short sleeves.

Today's CIA. Carmody thought they looked like small-town fight club contestants.

The bearded man nodded to him. "It's time to get underway," he said. "You have any special instructions?"

"No. I think you're good."

"Then we'll put on the prisoner's restraints and bring her out to the plane."

Carmody steadied his gaze on her. She sat staring at the wall opposite her, but he was sure she was paying close attention to everything in the room. He had learned that much about her these past days and nights. And maybe a little more.

"There's no need for cuffs," he said.

The bearded man looked at him. "You chose to extend certain privileges. But Opsec requires us to maintain physical control over her during trans—"

"The plan's changed," Carmody interrupted. "She's staying in my custody."

The freelancer hesitated, gave him an appraising look. "Nobody told us about anything like that."

"This is last-minute," Carmody said. "I heard from Langley en route."

The bearded man's features tightened. "I need to call in," he said. "Get confirmation."

The room was silent for what seemed a very long moment. Carmody glanced at DeBattista. "Guess I should've told you about the switch."

The white-haired man shrugged. "My job is to see that the planes fly to their destinations," he said. "The rest is none of my concern."

Carmody nodded at Outlier. As she rose from her chair, the bearded man stepped away from the wall, the other two contractors following him.

"I have my orders," he said to Carmody. "They're to fly the detainee back to the States."

"I told you," Carmody said. "Things have changed."

They stared at each other. The bearded man lowered his right hand almost imperceptibly toward his waist.

Carmody drew his Glock 19 from its concealment holster before the man's arm could drop any farther. Behind him, Dixon and Schultz entered the room with their Sig 9mm Rattlers out and leveled at the other two contractors.

"Don't even twitch a nose hair, Muffin Cake," Carmody said, holding the Glock straight out in front of him. His eyes flicked to the pair against the wall. "Same goes for you two bad boys."

Another few seconds passed. The three contractors stood motionless. Carmody nodded his head, and Dixon and Schultz came forward to frisk them. They collected three guns and two non-reflective combat knives.

"We all besties now?" Carmody said.

The bearded man locked eyes with him.

"Yeah," he said. "Sorry for any mix-up."

"It happens," Carmody said. And looked at Outlier. "We're heading out."

His Glock still trained on the bearded man, he reached behind him for the doorknob, turned it, pushed open the door, and nodded Outlier into the hallway. Carmody waited until she left to back through the door himself, Dixon and Schultz doing the same a moment later, their weapons pointed into the room.

When they were all out in the waiting area, Carmody grabbed a folding chair, kicked the door shut, and chocked the back of the chair under the doorknob.

"You want to stay, it's your choice," he said, glancing at Outlier. "Otherwise, we better step to it."

She left the terminal in silence. Carmody and his men went next, the four of them hurrying across the tarmac toward their aircraft.

II

Minutes after they boarded, the Gulfstream was soaring due west over the Tyrrhenian, then looping around on a flight path that would take it across the boot of Italy and the Adriatic to Eastern Europe.

Fox Team had stopped to get their gear from the Rover as they moved along toward the runway. Now Carmody lugged his backpack to where Outlier was reclining in a contoured leather seat, her face turned toward the window.

"Mind if I sit here?"

She glanced over at him and shrugged.

Carmody got into the seat beside her. Then he drew the backpack up, unzipped its main compartment, and slid out a laptop.

"My men recovered this in Malta." He held it out to her.

She took it from him, looking it over.

"It works fine," he said. "I suppose you know we checked it out."

She rested it on the seat beside her thigh.

"We'll be in Bucharest soon," he said. "You'll be able to pick up some fresh clothes after we land."

Her eyes met his. "Why are you bringing me there?"

"I'm not sure," he said. "We're going to hook up with somebody I don't like very much."

"And why are you telling me this?"

Carmody shrugged. "Not sure about that either," he said.

They were silent. The plane droned through the evening sky. Carmody leaned his head back.

"Listen," he said. "On the road last night. When I drove into the damn mountain. There really *wasn't* anything coming at us, was there?"

"No."

"That's not good."

"No," she said.

He kept staring upward. "I've been hitting something hard and need to lay off," he said. "Make that one more thing I probably shouldn't be telling you."

She didn't speak for a long time. Carmody looked up the aisle at the cockpit, glimpsed the Gulfstream's headings on a digital satellite map above the pilot. They were over the Kornati archipelago off the Croatian coastline.

"We're close," he said.

She turned briefly to look out her window, but the sky had

darkened. "Those men at the airstrip," she said, her eyes back on Carmody. "How did you know they wouldn't reroute us in flight?"

"To get you to the States, you mean?"

"Yes."

He shrugged his shoulders. "They probably tried. I know they would have called my superior."

"But?"

"I have a hunch Romania takes precedence," he said.

She studied him contemplatively awhile. Then she nodded.

"My name is Kali," she said. "Don't you ever dare call me Muffin Cake."

Carmody smiled a little.

"Deal," he said.

She leaned her head back, stretched her legs, and closed her eyes. After a few seconds Carmody did the same, neither of them saying anything more as the Gulfstream cruised on toward its destination.

18

Baneasa, Romania/Washington, DC
July 11, 2023

I

Colonel John Howard noticed the beetle crawling along the concrete walk seconds after he stepped outside for some fresh air. It was over an inch long, with thick antennas and something that resembled a triceratops horn growing straight out of its head.

One ugly little bugger, he thought.

He drew a breath, held it a moment, and heard his exhalation whistle softly through the gap between his upper front incisors. Lord knew why his mother never took him to get it fixed…*ain'no shame,* she would always say whenever she caught him self-consciously looking in the mirror. That had been her favorite motto.

Years later, it became his. Fifteen years here at the site attached to Janus, a full third of his life. Howard had gotten more than his nails dirty in that time. But the things that were done back in the day, the things *he* did…

He truly never regretted that part. The renditions brought over to him were the scum of Creation. If his methods of extracting information were just as hideous, Howard truly believed they saved thousands of American lives. He had carried those methods with him from one secret war to another, helping him to understand what was going on in the world's underbelly better than anyone.

The politicians had the luxury of debating till the trumpets of the Second Coming blasted them off their chairs. But an army officer was pledged to obey the orders of the President of the United States and the officers appointed over him. To defend the Constitution against all enemies. Foreign and domestic.

These days it was all about the cybers. The *technologie vampiri* in Eastern Europe were as corrupt and dangerous as anyone or anything that ever fell under God's sight—especially the hacking syndicate he had been tracking for the past few years. And its leader.

Vulfoliac.

The online handle—some kind of Goth horseshit—came up time and time again. He'd warned his bosses, sent all kinds of intel up the line, but would have been out of commission half a decade ago without the Duchess's quiet budgetary massages. And even so, he was down to eighty personnel, a quarter of them support staff. If she was sending Fox Team to assist, he did not intend to whine about it. He just had to make sure their fearless leader knew who was calling the shots.

Now Howard gazed past a fleet of manned and unmanned vehicles—military and civilian—to the compound's northern perimeter, where Nash the hedgehog was gliding along on patrol in the dimming light. Bristling with sensor arrays and mounted weapons systems, the autonomous robot sentries looked like king-sized versions of his beetle friend, and were hardened against physical and electronic threats. Howard respected their capabilities, and understood the need for them. But did he trust them?

Not one damned bit. Because *hardened* did not mean *invulnerable*. The two words were not interchangeable, and they never would be.

As he watched from across the parking area, Nash briefly paused to investigate something caught in the fence—a branch that must have snapped off one of the overgrown trees outside the line. Plucking it from the mesh with its pincer arm, the 'hog carried it off somewhere for disposal.

"Anal sonofabitch," Howard muttered under his breath. How many black funding streams had Morse diverted so he could replace his human patrols with 'hogs? But soldiers in flak vests and machine guns were obsolete, fighting yesterday's wars while today's enemies slipped through the back door.

Sighing, Howard decided to go back inside. Turning, he strode toward the short flight of stairs leading up to the steel entrance door...and paused a moment. The beetle had inched across the walkway to the bottom step and was probing it with one of its plated forelegs.

"Uh-uh," he said. "Sorry, you ungodly monster. No way I'm lettin' you crawl in the door with me."

He moved closer to the insect, raised his booted foot over it and hesitated.

A second passed. Howard's brow creased. Lowering his foot to the ground, he knelt and gave the beetle a long, close look. Watching as it got a small way up the step, fell to the ground on its back, and struggled to right itself on the concrete.

Howard frowned and took a deep breath; its legs were still wriggling in the air.

"You're gonna be stuck there till some damn toad comes along and eats you," he said, reaching to lift it off the cement, using his thumb and index finger like tweezers.

Holding the beetle between his fingertips, Howard carried it to the ragged patch of grass at the edge of the walk. Then he crouched again and carefully set it down.

"Go on," he said, and rose to his feet.

He turned up the flight of steps and touched his palm to the bioscanner, letting it read his hand and facial recognition nodal points. An instant later the door slid open and he walked through into the large climate-controlled room beyond.

Sergeants Pierce and Abrams were seated at a triple-tiered surveillance station, watching the feeds with their headsets on. Several were patches from the hedgehogs—Nash on the northern perimeter, Spree patrolling the south line, Earl on the eastern margin, and Walt at the compound's western edge—while others displayed pictures from IP smart sensors monitoring the base's approach roads and interior grounds.

Howard turned to Pierce. "Fernandez back from his outing yet?"

"No, sir," the sergeant said. "He left Bucharest at roughly oh-one hundred. ETA—"

"I know how long it takes to drive here." He grunted. "Anything else?"

Abrams swung around in his chair and removed his earpads. "Fox Team's in the air. If current weather conditions hold, they should arrive tonight." He paused. "Sir, there's more. The detainee is with them."

"*Outlier?*" Howard looked at him. "You sure?"

Abrams nodded. "The transfer was aborted at Amalfi. We received confirmation from Duchess stateside."

"That's it? She give you any details?"

"No, sir. I was just told to relay the information to you."

Howard was quiet. He'd been ringing the bell on the Romanian cybercrime gangs for over a year, warning that their leader, Vulfoliac, constituted a greater menace than any of the desert trash that once passed through his little backwater resort. It was high time the syndicate was taken down. Putting aside his personal feelings toward Carmody's team, Howard knew they could be usefully deployed against the circuit jockeys.

But Outlier was a total surprise. He hadn't counted on it.

Howard was silent another moment, the tendons at the hinges of his jaw bulging like cables.

He needed some time with his saxophone, he thought. Just the two of them. Alone.

"I'm going to my quarters," he said, turning to Pierce. "When Fernandez gets here, tell him I want to see him on the double."

And with that he turned away, leaving the sergeants to watch him stride rigidly off down the corridor.

II

"Madam President, these images are difficult to take," said Cody McDaniel, her National Security Advisor. "The attacks occurred sometime after midnight in Birhan. This area is Satair, in the Hagar area."

Yunes Abrika's precinct, Fucillo thought.

A cup of chamomile tea in her hand, her face stoic—as a female politician in the United States, you had to *learn* to look stoic better than any man—she sat at the head of the long conference table in the Situation Room beneath the West Wing, waiting for the video to roll.

"Thank you, Cody," she said. "If we're all ready, let's see it."

Nods from everyone around the table, a group of over a dozen top-level officials who had been summoned for this morning's meeting: Vice President Saul Stokes, McDaniel, Chief of Staff Randy Severin, and the entire National Security Staff, or secretariat. In chairs along the walls were various aides and deputies.

McDaniel glanced over at one of the aides, who keyed a command into an electronic console. An instant later, the widescreen wall monitor at the opposite end of the conference table flashed on, showing a medium close-up of a little girl—she was six or seven—in red pajamas. She was stretched on a tiled floor in a bare-walled room, flat on her back, her arms sticking straight up, her hands grasping at empty air.

"The images were shot by rescue workers, and uploaded to the Red Cross's ICRC database," McDaniel said. "We believe they were taken at an urgent care hospital facility about thirty minutes after the strike."

Fucillo felt her stomach tighten as the girl's mouth opened and closed, opened and closed…

Opened and closed…

"Sarin blocks the production of an enzyme that's a natural inhibitor to muscular and glandular activity. It puts the body into overdrive and then exhausts it to the point that it can't function." McDaniel cleared his throat. "She's exhibiting classic symptoms of nerve gas exposure. Convulsions, rapid breathing…what we see is the onset of respiratory paralysis."

The camera lens pulled out, its image jumping. The little girl—her legs scissoring together and apart in her baggy pajama bottoms—was now shown lying in a row of fifteen or twenty children that reached from one side of the room to the other. Some were spasming, their eyes rolling, hands over their cheeks. Others were completely unmoving, their stares vacant and sightless. Visible past their feet were the tops of heads belonging to an entire second row of victims.

"How many are there?" Stokes asked. The ex-marine and veteran of Afghanistan kept his voice neutral.

"Our information is that between four and six hundred people were transported to this center," said McDaniel. "We estimate the total number of casualties from Satair at almost a thousand. And if our reports are accurate, there were separate attacks at the Hagar refinery and a suburb of Port Birhan."

"So we could be looking at upward of two or three thousand," Fucillo said.

"Upward, yes."

The video camera panned around the room now to show more victims: a woman with her entire body rigid except for a single hand winding at her side. Another with blood streaming from the outer corners of her eyes. A young man sprawled on his stomach. Raised slightly off the tiles, his head lolled from side to side, his mouth hanging open. His arms were stiff and paralyzed, the fingers contorted. As the camera held on him, his movements slowed, his head sinking down and down.

"He's in the final stages of asphyxia," said the NSA. "Minutes from death."

"Is there *any* antidote to this?" asked Severin.

"Atropine can be effective. But it has to be administered very soon after poisoning. Or ideally before it occurs. I doubt any of these poor souls survived."

Severin rubbed the back of his neck. "God help us."

The sit room went silent as the video ran on. In her chair at the end of the table, Fucillo sat watching scores of men, women, and children in their spastic final agonies. Finally she closed her eyes.

"Okay, Cody," she said. "We've seen enough."

He nodded at the staffer with the computer, and the wall monitor went dark again.

Fucillo inhaled, exhaled, grateful that she could. She had known the crown prince of Birhan for two decades, and didn't want to believe he could be responsible for the atrocity the video substantiated.

She opened her eyes and looked at the blanched faces around the room, her gaze moving from one to the next. Then she pushed up from her chair.

"Ladies and gentlemen, our meeting is adjourned," she said.

Stokes glanced over at her. "I think we all agree something has be done," he said. "But what?"

"You'll know soon enough," she said, and left the room.

19

I

Alone in his master suite, Drajan sat before a large flatscreen display and saw a video conference ID appear in the call column.

"Quintessa Leonides," his digital assistant announced.

"Accept."

A window opened onscreen. Her pale blond hair pulled back, her eyes glacial blue, Leonides looked at him from a thousand kilometers away in the Latvian capital. Behind her, he could see wide glass doors and, through them, the bridges spanning the Gulf of Riga at the mouth of the River Daugava.

"Good afternoon, Mr. Petrovik."

He noticed her high cheekbones and long, slender neck, the skin smooth and pale above a diamond necklace. The photographs online offered mere hints of her stunning beauty.

"Drajan," he said. "If you please."

She smiled tightly. "Quintessa," she said. "On behalf of my

family, I would like to thank you for your business with Bank Leonides."

He gave a minute nod. "It's my thought to expand on our current dealings, and even partner on a certain upcoming venture."

"Yes?"

"I haven't considered another institution—and hope I won't need to," he said. "Your work is impeccable."

"Thank you again—but we prefer to be described as flexible." A shrug of her shoulders. "My government has a benign attitude toward its cryptocurrency brokers. That benefits us as well as our clients. We try not to set preconceived limits upon what is possible."

"Excellent," he said. "Let us talk, then, of shared possibilities."

II

"Spell it out plain and simple, Sofia," President Fucillo said. "What is my legal authority to send troops to Birhan?"

She was having lunch with White House Counsel Sofia Gudmund on the patio outside the Oval Office, an umbrella throwing shade over her bistro table.

Blonde, blue-eyed, almost six feet tall in flats—she played volleyball with the Swedish team in the Olympics—Gudmund was eating a plate of yellowfin tuna and salmon sashimi. She noticed Fucillo had not touched her platter of mixed sushi.

"It's mostly unambiguous...as long as we know what set of legalities we're talking about," she said. "As Commander-in-Chief you can order our armed forces into combat without congressional approval, period. But military action and war aren't always the same thing. In terms of US law, the Constitution leaves it to Congress to actually issue a declaration of war against a foreign power." She paused. "What's muddied this a little in the past half century is the War Powers Resolution...but *just* a little."

"I know all that," Fucillo said. "The courts say War Powers can't be enforced. Or at least that it's questionable...an infringement on executive privilege."

"And that includes the sixty-day limit after which Congress can theoretically require you to terminate the use of armed forces overseas," Gudmund said. "No president—I repeat, *no* president—has ever conceded any of this to legislators. Plain and simple? With a strike of short duration, it's your call."

"But it does give our senators and congressmen the ability to raise a furor," Fucillo said.

Fucillo glanced down at her plate. She couldn't muster the slightest appetite. Hours after leaving the Situation Room, she could not stop the horrific video from playing through her mind.

"All right," she said. "You mentioned other legalities."

"I was referring to international law," Gudmund said. "That's where it gets even murkier. The United Nations can and will mandate that a team of fact-finders visit Birhan and determine whether a chemical agent has been used there before any member nation takes action…unilateral or otherwise."

"And that could take weeks."

"Or longer," said the counsel. "The World Health Organization usually has to be on board. And the OPCW…the Organization for the Prevention of Chemical Weapons. The process requires the UN Security Council to review a report based on the team's findings and then make its recommendation."

Fucillo was quiet. She watched a large yellow bee spiral down to one of the ageratums in the gentle breeze, skipping from flower to flower as it gathered its pollen.

"Sofia," she said, "do you know all worker bees are female?"

The council looked at her. "No," she said. "I wasn't aware of it."

"Credit my insomnia. I saw it on one of those wildlife channels in the wee hours." Fucillo sighed. "They call them 'imperfect females.' I'm not sure why."

"Maybe a male bee scientist came up with the term."

Fucillo smiled wanly. "A worker spends the first part of her life tending to the brood, and the rest foraging for pollen and making honey," she said. "She'll only make a fraction of a teaspoon over the course of her lifetime. It takes thousands of worker bees to produce enough honey for a colony to survive the winter. You could say it's a cooperative effort…yet when you see an imperfect bee, she's alone."

"And this is apropos because…?" Gudmund let the question dangle.

Fucillo took a breath of fresh garden air. "Could be it's just a random thought," she said. "Two of the Security Council's permanent members are China and the Russian Federation. Do you think they're going to authorize the use of force against Birhan based on its government's human rights violations?"

"When pigs fly," Gudmund said.

Fucillo lifted her eyes from her untouched sushi to the counsel's face. "The NSA's preliminary analysis of the video evidence gives a near one hundred percent likelihood of sarin attacks at Hagar and elsewhere in Birhan. The small percentage of uncertainty only goes to whether a different chemical weapon—Novichock, tubun, or something else—may have been used. I will not let what happened there stand."

Gudmund sat looking across the table at Fucillo.

"Madam President, I am proud to serve you," she said after a bit.

There was a wistful quality about Fucillo's expression.

"However imperfect I may be," she said.

III

"We're starting right here," said the Secret Service agent. He was one of six men gathered on the sidewalk outside the New York Stock Exchange's official visitor entrance.

Harris noted his name was Day, as in the opposite of night. Agent Reginald Day, the bright sun gleaming off his tinted lenses.

It was an easy mnemonic for Leo, who had been into that sort of thing since college.

"POTUS and her security escort, along with all other protectees, will leave the building through this door shortly after the opening bell is rung at oh-nine-thirty hours. She will enter her limousine where it's parked over *there*—" he pointed to the curb almost directly in front of him "—and then drive west to Zuccotti Park with multiple components of the motorcade. The rest of the protectees will follow in separate cars. We're going to have additional vehicles join them on Nassau Street, which picks up where this street ends and leads directly to Pine..."

Harris wondered why Day felt compelled to tell a group consisting of two New York–based FBI commanders, a deputy police chief, and David Stiles, the governor's public affairs hack, the location of a street that they could all clearly see a few yards off to the left.

"...then turn left on Broadway, which is a one-way southbound," the Secret Service agent was saying. "This dictates that they head southwest to Battery Plaza, away from the park, and loop around on Greenwich Street to head back in its direction." He paused. "We currently expect POTUS's limo to halt at One Liberty Plaza, across the street from the park, then make her way to the outdoor stage and video setup."

"Ah...if I may interject." This was from Stiles. "I need to remind you that Governor Bender intends to decline motor transport and walk to Zuccotti Park after the opening bell ceremony."

"So we've been informed—and I want to be clear the we do not support this preference," said the other member of the Secret Service advance team. His name was Landen Nice, which rhymed with *spice, mice, vice, price, lice, twice,* and many more words Harris could think of, none useful from a mnemonic perspective. Unless you left it as it was, then paired it with his partner's name: *Nice Day.*

"The governor understands the service's perspective," Stiles said. "But we're expecting beautiful weather. And he prefers being close to the people."

"Governor Bender's walk is logistically unsound," said Lund, the Assistant Director of the Agency's New York field office, and Harris's direct superior. "It's going to divert and disperse our available resources…as I think Deputy Haines is best qualified to explain."

The tall, crew-cut man beside him nodded. Robert Haines was the NYPD's Deputy Commissioner of Special Operations. "To accommodate the governor, we need SWAT personnel stationed on rooftops along his walk path, an entire second line of police, Secret Service protection on the ground, and so on," he said. "Securing those office buildings is very complex, not to mention disruptive of the businesses inside them."

Stiles made a passably sympathetic face. "I'm sure the state can help defray the cost of added manpower for your department. And compensate firms that might be impacted by our choice."

Haines sighed. "Mr. Stiles…do yourself a favor and take a look around us," he said, his hand sweeping toward the NYSE security checkpoint in the middle of the roadway. "Don't be fooled by the fact that this street's closed to traffic…and that we had it cordoned off to pedestrians for this meeting. The event is on a Monday morning, the start of the workweek. When the sidewalks and office buildings are crowded with people."

Stiles shrugged. "The governor's office really does appreciate your concern. But the purpose of this whole thing is to rally popular support, and we want to be inclusive of—"

"The people," Harris said. "We get it already, Stiles. It's hot as hell out here, in case you didn't notice."

"Excuse me?"

"Bender can do whatever he wants." Harris glowered at the PR flak. "He likes a dog and pony show, okay. But do him a favor and let him know we all think it's a lousy idea. So nobody can say we didn't fucking warn him."

Stiles glared at him. "Would you like me to use those exact words to the governor? Or might you care to rethink them?"

Harris shrugged.

"You want to change 'idea' to 'brain fart,' be my guest," he said.

Stiles stood there looking furious.

"Governor Bender is taking his walk," he said. "You guys just do your jobs and keep him safe."

And with that he turned away from the group, stalking off toward his parked car.

"Good riddance," Harris said, watching him depart.

IV

"Carol, you still at your hotel?" Harris shouted into his Bluetooth.

"Why are you yelling?"

"I'm out on the street," he said. "It's noisy."

"Oh," she said. "Well, I'm leaving right now. In fact, if our connection drops off, it's because I'm getting into the elevator. My flight's in a little over an hour… I have a car service taking me to LaGuardia."

He turned to check out a sedan parked at the curb, reading the reservation card in its windshield. The name on it was C. Morse.

"Leo…what are you doing out here?"

Carol's voice was suddenly in both his ears. He spun back around toward the Warwick's entrance as she came toting her luggage bag past the doorman.

"You're starting to sound like Alex," he said. "Didn't I tell you I was on the street?"

"But not right in front of the *hotel*."

He shrugged. "I wanted to talk to you."

"Now?"

Leo nodded. The avenue around him blared with noise. He was thinking there weren't many places more secure from eavesdroppers than a midtown Manhattan sidewalk at eleven thirty on a weekday morning.

"It'll just take a minute," he said. "I hustled all the way up here from Wall Street."

"The walkaround?"

"Yeah."

"How'd it go?"

"It kinda got cut short." His shoulders went up and down. "Somebody pissed off the governor's lube monkey."

"Who?"

"Might've been me."

Carol smiled. Leo smiled back at her.

"So," he said, "you have that minute?"

She glanced at her wristwatch. "Not much more, Leo. I have two kids waiting at home."

"And hubby, I get it." He went over to the idling sedan, spoke briefly to the driver, then returned to where she stood. "It's about that favor we discussed yesterday. I wanted to know if you had an update."

Carol nodded, stepping closer so he could hear her. "I intended to call you after I got back to Washington," she said quietly. "We've got an MLE outside the Romanian capital. Don't ask how or why. It's a skeleton crew right now."

Harris stood there thinking. MLE was spookese for military liaison element; the Langley boys were even bigger on acronyms than their Bureau counterparts.

"What else?"

"I'm going to hook you up with the site commander. A Colonel Howard. He's a good man."

Harris nodded. "What's he got to do with my girl?"

She lifted a hand to cover her lips. "I redeployed the team that picked her up. To give Howard an assist with his ops."

Harris read her expression. "And she's with them?"

"Yes. That wasn't in the plan, but I'm letting it roll for now."

"Your boy again."

"Yes." She angled her chin at the waiting car. "Leo, I better run. I have to make my flight."

He nodded.

"We'll keep talking," she said.

He nodded again.

Then she gave him a quick hug and went hustling toward the car with her suitcase in tow, its wheels clattering on the pavement.

Harris watched as the car shot east toward FDR Drive, then turned toward the no parking zone where he'd left his own car a block away.

Things had gone pretty well, he thought. Everything friendly and professional between them. No weepy bullshit.

He missed her already.

V

The Gulfstream made its approach to Mihail Kogalniceanu Airport shortly after 8:00 p.m., flying dark over Lake Tasau on the Black Sea coast, its running lights cut off after it entered Romanian airspace. As the pilot banked over the airport's military sub-base, he flashed his red and green wingtip lights, waited for final radio confirmation, and then eased into a gentle descent, his wheels touching down with only the slightest of bumps.

Carmody unstrapped as the plane taxied to a halt. He had dozed for almost half an hour in the sky without benefit of the 'Rox—a small win, but one he would take.

He glanced over at Kali. "We're about two hours east of Bucharest."

"Yes," she said. "Constanta."

He raised an eyebrow. "You've heard of it?"

She motioned to the GPS map display in the cockpit. "I kept my eyes open while you slept."

Carmody nodded slightly. "Better get ready," he said. "I have an extra backpack for you. My guess is our rides are here."

Kali saw them as she climbed down the debarkation ladder. A pair of JLTVs sat idling in the shadows off the tarmac with their low-beams on, two US Army men in lightweight summer fatigues waiting in front of them. One was a tall, lank, fortyish African American with colonel's eagles on his uniform blouse, the other a man about the same age with olive skin, a modified Mohawk, and sergeant's chevrons.

"Colonel Howard." Carmody nodded at the tall man, but did not salute. "It's something to see you again."

Howard grinned. "*Something*, huh? Thought you might lie and tell me it's a pleasure."

Carmody stood there without replying. He noticed Howard closely scrutinizing Kali.

"I take it those aren't Company-issue Victorian riding boots you're wearing," the colonel said.

She stared at him a moment. "I'm not Company. What they are or aren't is my affair."

Carmody suppressed a grin. He turned to the other man who'd come to meet them and offered his hand. "How you been, Fernandez?"

The sergeant put his own hand out and shook. "Same shit, different year," he said, pointing to the JLTVs with his eyes. "You want to ride with me?"

Carmody nodded and motioned for Kali to join him.

"Our pleasure," he said.

VI

Denny Yalin stood inside the garage entrance and waved in an arriving automobile, reading the bar code on its windshield with his handheld scanner. It was about five o'clock in the evening near the end of a long, hot, draining day in a month that had changed his life forever. Changed it in more ways than he even knew for certain.

If he really wanted to trace the changes, Yalin supposed he would need to go back to when Lonel and Grigor Ilescu, a couple of guys from the old neighborhood, offered him the ATM card with a deal he could not pass up. Take the card to a bank, withdraw some money, and keep a percentage for himself... He knew what a cash mule was, and had been willing to become one. He'd do anything it took to help his daughter Tess.

But things didn't pan out. The card failed to make a withdrawal from not two but seven terminals at five different banks throughout the Bronx. When that seventh try didn't succeed, Yalin sleeved the card back into his wallet and drove home to his wife. He wasn't unhappy about it for his own sake. In his mind it was a low-risk gamble. He went for it, and lost, and it cost him nothing but time.

The disappointment he felt was all for Tess. Fifteen years old, she had excelled at high school track before life struck her a terrible blow, what might as well have been an asteroid falling out of the sky. Except Tess's asteroid was a drunk driver swerving into their lane while they were on the way home from a meet.

Neither he nor Sonia was seriously hurt, but Tess wasn't as fortunate. Her right leg was amputated on arrival at the trauma center, and for days her survival was touch-and-go.

Thankfully she made it. But nothing was ever the same afterward. Yalin and his wife maxed out their insurance coverage, paid tens of thousands in expenses that buried them in debt. It became a struggle just to keep a roof over their heads. But worse, far worse than anything else, Tess's life was turned inside out.

And so Yalin jumped at the fake cash card scheme. He understood it was nothing but bank robbery. All his life he had considered himself an honest man. But he no longer knew for sure what defined *honest*, and really couldn't worry about it. He only knew that he loved his daughter and would do anything for her.

After the unsuccessful ATM withdrawals, Lonel had insisted he was sorry and wanted to make it up to him. If Yalin really needed cash, Lonel said, he would introduce him to someone named Koschei, who paid more for simple favors than Yalin could ever have earned taking a cut of the ATM money.

Desperate, Yalin told him he was interested.

The limo was waiting one night after he left work—a driver in front, Koschei in the rear. A well-dressed man with a sharp chin, thick eyebrows, and dark, slicked-back hair, he handed Yalin a small carryall pouch and told him it contained everything he would need. Yalin never considered bargaining with him. Koschei looked like somebody who was used to setting his own terms.

Yalin brought the pouch back to his apartment and hid it

from his wife, waiting until she went to bed to open it. Inside, he found fifty thousand dollars in crisp new bills and an unsealed envelope. The envelope contained the jump drive and a folded sheet of paper with simple instructions. He was to plug the drive into the serial port on his handheld scanner at the garage, and send a Bluetooth data upload to the chain's internal computer network.

That was it. Everything. The job took under a minute.

Yalin was no fool, though. He knew he must have infected the network with something. But he didn't want to think too much about it.

Then, a few days ago, his supervisor told him the Feds had booked the garage for the upcoming presidential visit. That it would be reserved for VIPs attending the New York Stock Exchange and Zuccotti events. Somehow, Koschei must have known about it, Yalin thought. He seemed like a man who knew a lot of things. In any case, Secret Service agents and police suddenly were conducting security checks in and around the premises.

This morning was more of the same. Several officials pulled in early, including a hotshot named Stiles from the governor's office. After leaving his Chevy Equinox in the garage for about an hour, Stiles returned in a huff and insisted that Yalin pull it out right away. After waiting all of five minutes, he complained about it taking too long and drove off without leaving a tip.

Stiles and the others showing up today only reminded Yalin the presidential visit was less than a week off...and it made him nervous. One thing he did not feel, though, was regret. What he did, he did for Tess. How could he possibly regret that?

Now Yalin raised his scanner to yet another windshield, motioning the customer forward. In about a week's time, President Fucillo would arrive in the city, and he might find himself with some answers. Maybe they would be the kind that sent him straight to Hell. He didn't know.

The only man who could judge him was the one he saw in the mirror.

VII

His long hair hanging freely over his shoulders, his eyes puffy and tired, Bryan Ferago finished brushing his teeth, yawned, looked in the restroom mirror, and wondered if he ought to shave before catching some sleep. He had a razor in his overnight bag, and was thinking it would make him feel fresh.

He rubbed a hand over his cheeks. The truth was he didn't get any more growth on his face these days than he had at thirteen. But he tried to look neat. He wanted to be respectful of this laboratory, and of the two men who entrusted him with so much. No one had given him anything close to that kind of trust before.

Stifling another yawn, Bryan turned off the water and left the restroom. This was the third night in a row he was sleeping here at the lab, crashing on a couch in one of the lounges. He was thinking he needed to get out awhile. Do a lap or two around the campus, smell the grass, breathe some unprocessed air. The problem was that, except for when he grew so tired he couldn't keep his eyes open, he was unable to pry himself away from the virtual machines that he and Felicia Cheng infected with the Frankenbug. It was like no other entity he ever saw, and it made him worse than uneasy.

He stepped down the corridor to the vending machine, got an energy bar and an orange juice, turned toward the lounge… and then made a quick about-face for the Cyberlab, inputting his biometrics to unlock the door. Just a few more minutes at the machine, he thought. Then he would be off to Dreamland.

He sat down at the computer, crunching on his health bar. With Felicia's help, he had expanded the day-of-attack scenario well beyond their original three-machine, H&L Trust–Chloe Berne–botmaster configuration to a broadscale infection simulation. It was the equivalent of creating a test bed for a biological microorganism. A growth culture.

When scientists had cultured the polio, flu, and chickenpox

viruses, they used human cells for their substrate—the material on which a microbial colony was established. The cell strains were a homogeneous environment. But the internet was *heterogeneous*. You had computer networks with different memory and bandwidth capabilities, traffic flows, firewalls, and user safeguards. And you had mobile platforms like smartphones and Internet of Things devices, some of them without *any* security.

Bryan knew there was no way he could factor all of them into a manageable simulation. He didn't think anyone was capable of modeling it, not for the Frankenbug, except for Natasha Mori. Besides being the smartest person he knew, she was so good at predictive analyses, he would tell her it was her mutant power. After a while that got to be a joke between them.

He studied his screen setup, realizing how much he missed her at the lab. The prof had cleared it in a jiff when he mentioned wanting to talk to her about the Frankenbug. The only question was whether she was in town or touring. But Bryan had done a quick online check, and seen that her glitch act, Dev Zero, was doing a residency at Fallout under the Brooklyn Bridge.

It would be good to see Tash again, he thought, figuring he would head over to the club tonight and try to talk her into coming back.

Bryan washed down a mouthful of granola with a swig of juice. He'd made some progress with Felicia's help, creating a limited number of simulated environments, trying to vector in computer networks that might be expected to regularly interact with a bank like H&L Trust. It was an imprecise process, like figuring out which guests were liable to mingle at a party.

H&L was a large commercial lender. On an average business day it would connect with many high-end financial institutions. Bryan and Felicia's digital hot zone was therefore largely made up of the system configurations and programming languages those institutions might use. They had simulated JAVA, Python, C...even COBOL-based systems dating back forty years to when the old IT cowboys were designing them, and computer programmers still used punch cards. In fact, the COBOL sims were especially important, because H&L and most of the global financial sector still relied on that language for their depositor accounts, check-clearing, ATM machines, and credit and debit card networks.

He gulped some more orange juice. It was weird. The other day he had noticed the Frankenbug self-destructing, yet now it was sending out spores. That sort of thing wasn't so unusual in nature: fruits dropped their pits as they rotted, dandelions were goners once they blew their seeds, and there were any number of insects that died after egg-laying. But Bryan didn't know if he had ever seen malicious software behave that way.

Weirder and weirder. And for him the big question—or one of them—was whether the almost instantaneous maturation of the spores was an inherent ability, or occurred because of his sim's hyperfast rate of data replication.

Bryan's forehead creased. What if the dying Frankenbug's spores made the hop from H&L Trust to some other network in record time? How quickly might the infection spread? And what new and destructive forms might it take?

Staring at his monitor, he stuffed the remnant of his granola bar into his pocket.

He suddenly wasn't hungry anymore.

20

I

It was just past 10:00 p.m. at Fallout, and Dev Zero had lured out lower New York's smart and stylish to a full house. On the dance floor, frenetic club-goers were working up a sweat to Tasha's digital backbeats.

Tasha cut a striking figure behind the U-shaped sound station. Tall and waif-thin with deep-set emerald green eyes, she wore skin-tight black pants, a mid-length white shirt, a retro leather-string hippie belt and black high-top Converse sneakers. Her choppy white hair lashing wildly around her face, she swayed to her music—occasionally closing her eyes, typing on the keyboard with one hand, and waving her other in the air with a rhythmic flourish. The sawtooth sound wave tattoos on her wrists were based on one of her own improvisations.

Standing completely still beside her, Duncan Ulysses was Dev Zero's indispensable other half. His shaved head bowed in concentration, his stillness a counterpoint to her body's rhythmic movements, he worked his controls to turn her live digital code into a fantastical, constantly changing visual environment, bathing the room in projected light patterns and animations. It was Duncan who, once upon a time, convinced Tash that graphics would enhance, not mask, her raw codewriting. *Showmanship, baby...it never hurt a'one!* he would chide with his faint Jamaican accent.

His advice turned a struggling purist into a smashing success. But what really juiced Tash was their nightly experimentation, their improvisational merging of sound, light, and color. Every performance was a new beginning, and she never quite knew *where* it would take the room.

Tonight Natasha Mori was *soaring* to the rafters.

II

A final burst of light, a silver flash, and their set was over, cheers and applause filling the room.

Backstage afterward, Tash went straight to the small refrigerator against the wall. She was thirsty—a mad, demanding thirst.

A moment later Duncan followed her through the door. He wore a dark gray blazer over a white tank top shirt, black jeans, and motorcycle boots.

"Man, you were good tonight," he said. "Scary good."

Tash leaned into the refrigerator for a bottle of Riesling and two chilled wineglasses. Using the top of the fridge as a counter, she slowly poured it and handed Duncan his glass.

"Cheers," he said, holding it out for a toast.

"To being scary good," she said. Her fingers were long and slender around the glass, the nails cut short and painted with swirls of prismatic color.

They clinked and drank. After a minute she put her glass down, then reached for her smartphone, a pack of cigarettes and a disposable lighter. Checking her messages, she saw a missed call notification on the phone's lockscreen.

She dropped the phone back into her pouch and lit the cigarette.

"Everything okay?" Duncan said.

Tasha picked up the glass and sipped. "Yeah, why?"

"Thought I saw the word *Mom* on the display."

She shrugged.

"Moms suck," she said. "Next subject."

Duncan glanced at his watch. It was just after 2:00 a.m. "You want to grab a bite?" he said. "I'm starved."

"Can't." She drank more wine. "I'm meeting someone."

He flashed a huge grin. "Oh?"

"Not *that* kind of someone, so wipe the perverted look off your face," she said. "He's an old friend of mine. Bryan Ferago."

"Sounds familiar...where have I heard the guy's name?"

"I might've mentioned him once or twice," she said. "We met in grad school when I was studying data and probability analysis. Our professor was kind of a legend among geeks." She shrugged. "I'm not sure why he even wants to see me. We haven't spoken in forever."

Duncan grunted. "Someday you'll have to tell me why you took a walk on all that," he said.

"Someday," Tasha said. "It's a long story."

She lit her cigarette, silent thoughts going through her head.

"I thought you told me you quit smoking," Duncan said.

"I think I told you I was trying."

He grunted again. "If you want to cut back, I got a vape kit sitting in a drawer at home. Cartridges, batteries, the works. Never used the thing."

"Why's that?"

He shrugged. "Vaping sucks."

She gave him a small, crooked smile.

"Honesty's your third best quality, Duncan," she said. "But no thanks on the e-cigs. When I want to lose something, I make a clean break. Nothing else works."

A shrug. He glanced again at his watch.

"So," he said, "you gonna tell me my first and second best qualities before I go?"

Natasha took a deep drag off the cigarette and exhaled a stream a smoke.

"That's for another day," she said.

III

Fallout was a wide, vaulted space with a fifty-foot-high ceiling located under the entrance ramp to the Brooklyn Bridge, one of five nineteenth century storage chambers constructed inside its foundation near the Manhattan shoreline. Sometime during the Cold War, the Office of Civil Defense transformed it into a secret bomb shelter in case of nuclear attack...but it soon was forgotten, its stockpile of emergency supplies left to decay behind a padlocked steel door.

Half a century later, a city inspector stumbled onto it while conducting a routine safety checkup of the bridge. A subsequent relaxation of security restrictions opened the way for the club.

The fifty-five-gallon water drums, Geiger counters, and cartons of expired pharmaceuticals and stale survival crackers were photographed and trucked off by historical preservationists, as were two of the shelter's three galvanized steel fallout shelter signs. The photographs were enlarged and turned into wall murals inside the club. Cleaned of rust and grime, the third fallout shelter sign was remounted in its original spot behind the bar.

Now Natasha Mori sat opposite that sign, sipping her third wine of the night. Its yellow triangles stung her eyes. A tetrachromat, with an extra cone cell near each retina, she was sensitive to their yellow wavelengths.

Still, her gaze was drawn to the triangular fallout symbol, as her thoughts went to the era they represented. It was a time when the world came closer to the brink of annihilation than many realized, and it was also when her father was born in Russia.

She raised the wine to her lips. It was now almost 2:30 a.m. After saying goodnight to Duncan, she'd come here to the bar to wait for Bryan and mingle with a few admiring fans. A buzz on social media—and later a review in *New York Nightlife*—had gained Dev Zero a small but enthusiastic fan base, and that, in turn, led to their residency at the club. The attention was nice, but sometimes it made her uncomfortable.

Natasha drank in thoughtful silence, studying the dance floor. Then she finally saw Bryan pushing through the club-goers. He waved shyly as he drew closer, and she stood up, waving back. She put on amber-tinted glasses to filter the dance floor lights, but still avoided looking straight into them. The flashing colors were dizzying enough for someone with normal vision. She would see them explode into a thousand brilliant shades.

"Hey, hey," she said, hugging him. "How are you?"

"Good." He stood with his arms straight down at his sides, not hugging back, his eyes pointed down at the floor. "Sorry I missed your show."

"S'okay. Won't be my last." She noticed that his gaze was still downturned. "Ah, Bry, my eyes are up here," she joked. He nodded awkwardly, and she motioned him to a stool. "Want something to drink?"

"No thanks," he said, sitting down. "Well, I wouldn't mind a Coke."

"I see you're still on the hard stuff." She looked at him in his fitted T-shirt for about ten seconds, then gently touched his chest. "I also see you've been spending time at the gym."

Bryan nodded. "Tuesdays."

"What?"

"And most Thursdays," he said. "Those are the days I work out."

"Oh, right."

"The rest of the week, I run laps," he said. "There's a track on campus—"

"I remember." She smiled, and ordered a soda from Travis. "So. Tell me what brings you this far south?"

He looked at her a long moment, the music pulsing around them.

"We call it the Frankenbug," he said plainly.

"Ah."

"I kind of named it."

"Aha…"

"It acts like a worm, but also has characteristics of a Trojan, and it's mutating," Bryan said. "We can't figure out what it'll do next, because it penetrates systems in a deterministic way, seeds them with malware, and then deconstructs. But it's also automatic and designed to spread randomly. Like somebody has a target besides the one we know about, or think we know about, and wants to—"

"Uh, Bryan? You in a hurry?"

He looked at her. "No," he said. "I'm going too fast, aren't I?"

Natasha held her pointer finger and thumb slightly apart. "Maybe a little," she said. "By 'we'…do you mean Professor Michaels's involved?"

"The FBI too," he said. "It started as a *heavy* DDoS attack that was meant to hide an ATM card scam. But it turned out the card scam was cover for another theft." He paused. "Like, while it was going on, somebody stole fifty million dollars. From a single account."

"Wow," Tasha said. "How was it done?"

"A botnet setup."

"Zombies, redirects, all that classic stuff?"

He nodded.

"And how about the card withdrawals?"

"They were refused," Bryan said. "That's where it gets worse."

"Wait." She held up a hand. "How's it *worse* if the cards were no good?"

"Because they're carriers."

She looked at him. "Whoa, dude. These are *chip* cards?"

Bryan nodded. "They were programmed to handshake with the bank systems, and inject the bug," he said. "The problem is, I can't model its progression. Not like you. I don't know how to *build* your kind of predictive models. My simulations are mostly based on malware propagating through computer networks..."

"But that isn't how an infection spreads these days," she said. "Not in real life where *everything*'s connected."

He nodded again. "I ran a test to see if it would migrate between a mobile device and computer. First, I used a smartphone emulator. Then a physical phone to be on the safe side. The bug contaminated both times through a major firewall. It doesn't even need a USB cord or flash drive. It can use Bluetooth, near-field, anything. It probes for ways to make the jump."

Tasha was shaking her head. "Bry, I'm convinced. But I've got a lot going on right now—"

"I did the same test with AI assistants, using the top three on the market," he said. "Same deal—an emulator, then the real thing. And it jumped even faster."

She looked at him. "There has to be somebody else."

"Who?" he said.

She didn't hear any challenge in his voice. He wasn't trying to corner her, but was simply asking in his earnest, most innocent way.

"Listen," she said. "I don't do this anymore."

He sat drinking his cola. She hardly needed the prompt to finish her wine with a single deep gulp.

"One question," she said after a while. "Does the prof know you're here?"

Bryan nodded. "He knows," he said. "But it was my idea to ask you." He hesitated. "Tasha..."

"Uh-huh?"

"I can't do what you do. I mean, I can do other things. But not what you do. Even if you *don't* do it anymore."

A long moment passed. She was thoughtful.

"Say I agree as a favor. Just this once. When would you need me at the lab?"

His expression brightened. "How about we head up now?"

"*Now?*"

He nodded.

"With me half-crocked."

A second nod.

She broke into a sudden smile.

"Bryan," she said. "You're wings."

He gave her a puzzled look. "Does that mean you'll come with me?"

Tasha reached out and squeezed his elbow. "Yeah," she said. "We'll take the back way out to dodge the crowd."

IV

Drajan Petrovik was outside Emil's room when he heard footsteps down the hall. He turned in their direction and saw him approaching from the stairs.

"I've been trying to get hold of you," he said.

Emil stopped in front of him, his eyes glassy. "I'm sorry. I was in the village."

"All night?"

"I told you. I didn't hear the phone."

Drajan studied Emil's face. As youths, they had been inseparable, running together day and night. He was the wizard and leader, Emil his ready apprentice, a quick study with an eye for detail. Those days were long gone, and Drajan preferred it that way. But he needed a functional Emil. His exchange with Ansari Kem was a game changer.

"You should drink some coffee," he said. "Then meet me downstairs."

"Did you hear from my sister?"

The question surprised Drajan. "No. I assumed she would have spoken to you by now."

"Not a word since she left for Paris." Emil's pale lips tightened. "Stella isn't like us. She never was. I worry about her."

Drajan looked at him. Stella Vasile had played her own essential role in their order of three. Smart, clever, she was always willing to do anything on their behalf. Drajan knew this even as a boy, and used that knowledge calculatingly despite his fondness for her.

"Listen," he said. "Don't weigh yourself down with point- less thoughts."

"And where, instead, should I turn those thoughts?"

"West, Emil." Drajan's dark eyes gleamed. *"America."*

Emil looked at him.

"I don't understand."

"Of course you do—Hekate's been breeding for over a week," Drajan said. "Now have that coffee. Clear your head. We need to prepare for our strike."

BOOK III

THE INTERNET OF THINGS

21

I

At ten o'clock in the morning Eastern Africa Time, chief UN weapons inspector Bruno Christianson stood under a running shower in his room at the Panthea Hotel, scrubbing up before dinner with members of his joint OPCW-UN investigative team. The twelve-hour charter flight from The Hague to Birhan had included an extended stopover in Istanbul due to a summer dust storm. But overall, it was a smooth trip.

Most members of the team were famished. Christianson himself had only a light breakfast aboard the charter, and was instantly receptive when his deputy, Altha Whitehirst, suggested they all convene for a solid meal after checking into their rooms. At noon they planned to strike out with their private security escort and tour three coastal sites between Port Birhan and the Hagar Oasis, where it was believed sarin gas was used to massacre an untold number of human beings, nearly wiping out the ancient Satair and Beja tribal communities.

"It's wise to fill up good'n healthy," Altha told the group, speaking with her thick Scottish accent as they waited for their key cards at the reception desk. "Try to stay away from carbohydrates, and eat as much protein as you can. My hunch is that, after the site visits, we won't want undigested food in our stomachs."

Christianson did not doubt her for a second. Back in the Netherlands, they had seen video of the victims—hundreds upon hundreds of them—crowded into a small, understaffed urgent care ward, one of many such centers in the stricken areas. It was so appalling that two of the inspectors—Guadalupe Collins and Brad Sturgill—left the room green with nausea.

The sight of contorted bodies on the floor, of young children in the final stages of respiratory paralysis lying in pools of their own vomit and bodily waste...it would haunt Christianson as long as he lived.

Now he stepped out from under the shower spray, toweled dry, and stood at the bathroom mirror. As far as he was concerned, the pictures gave adequate confirmation that weapons of mass destruction were used in the attacks. For his inspection team, then, the questions really centered on whether the toxic material was indeed sarin or some other agent, how it was delivered, and if there were hidden stockpiles of the CW or its ingredients. Moreover, they would want to determine if those stockpiles consisted of Schedule One, Two, or Three controlled substances—generally outlawed in the first instance, and restricted in the other two. When their work was complete, their findings and recommendations would be presented to the UN General Assembly and Security Council, and, assuming the evidence was solid, help build a case for international sanctions against Prince Negassie's regime—and for tracing the weapon's chemical constituents to their sources inside and outside the country.

But that was a classic example of putting the cart before the horse. Today's visits to places that might have suffered a CW strike, or were linked to Birhan's suspected chemical weapons manufacturing program, were no more than preliminary scouting missions. Interviewing survivors and medical personnel, testing for precursor and trace materials, and collecting additional physical evidence was a lengthy, exhaustive process that could stretch on for weeks, if not months, before it concluded. In the meantime, Christianson's hope was that Negassie and his regime, mindful of penalties that could be imposed by the United Nations—and of the unilateral action threatened by the outspoken Fucillo administration in America—would suspend or completely terminate any use of CWs in anticipation of the inspection team's eventual report.

That was the best-case scenario, anyway. It was difficult to predict what would happen. A government could appear to be digging in its heels one day, and yield to international pressure the next. His natural optimism aside, Christianson knew it was all out of his control. Basic as it sounded, the only thing his team could do was their work.

Stepping out of the shower, he went over to his open suitcase, got out the coveralls he would wear for the site inspection, and put them on. Then he stepped out into the hall.

Guadalupe, who was in the next room down the hall, had wanted to phone her husband back in the Netherlands before joining everyone for lunch, so he strode past her door toward the block reserved for the rest of his team. Christianson had a bad habit of getting lost in big hotels like the Panthea, but he liked to claim his sense of direction had improved with age...and thought he might actually know where he was going this time.

Turning left, he rounded a corner in the hall, went past the emergency stairs and a bank of vending machines, and then started toward a second bend. As he recalled, Altha's room was one or two doors beyond it.

He was only a few steps from the bend when he heard the

voices on the other side. They seemed close—one of them low, gruff and male, the other Altha's unmistakable brogue.

Something was wrong, he thought. She sounded confused and agitated.

Puzzled, he turned the corner to see her standing outside her door, a half dozen armed troopers in dun-colored uniforms and red berets gathered around her in a loose knot. Her long, flame-red hair still damp from the shower, Altha was visibly distressed by their presence…and it was no wonder. The men belonged to the Birhanese National Defense Force, and they did not look at all welcoming or friendly.

He started toward them at once, wanting to find out what the problem might be—and then just as quickly froze in his tracks. The troopers had their backs to the hallway, and luckily so. But Altha saw him round the corner and shot a glance in his direction, her eyes full of urgent warning.

The troopers meant trouble, Christianson thought. It would do no good for him to stumble into the thick of it.

His pulse racing, he slipped back around the corner and reached into his pocket for his smartphone. A moment later he heard another familiar voice up ahead. Sturgill this time. His room was just a couple of doors past Altha's, and he must have stepped out to investigate the disturbance.

Christianson took a second to gather his wits, trying not to make a sound. Then he opened his Facebook app, selected the live video option, set it for "public," and started the stream. Raising the cell up to eye level, he held it ever-so-slightly around the bend so he could capture what was happening outside Altha's door…and watch on his display screen.

Sturgill had approached the troopers. Over six feet tall in his coveralls and ankle boots, the strapping New Zealander regarded them with mixed confusion and indignation.

"What on earth is going on?" he asked the men. "Who are you?"

His second question was rhetorical. Their garb was unmistakably that of Birhan's domestic military police.

"Please remember that you are a visitor in my country." The tall, thin trooper who turned to face him wore the breast insignia and shoulder bars of an officer. "I would advise you to show appropriate respect."

Sturgill just looked at him. "We're UN inspectors," he said. "Authorized to conduct our work here in an unimpeded manner."

The officer frowned testily. "I'll require your documents," he demanded. "Your phone too."

Sturgill didn't budge.

"This is insane," he said, and returned his attention to Altha. "Are you all right?"

The DCI nodded. "I'm okay," she said. "These bastards already snatched my phone and identification. They claim w—"

"Enough!" The officer suddenly drew his sidearm, leveling its barrel at Sturgill. "Give me the requested items."

Sturgill remained unmoving.

"Be quick!" the officer snapped, and gesticulated with his weapon. Moving closer to him, the other troopers brought semiautomatic rifles off their shoulders.

Glowering at them with angry contempt, Sturgill finally complied and unzipped his waist pack.

Christianson was still recording with his phone when he heard a sudden tramping noise behind him—footsteps. He straightened, tensing. There were several sets of them in the carpeted hallway, followed by the sound of someone insistently rapping on a door. Then a terse command, more knocking, the click of a lock opening, and a startled voice asking what was going on.

Christianson felt a droplet of sweat trickle down the back of his collar. *Guadalupe*, he thought. A second group of NDF troopers must have taken a separate elevator to roust her while she was calling home. They were coming for the inspectors, every last one of them, and missed finding him in his room by scant minutes. But how much longer could he avoid them?

He snapped a look over his shoulder. The emergency stairs were only a few feet behind him on the right, his room four or five yards back around the first bend in the hall. If he hurried, he might push through the metal door that opened onto them before the troopers came his way—*if* they came his way. He couldn't know where they were headed, or whether there were more troopers on the lower landings, down in the lobby, or guarding the hotel entrances. It was possible every way in and out of the place was covered. But maybe not. And even if they were waiting at the bottom of the stairs, his video would be live-streamed to the entire world. In fact, it *was* streaming...

Sticking close to the wall, he took a deep breath and told himself to stay put. He could hear the men that rousted Guadalupe from her room knocking on his door now. That would buy him a little time.

Outside Altha's door, meanwhile, one of the troopers tore Sturgill's phone and cardholder from his hands. He deposited the cell into his pack and gave the holder to his superior officer, who hastily pulled out the OPCW identification.

"Mr. Sturgill, we have received information that your inspection team has arrived in Birhan under false pretenses, and that it is your intention to conduct espionage against our nation," the officer said. "You will be detained as spies until further notice."

Sturgill was shaking his head in disbelief. "This is a criminal act. A violation of your agreement with the United Nations. You'll never get away with it."

The officer ignored him. "It would be best if you both come along peacefully," he said. "I prefer not to embarrass you by using restraints."

Sturgill kept staring at him. "You can't hold us," he said furiously. "You have no authority—"

Before he could finish, the officer issued an Arabic command to his troopers. All in an instant, two of them advanced on Sturgill with their rifles outthrust, the others pointing their weapons at Altha.

Christianson saw Sturgill take a protective step toward her.

He was paying no attention to the guns, reaching his arms out as if to somehow pull her away from the troopers...

The sharp crack of a rifle halted him midstride. A stunned, almost quizzical look on his face, Sturgill looked down at his chest, saw the bloodstain spreading across it, and crumpled to the hallway carpet.

"*Brad,*" Altha screamed. Her horrified eyes leaped to the officer. "My God...*what have you done?*"

"Shut her up—and get her out of here," he barked at this men, ignoring her. Then he nodded toward the service elevator opposite Christianson's spot against the wall. "Use only that elevator and rear corridors. I'll handle hotel security."

The soldiers obeyed at once. They shoved Altha up against the wall, wrenched her hands behind her back, and cuffed them, slipping a gag over her mouth to stifle her cries.

A moment later she was jostled up the hall at gunpoint.

Sick with horror, Christianson watched them move off with their prisoner. He didn't know where the troopers were taking her. But if they came his way and turned the corner, they would find him in a heartbeat.

He cast a desperate look over his shoulder. The troopers behind him were outside his door. Knocking on it.

His mind racing, he glanced at the emergency exit across the hall. The stairs on the other side would have thick concrete firewalls—and it was twenty-five long stories to the lobby. He *might* make it down there and slip out of the hotel, but the stairwell walls could block both his cellular signal and the hotel Wi-Fi, cutting out his livestream.

He would stay right here. Whatever the cost, he needed to show the world what was happening.

"*You! What are you doing there?*"

The voice was coming from the direction of his room. The knocking at his door had stopped.

Christianson took another look around, and this time saw

several troopers approaching him, moving fast, their weapons raised in front of them.

"What are you doing with that phone?" the trooper shouted. *"Drop it!"*

Mouthing a silent prayer, he turned it in the troopers' direction just as they opened fire.

Christianson knew terrible pain as their bullets ripped across his midsection—and then felt nothing but a strange sense of separation from his body. Before things dissolved into whiteness, he saw himself as if from a distance, the phone dropping from his hand, giving the troopers exactly what they wanted...

Or so they might have thought.

II

The tricked-out Sikorsky VH-60 helicopter that was Marine One sprang off the White House's south lawn at five o'clock in the morning for its flight to New York. A hot coffee in hand—black, no sugar—President Annemarie Fucillo was comfortably seated by a side window, deliberately ignoring the schedule Randy Severin had put in her hands as they boarded.

The schedule could wait, she thought. She intended to use her brief time in the air to mentally prepare for the day ahead...one she had thought until recently would be all hullabaloo, smiles, and a disarming dog.

Fucillo would still smile at the Stock Exchange when she rang the bell on the balcony above the trading floor. She would be smiling when Governor Kevin Bender introduced her onstage in Zuccotti Park, and would smile at appropriate times when she spoke to the lower Manhattan crowd about the Net Force initiative and a more secure future for the country.

So, yes, she would smile, and genuinely.

But toward the end of her speech, she would tackle something that had not been in her plans at all days ago...that was only added to her agenda after the Birhan incident. It would give her nothing to smile about.

She sipped her coffee. After a few minutes, she saw Randy leave his seat up front and come toward her in the chopper's aisle, passing the bevy of aides on the long, plush sofa to her right. He sat across from her, a tablet computer tucked under one arm, a can of Red Bull in his other hand.

"I thought you were off the high-test," she said, pointing her chin at the energy drink. "Just looking at it gives me the shakes."

The chief of staff shrugged philosophically. "What I really need is a whole new engine," he said. "The one inside me has fifty-four years of wear on it."

Fucillo looked at him. "Does it ever feel like a hundred fifty-four?"

"On a good day," he replied. "As my mother might have said... God willing, and the creek don't rise, it keeps working."

She gave him a commiserative look. "So," she said, "what do you have for me?"

"I've set up a call with Prince Negassie for seven o'clock this morning...two in the afternoon in Zayar City. Your breakfast with the governor and mayor is a half hour later. And there's the opening bell at nine...and everything else." He drank from the can. "You won't have much time on the phone with Negassie."

"I won't need much," she said. "I laid out his options before the nerve gas attack, held an open door for him. With what happened to those inspectors while most of Washington was still asleep, his country chose to walk through another." She shrugged. "My call is a courtesy based on our prior relationship, and the possibility that factions might be operating without his knowledge. But he is the leader of that nation. I'm going to recommend harsh punitive actions against it at the UN General Assembly this afternoon...and make it clear the United States is ready to initiate those actions, and more, with or without international support."

Severin regarded her for a long moment, then settled in against the sofa's backrest.

"I don't know how you juggle everything," he said, drinking his beverage. "Sometimes it seems too big to handle."

Fucillo looked straight into his eyes. "May I let you in on a personal secret?"

Severin nodded slowly. "If you please, Madam," he said.

"It's about the worker bees," she said. "They stay at it, no matter *how* big. As long as they make a little honey, it's all right."

III

Stepping off the deck stairs onto his driveway, Julia slightly ahead of him, a dressed-to-the-hilt Alex Michaels brushed a hand through the lavender plant growing alongside the bottom step, held it under his nostrils, and inhaled the relaxing natural perfume.

It was a hot, sunny morning, the squirrels in his yard looking sluggish from the heat as they scattered away from the big German shepherd. He opened the cargo door of his Grand Cherokee, unclipped Julia's leash from her collar, and let her in. Then he went around to the front, got behind the wheel, and transferred his security pass from the glove box to the top of his dashboard. When he reached the VIP parking garage on Hanover Street, the bar code on the pass would be scanned through the window glass and matched against a database of official visitors to the Wall Street and Zuccotti Park ceremonies. He wasn't exactly sure where Julia's name might be on that database, but had a feeling his canine show stealer would get through the screening process without a hitch.

Despite his aversion to publicity, and much to his own surprise, Alex found himself looking forward to the morning's events. His attitude had changed overnight—truly, overnight—when it occurred to him while falling asleep that the fuss would amount to a coming out party for Net Force. *That* was infinitely bigger than his discomfort at having the spotlight trained on him. Electronic security was America's Achilles' heel, and Annemarie Fucillo was giving him the chance to turn it into a revolutionary strength. It was a challenge, but most of all it was a humbling honor…and he was determined to prove worthy of it.

"Okay, Jule," he said, glancing at the dog in the rearview. "Big day ahead…let's rock it."

Although that was hardly on her list of Schutzhund commands, Julia settled down on her blanket anyway.

Alex told her she was a good girl as he backed down the drive. They were bound for the Big Apple.

IV

Natasha Mori took off her cyclist gloves, raised her hand to the reader to summon the elevator, wheeled her bike inside, and rode up to the tenth floor. When she and Bryan first cabbed it from Fallout two weeks ago, it had felt a little strange to find her bio-recognition data removed from the system. The truth was, it didn't surprise her; the professor would have been required to terminate her authorization after she quit grad school. That was her choice, and no one else's. But it was only while waiting for Bry to let her in that Tasha realized how thoroughly a part of things she once was.

Oddly enough, she felt *less* like someone who belonged once her access to the Cyberlab was restored days later. It was as if she was staying with a former roommate who changed the apartment lock, and let her borrow a new key until her visit ended.

Leaving the elevator now, Tasha walked the bicycle to the lab and repeated the hand scan to open its wooden door. It was eight thirty in the morning, and Bryan looked fresh at one of his virtual machines, his hair neatly piled in a bun.

She stood near the door, holding the bike's handlebars. She wore a lime-colored wide-brimmed helmet with a neck flap, dark lenses, a lightweight black cycling jacket, black riding tights, and cycling shoes.

"Tash…" He swiveled his chair around to face her. "Cool hat."

"It's an armored sunbrero," she said. "Get it? *Sun*brero? A pigment-denied cyclist's dream."

They traded smiles. It occurred to her that this was his happy place, a protective cocoon largely free of the challenging social situations that made things so tough for him elsewhere. For her it was in many ways the opposite. A reminder of the walls and isolation at the Russian *naukograd* where she was raised...of its strictly monitored routines and rigorous tests.

A moment passed. She leaned the bike against the wall, removed her cap and sunglasses. Each time she walked into the lab, every day since coming back, she would ask herself if it was a mistake. But Bry had a way of temporarily putting the question to rest.

"So, your text said you have a surprise for me," she said, approaching his workstation. "What's the good word?"

It took a second or two for his uncertain expression to disappear. "Your security clearance was reinstated," he said. "Professor Michaels forwarded me the email from JPAS. He got it last night, I guess."

Tasha considered that. Thanks to the professor's tacit nod, she had expected the official green light once her need-to-know application was processed. Her departure from the postgrad program fell within the two-year period the government considered current; a longer absence, and her status would have expired, making her go through the rigmarole of a complete background investigation. Still, the reinstatement meant she could openly access the lab's classified information and technology.

"This *is* big news." She pretended to make a muscle. "Now I can unleash my mutant power on an unsuspecting world."

Bryan looked at her without acknowledging the comment or gesture. "I logged you into the HIVE," he said. "Full user privileges."

Which was something the professor had restricted up to this point, since her linking to and transferring data between and outside classified networks could have pinged their hosts. That included parties who weren't overly thrilled about Alex Michaels being tapped for the Net Force thing...and might decide to play dirty politics by accusing him of lax security protocols.

"I'd like to input the models we've set up," she said. "Utilize some of the HIVE's computing power and VR capabilities."

Bryan nodded. "It's done," he said. "I figured I'd give us a jump, so we could watch the President's speech this morning without losing any time. Well, if you want to watch."

Tasha realized she was eager to get to work. She had been burning it at both ends, spending several nights a week at the club and most days at the lab. Trying to foresee what the Frankenbug would do was a complicated problem. But for all her reservations, she enjoyed the process of trying to solve it. It was like being a detective working to solve a mystery that was yet to occur.

"There any blah, watery office coffee available before we start?" she asked.

Bryan quickly stood up. "I just brewed a pot!" he said.

Tasha *knew* he wasn't trying to be funny.

Just different, she thought, smiling behind him as he went to pour their cups.

V

"Ansari."

"Yes, Highness."

The cell phone to his ear, Kem sat forward and plucked a plump brown olive from the bowl on his terrace table. "How is it in the capitol?"

"As you would expect," said Negassie. "When will you arrive?"

Kem frowned when he considered yet another helicopter flight. But what choice was there? He had been summoned. "I'll be on my way within the hour."

"Very good," Mustafa said. "Have you any more information about the incident at Hotel Panthea?"

"No," Kem said. "I'm awaiting initial reports."

"It cannot be difficult to identify the rebellious unit that conducted the violence against the inspectors."

"That would be my expectation." Kem chewed the olive.

"But I have seen where insubordinate cells can wipe their tracks clean."

"Do not minimize what happened as insubordination," Negassie said. "Along with the missile strikes against Hagar, it was a violation of international law. A ruinous act of rebellion against my sovereign authority."

Kem heard a rare anger in the prince's words.

"I will get to the bottom of things," he said. "You have my pledge."

"Good." Negassi paused. "There is something else. President Fucillo phoned from New York minutes ago."

"And?"

"She intends to recommend a comprehensive list of sanctions against our country to the United Nations General Assembly this afternoon. The freezing of our assets in foreign banks. A cutoff on military aid, an embargo of oil-refining equipment. If these measures are adopted we will be politically and economically isolated…and that is only the beginning."

"In what sense?"

"She has reserved the option of a unilateral military reprisal by the United States," Negassi said. "I have known this woman many years. She does not bluff."

Kem nodded to himself. The prince's estimation was accurate. Fucillo played the cards she held or did not play at all. But if Drajan Petrovik succeeded with his plans, she would never have a chance to address the United Nations. The Assembly would not hold its emergency session. New York—indeed, all of America—would have something other than Birhan commanding its full attention.

He took another olive from the bowl and rose off his chair. "I must prepare for my departure," he said. "We shall avoid the worst, Highness."

"I wish I shared your confidence."

"Rest assured," he said. "The dust from a storm always settles. And when it does, our course will be clear."

VI

Drajan Petrovik sat at a workstation in his sublevel basement listening to the Third Movement of Richard Wagner's *Symphony in C Major*, its stirring martial tones raised to a cacophonous peak by Apocalyptica's gothic metal strings.

Though Clara had brought his usual *cafea turceasca* and raki, Drajan hardly needed it today. Soon it would be three thirty in the afternoon by his clock, nine thirty in the morning in New York...coinciding with the start of the American President's speech in Zuccotti Park.

He was ready. *More* than ready.

Lowering his eyes from the wall, he turned to regard Emil. In the old days they would have amped themselves with MDMA—two hundred milligrams in a single pill wrapped in paper, then another hundred when they were ready for their hack. By parachuting the first dose of the drug, they would ensure its effects would hit them all at once.

And now? But Emil moved beyond that, had done something to elevate. The neurotech implants and the advanced drugs. Thin, pallid, he looked like a fading apparition. Like Drajan's recurring dreams about Turkey, the Sacred Road, the temple...

And Kali.

He breathed, sipped his coffee, lifted the raki glass off his desk, and drank. Then he pressed his headset's muter.

"I'm up for this, Emil," he said. "It's as if we've been moving toward it, always."

Emil looked at him, his pupils unnaturally dilated. "There will be no going back after today."

Drajan gave a shrug. "The synchronicity of events in Birhan and New York... I won't ignore them. No, Emil. The stars scream for us to *stride*."

Turning back to his computer, Drajan released the muter to let the music rush back into his ears.

An hour and counting, he thought. That was all. And heavens would fall.

22

New York City/Satu Mare, Romania
July 27, 2023

I

Denny Yalin was scanning the windshield of the Grand Cherokee when he noticed the huge German shepherd in the back seat. A service dog wasn't in his database. So, then, how had it gotten through the street checkpoints?

He read the name off the dashboard security card, went around to the left side, and leaned forward as the window slid down.

"Mr. Michaels," he said to the bearded driver. "I'm afraid we can't allow a dog..."

"It's fine." This from a Secret Service agent hastening up to the car. "Professor, if you'll please leave your car to an attendant, I'll have someone escort you and your special guest to the Exchange."

The driver smiled. "Thank you," he said. Then he gave Yalin a nod. "Appreciate you being on top of things. Better safe."

Yalin nodded. "I'm only doing what I have to, sir," he replied. As he saw things, it was the absolute truth.

II

Bryan couldn't tear his eyes from Natasha's 3D model. It was like a science fair project in which you poured salt and food coloring into a bowl of water and watched as crystals grew over its sides...but right now he was at the center of the bowl, watching the geometrical lattices take shape around him.

"This," he said, "is amazing."

"The Game of Life," she said, floating beside him in virtual space. "On steroids."

Minutes ago, they entered the HIVE to run her construct. A cellular automaton based on the famous zero-player game developed by John Herald Conway, it was a kind of mad scientist's version of solitaire.

Once upon a time, the British mathematician had drawn a grid of squares on a sheet of paper, calling each square a cell. Cells existed in one of two possible states, alive or dead. A *live* cell was covered by a board chip, a dead cell left empty. Each cell had eight neighbors—the squares, or cells, that were horizontally, vertically, and diagonally nearest on the grid. Together they formed a neighbor*hood*.

If a cell had four or more neighbors at any given time, it died of overpopulation. If it had only one neighbor at a time, it died of isolation. But if a dead cell had three live neighbors—no more, no fewer—it would be *born*.

Conway did not invent the game with computers in mind. But the growing use of mainframes in the 1970s gave his exercise a popularity he never foresaw. Computer scientists enjoyed watching successive generations of cellular automata go through their patterns of evolution. Their behavior accelerated in visually entertaining ways, neighborhoods would glide infinitely across the grid (or plain, as Conway sometimes referred to it), build copies of themselves, grow in size, or might even die off.

Tasha's variation on the game was far more complex than Conway's. Her cells represented not living entities, but intelligent *machines*—computers, tablets, smartphones, AI assistants, and all sorts of Internet of Things nodes. She used hexagonal cells instead of squares, their larger number of sides representing the various avenues of malware transmission possible through networks and device-to-device contact. The states, or conditions, of her cells vis-à-vis infection were defined as susceptible, exposed, carrier, interrupted, and removed…with other states imposed depending on the bug under investigation.

She wouldn't have called the model she designed to study the Frankenbug's possible dispersal and evolution "fun." But after working on it for almost two weeks, Tash was satisfied that it might shed some light on the Frankenbug's reach…and, with added tinkering, become honed into a highly effective tool. But she also knew they were running against the clock. There were no patches for the infection, no firewalls able to contain it. Although it quickly burned through its artificial lifespan, she did not know enough about its makeup to calculate how it might seed computers and networks with undetected spores—bugs that would eventually incubate and swarm through cyberspace.

She watched her automata race across a satellite relief map of Manhattan. Glowing tendrils spooled outward, wound together like threads, overlapped, merged and separated again. It was the perfect mimicking of a tech virus.

It was the mobile hosts, she thought. *The phones and tablets.* Their traffic in a concentrated population center like New York imparted a high degree of randomness to the spread of infection.

She looked at Bryan. The two of them could have been riding magic carpets above the city. "What we see is just the initial outbreak," she said. "The likely migration of the Frankenbug from Chloe Berne's computer to its neighbors over the July Fourth holiday," she said. "Its internet connection was active that whole time."

Offering the bug countless routes for scattering outward…
even before its dissemination through the counterfeit bank cards.

Tasha was thinking about the show she did that weekend.
Say somebody came into town to see the fireworks, then tear it
up at Fallout afterward. What would it take to spread the bug?
A beer and burger in midtown, Wi-Fi for directions to lower
Manhattan, drinks at the club, and an NFC phone app to pay
for everything.

Sneezes between devices. *Contact, transmission, infection.*

"Eve, accelerate the model," she said. "One week postemer-
gence."

"Coming up."

The pattern formation sped up. She watched from an aerial
vantage as filaments of contagion radiated out and out across
the city.

"Eve," she said. "Accelerate. Present time stamp, wide view
geo-layering."

A glowing membrane covered the street grid, crisscrossing
the waterways into the outer boroughs and New Jersey.

Anatomy of a pandemic.

Natasha looked at Bryan through her VR glasses. They'd
both had enough for now.

She told Eve to cut the sim, and suddenly they were in a room
that was, for all its interactive tech, only a room. Her body settling down as if after a flight, she sat for a minute before turning to Bryan.

"You okay?" she said.

"No," he said.

"Can't say I blame you," she said, removing her VR glasses.
They sat quietly again.

"The prof should be taking the stage downtown any minute,"
she said. "We should get ready to watch."

"So, what do you think about the model, Tash?" he asked.

"It's a rough draft, good for starters." She shrugged. "I can model the bug's progress. But to kill it, if we *can* kill it, we're going need somebody who knows what it *is*."

Bryan looked at the floor. He was rocking a little. She gave him a moment.

"If there's a purpose for the Frankenbug's release, a *target*... why would you drop a nuke instead of a hammer to crack a nut?" he said. "Even if it's a macadamia nut?"

She didn't say anything.

"That's the toughest nut to crack," he explained.

"I know, Bry. So, what's the point? Why do it?" Natasha thought a moment before she answered her own question. "I think because you want to shake the world," she said at last.

III

"You're good to go, Mr. Rainey," said the garage attendant. He gave a claim ticket to the Tesla's driver, the sled scanner in his other hand. "This is for you."

Standing outside the car, Anton Ciobanu slipped the ticket into his laptop bag.

"Thanks," he said.

"Call us about fifteen minutes before you're ready for pickup." The attendant nodded at the long line of vehicles backed up from the entrance onto Hanover Street. "Otherwise it might be a wait with all this commotion."

Ciobanu thanked the attendant—his name tag read Yalin— as the Tesla was driven off toward its slot. He never intended to reclaim it.

Glancing past Yalin into the packed indoor garage now, he saw an NYPD Special Operations officer in a black uniform and flak vest walking up one of the aisles with a handheld chem-sniffer that looked like a ruggedized smartphone. When Cio-banu had pulled in from the street moments ago, an identically clad patrolman passed a long-handled vehicle inspection mirror under the Tesla as a routine check for an IED.

They were looking in the wrong places. The military-grade

Crystex plastique he was carrying had the highest detonation ve-
locity and lowest vapor pressure of any nonnuclear explosive on
earth. That made it incredibly powerful and hard to detect...and
Ciobanu's shaped charge was enclosed in a hermetic plastic wrap
to make it harder. But the HDX/CL-20 hybrid was not *beyond*
detection, and he didn't want the sniffer anywhere near him.

Dressed in a plain blue suit, the laptop bag over his shoulder,
he turned toward the garage exit, adjusting his hearing-aid-sized
earclip computer, and then checking that his credentials were
easily visible around his neck. These included a forged Stage-
Works Professionals photo identification for John Rainey, as well
as a separate dated, laminated name tag issued by the Office of
the Police Commissioner. Another tag embossed with the commissioner's official seal was pinned to the bag.

The second and third pieces of ID were spit from printers
in government offices. Twenty-four hours earlier, Rainey had
come into existence within the NYPD's official computer system, born into the world as a thirty-six-year-old man. The other
tag was simultaneously created in StageWorks' employee database, complete with a full personal background and detailed ré-
sumé that included his current position of event manager with
the corporation.

"Turn right onto William Street for the checkpoint," the attendant was telling Ciobanu. "I suppose you already know your
way to the park."

Ciobanu gave him a questioning look.

"Your credentials," he said, indicating them with eyes. "Stage-
Works crews have been here all week setting up for the President."

Ciobanu nodded, looking past him again. He had noticed
the Special Operations cop with the sniffer walking back in his
direction.

"Thank you," he said, and quickly turned to leave.

Yalin watched as he disappeared amid the bumper-to-bumper
vehicles outside the entrance. Rainey was a latecomer—Stage-

Works had set up a giant mobile stage and video screen for the President's appearance in Zuccotti. But most of the company's employees—the ones who weren't in trucks outside the park—arrived hours ahead of time to do their work.

So, he was late. The job title on his ID was Manager. Probably he had nothing to do with the nuts and bolts of putting together the stage. He might not have to get there early. And why even worry about it?

Why worry? There were plenty of reasons. He knew what he was doing. Fifty thousand dollars for a minute's work. Fifty thousand *cash.*

With an inward sigh, the attendant waited for the cop outside to finish sweeping his mirror under another car and then motioned it through the entrance. The parade of vehicles was endless. There were hundreds of people arriving for the event.

Yalin could only pray to God that he would see all of them back here in one piece when it was over.

IV

Standing above the main trading floor of the New York Stock Exchange, Governor Kevin Bender could hardly believe he was playing second fiddle—actually *fourth* fiddle—to *a dog* at the opening bell ceremony.

There were six people on the balcony: President Fucillo in the middle of the podium, Professor Michaels to her right, and Bender to her left. NYSE Chairman Roger Owen stood a polite step to one side at the balcony's marble rail, and three White House Secret Service men were against the wall behind the luminaries. The monstrously huge canine, Julia, was heeling between Fucillo and Alex.

The governor eyed the beast with disgust. She was closer to the bell's control button than he was. In fact, if she stood up on her hind legs, she would have had an easier time reaching over to press the button. How was that proper decorum? Wasn't this supposed to be *his* day? How had it gotten stolen out from under him?

"She's magnificent, isn't she?"

Bender looked at Fucillo's smiling face and forced a grin. The dog was wearing a vest emblazoned with Net Force's departmental logo—a stylized *NF*, with an integrated circuit pattern inside the *N*, and patriotic stars inside the horizontal bars of the *F*.

"I think it, ah, *she*, is a sight to behold," he said. "So, if I understand things...we have a German shepherd up here with us today because...?"

"Julia is a Schutzhund. She's reliable and dedicated and highly trained to protect against intruders," Fucillo said. "Very emblematic of Net Force's declared mission, isn't that so, Alex?"

He was looking down at the trading floor with its kiosks and brokers. These days most trading was done online, making the physical Exchange a kind of anachronism. Still, how many people got the chance to stand on this balcony when the opening bell tolled? Alongside the President of the United States, no less?

He felt...privileged.

"The German word *schutz* literally means to guard and protect," he explained. "I would agree about the symbolism."

Bender bit down on his tongue, thinking the blame for this outrage fell on Stiles. He should have been informed ahead of time of the dog, the vest, and the logo. If he had known ahead of time about the garish stunt, it could have been trumped.

He sighed. It was a minute or two before nine thirty. He listened in as Owen moved closer to Fucillo and explained the bell-ringing procedure.

"You need only concern yourself with the green button, Madam. Hold it for ten seconds," he said. "The red is a backup, and the orange initiates a single clang for a pause in trading—a moment of silence, for example."

Bender was thinking he had not come here to be overshadowed. He checked his wristwatch. 9:29. He had a stroke of inspiration.

He watched Owen nod for Fucillo to press the control button. She thanked him and started reaching for it.

Bender shot an arm out in front of the President and jabbed a finger at the button, partially displacing hers so they were both pressing it at once. Fucillo looked at him with surprise as bells began to clang around the hall and the brokers below erupted into enthusiastic cheers and applause.

"Well, that was mature and gentlemanly of you, Kevin," she said, moving her lips as little as possible.

Bender feigned innocence. "Whatever do you mean, Madam?" He kept his finger right there with hers. "This is a fabulous day. And I'm *thrilled* we're all here to share its excitement...*together.*"

V

As he prepared to send his packet, Drajan Petrovik allowed himself a double measure of cold raki, chasing down his coffee with the strong Turkish liquor. The music in his headset had segued from Apocalyptica's electrified Wagner to the Velvet Underground's "Venus in Furs." The violinist's bow was a sharpened claw raking at the strings, tearing its exquisite notes from the very guts of Hell.

Does God dwell in darkness or light? Kali had mused once. In one of her deep moods, she had explained that it was an age-old question debated by religious scholars, a question arising from the first words of the ancient Vedic scriptures.

Drajan wondered if she ever found her answers...but there was no place for Kali in his mind now. Enough that his recent nights had been haunted by dreams of their crossroads outside the temple of Hekate, and a promise he made while knowing it would not be kept.

He sat listening to the music, feeling mildly elevated as the raki worked its way through his system. The computer monitor showed a live CNN news stream of the crowd gathered at the outdoor stage in New York's financial district, where the

President of the United States was minutes away from her presentation.

Drajan turned to the rail-thin figure beside him and fingered his Mute button.

"Where are we with the upload?"

"Right on target." Emil glanced over from his laptop. "I've pinged all the smartphones on the MEID database. Once I hit the ones we need, and isolate their location, it will take under a minute to—"

He broke off midsentence, staring at his monitor.

"Emil?"

"It's done. I have our cell tower." He angled the laptop toward Drajan. "See for yourself."

Petrovik scanned the map of the United States that filled the screen. The list of numerical sequences on its left pane was a list of MEIDs—mobile equipment identification numbers resembling IP addresses. These were the unique footprints of the phones. In a pane on the bottom of the screen was a set of coordinates:

> *Latitude: 40 43 19 Longitude: 74 00 28*

"That's lower Manhattan?"

Emil nodded, tapping on his keyboard. An arrow flashed on a precise location on the map—the intersection of Hudson and Varick Streets. "Stella's apartment wasn't far from there."

Silence. Drajan did not want Emil distracted with thoughts of his impulsive sister. "How many phones did you hit?"

"Thirty," Emil said. "We have built-in redundancy. There's no downside."

Petrovik's eyebrow ticced upward. It wasn't the number of hits that surprised him—he was a believer in extreme redundancy—but the thought that he could still be awed by his own reach. No government on earth could resist, no military force could defend.

Today the American people would have their first glimpse of the redefined landscape…but *only* a glimpse. They would think it the storm…when it was only the air stirring before its arrival.

"The upload will take under a minute—it's a simple remote activation program," Emil said. He looked drawn but almost preternaturally alert. "We'll be ready."

Drajan turned back to his computer. The President's motorcade was even now arriving at the park to a waiting crowd of security personnel and civilian onlookers.

"Ready, Madam President," he mouthed silently.

VI

Leo Harris stood in the scalding sun outside Zuccotti Park, pulling a handkerchief from his jacket to mop his brow. There had to be three dozen perspiring bodies around him inside the security cordon—additional Bureau personnel, Secret Service men, and plainclothes and uniformed NYPD, all assembled to protect President Annemarie Fucillo and the dignitaries she was bringing to the festivities.

Leo scowled in sweaty discomfort. Another thing he hated about the weather—wearing his jazziest summer clothes to POTUS's jamboree suddenly didn't seem like the best idea. But here he was in sharp white linen trousers, a navy blazer with shiny gold buttons, a pale blue shirt with big white polka dots, and a matching polka-dotted tie.

With the ceremony not yet underway and Fucillo's fifteen-vehicle motorcade having just this minute swung off Trinity Place toward the park, Harris was thinking his whole ensemble would turn into a soggy pile of laundry long before the day was over.

He checked his watch as the convoy approached. 9:40 a.m. POTUS and her entourage had taken half an hour to get from the Stock Exchange to Zuccotti Park…a five-minute stroll on foot. But the streets of the city's financial district were laid out like a ball of yarn that had been unwound by a crazed cat, and the choke points established by the Secret Service and NYPD advance teams compounded the usual difficulty of getting from one place to another. That forced the President to take the long and winding way around.

Harris watched the convoy make slow, halting progress along the northeast side of the park, guided by a Kevlar-clad officer with his hands waving in the air. A fleet of police cars and motorcycles led the pack, followed by a group of black Secret Service SUVs, three limos carrying POTUS, her aides, and her VIP guests. Bringing up the rear was a counter-assault van loaded with SWAT cops, a couple of emergency medical vehicles, and a few trailing motorbikes.

As the limos pulled up to where Harris stood in position, his gaze went past them to One Liberty Plaza across the street. With the entire block cleared of civilian traffic and parked cars, he had an unimpeded view of the fifty-four-story office tower and its wide front court, which had become an assembly area for K-9 police, counter sniper support units, and other uniformed and nonuniformed security personnel. Mobile law-enforcement command posts and television news vans sat at the curb, satellite antennas poking from their roofs.

Harris craned his head back, raising a hand to screen his eyes from the sunlight as they climbed the skyscraper's black steel facade. One Liberty's tenants were mainly financial and insurance powerhouses—NASDAQ among them—that had remained open for business as usual, and he could see office workers gathered at the windows for a look at the President.

This didn't thrill him. He assumed One Liberty maintained tight internal security. Secret Service would have swept its offices with their magnetometers and chemical trace sniffers. But every person coming in and out of a place loosened the seal a little…and there were hundreds of men and women working in the building. Swipe cards, ID checks, biometrics, you name it, they were all vulnerable to compromise.

He elevated his gaze some more. He could distinguish the tiny silhouetted forms of FBI-Counterstrike sharpshooters along the edge of the building's rooftop, their long-range rifles ready in case of trouble. Higher up, an NYPD surveillance helicopter held a stationary hover.

Everything that had to be covered was covered. Not only here, onsite, but elsewhere in Manhattan. At headquarters, Ki Martin's crew would be monitoring key points of possible attack on the infrastructure. The energy grid, communications networks, transportation and water systems, anything that might be targeted with POTUS in town.

A tight net, Harris thought. *But one single opening, one lunatic who manages to wriggle through, and none of it's worth a damn.*

He was suddenly jostled around by a drove of Secret Service personnel, the black suits shoving past as if he was invisible. They converged around the limousines, getting set to whisk Fucillo and the rest of the dignitaries toward the stage. Irritated, he reached down to the two-way clipped to his belt and opened the channel dedicated to his roving agents. Invisible Man or not, he had his own job to do.

"Musil, you read me?"

"Yes, sir."

"Where are you now?"

"Moving north on Trinity Place, sir."

"I want you closer in."

"Yessir. I was waiting for the motorcade to pass—"

"You hear me ask for an explanation?"

"No, sir..."

"So don't explain," Harris said grumpily.

Probably he shouldn't have vented his frustrations on Musil. The Washington desk jocks wanted him and Fahey on enforced leave after Brooklyn, and neither agent needed more crap.

The limousines were emptying out now, Secret Service agents hustling Fucillo and her Director of Homeland Security, Cliff Parsons, through the security zone bordering Zuccotti to the fifty-foot-wide stage. The governor and his people were in the second car, followed by Professor Alex Michaels in the third and last limo… Alex's German shepherd springing from the door ahead of him.

As Harris understood it, Fucillo wanted the shaggy monster to become Net Force's official mascot. Politics in the US of A.

Surrounded by agents, his dog on a short lead, Alex was walking across the sidewalk toward the park. Harris hurried to catch up, moving briskly along with the black suits and VIPs.

"Hey, Prof!" He raised his voice above the noise of the crowd. "Hold up!"

He pretended to be oblivious to the baleful glances he was drawing from the Secret Service men. They didn't like him in their space. Except the FBI ID hanging from a lanyard around his neck told them it was his space too.

"Just want to wish you luck," he said.

Alex smiled a little and paused a step, heeling Julia with a quiet command. They were at the foot of the stage ramp. "Thank you, Leo. Sincerely."

Harris started to put out his hand for him to shake, then froze. Julia had moved between them, putting him on notice with a defensive stance. Her neck raised high, her triangular ears turned stiffly forward, she locked her brown eyes on him above her massive snout.

Alex tugged on the shepherd's leash, leaning over to rest a hand on her chest.

"Be 'Seder," he commanded.

She visibly calmed at once, lowering her forequarters and returning to her master's side.

Harris grunted, carefully watching her. "What'd you say to her?"

"That everything's okay." Alex looked up at him. "It's Hebrew command training."

Harris nodded, and Alex and the dog were swept up the ramp to join the President and her other guests on stage.

The SAC watched him for a second, then turned and strode back to the cordon, his eyes scanning the crowd of onlookers.

Be 'Seder, he thought. *Like* babysitter.

Not the best mnemonic. But passable on the fly.

VII

"In a moment, we'll all share the honor and privilege of hearing Madam President's visionary plan for American cyber-security," Governor Kevin Bender said. "But I want to thank everyone for the magnificent turnout. I know it's hot, and I know it's a workday, and I appreciate all of you being here with us."

He smiled, giving the crowd a chance to applaud. Behind him, Fucillo sat beside Alex Michaels and his baleful-looking shepherd. What choice was there but to play along...and hopefully avoid getting upstaged by a fleabag dog?

As the applause died down, Bender flashed another Chiclet-white grin.

"People say my cryptocurrency program is a trailblazing model of protection for the global financial community," he said. "A coordinated, integrated online backup for *physical* currency in the event of a natural or man-made disaster. They tell me I did something special by establishing such a failsafe in this great state of New York..."

In her seat onstage, Annemarie Fucillo was tempted to shoot Alex a discreetly amused glance...and in their old college days she would have. But the slightest inappropriate twitch of the lips could be—and usually was—captured by someone's phone and posted online for mass dissection.

Gazing out at the crowd beyond the barricades, she ignored the governor's pomposity and instead focused on upsides. Kevin Bender's relentless pitching of his program had grabbed media attention, building momentum for her own Net Force reforms. A top-to-bottom restructuring of the country's anti-cybercrime/cyberterrorism efforts would not be tax-dollar cheap. But the biggest obstacle in winning public sentiment wasn't cost-related; it was the

American people's widespread ambivalence toward stronger governmental internet surveillance, and concerns about their privacy being whittled away. Fucillo only hoped she could leverage her high public confidence ratings to provide enough reassurances.

She continued to gaze out at the crowd. There were so many people, yet they only represented a fraction of the national audience watching on television or internet livestreams. How many had come to hear about the cyber initiatives, how many were drawn by the spectacle, and how many fell into both categories? She tried to read their faces and gauge their mood, but it was hard with the sun blazing in her eyes.

Grateful for the large, drum-shaped air circulators at the wings of the stage, Fucillo returned her attention to the governor, who had finally dawdled around to her introduction. She felt ready to go.

"...and now I'm delighted to welcome a fellow champion of internet security, a friend of mine and every other New Yorker... the President of the United States, Annemarie Fucillo!"

Fucillo looked at Alex as she rose, and wasn't at all surprised to discover that he was looking back at her.

"This is it, Annemarie—our start," he said. He indicated the gigantic video screen overhead with a tip of his head.

She paused, sparing a glance up at the screen, where the Net Force emblem had materialized in letters at least six feet high. Then she lowered her eyes to the professor's face and gave him a small, confidential nod.

Theater and showmanship, she thought. They were the spiffy packaging that sold what politicians had to offer. But without having the goods, it was all razzle-dazzle.

Fucillo hadn't spent a lifetime in public service for that. Ready to deliver, she stepped toward the podium.

VIII

Watching the livestream feed from Zuccotti on his computer, Drajan Petrovik saw the President briefly turn to the man beside her, and then glance over her head before taking center stage. The video feed instantly cut in the direction of her gaze, owing, no doubt, to an observant news director.

Drajan turned up his audio.

"—'pears we have a few seconds before Madam Fucillo makes her announcement, we want to show our viewers around the world the fantastic jumbotron above the stage. The image of the Net Force badge is quite an eyeful…"

Drajan felt the snap of jaws inside him when he saw it on-screen.

"No," he said. "Not a badge…a shield. In some minds."

He sat typing beside Emil, so in synch with him it was like he possessed an extra pair of hands. Infecting a single computer system with malware was a relatively simple thing. But he had engineered Hekate's spread—directed and random—to multiple systems, a far more complex task.

The parking attendant was a trained flea out of the box, a carrier infecting the garage chain's main server. That system interfaced with the Office of the Police Commissioner's internal network to download the list of VIPs with parking access. There were politicians, private donors, stockbrokers and celebrities, friends and family members of the dignitaries…as well as dozens of personnel from the firm contracted to produce and manage it.

Drajan had accessed StageWorks' intranet to create the Rainey alias for Anton Ciobanu. That was vital. But his penetration of its Internet Protocol Television network was a yield not originally considered—or one he'd even cultivated.

It happened that way sometimes. He would reap his richest harvests after sowing unpredictability across systems, then probing those systems for the various outcomes. When one evaluated systems from a nonlinear perspective, and saw how small alterations within them might ripple off to effect greater consequences, one could also understand that the seemingly unconnected was always connected.

Drajan studied his computer screen, having logged into the

IPTV network with the same hacked information he used installing his codec. He was prepared to deliver an audiovisual packet Hekate had been designed to decompress and run.

"I'm set," he said, glancing over his shoulder at Emil. "Is the upload complete?"

"The mobile devices are ready."

"And Ciobanu?"

"I'm tracking him right here." His gaze moved to a map of the target zone on his screen. A red GPS dot representing Anton Ciobanu was gliding through the maze of streets near Zuccotti, toward the stage setup. At the upper corner of the map, a digital accelerometer readout from the wearable ear clip computer showed him to be walking at almost five kilometers an hour—a brisk but inconspicuous pace. "He'll reach the target zone in minutes."

"Then we're only waiting for POTUS."

Drajan went back to the live news feed. In minutes, he would strike his opening blow, a clear declaration that the cybersecurity shield emblazoned above the stage meant nothing to him.

He watched as Fucillo began to speak. A single set of shocks to a system, or network of linked systems—biological, political, electronic, it made no difference—was not a true epidemic, though it might be crippling to all that were struck. By definition, an epidemic only occurred when the initial shockwave set off a chain reaction in systems that *did not* experience the original blow. His ultimate success would hinge on identifying vectors of transmission, arriving at a predictive factor for successive outbreaks, and knowing precisely when to exploit them.

The contagion would start in New York, to be carried across the length and breadth of the United States...

And then, spreading across the globe, it would make the next leap in its evolution.

IX

Anton Ciobanu stood amid the onlookers outside the security cordon, facing the stage, his head turned slightly to his right as he watched President Fucillo ease behind the podium. Minutes earlier, he had swung east from Trinity Place onto Liberty Street, his identification tags easily letting him bypass the NYPD Special Operations guards stationed at the corner. There was a tense instant when one of the black-clad officers came close to him with a Labrador—the city deployed the scent hounds almost exclusively for explosives detection—but he hurried along without incident. It either could not pick up a vapor wake from his computer bag, or was not trained to recognize it as being given off by bomb material. The second possibility was a strong one; Koschei had reassured him that 70 percent of the bomb dogs were not trained to identify Crystex's unusual chemical bouquet.

Still, he breathed a sigh of relief when he made it past the dog.

Bumping through the crowd now, he moved up to the far end of the stage, where he saw a small opening between two barricades. Beyond the barricades, a cluster of large road cases for transporting production equipment sat on the ground near the edge of the stage. Some were closed, while others sat on the ground, their lids raised, industrial cables coiling from inside them. The stickers on their sides all bore the StageWorks logo.

His nerves humming, Ciobanu eyed the security line and counted three uniformed police spread out loosely behind the gap. He suspected others of being NYPD or FBI plainclothes, and there would be several more undercover law-enforcement personnel.

He shifted his attention to the path he would take through them. Onstage, the President was making some polite remarks to the governor and New York Stock Exchange officials who had organized the morning's program.

He waited. The packed bodies around him seemed to have amplified the heat until it was almost dizzying. But he would not have to endure it much longer. It was almost time. When his cue came there would be no mistaking it.

He was eager to drop the bag and get out.

X

"...New Yorkers, fellow Americans, friends around the world, I'm proud to see how many of you have turned out today," President Annemarie Fucillo said from the stage. "Proud and humbled to stand with those who share this physical space with me—this very *hot* space—and those watching from a distance on televisions, computers, tablets, or smartphones...hopefully with cold beverages within reach."

She paused, smiling, as laughter rippled through the crowd. Her comments about the turnout weren't mere speechifying. There were, she guessed, a thousand onlookers standing in the street, along with about a hundred fifty invited guests in three or four rows of folding chairs in front of the stage. What made it especially gratifying was that this was a Monday, the start of the workweek, meaning most of those in attendance unquestionably had other things to do besides listen to her hold forth about internet security...yet they had come.

Her expression growing serious, Fucillo went on. "I'm old enough to recall how things were before the internet...or before it became accessible to average men and women," she said. "I can also remember how it felt when I logged on for the first time. There was an exhilarating sense of wonder and discovery. It made my reality simultaneously expand beyond anything I could have imagined, and shrink so the world was at my fingertips. I could instantly reach across international borders, share my thoughts with a person who was far away in terms of miles, and at the same time bring that person into my near and immediate space. A space with undefined boundaries...or boundaries that might require a new definition."

Fucillo paused to let that settle over the audience.

"Before we can discuss reexamining internet security, I think we need to look back," she said now. "Back in the late 1960s, computer scientists at university think tanks developed an electronic network that could quickly exchange information with other networks across vast geographic distances. They saw it as a tremendous asset to their research. But remember, their work was funded by the Department of Defense. With the Cold War at its height, the US military conceived of this network as a potential communications system that could survive the failure of all other communications systems if World War Three broke out.

"So, from its birth, we had two very different visions of the internet. Our scientists sought a gateway for an open, free-flowing exchange of information. Our warriors wanted a secure channel of communication that would withstand any sort of attack.

"Free-flowing information. Unassailable security. These concepts would seem to be in radical opposition. But are they?

"When the internet's creators were doing their early work, who would have thought we'd be spending so much of our daily lives in that space? That it would become essential to our global infrastructure and economy? And, regrettably, that criminals and enemies of democracy would seek to exploit its weaknesses for their own advantage? Who would have *imagined* the heated debate Americans now have over how to safeguard that space without infringing on our privacy?

"But for our own welfare, for the health of the Space—capital *S* now—it's high time we *come together* to protect it in a reasonable, coordinated, and comprehensive way."

The Net Force initiative was anything but hush-hush. But everything that came before was a preview. Today was its official premiere. Its reception would determine whether she could garner the momentum needed to propel it through Congress.

Stepping back from the podium, she prepared to raise her hand toward the jumbotron. The gesture would signal its operators to increase the screen's brightness, making the huge Net Force graphic radiate more sharply in the ambient sunlight.

She took another breath, letting herself enjoy the moment, absorbing everything about it. The crowd was silent, waiting for her. Finally, she motioned to the screen.

"Friends," she said, "you see here the symbol of our commitment and responsibility for a safe, buoyant internet. The symbol of—"

XI

"War," Drajan said, completing the President's sentence. He swiveled to look at Emil, who gave a simple nod toward his laptop. The magic packets implanted in the smartphones were about to be triggered.

Drajan turned to his own keyboard, clicking a key for the IPTV takeover.

The savage thing he had fathered was about to *roar*.

XII

Andrew Jackson Marshall frowned. After turning down the hall into the cubicled workspace shared by his analysts and portfolio managers, he noticed that nearly all had left their desks, lining up at the windows to watch President Fucillo.

As founder and CEO of Collier Bay Investments, Marshall wondered if he should have listened to the President's advance team when they approached him about closing down today. But Collier Bay was a global enterprise, and its investors and capital partners throughout the world expected the company to make prompt, effective decisions on their behalf. Those clients deserved nothing less than his staff's consistent attention. A political speech was no excuse to lose focus.

Unfortunately, Marshall thought with annoyance, his employees seemed to have done just that this morning.

A tall, stern man of sixty, he stood scowling into the office space. The half-dozen or so staffers in this division were all kids who'd held smartphones in their hands since they set aside their baby bottles. While Marshall knew his firm's critical edge in the marketplace relied on the latest technologies, it irked him to see them at the window right now, taking videos and snapshots with their phones when there was work to be done—especially because the cells were company-issue equipment.

"I hope everyone's enjoying the event," he said, surprising them. "Go ahead and soak it up—you'll all be staying late tonight."

They turned, looking like ambushed rabbits. Ariel Hanigan, a commodities specialist who generally impressed Marshall with her shrewdness and chutzpah, was so taken aback she kept her phone raised to shoulder height, its lens pointed at the floor-to-ceiling window. He could see a zoomed-in video image of the crowd scene below on the display.

"Sir, we were just—" She broke off, straightening her posture. "Check that. It isn't every day that the President of the United States is across the street, and we wanted to see her. No excuses."

Marshall knew better than to lift his frown. Still, he liked her accountability.

His eyes went from the phone in her hand to those held by the others. Many were still recording...but he would address that issue later. He was passing through on his way to a senior executive's office and was eager to get on with business.

"Fair enough," he said after a moment. "But don't let this happen again. Any of you. Is that understood?"

A nod from Geoffrey Kline, one of his rookie portfolio analysts. "Completely, sir...and we're sorry."

Marshall noted that he was still aiming his phone at the window. Fucillo was popular, say that for her. Though he wondered if she was about to squander much of that currency with the political crisis in Birhan. No one gave a damn about an African uprising, especially when it might lead to US military involvement.

But that was her problem, he had his own share to keep him occupied. Acknowledging Kline's apology with a curt nod, he started to turn back toward the corridor...and then suddenly stopped.

He'd heard the rapid electronic beeps of a number being dialed into a phone.

His brows arched. No, not one phone. Several. Including the company cell in his trouser pocket. Glancing at the phones in his employees' hands with utter mystification, he saw that their camera applications had closed, their displays switching to the basic digital phone keypads.

They had all dialed at the same time. And from what he could see, each of the numbers had the Colliers Bay organizational prefix.

What's going on? Marshall thought. It was as if they were all calling each other.

He was quizzically pulling the phone out of his pocket when the explosion ripped through One Liberty's twenty-seventh floor, blowing out the windows where the young staffers stood looking down at the park, sweeping them and Andrew Jackson Marshall and so many more into its roaring, consuming white heat...

And then into darkness.

XIII

Fucillo was turned halfway toward the video screen, her eyes angled upward, when she saw the flash out of the corner of her eye—a dazzling brilliance that immediately made her spin back around to look at One Liberty Plaza across the street.

She had no sooner done so than a gout of fire and smoke shot from the middle of the skyscraper. Then there was a deep, rumbling boom and a terrific crash that she recognized as the sound of breaking glass.

The windows, she thought. *That building is all windows.* It was as if a huge fist had punched them out. The shards of tinted glass blew through the air, darkly catching the sunlight as they rained to the ground.

And the people who had been watching her...

They were gone, vanished in the flames.

The vibration, the one that felt like an earth tremor, came a heartbeat later. It rattled the stage, shaking everything on it.

Instinctively seeking something to hold on to, Fucillo reached for the top of the lectern with both hands. But before her fingers made contact, she was swarmed by Secret Service men, the agents surging over her, closing ranks, almost sweeping her off her feet. There was a barrage of noise: the agents speaking rapidly into their radio microphones, police shouting commands, people screaming, sirens, all of it overlapping in her ears.

Fucillo let herself be hustled to her right, the Secret Service men speeding her along. Then she heard another sound from overhead, a rumble like a thunderclap, and angled her head up toward the sound.

Annemarie Fucillo was not a woman who frightened easily, and *showing* fear was even less a part of her makeup. But what she saw on the video screen made her jaw drop.

"Oh my Lord," she said. *"What is happening?"*

XIV

Ciobanu had been given some knowledge of what to expect, but he was still almost frozen by the scene unfolding around him.

In the seconds after the blast in One Liberty Plaza, he moved ahead as planned, quickstepping toward the gap in the security barricades as all eyes around him turned toward the skyscraper. Then with the explosion still echoing in his ears, he heard the thunderous boom above the stage and found himself looking up at the giant video screen.

His eyes gaped open. The static Net Force emblem it displayed had been replaced by a circle of darkness, surrounded by seething red and white crackles of energy.

The black disk grew larger and larger on the screen—and then disappeared all at once, the entire visual gone in a heartbeat. On the screen instead were a few simple words, black against a white field:

GOD IS NOT WILLING TO DO EVERYTHING

Ciobanu tore his gaze from the screen, knowing he had to move fast. The milling crowd, the army of Secret Service men and police guarding the barricades, all were twice distracted, their attention split between the video screen and the burning office tower opposite Zuccotti.

He edged between the barriers, not glancing at the uniformed personnel around him, hoping to avoid drawing their notice. The road cases were straight ahead of him, and he strode directly over to the one with the open lid, sliding the computer bag off his shoulder and letting it drop to the ground beside the case.

That was it. His assignment was executed. All that remained was to hurry off before the second bomb went off.

But there wasn't much time. The tiny wearable computer on his ear, linked to his smartphone using a Bluetooth connection, had become a wireless detonator, its transformation remotely initiated across a distance of over four thousand miles.

Ciobanu started anxiously past the stage, wanting to gain some distance fast.

XV

Coughing hard in the smoke from One Liberty Plaza, Harris had reacted to the explosion and the bizarre images on the giant screen with a combination of shock, horror, and incredulity. His mind went back to the 9/11 attack over two decades ago, when he was a much younger man—but only for a moment.

Now his trained instincts took over. Whatever the hell was happening, he wasn't here to stand and gawk. He had to get a grip.

He reached into his jacket for a particulate mask, slapping it over his face, glad he was wearing his sunglasses. Without them, he would be half blind from the soot and ashes floating in the air. Still between the sawhorses and stage, he was searching for suspicious faces, anything out of the ordinary. For all the security personnel around the park, most had been distracted by the explosion, and then the noise and images on the screen...

And maybe that was the whole point.

The thought no sooner occurred to Harris than he noticed the guy in the blue suit near the ramp at stage right. Somehow, he slipped between the barriers…slipped between them carrying something over his shoulder.

It was a bag. A laptop computer bag. Perfect for an IED.

He took a step toward the guy, then another, and by his third step went from a measured walk to a trot. Blue Suit had dropped the bag, let it fall behind a road case with the raised lid, and then started moving again.

"Hey! Hey, *you*! Stop where you are!" Harris shouted, realizing at once there was no way the man would be able to hear him in all the surrounding noise. He kept hustling straight past the ramp toward the rear of the stage.

The SAC raced after him, bringing out his wallet and holding it high over his head, displaying his Bureau ID through its plastic window.

He would never know whether the guy sensed him coming up on his tail, or caught a sudden glimpse of him, as he hooked right behind the backstage scaffolding toward the northwest side of the park. But for whatever reason he paused there for a second, staring at Harris.

Then he took off running.

XVI

"I don't know what's going on," Emil said. His eyes flicked from his screen to Drajan. "The accelerometer has Ciobanu clocked at almost twelve klicks per hour."

Petrovik studied the readings. Koschei's man had been walking normally a minute ago. Now he was sprinting…and toward the park's northwest exit.

"Someone's picked him up," he said without a ripple of disturbance in his calm. His eyes shot to Emil's face. "Trigger the bomb."

Emil nodded, and keyed in the coded sequence.

XVII

"Oh my Lord, what is happening?"

Even as the words left her mouth, Fucillo felt a shove—the Secret Service detail was suddenly moving her to the left, doing a complete about-face. One of them, a tall, broadly built man, wrapped his muscular arms around her waist in a kind of bear hug.

Carrying her against his body, holding her to his chest, he launched himself across the stage, running, his feet pounding out an urgent, hurried rhythm.

Then the second bomb went off, nearby this time. The agent kept moving, his arms wrapped around the President, holding her close, *moving*—

There was a prolonged, rumbling roar, a vibration that rattled the ground under the agent's feet. He staggered forward another step or two and went down hard with the President still in his arms, unable to go any farther as the blast wave overtook them.

23

I

Leo was hustling after Blue Suit when a second explosion rocked the stage. Just moments before, he'd radioed the Secret Service to warn them about the man dropping his computer bag near stage right. In trying to get Fucillo into her armored limo, they were unknowingly moving her *toward* the suspicious bag.

Glancing back, he could only hope the agents got the message in time. As the blast reverberated between the office towers around him, he heard people screaming in terror as the stage heaved upward and its right wing was engulfed in flames.

The SAC's first instinct was to hurry back toward the park and assist. But fire trucks and ambulances were already howling up Broadway in response to the One Liberty explosion, and he could see an entire fleet of NYPD vehicles racing toward the park. Those responders were trained and equipped to handle the situation. As far he knew, he was the only one on Blue Suit's tail.

Harris willed himself to stay on his man, shoving through a crush of shellshocked bystanders as Blue Suit turned west onto Trinity fifty or sixty feet up ahead.

"Musil, you with me?" he shouted into his radio headset. "Suspect's heading uptown on Trinity."

"Roger, sir..."

"I'm gonna need assistance."

"Yes, s—"

"Out!"

Harris pressed forward. Both sides of the street were mobbed with pedestrians, everybody gathered to see what was happening at the park, or running for cover, or looking around with stunned, vacant expressions. All of them getting in his way.

Flashing his ID so they would clear a path for him, Leo swept his gaze left and right, searching for Blue Suit. He noticed all the stoplights on Trinity were out of commission, hanging dark and dead as the cops tried their best to direct traffic.

Power's down, he thought. But there was no time to think about the implications as he picked up his quarry again, saw him turn east onto the pencil-thin strip of pavement that was John Street.

Leo jostled around the corner behind him. There was an enormous high-rise dorm at the southeast side of the street, and a hotel opposite. If the electricity was out—if it was out *everywhere*—it would mean there was no elevator service in the buildings, and *that* meant people would cram the emergency stairwells trying to evacuate. It was a dangerous situation that could easily turn into a stampede. This was lower Manhattan, within eyeshot of where the hijacked planes once struck the Twin Towers, and not a soul here would ignore that fact.

But he couldn't worry about that now. Increasing his pace, struggling to keep Blue Suit in sight, Harris shouldered through the crowd with his cardholder raised high in the air, shouting he was FBI at the top of his lungs. The heat, the reek of fire and smoke, the howl of sirens—it all swirled around him as he pushed up the street. He doubted his backup would reach him in time. Blue Suit was plunging ahead full-tilt, crashing into people as he ran toward the tangle of streets bordering the highway and East River.

Leo realized he was nearing the end of the block. The crowd thinned a little here, restaurants and bars replacing the taller office buildings shadowing the streets behind him.

He would never know whether that was when Blue Suit finally picked him up, or if he'd spotted him as far back as Zuccotti—and he supposed it didn't make a difference. What mattered, *all* that mattered, was the weapon that suddenly appeared in his hand, coming out from under his sport coat. It was a machine pistol. Dark and just slightly reflective. Leo thought it might be one of those superalloy computer-printed guns.

He reached under his jacket to unholster his nine-mil service gun, hoping to God his man wasn't enough of a lunatic to open fire with the sidewalk full of people. But then he abruptly stopped running, spinning around with the semiauto held out in front of him.

Their eyes locked, Leo halting in his tracks. Of course, he was crazy enough. He'd tried to take out the President. *The President of the United States.* And for all the SAC knew, he might have succeeded.

Harris stood there holding his gun in a two-handed shooter's grip. A moment passed. Another. The two men staring at each other, weapons steady in their hands. And then, suddenly, Blue Suit angled his machine pistol inches to Harris's right, triggering a single shot from its snub-nosed barrel.

Harris saw a young woman go down, crumpling onto the sidewalk. There were screams all around him.

Then Blue Suit gave the slightest of nods, his gun trained on Leo again.

Your choice.

Harris stood with his hands wrapped around his gun. People were running everywhere, scattering wildly between them, making it impossible to get a off a clean shot. Blue Suit was challenging him. Daring him to get into a firefight here on the street. If bullets started flying, it would be a bloodbath.

He glanced at the woman sprawled on the concrete. He could try to help her. Or do something that would lead to many more civilians being wounded.

Your choice.

He made it in an instant, hurrying over to her, kneeling, turning her onto her back. The bullet had struck the left side of her chest, and blood was pumping from the entry wound, already saturating her blouse, forming a puddle underneath her. Holstering his gun, Harris yanked off his jacket and bunched it against the wound, trying to staunch the bright red flow. He called for urgent medical assistance on the two-way, shouted for someone in the crowd to bring water, and then lowered his voice, saying whatever he could to comfort her. *You'll be okay, we're getting help, hang in with me.*

Someone rushed from one of the waterfront pubs with a bottle of water, and Leo took it, raising the woman's head up slightly, urging her to sip, not wanting her to dehydrate.

She took a small swallow, a second, gave a weak smile, and then let her head sink back down in his hand.

He was still crouched over her when she died there on the sidewalk a minute later.

II

"Sir, please, you have to come with us."

Alex Michaels looked dazedly at the Secret Service agent to his left, holding on to Julia's leash. He was speaking through a particulate mask, but that didn't explain why his words seemed to be running together. They were slurred and garbled, like a voice recording played back at slow speed.

Alex wondered if there was something wrong with his hearing. He thought he remembered an explosion…but wasn't certain of it. Things were disordered and confusing in a way they normally weren't for him.

"...this area's being cleared..."

He looked at the agent. What was he saying? Alex didn't understand. His face felt warm...

"Sir, we'll get you a wheelchair," the agent said, taking a half step closer.

Julia launched toward him, tugging against her leash, producing a low, assertive growl.

"*He'sha'er.*" The professor gave the Heel command. He'd felt a sharp pain on the side where he was holding the leash. "I don't...need a wheelchair."

The agent fixed his gaze on him. "Sir, listen to me," he said. "We need for it...the dog...to stand down. You've been injured, and it's vital you get to triage—"

"No. I'm fine. *Wherrrre* is Annemarie?"

Before the agent could reply, Alex found himself looking around for her. He recalled that she was at the podium, speaking as he listened, sitting behind her with the others onstage. And then...

The flash across the street. At One Liberty. There was a noise, a loud rumble. He recalled that now. Recalled the stage shaking underneath him, and then...

What?

He struggled to fill the hole in his memory and could not. Then he noticed a second Secret Service man—he also had a mask over the bottom half of his face—approaching in front of him. The agent moved slowly, carefully, mindful of Julia's attentive eyes and taut form.

Alex's gaze drifted past him. He saw police, firefighters, emergency medical techs in white uniforms. Across the street, outside the office tower, dozens of them were clustered behind ladder trucks and ambulances, scrambling over blown-out glass. Thick braids of smoke were roiling from midway up the tower.

What happened here? he thought. And tried again to rewind his memory. Eve had been giving her speech and—

No. Not Eve. That wasn't the President's name. Eve lived in a hive somewhere...

A hive? What did that mean?

He didn't know. Things were very jumbled in his mind.

Frustrated, he tried to concentrate. He was dizzy and felt a tightness in his throat and chest. It was the smoke. It had to be. Besides the uniformed people outside the tower, he could see cops in body armor, EMTs crouching over sprawled bodies amid the debris on the pavement. Blood everywhere...

Alex shifted his eyes back to the agent. "Where is she?" he insisted. "Where is the President?"

"She's safe," the agent said. "Again, sir, we need to move you."

He reached into a trouser pocket for his smartphone, thinking he had to call the lab.

"That won't work," said the agent through his mask. "We've gone dark...the cells are out." He nodded at Julia. "We have to get past the dog now, sir. You're hurt and need medical attention."

Alex looked at him. *Gone dark?*

He glanced down at the phone and saw a droplet of red land on its screen. Then another. Another...

Blood. It was his blood. Dripping onto the phone.

Hurt, he thought.

He looked up at the agent, warm blood running down his forehead, getting into his eyes, blurring everything...

Alex sagged at his knees, the phone dropping from his grasp as Julia's leash slipped from his other hand. He saw a medical tech rush toward him, his arms outstretched, and then Julia was lunging, snarling ferociously, stopping him in his tracks.

Alex was dimly aware of the EMT talking urgently to the agents. Then he felt his legs turn to melted wax. The whole world around him was fading, fading...

And that was all before everything around him went away.

III

On the barricaded street outside One Police Plaza, President Annemarie Fucillo sat in the back seat of her executive limousine, known as The Beast to the White House security detail. A Blackhawk military chopper wheeled overhead, and a small army of SWAT cops and Secret Service agents in black SUVs surrounded the heavily modified Cadillac Escalade. It was now Fucillo's mobile command center.

A Cognizant GlobeNet satphone in her hand, she was on a redline conference call to Vice President Saul Stokes and Chairman of the Joint Chiefs of Staff General Luther Fowler at the Pentagon. Their communication was as secure as technology allowed, scramblers in the car's armored panels having thrown an electronic screen around it.

"Annemarie, I'm advising you to get out of Manhattan," Stokes was saying. "You're in the middle of the dark zone."

"No. What will they think if I bolt?"

"Madam President, we understand your concern..." This was Fowler, his deep voice filling her ear. "But our primary focus has to be *national* security."

"I have confidence that Homeland has everything in place, General."

"Still, Madam...my recommendation is that we have Marine One fly you to NORAD EADS in Rome, New York. From there—"

"I've made my decision," Fucillo said.

A brief pause. Then the veep chimed in. "Annemarie..."

"That's it for now," Fucillo said. "I'll be in touch shortly."

She got off the phone and let her eyes close for a moment. A saline IV hung above her window, its line running from the bag to her wrist. Were her injuries more severe, a bag of her own blood could have been removed from a refrigerated compartment under the seat. As it was, she had a minor gash on her arm, second-degree burns, and some facial lacerations from the first explosion. But she considered herself blessed. Governor Bender and two of his aides were killed onsite, and she would have died with them if not for her Secret Service escort, who converged around her and took the explosion's brunt. Three members of the team were wounded…and the man who lifted her into his arms was another casualty.

Special Agent Gustavo Marquez, she thought.

Marquez. Married just over a year. A month or so ago, he had shown Fucillo a photo of his daughter.

Now his wife was a widow, their child fatherless.

It all occurred so quickly. One moment the agents were rushing her toward the ramp at stage right, near her parked limousine. The next, they reversed and carried her off to the left. Then the bomb went off precisely where she would have been if they had stuck to their original evac route.

Fucillo expelled a long breath. How had they known to go the opposite way? Did they see something that clued them to where the bomb was planted? *Or receive the information from someone else?* She had many questions…but they could wait until later. What she knew was that she owed her life to her entire guard detail, and especially to Marquez. It was a debt she would not fail to honor.

"Tom, put me on to somebody at Zuccotti," she said, handing the phone to the special agent beside her.

He nodded. Recently installed aboard the Beast, the Broadband Global Area Network—or BGAN—terminal designed by Cognizant's Adrían Soto was identical to the laptop-sized units carried by NYPD and FBI emergency communications vehicles. These allowed mobile satphone communications even if their surroundings were without power. The only predicate was an unobstructed line of sight with the satellite.

The agent pressed in a number as Fucillo waited. Her arm hurt like hell, but she had refused anything stronger than Tylenol. She needed to stay alert.

"Madam President, I have Lieutenant Vincent Dunn on the

line," the agent said after a moment. "He's the NYPD emergency liaison onsite."

She took the phone from him. "Lieutenant Dunn, I'll make this quick. You're familiar with Professor Michaels?"

"Of course, Madam," he said. "He was one of the dignitaries at the ceremony."

"I'd like an update on his whereabouts and condition. ASAP."

"I can give it to you now," Dunn said. "He's alive, but unconscious. We don't yet know the extent of his injuries."

The President took another deep breath. *Alex.*

"Why not?" she asked. And hesitated. "Is he trapped in the wreckage?"

"No, ma'am. That isn't the problem."

"Then what is?"

"It's his dog. It won't let anyone get near him."

"His…" She took a breath. "How will this be handled, Lieutenant Dunn?"

"NYPD tactical is on it. They'll either sedate the canine or take it out. Whichever is faster—we are strongly considering the second option."

Fucillo was silent. Alex loved that damned brute.

God is not willing to do everything, she thought. Ringed by special agents, she never saw those words appear on the video screen. Tom only briefed her after they were safely clear of the park, and she still had no real idea what any of it meant.

Tasting acid, she watched an ambulance come screaming toward a triage tent up the street. Alex Michaels had attended the Crypto Wall Street event at her urging, not to say insistence. If the decision were left to him, he would have happily spent the morning at his lab…

But that wasn't what brought the bitterness into her mouth. Not at all.

Asking Alex to come was one thing. He was her pick to lead Net Force, and public appearances—along with their associated risks—went with the territory. As President of the United States, she well understood better than anyone.

He had willingly accepted the candidacy. More than willingly...he did it eagerly, accepting it as a patriotic duty.

That was his decision, and Fucillo knew he would have no regrets.

But it was her bright idea that he bring the dog.

IV

Adrían Soto was out for his morning jog in Central Park when he heard the ringtone on his sat/switchable. As he unclipped the phone from his running belt, he saw that it was Stan Freeman, his VP of Operations at Cognizant.

"Stan," he said. "What's up?"

"You *merrm... ttrd...*?"

Soto frowned. "I can hardly hear you," he said. "I'm at the reservoir. The tower reception's bad."

"*Trm...* Zuccotti *splisnnn.*"

"Sorry...all I got from you was 'Zuccotti,'" Soto said. But that wasn't really all. He didn't like the nervousness in Stan's voice, knowing the President had been scheduled to deliver a speech there. "Hang on, I'm going over to sat mode." He touched the button on his display. "Okay, let's try this again. What's happening?"

"Trouble, Adrían." The changeover did the trick. Stan's voice was now clear, bouncing off their company's proprietary satellite. "All kinds of trouble."

Adrían suddenly noticed the sounds behind him. Footsteps on the cinders, people talking agitatedly. He turned to see the joggers and fitness walkers coming off the paths.

His hand tightened around the phone. "Lay it out for me, Stan," he said. "Make it quick."

He gave a rapid summary of events downtown. The bombings, the apparent hacking of the jumbotron, the unknown number of casualties and indefinite status of President Fucillo and the governor...

Power was down, Freeman explained, and civil and military authorities were implementing a general evacuation. Cognizant's headquarters was in the heart of what was being called the "dark zone," and its senior managers instructed all nonessential personnel to leave the building—over four hundred employees. The exceptions to that order had been technical support teams, who were swamped with emergency calls about major service disruptions to the national telecommunications infrastructure. If there was a positive bit of news, it was that the building's state-of-the-art solar backups were generating enough electricity to sustain bare-bones operations.

The phone still to his ear, Soto saw more people approaching the track. Overhearing parts of their agitated exchanges, he realized they had also gotten the news one way or another. He understood why they were all showing up now. The gatehouse was a kind of informal gathering place for runners, and it seemed only natural that they were coming from around the park as if drawn by some instinctive connection, seeking comfort among friends and familiar faces.

"Stan," Soto said into the phone now, "I'm heading over."

"I'm not sure that's possible. The neighborhood's in lockdown."

Soto blew out a breath. "Look," he said. "God willing, the President's okay. We have to get through to her."

"Adrían, under the circumstances, I don't see how—"

"If you can't contact her directly, go through the DoD. Tell the secretary I'm making a personal request. That I think Cognizant can be of assistance. Keep me posted—I'll see you soon."

Soto put away the phone. Cognizant was an information, communications, and media technologies systems designer with clients in the public and private sectors—including the United States Army, the Navy, and Department of Defense. If the interconnected government and military systems had been compromised by a cyberattack, he needed to be where he could be most effective getting them back up—and his headquarters was the best option.

It would be a difficult task. Stan was right about that. There would be no mass transportation, and surely no southbound streets open to traffic. But he needed to find a way. He could not stay where he was and do nothing.

One foot in front of the other. That's how you start.

Nodding slightly to himself, Soto turned away from the reservoir and aimed downtown.

24

Bucharest, Romania/New York Metro Area
July 27, 2023

I

It was 5:00 p.m. sharp in Bucharest when Mike Carmody entered the Opal Cybercafé outside the campus of the King Carol I Central University off Bulevardul Magheru, a commercial strip running north to south through the city's heart. Wearing darkly tinted smart specs, a leather carryall over his shoulder, he saw Kali behind her laptop at a rear table, motioned to let her know he'd arrived, and ordered a black coffee from the barista.

The television on the wall opposite the counter was tuned to *CNN International*, showing live images from the Wall Street area in New York City, where President Fucillo was touting her internet security proposal. Carmody wasn't a political animal, but he had followed the Net Force story knowing Carol Morse was involved in it—and figuring he eventually would be too.

He took his coffee and carried it to Kali's table.

"You cut your hair." He slipped off the glasses, pulling up a seat opposite her. "It threw me for a second."

She shrugged. When he left her a couple of hours earlier, it had fallen well over her shoulders. Now it barely reached the base of her neck.

"I've no time to fuss with it," she said. "I found a fat, jolly barber with scissors and an electric razor. He took five American greenbacks." She paused. "So, was your errand successful?"

"I got what I needed." Carmody reached into his carryall for a paper sack. "Picked this up for you. Thought we might have it with dinner."

Taking the bag from his hand, she opened it and sniffed the still-warm bread inside. Its fresh, grainy aroma carried a hint of malt.

"It's traditional Romanian country bread. Fired in a brick oven."

She looked at him, recalling the hard-crusted *pane cafone* he brought her in Naples. "Shall I expect baked offerings wherever we go?"

He grinned. "I like fresh bread. And I like sharing what I like with certain people."

Kali smiled a little and crumpled the bag shut. She had on a black T-shirt, army fatigue pants, and black paratrooper boots purchased at a military surplus store on the Pieta Romana.

He motioned at her computer. "How's it working?"

"Well enough." She brought her eyes up to his. "But it was sharing far too much."

Carmody said nothing. They sat looking at each other for almost a full minute, neither breaking the silence. Finally, she lifted her knapsack off the floor and reached into one of its outer pockets. Her hand emerged holding a small, folded napkin, then slid back inside and produced a USB power cord.

Still without a word, Kali set both items down on the table. The metal plug had been removed from the cord, leaving only the connector's hard plastic base.

"You've kept busy," he said. "How'd you pull that thing apart?"

"I did it, that's all," she said, and picked up the napkin. His eyes were attentive as she unfolded it on the tabletop.

The shiny copper square inside it was smaller than her thumbnail. She plucked it up with her fingertips, bending it slightly between them.

"I took this from inside the plug," she said. "An ultrathin, flexible circuit board. The material looks to be copper-clad laminate."

He shrugged. "I don't get into the tech."

"An out-of-the-box user?"

"Whatever. I just know it works."

Her dark eyes went to his. "'It' being a transceiver."

"Yes."

"Range?"

"About eight miles."

"Before it relays to a remote operations center, I would guess. So my computer can be tapped when I'm offline. Or have spyware infiltrate and exfiltrate it through a radio pathway."

He nodded. "After my men retrieved it, the laptop went into a Company shop for analysis. I told you that."

For a moment, neither of them spoke. Then she bent the square a little more and snapped it through the air at him. It bounced from his chest to the tabletop.

"I came here out of my free will," she said. "I could have left you on the road to Amalfi."

"Let's not make it about that." Carmody lowered his voice. "I obviously trusted you enough to bring you out on recon."

"Babysit me, you mean."

"No. I needed your help—"

She shook her head. "I won't be monitored. I can't allow it."

His face remained still. He was wearing a green button-down shirt with an open collar and rolled-up sleeves and a pair of faded indigo Levi's. As he lifted the tiny metal circuit board off the table, she glimpsed the lower edge of a tattoo above his elbow.

Lilac and blue. The colors, and the asymmetric curve of the line, reminded her of wing feathers.

He dropped the board into his pocket, and the sleeve rode down to cover the ink.

"We should finish our coffees and head over to the Piata Romana station," he said after a moment, glancing at his chronograph. "Our train's scheduled for…"

He abruptly stopped talking and turned toward the front of the café. A sudden, nervous commotion there had drawn his attention—it was the students he passed near the door. They were all watching the flatscreen, some abruptly rising from their chairs, others pulling out their cells. Carmody spoke limited Romanian, but the word *telivizione* needed no translation.

"Mariti volumul!" one of the young men told the barista. He motioned with his hands, prompting him to raise the set's volume.

Carmody looked at the television and saw a herky-jerky video image of people running wildly in different directions. There was heavy smoke, and the orange glare of a fire—a large one.

After a second, he read the crawl bar near the bottom of the screen:

ZUCCOTTI PARK EXPLOSION—
LIVE POOL FEED FROM NEW YORK

Rising off his chair, Carmody shouldered over to the TV and manually raised the volume.

"—can you tell us anything about President Fucillo's status? Is there any indication she was hurt?" a British inflected male voice said through the speakers.

"We have no official word." This was a female, an American. "I'm told by several sources that she was rushed into the executive limousine and driven from the area. But these are unconfirmed statements. I should point out that she was accompanied onstage by a large group of aides and dignitaries. Kevin Bender, the governor of New York, was among the notables. Also Professor Michaels, whom Madam Fucillo handpicked to lead the government's projected new internet security arm. Net Force, as they're calling it…"

"And do you know anything about the condition of these people?"

"There have been conflicting eyewitness statements, but I won't speculate on which are accurate—"

"What about what's being called a video hack of the jumbotron above the stage? I'm referring, Sheila, to the image takeover and the words that subsequently appeared…for viewers just tuning in, I think we should show them…are we able to bring up that shot…?"

Carmody had the presence of mind to glance over at Kali. Her body signals were far less pronounced than the average person's physical cues; he'd realized that about her almost immediately after her capture. But his interview-and-interrogation training keyed him to their subtleties.

She was leaning forward over the table, her eyes narrowed.

"Okay, we have it onscreen. To give everyone a sense of how this appeared at Zuccotti Park, the words were five or six feet tall on the 'tron—"

"'God is not willing to do everything,'" Carmody read in a low voice.

Kali raised her chin slightly.

"Sheila, we aren't able to get you on camera, but are you still able to hear me?"

"There's a lot of noise around…it's hard to describe the sirens and horns…but you're coming in all right."

"Good. Sheila, on that phrase…correct me if I'm mistaken, but hasn't its source been identified?"

"Yes, I'm told it's from Machiavelli's most famous—some would say notorious—work, *The Prince*…"

Carmody edged over to their table, sat down opposite Kali, and regarded her in silence. Her eyes were coldly distant, reminding him of how they looked in the helicopter from Malta, when she had seemed to turn deep inside herself.

"Better gather your stuff," he said to her. "We have to get back to base."

She just looked at him, her eyes not deviating from his. Then she finally nodded, shut her computer, packed it away, and rose from her chair without a word.

In a moment she was pushing through the college kids around the television, Carmody hurrying out behind her.

II

Shortly before 9:30 a.m. in Montclair, New Jersey, a half-hour's drive across the Hudson River from New York City, Tyrone Vaughn, a vacationing construction manager with the general contracting firm of Baron, Rollins & Sims, came in from watering his lawn to find his wife Cheryl's oh-so-fricking-wonderful smart fridge acting up.

The virtual-assistant-enabled Cybercool 3000 had been his big—almost *four thousand dollars'* worth of big—gift to her the previous Christmas, and did everything but wolf down the food on its shelves. That included autoregulating its power levels, remembering purchase and expiration dates, and even pulling recipes off the internet for the smart oven Tyrone couldn't yet afford. To Cheryl's delight, it also connected to their cell phones when they were at the supermarket, reminding them whether they were low on eggs, ketchup, cheese, and whatnot. And naturally its touchscreen bulletin board displayed the current and extended weather forecasts, stock reports, and major news headlines, while allowing Cheryl to send email, order catalog items from online sellers, and download music, movies, and e-books. Depending on her mood and whim, she could stay informed, rock out, or escape into one of her steamy vampire novels.

The problem right now, though, was that this stainless steel

Stephen Hawking of refrigerators seemed to have gone wonky. *Seriously* wonky. Tyrone noticed that the LED on the Cyber-cool's door wasn't showing its regular homescreen, with a photo of their cat Sprinkles, and local time and temperature readings.

Instead, its background had turned a bright, glowing white and had seven large words floating randomly across it:

GOD IS NOT
WILLING
TO
DO
EVERYTHING

Tyrone pressed a finger against it to see if that would restore it to normal. But the words kept drifting in random patterns. Trying to make sense of it, he reminded himself that Cheryl was *h-e-a-v-y* into some positivity guru. Maybe she'd downloaded an affirmation or something...

But even if he was looking at a screensaver...what *kind* of screensaver didn't go away when you wanted to be rid of it?

Tyrone scratched behind his ear, figuring he would ask Cher about it later. As long as he could have himself a nice, cold can of soda, Cybercool here could go ahead and call him rotten names if it wanted.

He grabbed the handle, pulled it open...and frowned. The instant the door swung back in his hand, he realized there had been no familiar blast of chill refrigerator air from inside.

"Why?" he asked aloud. "Why you gotta do this to me?"

"GOD IS NOT WILLING TO DO EVERYTHING!"

Tyrone almost jumped out of his sneakers. The deafening female voice belonged to Dina, the complimentary online voice service—cum—virtual assistant that came with Cheryl's GoBuy Premiere membership.

"Dina, lower the volume," he said.

"GOTT IS NICHT BEREIT ALLES ZU TUN!" the VA trumpeted.

Tyrone flinched again. Was that *German*?

Frowning in bewilderment, he decided to finish checking out the Cybercool. Once he was done with it, he could head into the living room for a look at Cheryl's GoHub—the Wi-Fi computing device that connected Dina to their home. Maybe *it* would turn out to be the cause of his problems.

He leaned into the fridge. The interior wasn't exactly warm, but it wasn't cold, either...and the light was just dimly on. Almost like something was draining its power, he thought.

He decided it might be a good idea to call Cheryl before taking the hated customer service route. With her being an admin at the FBI's NYC field office, and the President visiting town today, he figured she was busy enough without him bugging her. But she was a stickler for reading user's manuals, and he was thinking she might have some tips. Who knew, maybe the fridge had a reboot button or something for an easy fix? A quick call wouldn't hurt.

He reached into his jeans for his smartphone, raised it to press in his wife's number...and then stood there staring at its screen, dumbstruck. The image it showed was identical to the one on the fridge, those same words floating around a white field:

GOD
IS

NOT WILLING TO DO

EVERYTHING

Tyrone felt a sudden unease. With Dina getting weird on him too, it stood to reason they could have picked up some kind of computer virus. The devices in their house were all cloud-synched. But if that was the explanation, *what kind of weird bug was it?*

"What the hell's next?" he muttered under his breath.

At that precise moment, heat started blasting from the central air vents.

III

At 9:55 in the morning, a gravely distressed Judge Charlotte Pemstein was driving her BMW Coupe on I-84 East, Rachel in the back seat.

This was supposed to be the start of their vacation following the weekend at Mohonk, but given the news coming over the radio, all she wanted now was to be safely off the road.

Pemstein had been approaching New Haven, roughly a third of the way to the north shore of Massachusetts, when she heard the earliest reports. Explosions in New York, the President's status uncertain, Governor Bender and dozens of others killed. It was almost beyond belief.

Concerned, she had called her friend Genie Sandoval. Genie's law office was down there in the neighborhood. She could have easily decided to walk over for her speech.

Pemstein made three attempts at calling her, each time getting a notice that service was interrupted. Next, she phoned her administrative assistant's landline without success. After calls to several other friends yielded the same frustrating results, she began hearing reports about disruptions in the area's power and communications grids.

By then, her concern had deepened to worry, and not just for those closest to her. Although more than half of her fellow Southern District magistrates were on vacation this week, there still was a packed docket at the courthouse on Pearl Street, a five-minute stroll from Liberty Plaza and Zuccotti Park. It would be full of clerks, attorneys, freshman judges, and dozens of other legal, security, and maintenance personnel. Any of them could have been near the park when the bombs went off.

Pemstein had briefly considered pulling off the road, turning around, and heading back. But that made no sense. The city wasn't safe. She needed to think about keeping Rach out of harm's way.

It wasn't long before the idea became moot. Soon after hearing the earliest reports of the bombings, she noticed that traffic in the opposite lanes was a near standstill. The radio confirmed what she suspected. All toll plazas and bridges into New York were closed, completely sealed off to inbound and outbound traffic. The city was in lockdown.

And so, she stayed on the highway into New England, figuring she would make some calls once she and Rach checked into their bed-and-breakfast. In the meantime, she would keep her ears glued to the radio.

Unfortunately, nothing Pemstein heard gave her cause for relief—and her concern only worsened when she thought about Leo Harris. When they last spoke a week or two back, Leo had mentioned he would be onsite with the bureau contingent at Zuccotti.

She tried not to think about her old friend possibly getting injured—or worse—in the bombing. She needed to stay focused. A big, rumbling semi behind her was too close for comfort, and a glance at her heads-up display showed she was already doing sixty. By no means would she toe the gas any harder for the driver's sake.

The trucker wasn't the only one making her nervous. Connecticut motorists were crazed at best, and their obvious panic didn't help matters. They were speeding like maniacs, cutting wildly between lanes. Almost certainly they were getting the same news she was, and wanted to get off the highway.

"How're you doing, honey?" she asked, casting a glance at Rachel in her rearview mirror.

Rachel was strapped into the back seat. Her travel tote beside her, she held an apple juice box in one hand, and had a coloring book on her lap.

"Okay," she said. "But I'm scared for Sophia."

Pemstein felt a small catch in her throat. Sophia was her best pal from up the street. It wasn't the kid's concern for her friend that took her aback, but the fact that she was obviously paying attention to the radio. Rachel was as smart as a whip.

"Her mom and dad take good care of her," she said. "I think she'll be all right."

"*Really?*"

"Yes," she said. "Tell you what, though… I was going to make some calls when we get to the inn. Just to check up on people we know. So let's dial Sophie's number and have you talk to her. How's that sound?"

Rachel gave her a smile of unadorned gratitude. "Okay!" she said happily. "I…"

She abruptly stopped talking. Glancing into the rearview, Pemstein saw that she was staring straight ahead.

"Hon," she asked, "what is it?"

Rachel pointed at the windshield. "Aren't we going to Massachusetts?"

Pemstein realized her daughter was motioning to the HUD display—and a quick glance told her why. Its white odometer, real-time traffic, and destination readings were gone.

Replaced.

Her brow grooved with confusion as she read the same words that the news stories were saying had flashed on the giant video screen at Zuccotti:

GOD IS NOT WILLING TO DO EVERYTHING

Pemstein told herself to stay calm, not wanting to frighten her daughter.

"One sec," she said, wanting the VA to run a diagnostic. "Dina, is there a problem with the HUD readings?"

The response was instantaneous.

"*God is not willing to do everything,*" it said in its digitized female voice. And then again: "*God is not willing to do everything.*"

Pemstein felt cold. She was afraid to look down at her dashboard display but did so anyway.

Floating across the central panel, black against a white background, were the same seven words she'd heard from the VA. The same words that replaced the normal readouts.

Charlotte took a breath. The VA was repeating itself over and over, like an old phonograph album with a scratch.

"God is not willing to do everything. God is not willing to do everything. God is not willing to do everything..."

"What's Dina saying about God?" Rachel asked from the back seat. "Mom... I'm scared."

"Can't talk, Rach. I have to concentrate."

The tailgater in the semi still wasn't giving her any breathing room. There was a breakdown lane to her right, and an exit about a hundred yards ahead. She would swing across the right lane, pull to the shoulder, and drive to the exit. Once she was off the highway, she planned to park the car somewhere and figure out what to do next.

Glancing over her shoulder, she saw an opening in the right lane and hit the turn signal.

That was when the BMW surged forward, its turbocharged engine revving loudly.

Terrified, her heart thudding in her chest, Pemstein stepped on the brake but it didn't respond. She heard Rachel screaming, *shrieking*—

She was turning frantically around to look at her when she heard the bellow of the tailgating semi's air horn. Then the truck slammed into her rear end with a terrific, grating crunch of metal that drowned out the horn and the screams inside the car and the endlessly repeating voice of the VA and every other sound in the universe.

IV

"Musil, you read me?" Harris shouted over the command net. "We need Lulu in the air."

"We don't have clearance, sir. It's the situation at the Brooklyn Bridge."

Leo didn't need Musil to tell him about it. He was only a few hundred yards from the East River, where a swarm of police vessels and fireboats were converging to establish a perimeter around the bridge. Like everyone around him, he had heard the terrific, ear-splitting screech of the NYPD chopper's engine, then looked up to see it shoot over the water in an uncontrolled tailspin.

Several heartbeats later it collided with the suspension wires radiating from the bridge's Manhattan tower. As the wires snapped from their stays and twisted around its airframe and rotors, the bird had plunged down toward the water, its fall stopping about a hundred feet above the surface when the suspenders jerked it back up into the air.

The helicopter hung over the river now, caught in the wires, thrashing like a fly trying to escape a spiderweb. The stress on the airframe had partly snapped off its tail section, and it dangled crookedly from the front of the chopper.

Leo saw licks of fire through the smoke brewing against the windscreen, and tried not to think of the pilot and crew trapped in the cabin.

Meanwhile, the situation up on the bridge's approach ramp was no less surreal. Stalled cars, SUVs, and taxis jammed its lanes, at least a couple on fire and sending up columns of thick black smoke. One car had smashed halfway through the concrete safety barricade along the edge of the road, its front end teetering over the street below. People were swarming from their vehicles, abandoning them in confusion, even climbing up onto their hoods and roofs to try and shortcut past the crowd flooding out into the lanes.

The cumulative effect boggled Leo's mind. He felt as though he was watching a disaster simulation created by Alex's HIVE. But he could only have wished it was something like that. The horror and insanity of the scene was as genuine as the woman's blood smeared on his hands.

"This is bullshit, Jot," he said, barely able to hear his own voice over the megaphone-powered announcements blaring from the river. "What's the use of a cyber-hardened bird if we can't send her up?"

"I share your frustration, sir. But Emergency Management has grounded everything...including *non*-internet-connected aircraft."

Harris didn't give a damn about the playbook. This was not going to be OEM's call. He wouldn't let it be.

"Did you put Ki on it yet?"

"No, sir, I—"

"Then do it."

Harris signed off. His hub man was a certified black belt at cutting through bullshit. He knew which strings to pull.

Meanwhile he needed to keep looking for that son-of-a-bitch in the blue suit.

He ran another few yards to the corner of South Street and swung right opposite the new waterfront esplanade. The FDR was almost directly above him now, the bridge several hundred yards up ahead. Beyond the docks, police and fire rescue crafts continued to blare amplified warnings over the river.

Harris found the esplanade eerily deserted. There was no sign of Blue Suit.

He frowned. Four or five minutes must have passed since the killer left him behind, long enough for him to have found any number of hiding places on the waterfront. There were several blocks of run-down storage warehouses and low-income housing projects, butting up against the chichi hangouts and attractions. Beyond the projects, a twelve-foot wooden wall cut South Street off under the bridge ramp, keeping trespassers out of the stalled construction site where the old Fulton Fish Market once stood.

Leo ruled out the possibility of Blue Suit going over the wall. Too high, too hard to climb. *So where the hell was he?*

Turning to the public housing complex on his right, he saw concrete walkways between the buildings, a parking lot out in front of them, and a small, neglected playground behind a low chain-link fence. Swings, slides, weeds, park benches, and more weeds…

Leo suddenly noticed something on the ground under one of the benches. Something blue, visible through the fence.

He told himself it probably wasn't what he thought it was. But it was the right shade of blue. Ex*actly* the right shade.

Turning into the playground, he trotted over to the bench, holstered his pistol, and slipped on his vinyl evidence gloves. Then he knelt to the ground and reached under the bench.

Bingo.

Folded into a clear plastic bag, the sport jacket perfectly matched the killer's. Leo was sure it was one and the same.

He pulled the jacket out of the bag and immediately smelled fresh sweat and cologne. The cologne had a citrusy tang and wasn't cheap stuff. Neither was the jacket. Its tag read FENDI. He was holding half a five-thousand-dollar suit in his hands.

Quickly examining the outside of the jacket, he noticed hairs on the collar, and the slightest rectangular bulge in its right pocket.

He reached into it and pulled out the photo credentials that had been hanging around the killer's neck. There were two separate laminates for a John Rainey, one of them from something called StageWorks Professionals, the other a police pass for anyone besides official security personnel with close access to the Zuccotti event.

Harris's brow creased. He figured Rainey was a bogus name, and thought it fifty-fifty that StageWorks would be too. But the NYPD tag had all the right identifiers, including holos. It looked authentic to his eyes.

Taking a couple of Ziplocs out of his pants pocket, he put the laminates into one of them, dropped a couple of the hairs into another, then returned both baggies to his pocket. After hastily feeling through Blue Suit's jacket and finding nothing more inside or out, he folded it back into the plastic bag. He would call for someone to collect it, hoping it wouldn't disappear in the meantime. He couldn't carry it around lower Manhattan. He needed his hands free.

Harris thought for a moment. Blue Suit probably wouldn't have ditched the creds unless he had alternate ID with him. Without the jacket he was just another guy in a button-down dress shirt. Leo couldn't even be positive what color it was. His memory registered it as white, but it could have been one of a thousand shades of businessman bland.

Leo stood up and hurried out of the playground. If the killer didn't jump the construction wall, he must have run into an apartment building or cut through the projects. Either way it would have meant turning off the esplanade. Doubling back toward the financial district.

It made sense. Here he might as well have a flashing light on his forehead to draw attention. But he could hide in the streets outside the office buildings and courthouses, just another collared shirt in the mass of thousands that had spilled onto the sidewalks.

Harris stared down South Street. The downtown heliport was only a few blocks past the construction site. Lulu could have been up in the sky by now. Could have been tracking the killer.

He needed that aerial surveillance.

Sweat pouring down his face, legs stiff from running, Harris turned west off the esplanade, betting his quarry had done the same.

V

Clad in full SWAT garb, Special Agent Gary Wilkerson, FBI Tactical Operations, raised the M25 sniper rifle's barrel and prepared to fire a 7.62mm NATO round into the German shepherd's heart. He had detached his unneeded scope from its mounting rail and slipped it into a gear bag. From where he stood just yards from the shepherd, he could make the kill without looking—and he almost wished he didn't have to.

He hated this assignment. Taking out the animal would break

his heart. But his on-scene commander had decided against using tranquilizers. Wilkerson couldn't blame him. A trank would take time to work, especially with the dog pumped up on adrenaline. And someone's life was at stake. They needed to do what was best for the human being.

In front of him, behind the wooden police barricades, an unconscious Professor Michaels was curled on his side in a fetal position, blood covering his bearded face. The shepherd, in her special Net Force emblem vest, sat erect on the ground on his right, staring at the men she thought had gathered to threaten her master.

Wilkerson admired the dog's loyalty and protective courage. But her faithfulness was killing Alex. He needed immediate medical attention.

"In position," he said into his headset mike, balancing the stock lightly on his left hand, his right index finger poised over the trigger. "Ready to fire, over."

"Let's get it done, Wilk." This was from the OSC. "At your discretion, take the shot."

Wilkerson pressed the weapon's synthetic stock against his shoulder. The barricades arranged around Alex and the dog in a U-shape formed the boundary of an area about three yards wide that had been cleared of everyone besides essential personnel—a handful of Secret Service agents, fellow members of his tac unit, and a group of EMTs standing near their ambulance with a gurney. All giving the professor and his shepherd a wide berth.

Wilkerson inhaled, then exhaled—his practice breath. He would pull in another, hold it a second, and fire on the exhale.

"Good dog," he said in an undertone. "This won't hurt. I promise."

Peering down the barrel of the rifle, he took his breath.

VI

At Cyber HQ in 26 Federal Plaza, Ki Marton was on the phone with the agency's Critical Incident Response Group.

"ASAC Marton?" It was Vanessa, the executive assistant. "Are you still with me?"

"Yes." Pulling himself together. "With you."

"Chief Hardin apologizes for the delay," she said. "He's on the line with Washington... We're inundated, as you can imagine."

He could, of course. In a domestic emergency, CIRG had operational command of all FBI elements deployed to the crisis areas, including Cyber and the Surveillance and Aviation Section. Special Agent Rich Hardin was its section chief in New York City.

"I'm going to put you on hold," Vanessa said. "I won't be long."

Ki hoped not, thinking that it had been half an hour since he got through to his friend, Sharon Bennett, at the hospital. As head pre-op nurse, Sharon had promised to keep him updated on Mark's surgery.

She did that as long as she could, but her last call was dire. Within minutes of the Zuccotti explosion, electronic systems, computer networks, and large sections of Con Edison's energy grid started crashing throughout the financial district. For some inexplicable reason, the hospital's backup generators had remained offline. The lights and air conditioning were out, she said. Worse, patient monitoring and life support systems were down. She'd told Ki she had her hands full coping with the emergency, but would hurry over to the OR to learn what she could—and that was the last he heard from her. When she didn't call back after half an hour, Ki dialed her cell and briefly got through. That time, the call dropped. And dialing the hospital's main number only resulted in a busy signal.

Ki stared out his window at the green-clad FBI SWAT personnel seventeen stories below, forming an armed line of defense around 26 Fed.

Nothing in his experience had prepared him for this.

First Mark's headaches and forgetfulness. And then the diagnosis: a grade four anaplastic astrocytoma. A mass at the back of his brain. Somehow the X-rays missed it, but it showed up with spiteful clarity in the follow-up CT scan. The doctors rushed to schedule him for surgery.

"...Marton, you still there?"

Ki snapped to attention. "Sorry, Rich. I got distracted."

"You've got good reason," Hardin said. "This looks like everything we've been afraid of...a complex, sophisticated cyberstrike. We don't know where it's coming from or have any real idea about its scope and purpose. That scares the hell out of everyone, and it should. But all the congressmen want to know is our evacuation plan for the Hill."

"Priorities."

"There's nothing else to expect from those assholes." Hardin sighed. "Anyway, what can I do for you?"

"I have to ask a favor, Rich," he said. "We need a bird."

The chief hesitated. "I can't," he said. "That's beyond me."

"Little Lulu's on station. It doesn't make sense that we can't use her."

"Ki, we've known each other since Quantico—"

"That's exactly why I came to you..."

"Let me finish," Hardin said. "A chopper's crashed into the Brooklyn Bridge. Two more helicopters have gone down in Connecticut, and a small plane in White Plains before they shut the airports. These are just in the New York area. Sending anything into the air is a public hazard, and what you're asking violates incident management protocols."

"Technically, I suppose."

"Technically?"

"OEM establishes the guidelines. But this situation's unprecedented. CIRG has operational command on the ground..."

"And you're an expert on this since when?"

"Rich, I'm making my request on behalf of the SAC," Ki said. "He's on the target."

"Are you *serious*?"

"He picked him up at Zuccotti. But we need a floating box

around the guy with aerial support. There's no other way to track him. The streets down here are a maze."

Hardin was silent a second. "I'll give you microdrones. You'll have them right away."

"No good," Ki said. "The situation's too fluid. We need real-time human judgment."

"Ki, take what I'm offering. It's the best I can do. I won't put our personnel at risk—"

"Please, Rich. Give us Lulu. She's hardened against cyberattacks. I'm talking Cognizant firewalls. *This situation is why she exists.*"

Hardin was quiet again. Ki waited, letting him think things over. Meanwhile, he had just reached a decision of his own. He would try the hospital one more time after this call. If he didn't get through—

"Okay," Hardin said. "She's yours. And, yes, you owe me."

Ki straightened so quickly he slammed his knee against the bottom of the desk. "Rich..."

"Don't shower me with gratitude just yet," Hardin said. "I won't have this all on my back, Ki. If things come down heavy, your SAC's taking his share. And then some."

"Got it."

"Not so fast," Hardin said. "It works the other way too. You nab that motherfucker, I want him turned over to CIRG. Harris's nothing but a glorified brick agent in my book. He isn't basking in the afterglow. You better make sure he understands. I'm not someone he wants to piss off."

Ki sat a minute, surprised by the sudden edge in Hardin's voice. He had never heard him sound like that.

"I'll tell him," he said.

"All right. Give me five minutes and you'll have your bird on the net."

Ki tapped his foot pedal and switched to the two-way. He needed to contact Musil and Harris.

VII

Trooper Greg Rhodes, Connecticut State Police, hated to look at the little girl. But his eyes followed along as the techs rushed her from the mauled BMW to the ambulance. He couldn't help himself. The mother finished, the kid looking close to it—this one was ugly. As far as he could tell, the car had gone straight into a tractor trailer, causing the truck to jackknife across the highway, which sent other vehicles swerving to avoid it.

Rhodes stood watching the EMT crew load the diminutive body on the stretcher into their wagon. The woman had been all busted up when they pried her out of the front seat, every stitch of clothing on her body soaked in blood. She must have been killed instantly.

"Greg, we have the driver's ID. Got it out of her wallet."

Rhodes glanced at his partner. Trooper Ron Dillon was sweating heavily as he strode over from one of the other highway patrol cruisers, shattered glass crackling under the soles of his boots.

"Who is she?"

"Charlotte Pemstein, a New York federal judge," Dillon said.

"Does her daughter have a name?"

"Rachel. Rachel Alyssa."

Rhodes nodded somberly and stood listening to the squawk of two-way radios inside the cruisers and emergency vehicles lining the highway.

"Do we have any clue what caused this mess?" he said.

"Only thing I know for sure is that rig was on the Beamer's ass." Dillon cast a glance down the road at the truck. It had skidded out of control and almost plowed through the highway divider separating the eastbound and westbound lanes.

The shaken driver was giving his statement to another team of staties outside his cab.

Rhodes was peering over at the truck when his partner's

handheld beeped, then squawked out the call sign from Dispatch—"Andy one-oh-four, Andy one-oh-four, do you read?"

Bringing the radio up to his ear, Dillon rogered, listened and frowned. "Com, could you repeat that?"

A brief silence. His frown deepened.

"Com, I think there's been a mix-up," he said. "We're currently with other units at an A-11. Interstate 84 E, Exit Three-Three, south of New Haven. I'm standing by a blue late-model BMW Coupe..."

He stood listening again, fired Rhodes a baffled look, hit Transmit. "Any other details?" Another pause. "Okay, roger—that's positive. We're heading over. I'll notify you when we're on scene."

Rhodes watched as he clipped the radio back onto his belt. "What's going on?" he asked.

"A multivehicle accident," Dillon said. "About ten miles north on I-91 S...outside Hamden. They need additional units."

"Goddamn," Rhodes said. "This is crazy."

"It gets crazier," Dillon said. "Another car went out of control. Can you believe it? At first I thought Dispatch was talking about this accident. Figured they got the location wrong or something."

Rhodes stared at him. "Are you sure they didn't?"

Dillon nodded. "Eyewitness say it accelerated all of a sudden, went into a biker," he said. "Then it was like dominoes with the other vehicles on the road. Same as we've got right here."

Rhodes heard the whoop of a siren as another ambulance left the roadside for the exit.

Dominoes, he thought, hurrying toward their cruiser.

25

New York City
July 27, 2023

I

Special Agent Faye Luna and Special Agent Ron Cobb had been a tandem with the FBI Surveillance and Aviation Section for almost a year, since they first drew the assignment of crewing Little Lulu or Lu-bird, as they nicknamed the section's advanced Boeing 500 NOTAR (no tail rotor) helicopter variant.

Their instant bonding as partners was probably related to their similar backgrounds and career paths. Both were military veterans who attended college on the GI Bill and held US Army B4-ASI Sniper certs along with FBI precision marksmanship qualifications. Both proved naturals at flying on completion of the helicopter pilot course required for hostage/rescue assignments, and were tapped for SAS because of their outstanding proficiency at aerial maneuvers. Both were obsessive about physical fitness, possessed strong competitive streaks, and held a zeal for long-distance running that had led to them to train together, meeting early Sunday mornings for laps around the Central Park reservoir.

They also shared a passionate love of baseball. One Friday night the agents hit a sports bar to watch a game. What happened that night caught them both by surprise, which was almost predictable, considering how much else they shared.

At Luna's Chelsea apartment building, where Cobb normally split off to the subway, their heated debate over an umpire's game-ending call somehow morphed into a fiercely ardent kiss. It lasted all the way through the building lobby, into the elevator, up to her door, and into her apartment.

They had been an item since that night, although neither was ready to use the word *couple*. Because the Bureau discouraged dating between agents in the same section, particularly teammates, Cobb told only his older brother. Luna confided in no one, and wasn't sure if their thing had an expiration date. But however undefined their relationship, they enjoyed it, and wanted to see where it took them.

On the morning of President Fucillo's Zuccotti Park speech, the two jumped out of bed and dressed in a hurry. With the President in town, they were reporting to the Downtown Manhattan Heliport. Little Lulu was one of five whirlybirds CIRG kept on station there—the others being a pair of Blackhawks, a Bell Huey, and a Sikorsky S-92 Search and Rescue chopper—and they had to be ready for deployment at a moment's notice.

The agents had no reason to think it would be necessary. In New York, as in most major cities, any visit from a high-profile dignitary triggered an elevated security alert, and it was raised to a maximum when the dignitary was POTUS. Putting the SAS's local task force on standby was standard procedure, and Luna and Cobb had been through the drill several times without going airborne.

Still, they took nothing for granted. They were a hyperelite team and conducted themselves like one. When called upon to report early, they showed up earlier than early. Their selection as Lu-bird's exclusive flyers did not come on a whim.

The tiny ovoid chopper needed to be handled with care. Her stealth modifications were shared by a small fleet of CIA and military aircraft, but she alone carried an integrated multiple-biometric high-definition surveillance and targeting suite, or MBHD/ST. Before training in the black tech's use—or even learning of its existence—the agents had required Sensitive Compartmented Information clearances that rose above and beyond the Top Secret clearance required of all FBI personnel.

Luna and Cobb were proud to crew the prototypical aircraft, considering it a mark of honor—the best entrusted to the best. They flew countless training runs to stay sharp, but knew that if they ever took her out in an operational role, it would mean they were dealing with a crisis of the gravest order.

Luna got the radio call from Chief Hardin at CIRG's Washington office, where the power had not yet so much as flickered. Along with other FBI pilots waiting in reserve, they had intermittently left their lounge at the terminal to stand with the police teams looking upriver at the burning helicopter suspended from the bridge. Because the chopper was based in Midtown, the Bureau flyers weren't certain they were acquainted with its crew. But that made no difference as they joined in prayer with the NYPD boys.

Hardin's instructions to Luna were terse. She and Cobb were to launch immediately and place themselves at the disposal of New York Cyber, who would apprise them of their specific mission over the ComNet.

Lu-bird was in her circle on the pier. Luna's higher score in situational adaptivity tests had earned her the pilot's seat, and Cobb was comfortable with sidekicking, secure in his ability to execute her orders with precision.

In the cockpit, they donned their lightweight HUD helmets, ran through the checks, and got Lulu warming. With the wind blowing in a northerly direction, the smoke from the NYPD helicopter wasn't too bad. But their FLIR guidance systems would allow them to cruise through black ink.

The bird was ready in three minutes. Outside on the rubber, the rest of the pilots watched. Grabbing the cyclic, Luna reached a hand out to Cobb, keeping it low between their seats so no one outside would see.

"You ready, sugar?" she said.

"Let's do this," he said, giving her fingers a discreet squeeze before takeoff.

II

Sweaty and winded, Leo Harris stood on Broadway opposite St. Paul's Chapel, watching a river of humanity being channeled uptown toward a series of evac points. Leo saw no end to the masses, and was looking at sheer mayhem up past City Hall Park, where thousands of people at the barricades were trickling through.

He pushed and weaved his way up the street. Blue Suit was gone. He could have easily melted into the crowd, disappeared. *So, what now?*

Harris tried to figure out his next move. After inputting Blue Suit's ID photo to the NGI database, he had ordered face scans of anyone at the checkpoints that generally matched his description, knowing that nine out of ten businessmen from the office buildings down here would fit the general mold. Also, the regular cops at those posts would have serious manpower issues trying to carry out his order. They weren't equipped with satphones or satellite-linked readers that would work with the terrestrial cell net out of commission, leaving the spot scans to a relative handful of FBI and NYPD Special Operations personnel and adding to logjams at the checkpoints. The odds of actually catching his man weren't good.

He was standing flat-footed, pulling together his thoughts, when he heard the chop of helicopter rotors overhead. *Lulu*, he thought, squinting up into the sky. The stealthy little copter's egg-like shape and fainter-than-normal noise profile would have been distinctive even if she wasn't the only aircraft cleared for flight.

One hand shielding his eyes, he opened the assigned channel on his two-way and identified himself.

"Roger, sir, we've expected your contact," a female voice replied. "This is Agent Luna."

"Agent, did you upload that badge photo I found into your onboard?" he asked, getting right to it.

"Yes, sir. John Rainey. There were no AIFIS/NGI matches."

Harris wasn't surprised. Whoever had planned the Zuccotti strike had been too smart to use someone whose face was on the FBI's biometric database. "Can you do a comparison with that picture? If your cameras pick him up?"

"Sir," said a male voice. "This is Agent Cobb. I'm the spotter. We plan to do parallel track sweeps. South-north, river to river. We're presently over—"

"I can see you without straining my neck," Harris said, watching the bird shoot closer. "Is it yes or no on the comps?"

The spotter paused. "We should be able to generate composite images of the crowd and compare their face landmarks to the ID photo."

"Why 'should'?'"

"A second-gen, 2D image isn't great. Low-def, blurry…we'll cross our fingers."

Harris angled his head back, saw the helicopter directly above him. He had a thought. "Musil, you read me?"

Nothing but static in his earbud. His scowl deepening, Harris turned the corner and hurried downtown against the flow of men and women on Broadway. He might not know Blue Suit's whereabouts, but wanted to check on Alex's. Zuccotti was just a few blocks south.

"Musil, I repeat, do you read…?"

"Here, sir, yes. Sorry. I'm having difficulties with—"

"Listen up," Harris cut in. "There were news cameras at the

park when the shit hit the fan. Figure some got shots of the guy who left the bomb. I want the video."

"Yes, sir. We can request—

"I want it *now*." Leo glanced up at the sky, saw Lulu making her way west toward the Hudson. "Cobb, you with us?"

"Roger."

"The video caps…what'll they do for your chances of a positive match?"

"They're gold if you can get them to us right away, sir."

Leo grunted. That was a big if with electricity and telecom down in the area.

He was now within a block of Liberty. Smoke from the explosions hung over everything. Up ahead were the police barricades, emergency and tac vehicles parked behind them. The elite units had secondary power sources and satellite links, and the National Guard would bring in field generators besides. But fishing for internet videos was a crapshoot. The news trucks might or might not have working generators, and their cameramen wouldn't have brought a huge supply of backup batteries.

So, what then? If the mobile studios were already dark, it meant the video equipment and technicians would have to run over to law-enforcement vehicles to get the job done…assuming they had juice to spare. What were his agents supposed to do when the batteries in their two-ways, satphones, and bioreaders ran dry? Stand in line waiting for recharges? And that would still leave them better off than the regular NYPD cops strung along the barricades. With their cells knocked out, and no satellite phones, how were they supposed to communicate?

Fucillo's speech had been right on the money. Nobody was prepared. Nobody had planned for this sort of thing. And the bad guys knew it.

"Musil, where are you?" he asked the agent.

"The City Hall Park checkpoint, sir…"

"Fahey?"

"Church Street," said the other agent. "The west checkpoint."

"All right, keep your eyes open. You see camera crews, tell them what we need. I'll shake loose what I can at Zuccotti." Leo took a deep breath and tasted ash and melted rubber. He would need his particulate mask here. "You get hold of anything, be ready to beam it up to the chopper."

"Sir?" This was Luna in his earpiece now. "Can I interject?"

"I'm listening."

"We've got an active satellite link to headquarters. It ought to be unhackable. Long as your men keep an open channel with us, whatever images of the bomber they get—or *we* get—can be analyzed and shared in real time."

Harris had reached the corner of Liberty and was back to flashing his ID, the uniformed personnel at the barricade parting in front of him.

"Eye in the sky, huh?" he said into the phone.

"And wherever else we can put one," Luna said.

III

Anton Ciobanu moved north with the vast human herd on Church Street. Rising high to his left was the Millennium Hilton; on his right, just ahead, he saw the 9/11 Memorial. Beyond it, the swarm of evacuees thickened near a constellation of red-and-yellow lights. *Law-enforcement vehicles.*

Fatigued from the chase, Ciobanu willed himself to keep his breathing steady. He needed to blend in.

Noticing a man in a green doorman's blazer close by, he instinctively softened the predacious look in his eyes. He wanted information, and doormen were always good sources.

"Looks like a mess," he said, and nodded toward the walkers gathering at the lights. "What do you think is going on?"

The doorman looked at him. "They're stopping everyone at the barricades. Then letting people through a few at a time."

"Really? Why?"

"Not sure. I heard they got scanners or something."

Ciobanu supposed they might be explosive trace detectors,

but he doubted it. Their sensors ranged to a distance of ten meters and would scan large areas in one sweep. That wouldn't appreciably slow the people passing through the barricades. Nor would it serve the purposes of the guards. Their focus would have shifted from finding somebody with a concealed explosive to finding the person who successfully *detonated* one.

More likely the units were biometric readers. Exactly the sort of devices that *had* to be utilized for spot checks at the crossing.

"I guess we're all stuck with this situation," Ciobanu said, approximating the doorman's fatalistic tone.

"You got it." A nod toward the towering hotel to their left. "That's where I work. Guests are already emptied out."

Ciobanu looked. Overburdened with luggage and garment bags, the confused, displaced guests milled around a small crowded side courtyard.

He brought his eyes to rest on a woman with a stroller. There was an infant inside it, a young boy of perhaps six or seven holding its frame. As Ciobanu watched, the woman bent to lift the crying baby out of the stroller. She grabbed a diaper bag off its handle, then turned and laid the baby on a cushioned pad she set on one of the planters.

An odd, flat expression on his face, the little boy stared vaguely into the crowd, let go of the carriage, and then wandered off a few paces.

Ciobanu noticed the words printed on the front of his T-shirt. They read:

SHINING A LIGHT
ON
AUTISM
The SunBright Children's Foundation

"I feel for those people," the doorman said. "Don't know how long they're gonna be stuck there, or where they're supposed to go."

Ciobanu kept the hawk out of his eyes.

"Actually," he said, "I'm picking someone up."

"Oh." The doorman looked surprised. "Want me to help find the person?"

Ciobanu shaped a smile. "You already have," he said.

IV

The baby girl bawled the entire time they were making their way downstairs to the hotel courtyard. It was easy for Doreen Morgan to see why.

Olivia was wet even before the alarms sounded inside the Millennium and everyone was told to evacuate—which for Doreen, Olivia, and Cody entailed descending fifteen long stories in an un-air-conditioned emergency stairwell.

Cody handled everything okay considering the frenzy, although he stopped talking by the time they reached the stairs. He was normally pretty verbal. But when the loud, shrill racket of the alarms started to overwhelm him, he simply clammed up.

That part did not overly concern Doreen. When unexpected things happened to make him feel stressed or afraid, Cody's first reaction was to go silent...though like many kids on the spectrum, he sometimes melted down after a while, as if all the inexpressible thoughts and emotions bottled inside him were brewing free at once. The deeper the silence, the more severe the outburst. Doreen hoped he didn't completely slip into his own world, because that could be the calm before the storm. But so far, he appeared to be staying with her.

Cody's heart was a greater worry. The SunBright Foundation had flown him to New York a full week ahead of his surgery for a flurry of sightseeing excursions. God bless them, they wouldn't have done it if he weren't facing a life-threatening situation. His mitral valve had almost stopped functioning and needed to be replaced.

Glancing back over her shoulder, Doreen saw him standing

by the stroller a few feet behind her. He had let go of the carriage's frame.

"Cody!" She made a gripping motion with her hand. "What did I tell you to do?"

The boy took hold of the stroller again, withdrawn but responsive.

Taking the wipes out of her diaper bag, Doreen quickly cleaned Olivia up, got her back in her sun dress, and lifted her in both arms. Then she turned back to where she'd left the stroller.

Her expression abruptly became confused. The stroller was standing there by itself. Cody—where was he?

Her eyes darted around the courtyard.

Where was he?

Holding Olivia to her breast, she rushed over to the stroller in a panic, searching for him in the crowd without success.

"Cody!"

Faces turned in her direction.

"Has anyone seen my son…a little boy? *Anyone?*"

No one answered.

"Cody… Cody where are you?" Doreen was screaming now, drawing glances. *"Cody!"*

"We better call the police, ma'am," said a man nearby.

He took his cell from his pocket on impulse—and then gave Doreen a look of cold apprehension. The phone was dead. There had been no cellular service since the bombing.

Without another word, he pushed off into the crowd to find a police officer.

V

Ciobanu, holding the boy's hand, left the Millennium's courtyard and moved east with the swarm of people heading toward Broadway.

The snatch was clean and easy.

"Hi, I'm with the SunBright Foundation," Ciobanu had said

with a smile, reading the lettering on the boy's tee. "We're going to have fun today. But we have to hurry."

The boy had looked at Ciobanu vaguely.

"My name is Fred," Ciobanu told him. "What's yours?"

No answer. Nor did the boy say anything when they left the courtyard. But he went along calmly as they melted into the crowd.

Now Ciobanu turned onto Broadway. There could be no better disguise than the boy to help him avoid a spot check. His hunters were not seeking a man with an autistic child.

"We'll be at our place soon," he said, bowing his head so the boy could hear him above the commotion.

The child brushed his face with a flat, withdrawn glance and kept walking.

Ciobanu narrowed his eyes on the checkpoint, moving toward it as quickly as possible.

VI

It was almost ten thirty in the morning when Harris returned to the smoke-enshrouded devastation outside Zuccotti Park. With uninjured civilians moved off on foot, and those in need of urgent care sped to triage centers, only a few people with minor wounds were still getting first aid on the street. But there were official personnel milling around everywhere.

Leo edged up to sawhorses and yellow tape outside the park, displaying his creds to the cops in riot gear guarding its perimeter. As they moved the barricade to let him through, he looked around at the regular and special ops police, plainclothes detectives, Secret Service agents, firefighters, and medical rescue workers hurrying past him, trying to figure out who was in control of the scene. He only knew that it wasn't him.

"Harris."

He turned toward the voice, realized it belonged to the Secret Service advance man who had arrived from DC a few days before. What was his name? *Opposite of night.*

"Day."

The agent nodded. "Hell of a thing we have here," he said.

Harris looked at him. "You running the show?"

"I'm with the President's protection detail. It's my responsibility to assume site command in the present situation." Day stood with his shoulders straight. "Where have you been?"

"I was on the comnet. You ought to know."

"I know you went off after a suspect prior to the second explosion." Day was staring him. "Thanks to radio trunking I know he shot a woman to death. And I know you lost him." He paused. "Your people didn't exactly loop me in."

Harris ignored his remark. "How's the President doing?"

"She's stable."

"And the people on that stage with her?"

"Governor Bender is dead," Day said. "Two of his aides were also killed. At last word, several others were in critical condition."

Harris braced himself. "What about Professor Michaels?"

"The EMTs brought him to the triage in an emergency vehicle. He was unconscious and didn't appear in great shape. But he was alive." Day shrugged. "If the professor makes it, he might owe his life to a police sniper. Chalk it up to the benefits of cooperation."

Harris took the bait. "What the hell do you mean?"

"Alex was down on the sidewalk." Day pointed at the spot. "His guard dog wasn't letting anyone close to him...he would have bled to death if it wasn't taken out." He nodded toward a black Chevy Suburban. "They needed three men to lift the animal inside. I think the tac who did the job is still somewhere around."

Harris turned toward the Suburban, thinking the dog should be the last thing on his mind. But the prof had loved the animal. He wanted to be sure the remains weren't lost or mishandled.

He walked past the front of the vehicle, saw no one in the driver's seat, then went around to the heavily tinted back window and peered into its cargo section. He could make out the huge form of the dog stretched lengthwise on the floor. An ESU cop squatted next to her, his helmet balanced on his lap. There was an M25 rifle on the floor mat at his feet.

Leo held up his ID and rapped on the window. After a moment the sniper raised the hatch for him,

"Sir," he said. "I'm Sergeant Wilkerson."

Leo grunted in acknowledgment. His eyes widened as he saw her ribs rise and fall.

"She's *alive*?" Harris looked at the ESU, then at the weapon alongside his foot. "What did you hit her with? That's no trank gun." Wilkerson unslung a second rifle from behind his back. "This one is, sir. A Marlin capture gun," he said. "My orders were to kill and then they weren't. Unit command says the hold came directly from Artemis."

"President *Fucillo*?"

"That's my understanding, sir."

Harris felt a weight lift from his chest. "Give me some room. I want to check her out."

The ESU moved aside to let him climb into the vehicle. Shuffling up to the dog's head, Leo noticed she was muzzled, and that her large brown eyes were open but glazed. As he knelt over her for a closer look, her forelegs twitched slightly.

"I hit her with acepromazine," Wilkinson said. "A heavy dose."

Leo glanced up at him. "They use that shit on *horses*."

"Yes, sir. But it was either that or a bullet." Wilkerson gave him a direct look. "We needed to put her under fast and get the professor to an aid station."

Harris lowered his eyes back to the dog and then put his hand on her side, feeling her muscles tense under his fingers. She made a sound deep in her chest—a kind of rumbling growl.

"She's coming around," Wilkerson said. "But she'll be groggy awhile."

Leo kept a hand on her flank, recalling the Hebrew command Alex had used to calm her.

"*Be 'Seder,*" he said quietly. "Remember me, Julia? I'm your dad's pal." He thought her body relaxed a little. "Bet you're thirsty as hell."

Harris began unbuckling the muzzle's leather strap behind her head.

Wilkerson hesitated. "Sir, that's a powerful animal. If she clamps those jaws down on y—"

"Don't worry about it." Leo crossed his fingers. "Me and the mutt are tight."

He finished slipping off the muzzle, set it down, and waited some more. Julia started a little, rolled her copper-colored eyes onto his face, and tossed her head, the rise and fall of her chest quickening.

Harris gently stroked her side until he felt her settle down. *"Be 'Seder,"* he said. "Everything's okay."

He reached into his pocket for his half-full water bottle, cupped his hand, poured some water into it, and lowered it in front of Julia's snout.

"Go on," Leo said. "Take a drink."

She regarded him sluggishly another moment, licked her lips, and then lapped at the water in his palm. He angled the bottle, poured more onto his hand. Then a little more.

"Good girl. Good girl…"

Julia kept lapping up water. She licked her lips and nose several times, huffed out a warm, tapering breath, then dropped her head onto the floor, falling under the tranquilizer's effects again.

"She's gonna be all right," Harris said. He looked around at Wilkerson, one soothing hand on the dog's side. "I'll put the muzzle back on now—"

He heard a voice in his earbud and abruptly fell silent, realizing it had slipped out of position.

"…sir, can you read me?"

He adjusted the bud with a fingertip. "What is it, Ki?"

"Sir, there you are, good." The ASAC's tone was urgent. "I'm hearing from the triage area at One Police Plaza. You're being asked to report there immediately—"

"Wait a minute," Harris said. "Who's asking?"

"Sorry, sir, you must not have heard me," Ki said. "The request's from POTUS herself."

26

I

Carol Morse kept an LED photo frame on her desk at Langley, its memory loaded with family pictures. But she had a second photo frame that was hers alone to see. One she shared with no one on earth. This one existed not in physical space, but in her mind's eye.

She had been Mrs. Leo Harris for over a decade, and carried a great number of pictures of him—of the two of them as a couple—in her memory. Carol loved her husband dearly, but Leo was Leo. She didn't have a word, or phrase, for what he meant to her...or if she did, she resisted using it, even in her secret thoughts.

All Carol did know right now was that she was very concerned about him.

In the two-plus hours since the Zuccotti/Liberty Plaza bombings, she had hastily queried her people in the field for available intel, and left two unanswered voice mails on Leo's cell. Back from the assistant director's office after the briefing, she took a quick break from data bagging, received a call from Carmody in Romania, left a third voice mail for Leo, and then wound up staring worriedly at the wall across from her.

It had come as a tremendous relief to find out Annemarie was safe. Now she was hoping Leo would return her calls, so she would know he was likewise okay.

When her direct phone line rang at twelve fifteen, she almost lunged for the receiver.

"Yes?"

"Carol, it's…"

"My God, I was just thinking about you," Carol blurted. "You must be psychic."

"That would make my job a whole lot easier, wouldn't it?"

Carol smiled soberly. She had known Annemarie Fucillo since her time at the State Department, when both their careers were on the rise. Annemarie hadn't needed extrasensory abilities to become who she was today. She did it with heart, brains, and plenty of brass.

"I don't need to read minds to know you're worried," Fucillo said now. "I would be if our situations were reversed."

Carol exhaled.

"Until a little while ago, I only knew you survived the blast," she said. "My reports were all over the place on how badly hurt you might be."

Fucillo was quiet a moment.

"The governor was killed," she said. "Along with one of his assistants. They were onstage with us."

"I know…"

"And those people in that building across the street. I saw it explode, Carol. I saw their faces disappear in the flames and smoke. They were lined up at the windows to see me…and then they were gone."

Carol held the receiver. "I'm sorry, Anne. I... I don't know what to say."

"You listening is enough," Fucillo said. "It was true when I lost my son. Just you listening. Because for the rest...for everyone else... I have to be strong."

Silence.

"I'm your friend," Carol said. "Proud of it, prouder of you."

"You know," Fucillo said, "there's a political slogan in that somewhere."

"Use it and you're springing for dinner next time."

Fucillo chuckled and was briefly silent.

"Carol, I barely have a minute. There are a thousand things waiting for me. But I want you to know that I would not be alive if not for your ex."

"*Leo?*"

"Is there another you haven't informed me about?"

Carol laughed a little giddily, relief swelling up inside her. "I've been trying to call him. To see how he's doing. I knew he would be near the stage..."

"He spotted the bomber right before he dropped the IED, and then warned my Secret Service detail in time for them to get most of us safe. Then, I'm told, he somehow obtained the bomber's identification," Fucillo said. "You could not have been more right about him."

Carol was thinking that if Leo ever found out she had lobbied POTUS to tap him for Net Force, he would be livid.

"I wish the circumstances were different," she said. "But, yes, he's the goods."

"And the person I'm going to need moving forward."

"Yes," Carol said. "I believe so."

"For this, dear friend, I owe you more than dinner," Fucillo said then. "Leo's on his way to meet me... I won't tell him we spoke. Stay strong. We'll talk later."

Carol held the phone for several seconds after Annemarie clicked off, her mind drifting back to her imaginary photo album.

Leo was all right.

Thank Heaven, she thought.

About that, she could not have been happier.

II

For nurse Sharon Bennett, what was happening at Shelstrom Medical seemed worse than any nightmare.

It was shortly after nine thirty in the morning when the lights and air-conditioners were knocked out, the elevators simultaneously stopped, and the computers and medical equipment shut down across the board. Operating rooms and intensive care units lost electricity, their dedicated backups inexplicably failing to kick in. In the ICUs and step-down wards, mechanical ventilators, dialysis machines, and feeding pumps all ceased to function.

At first, Sharon could barely credit it. Then she heard the first shouted alert in the hallway. It was intended to be broadcast over the public address system, but the PA system had died as well: *"Code Purple, Code Purple, Code Purple..."*

The hospital should not have gone dark. As head of pre-op nursing, Sharon was thoroughly versed in the emergency system specs, and knew power was supposed to be restored to most of the building within a minute—less for areas on the critical energy bus. She couldn't understand how the backup generators failed.

Slammed with the inescapable reality of the situation, she had rushed to the beds of life support patients with dozens of other nurses and aides. A compact, full-figured woman of thirty-eight with dark skin, tightly braided black hair, and large, attentive brown eyes, Sharon was no stranger to working under pressure.

Carrying manual resuscitators and battery defibrillators, they bagged the patients at once, disconnecting their breathing tubes and slapping ventilator masks over their noses and mouths. There were forty-seven patients at the center on full life support, and several were lost almost immediately, going into cardiac and respiratory arrest. Fearing most would die unless power was quickly restored, Sharon tried dialing 911 on her cell to report what was happening—but the phone wasn't working.

She had put the useless cell phone back in her pocket, and rushed five flights up to the administrator-on-call's office using the emergency stairs. The air in the hallway and stairwell was stifling, and she realized the heat would soon be a grave problem.

Sharon had pushed through a set of double doors into the administrative wing and found the AOC's doorway filled with almost a dozen other members of the decision team—fellow nurses, physicians, security people, EMS staffers, and heads of the hospital's managerial and administrative departments. The AOC, a gray-haired man named Weatherfield, stood in front of his desk motioning for them to gather around him.

Their meeting took under four minutes. The overriding imperative was to keep the hospital open. They could provide triage services and shelter to the community even without power. But the increasing heat and inability to provide basic life support made it necessary to attempt getting the most critically ill patients to facilities outside the city. Weatherfield had already put in a call to the Office of Emergency Management for a medevac exception to the city's no-fly rule. He also spoke to the fire department about sending ambulances to bolster the hospital's fleet, but was advised that it would be difficult with so many committed to Zuccotti and Liberty Plaza.

Frank Morales, the chief of EMS operations, offered a solution. He had already tried getting hold of a large, mass-casualty ambulance. One was trying to make its way down from Connecticut, but conditions on the highways were supposedly worse than those on the local streets.

"A dispatcher in Hartford told me about car collisions...a plane burning on I-84," Morales said. "But I think we can trick out an eighteen-wheel rig. There's a truck depot just east of here. If we can anchor our cots and IVs so they don't roll around the trailer, we're good."

Weatherfield had agreed it was worth a shot. "Prepare the

most urgent cases for transfers—pediatrics—first," he said, looking around the room. "Questions?"

There weren't any. Everyone knew the job ahead would be staggeringly difficult.

As the meeting adjourned, Sharon had headed straight for the stairwell.

That was when the cell phone rang in her scrub jacket. *How could it be working?* Somehow, its tower must have come back online. Its caller ID showed Ki's name.

"Ki... I'm on my way to check on Mark," she said. "Can you hear me?"

She would never know. Her friend's words were garbled and broken.

Within seconds, the phone cut out again. She tried dialing Ki back, got a Call Failed notification, and then was back to descending the fire stairs. There were other staffers on them with her, doctors, nurses, orderlies, and volunteers clambering in both directions, lugging medical supplies, fold-up gurneys, water cooler bottles, all sorts of things. It seemed several degrees warmer than before.

The neuro operating room was on the third floor. She ran along the windowless corridor leading toward its entryway, dim without functional overhead lights...

And then suddenly there *was* light. Streaming through the vertical glass panel in the middle of the swinging door. Sharon pushed through, and noticed that the OR's ceiling fluorescents were out, the room dark beyond a small pool of brilliance around the operating table. The light was all radiating from there.

She squinted into the glare. A group of doctors, nurses, and technicians were assembled around the neurosurgical operating table, with its real-time MRI, and surrounding thicket of flatscreen monitors. Some shone handheld spotlights on the table.

Sharon moved in from the door, stepping gingerly over some heavy-duty electrical cables coiled on the floor like tangled vines. She saw the scrub room behind a second door to her right, a collection of anesthesia machines, spare monitors, and other standing units to her left. She recognized a portable generator of the type she'd mentioned to Ki. A multiple outlet power strip was attached to it, the snarled cords underfoot running to the operating table. They were feeding power to the lights, MRI machine, and computers.

Sharon could discern little else with the blinding brightness in her face. But as she continued deeper into the room, leaving the noisy, humming generator behind, she heard tense voices around the operating table. It made her uneasy.

She hurried forward. Half an hour ago, the technicians were seated at their computers, preparing for surgery. Now they had vacated their stations to assist the doctors around the table.

But Sharon knew they shouldn't have budged, not with the generator providing current to the room. Their monitors were meant to show images of Mark's brain anatomy, revealing his tumor from different angles, helping the surgeon navigate. Once upon a time Mark's tumor would have been inoperable. That was still true without the precision mapping images. *Why had the techs abandoned their stations?*

Sharon glanced up the monitors hanging from the ceiling— and froze where she stood.

They were, in fact, lit up. But there were no images on them. Only words, their black block letters drifting against a plain white background…

GOD IS NOT

WILLING

TO

DO

EVERYTHING

Sharon's first bewildered thought was that she was imagining what she saw on those screens. But a piercing electronic whine from deeper inside the room snapped her from her stunned paralysis. She propelled herself toward the operating table, drawing the attention of one of the nurses around it, the nurse turning to face her, the two looking at each other over their surgical masks.

Sharon had known Laila Iram for years. Now she faced her in silence as the sound of the charging defibrillator gained intensity like shrill feedback.

After a second she heard the slam of the discharging paddles and looked toward the table. She glanced between the gathered OR personnel to see Mark's body arch convulsively from the high-voltage flow of electricity into his heart.

The surgeon leaned over Mark with his stethoscope. *"Again, up five joules!"*

The whine again, then the slam of current pouring into Mark's chest.

Sharon waited tensely.

"Nothing, damn it." Grim acceptance creeping into the surgeon's voice. "Once more—another five..."

Sharon started forward to get closer to the table. But Laila's gloved hand took hold of her arm.

"Give them room to work," she said.

She nodded, took a breath.

More waiting. The wait stretched on much too long.

Sharon felt the bottom drop from her stomach even before the surgeon spoke again.

"Okay...that's enough," he said. "We lost him."

Laila relaxed her grip on her arm.

"I'm sorry," she said.

Sharon started to nod, but her head seemed too heavy to lift, and sank until it was resting on Laila's shoulder.

Seasoned nurse that she was, it took her a moment to recognize the sobs she heard as her own.

III

NYPD Officer Alberto Santini was among a dozen or so cops hurriedly shifted from Zuccotti to Checkpoint Broadway, where the guard detail was in urgent need of reinforcement. As they pushed toward the barricades, the evacuees numbered almost twenty abreast, mobbing the traffic lanes from one side to the other.

Santini was at the checkpoint maybe five minutes, when he heard a child's high, screeching cries in the crowd. Craning his head, he spotted a man with a young boy. He was having a hard time, trying to hold on to the boy's hand while he threw a full-fledged tantrum—kicking, thrashing, making a huge fuss.

After moment, Santini noticed the boy's T-shirt. It said:

SHINING A LIGHT
ON
AUTISM
The SunBright Children's Foundation

"That kid's in a bad state," said one of the black-clad special operations cops beside him. He gestured at the crowd on the other side of the sawhorse.

Santini nodded. "Wonder if we should help?" he said.

The cop thought a second. "Let's move them to the front," he said. "I'll hold up the line. You escort 'em through."

Santini nodded again. The kid and his dad were stalled in the densely packed throng of evacuees.

"Here goes nothing," he said, plunging into the crowd.

27

New York City
July 27, 2023

I

"Faye, hold up." Cobb peered through Lu-bird's canopy, motioning toward a disturbance outside Checkpoint Broadway. "It's probably nothing. But I want to see what's going on."

She nodded, working the sticks to put them in a stationary hover. "Maintaining altitude," she said. "We don't want to panic the crowd."

Cobb kept his eyes turned toward the ground as she stabilized their chopper above the rooftops. What he saw below was, in fact, none of their concern. Just a kid giving his dad a hard time outside the checkpoint and a sympathetic cop coming to the rescue—

Cobb's brow suddenly furrowed, his gaze settling on the father. His face...

Could it be? What were the odds?

He looked down at him another moment. His face resembled the one in Harris's ID badge photo. No question about it, screw the odds.

Magnifying the scene on his HD heads-up display, Cobb read the lettering on the kid's shirt and immediately realized why the cop was getting involved. The boy was autistic. Meaning he wasn't having a bratty conniption, but a severe behavioral episode. But what would his man be doing with him—if it was *really* his man?

Cobb trained his FR/Bio sensors on his face and snapped off a series of digital photos for analytic comparison. Lulu's onboard unit would map the face in the photo, extract its landmarks, then handshake with the FBI's biometric database via satellite link. Not only would it seek a match with the ID photo, but with the rest of the fifty million faceprints in the database.

It would take less than five seconds for the system to decide whether it had a positive. Cobb didn't wait that long to alert somebody on the ground.

II

Agent Jot Musil stood fifty or sixty yards behind the Broadway checkpoint, watching the crowd move past through his FR/Bio sunglasses, holding their mobile scanner/control unit in his right hand. The bridges and tunnels out of Manhattan were closed, the ferries shut down, the downtown subways halted due to power outages. All the evacuees could do was follow the basic instructions issued by civil authorities. *Leave the dark zone. Walk north.*

There was nothing else to tell the people.

Musil remained on the alert for anyone matching the Zuccotti bomber's description. The crowd would be his best disguise. Brown haired, Caucasian, light-colored shirt, blue dress trousers…the man was like a drop of water in the ocean.

"Excuse me, Agent. Someone's asking for you."

Jot turned toward the sound of the voice and saw a cop from one of the ad hoc crowd control details approaching from the left, where a row of news vans were parked outside City Hall. With him was a short, heavyset man with a leather messenger bag slung over his shoulder.

Musil recognized him as a video editor named Lang. Acting on the SAC's orders, he had stopped at the news truck to request footage from Zuccotti and found Lang eager to cooperate—with the stipulation that he would need a green light from station management.

"Mr. Lang." He waved him closer. "How did it go?"

The man's uncomfortable expression said it all. "I spoke to our vice president on the satphone." He paused. "He says he can't turn over the video without knowing why you want it."

Musil regarded him calmly. "Did you tell him it was requested by the FBI?"

"Yes."

"Then he must appreciate the urgency of this matter," Musil said. "We won't know if the footage we need exists until we review the video."

The editor gave a commiserative nod.

"He gets it. But he feels it's bad legal precedent for us to supply video to law enforcement without a court order."

"The courthouses have been emptied out," Musil said. "We have no way to obtain a subpoena."

Lang nodded again. "The vice president makes the call. I'm just telling you what he expects."

Lang slipped the messenger bag off his shoulder and stepped forward, holding the bag between himself and the agent. "Wouldn't you know it, though... I downloaded the fifteen, twenty minutes of footage you wanted onto an external drive. Just *in case* the execs agreed to share it. Then I put it aside for a sec, and with all the craziness going on, I got distracted and lost the thing."

Musil let the man's words sink in. Then he took the bag from him, strapping it over his own arm.

"I'm sure it will turn up," he said gratefully. "Thank you, sir—"

"Agent Musil, do you read? It's Cobb."

Musil broke away, adjusting his earpiece.

"Yes, I hear you, over."

"We have you at five-oh yards north of the checkpoint. Is that accurate?"

"Yes."

"Can you see the barricade from your position?"

Musil craned his head to look past Lang. The crowd had thickened about a block south of them. "What's happening over there?"

"Probably nothing. A guy with a kid that's acting up. He resembles the one in the credentials, but so do a million other guys."

Musil drifted away from the video man for a better look. "Did you run his facials?"

"Yes, and we're getting a negative. But the ID badge sample's so low-res, it might be worth an eyeball."

Musil walked toward the barricade. "Do you have a photo capture?"

"Affirmative," Cobb replied. "Relayed it to you and the SAC. If he verifies it's the same man, we'll extract a new template, mark him as our suspect..."

Musil picked up his pace, tapping his scanner to download Cobb's image. It appeared at the upper corner of his lenses.

"Stay with me, "he said. "I'm heading over to the checkpoint."

III

"Sir? Is the boy all right?"

Aware of the helicopter overhead, Ciobanu read the name tag above the cop's badge. Santini. He had come through the barrier and cleared a small spot around him of evacuees.

"Yes, thank you," he said, clasping the child's hand. "He's having a rough time."

The officer squatted to look into the boy's face. "Hi there," he said. "How about I walk you and your dad up the street?"

The boy stood there wailing uncontrollably. Ciobanu thought the loud voices, sirens, and flashing ambulance lights must have set him off. Whatever the trigger, he was convinced his father charade would get him through the checkpoint. If he could reach the other side, he would release the boy and lose himself among the masses.

Ciobanu knew how to hide in the open, seen and unseen, invisible to pursuers and prey alike. He knew because his life so often depended on it.

He carefully watched the police officer rise from his crouch. Though he was steps away from freedom, he would take nothing for granted.

"Wish I could have that bird up there fly you and your son out of this stew." The officer jabbed his chin up at the little helicopter casting an oval shadow over the crowd. "But I can hustle you through the barricades."

Ciobanu shot a quick glance skyward. His understanding was that even the police and FBI fleets would be vulnerable to the cyberstrike. What was the aircraft doing in flight? Why was it hovering overhead?

He felt a tingle of unease. The chameleon survived because it was adaptive. Instinct told it when to climb, run, or change colors.

Ciobanu trusted his instincts.

"Officer, my son needs something to calm him," he said. "I left his iPad in my office...it's a half block south."

Santini shook his head. "I'm sorry. I can't allow—"

"Please. He's having a meltdown."

The cop glanced down at the boy, his eyes lingering on his face.

"I could have my head handed to me for this," he said. "Go on. Get your son's iPad. But then I want you on your way."

Ciobanu summoned an expression of gratitude from his tool kit. "Thank you."

The cop nodded, smiling at the boy.

Ciobanu lifted him off the ground. Overhead, the helicopter remained in a stationary hover. He did not like it.

His kicking, flailing human shield against his side, he turned away from the officer and hurried back downtown.

IV

"Musil." It was Cobb again in the bird. "We've got a problem—"

"Copy that." Musil was now within fifteen yards of the police barricade. "What's going on?"

"The target's about-faced," Cobb said. "Bearing south on Broadway."

Musil jostled toward the barricades, trying to seek him out in the crowd. But there were too many people between them.

"Does he still have the boy?"

"Yes. He's carrying him now. Agent, I'm starting to think he's our man."

Musil quickened his pace. He did not know what his target was doing with the boy. Nor could he even think about it.

Right now he just needed to find him.

V

At the corner of Broadway and Park Row, a half block below the checkpoint, Ciobanu paused with the struggling child in his arms and again glanced up at the helicopter. It had jumped south along with him.

He scanned the thoroughfare for escape routes. City Hall Park was on the east side of the street, no more than three yards to his left. He had scouted its entrances, and one was uptown, past the checkpoint. But the downtown entrance was just around the corner.

He carried the boy toward the park entrance, moving as quickly as possible.

VI

Edgy as they were, the three cops posted at City Hall Park's south entrance felt limp and sluggish from the pummeling heat.

Stationed just blocks from the Zuccotti explosions, they had done little besides stand pat on the sunbaked pavement, wilt away in their uniforms, and wave off anyone who ignored the steel barriers at the entrance. Until now, no one had been clueless enough to try, so the officers were mildly surprised when they saw the guy trot up to the barricade with a boy hoisted in his arms.

"Sir," one of them said. The kid seemed in an awful state, his legs tucked up like he was trying to curl into a ball. "Is he okay?"

"My son needs water," the man said, breathless. He nodded toward the large ornamental fountain and pool down along the park's main walking path. "I thought he could use the fountain."

The cop noticed the writing on the boy's T-shirt. "We can't let anyone in—the groundskeeper's on his way to padlock the gate," he said. "I can radio for an ambulance. Or you can bring him to an aid station."

"Okay, thanks," the man said. The kid twisted against his side. "Can you tell me where to find one?"

One of the other cops gestured east toward the river. "I can show you," he said. "It isn't far—"

The man's right hand flashed behind his back, reappeared gripping the black machine pistol. The officers barely had a second before he opened fire.

The cop motioning up the street was first, a burst to his face taking him down to the pavement. The second and third fell simultaneously in a shower of red, the gun shivering in the killer's hand as bullets tore into their heads and chests.

Ciobanu could not waste a moment. His shots had sent people on the street scattering in all directions. The stampede would be noticed from above, and there was nothing he could do about it. But it would also slow his pursuers, and that was an advantage.

The boy shrieking now, Ciobanu tightened his grip on his waist, went around the barrier, and hurried past the draining bodies of the officers into the park. If he was quick he might still make it to freedom.

VII

"Agent, this is now a Code Red. Do you copy?"

"Affirmative, I'm at the checkpoint." Jot was pausing to display his FBI credentials to the police when a wild commotion erupted opposite City Hall Park, on the downtown side of the barricade. "What can you tell me?"

"Target's at the south entrance. We have gunshots, officers down."

Musil tapped his handset display for the chopper's livestream. It instantly appeared in his glasses. "I'm going after him."

"We need to get you support, Agent—"

Musil was now within a foot of the barricade, the panicked mob on Broadway surging toward it. Several officers were pushing back with their riot shields, fighting to hold the line in the escalating chaos.

"I can't wait," he said. And clipping the FR/Bio handset to his belt, Musil grabbed the top of a sawhorse with one hand, then boosted himself over it into the churning multitude.

VIII

Cobb had taken months to get the hang of the HUD's eye-blink control, and still wasn't altogether comfortable with it—but it was faster and cleaner than jabbing a touchscreen. A long wink to bring up a GPS map, and he saw a fast moving dot—the signal from Musil's FR/Bio reader. "He's turned the corner of Park Row."

"On the bomber's ass," Luna said. "We need to get over to him."

A quick hook to the right as she opened the throttle. Then the lush green patch of City Hall Park was dead ahead.

Cobb blinked his left eye twice to zoom in on the park entrance. He saw a gathering of police on the street, a smaller number of men in dark suits peppered among them. *Secret Service.*

"Update me, Ron."

Overlaying the GPS map on the high-def video, Cobb tracked the dot representing Musil.

"He's already inside the park," he said. "With that fucking maniac."

IX

Musil reached the park with his Glock 22 drawn. He could not afford to wait for backup. The target had blown up a stage on which the President was speaking, killed an innocent woman, shot those officers down in cold blood.

And now he was in the park.

Musil could not help but think of Han Jingrui slipping away from him on the rooftop. Holding the service pistol in a two-handed regulation grip, he jogged through the entrance and found himself on a flagstoned central walk. The park looked deserted. No sign of his quarry.

His eyes darted left and right, taking in the thick foliage bordering the path.

Nothing. No sign.

He took a step forward, another, and then halted again, sweeping the Glock back and forth at full extension. He did not know how the man got hold of the boy. Probably he had abducted him and was using him for cover. But whatever his motive, Musil did not have the slightest doubt that he would kill the child if it suited his ends, murder him as pitilessly as he snuffed out the lives of his other victims.

He would not lose him. Not if it could be helped. *Not this time.*

A second or two passed. Musil remained motionless. He eyed the fountain's square granite pool, filled with two or three feet of water despite its spouts being silent and dry.

Once again scanning the foliage, he grew aware of Lulu's rotors above him.

"Agent, do you read?"

"Roger." His voice was barely above a whisper. "I hear you."

"We have you on GPS. Assistance has reached the scene."

Musil glanced over his shoulder and saw them on the street approaching the entrance—uniformed special forces officers, Secret Service men.

No, he thought. *Not now.* Their competence went without question, but it was unclear how the killer would react to their presence. And he had the boy.

Musil faced front again. Cobb was sending him a thermal of his target. Right side of the pool in the pine hedges. About five yards north.

"Are you in contact with the blacksuits?" he said into the two-way.

"Affirmative. They have satphones."

"Advise them to form a perimeter outside the park. Seal the exits, no gaps."

"Agent, the man is—"

One in the chamber, the hammer cocked, Musil scanned the brush along the path, lining up the thermal imagery and what he saw with his naked eye…

Then he registered the shadows. Trembling on the flagstones over by the pines, quivering in the breezeless air.

There. There.

The target's thermal resembled a ghost. A yellow-orange ghost shimmering behind the blue low-energy emissions of the pine hedges. The child hoisted in one harm, his opposite hand rising…

Musil no sooner saw the weapon than his man pushed through the foliage and opened up on him.

X

Cobb pulled in a breath. Directly below, the murderer he'd been hunting since takeoff emerged from the pines, moving straight toward Musil, his machine pistol spurting fire.

Cobb peered down through the chopper's canopy.

"Faye—I'm getting out my rig."

She looked at him, her eyes steely.

"Do it," she said.

XI

"We have to get backup into the park," Day said. "Right away."

Harris wasn't convinced.

They were speeding from Liberty Street to the President's triage outside 1PP, Harris in the Suburban's back seat, Day in front of him, a second Secret Service man driving. Julia was still tranked out in the cargo section.

Knowing Alex, he would ask to see the dog if he was even halfway conscious.

Leo didn't need biometrics to confirm the guy in the park was their man. Matching them up to Lulu's video cap was the only facial recognition system he needed.

He didn't blame Musil for going after him alone. But the agent was young, and under major scrutiny.

At the same time, Blue Suit couldn't be allowed to escape. He had killed a woman in cold blood, three cops, an unknown number of civilians…and come close to taking out the President. It was a sure thing he would kill more given the chance. Beyond that, he was the best source of information about whoever sent him.

Stopping him was the priority. That screamed for reinforcements.

Day turned halfway around in his seat now. "Say what you need to."

"The park's cordoned off," Harris said. "That killer's not going anywhere. I want to give my agent a shot at doing things his way."

"And why would I go along with this?"

Leo put on his best bluff face. "Your job's to protect the President. The rest is mine."

Day bristled.

"I won't waste time arguing protocols, Agent," he said. "There is no guidebook for this situation."

The SUV turned another corner. The streets here were in lockdown. With President Fucillo triaged at the end of the road, it was like a military control zone.

Day was still looking over his seat at Harris as the vehicle slowed in front of 1PP.

"Okay," he said, resigned. "We'll give your man a window."

XII

Musil reacted to the TI in a heartbeat, scrambling behind the right side of the pool an instant before his man appeared from behind the shrubbery.

Kneeling for cover, he took aim over the fountain's low granite wall. The killer was keeping the boy partly in front of him with one arm, using him for protection as his gun spit out another burst.

The bullets slammed into the wall, ricocheting in different directions.

A second or two passed. Musil remained crouched behind the wall, holding his fire, aware of the helicopter circling overhead, the law-enforcement and White House security personnel assembled at the park entrance...and above all, the man and boy on the other side of the pool.

"Jot, you read me?" A new voice in his earpiece now. But a familiar one. Harris. "Jot—"

"I read you."

"You got this one, kid. I'll hold off the cavalry."

And that was it. The two-way went silent.

Taking another breath, Musil came up a little more behind the wall and saw the killer take a step closer to the pool. His semiautomatic held out in his fist, the man spared a quick look up at the hovering chopper and then leveled his attention at the crouching agent.

Musil held his own weapon steady, watching him...

His eyes dropped to the boy. His face leached of color, he was gasping for air, his scrawny chest heaving under his T-shirt.

Musil thought he almost looked as if he was having a seizure.

"Let him go," he said, peering over the nub of his gunsight. "This won't help you."

The man shrugged. Lifting his weapon, motioning it vaguely behind Musil toward Broadway.

"I think it will," he said. "The boy and I leave together."

Musil was thinking the park's north entrance opened hundreds of yards beyond the checkpoint's barricades, allowing anyone who got through to bypass them. If the killer had scouted the park, he would know it.

But *could* he get through? By now the police guard at that entrance would have been bolstered. Musil doubted he could escape. But he still held the boy.

Jot held his gun steady, the sun beating down on him. He thought about Han Jingrui slipping from his grasp on the sun-baked rooftop. Then he thought about Harris's words to him. His confidence in him.

He gripped his weapon, peering down its barrel. He could aim for the middle of the man's chest. Or his head.

On the other side of the pool, the killer lifted the boy higher against his body.

Heart or head, Musil thought. A clean kill.

Unless the killer raised his captive a mere inch or two in his arms. Or the boy thrashed violently at the last instant. Then *he* might be the one to die.

Musil would not lose him.

Pivoting on his heel, he angled his gun down at the killer's legs and squeezed the trigger of his Glock, catching him in his kneecap. His target instantly started to crumple, the machine pistol stuttering in his hand.

At least one of its rounds found its mark. There was a sudden *whack* on Musil's arm below his shoulder, and he was knocked off his haunches from the impact, falling backward, his head hitting the flagstones. On the opposite side of the fountain, meanwhile, the killer was halfway down, his legs folded underneath him. He was still gripping his machine pistol in one hand, holding his shattered knee with the other.

Musil pushed up on his elbows, trying to rise to his feet. But there would not be enough time. Staring at him across the plaza, the killer started turning his gun toward the boy's head.

XIII

Up in Lulu's cockpit, Cobb did not hesitate. Everyone wanted the murderer alive for interrogation. So did he. But not if it meant losing the kid.

The lightweight synthetic stock of the MK 15 Mod 7 sniper rifle braced against his shoulder, its long barrel balanced on the cross straps of his rig, he fired a single .300 Win Mag into the back of the man's head and watched him go down.

"It's over, Faye," he said. "Fucker's done."

XIV

Somehow back up on his feet, Musil ran around the pool, his gun holstered.

The killer was dead, the crown of his head gone, his clothes splattered with gore and bits of skull tissue. But Musil would not stand gawking at him.

"Medic's on the way." It was Cobb's voice in his earbuds. "So are we. Hang in."

Musil had no time to wait. The boy needed oxygen. His arm throbbing, the sleeve of his sport jacket soaked with blood, he pulled the boy's shirt up almost to his collarbone, pressed the heel of his right hand in the middle of his chest, placed his left hand on top of it, and began his compressions—a hundred a minute, thirty until mouth-to-mouth, *One-two-three, four-five-six...*

Pushing, pushing, but the boy didn't seem to respond. Musil

saw the blue-gray discoloration spreading from his mouth to his cheeks, heard him wheezing, and kept working on him, ignoring his own blood loss and the numbness in his right arm. *Seven-eight-nine push*, grunting with exertion, *ten-eleven-twelve...*

Thirty compressions in, the first CPR cycle complete. The kid was still struggling for air, but Musil thought he wasn't laboring quite as much as before. Tilting his head back, pinching his nose shut to create a seal, he gently tugged down the boy's chin, covered his mouth with his own, and blew into it, a quick expulsion of breath. He checked to see that his chest expanded, shared another breath with him, and then went back to the compressions. *One-two-three, four-five-six, seven-eight-nine...*

Musil was conscious of men running up close. Then a breeze that wasn't a breeze swept over him, cool against his sweaty face, flapping his blazer around his body.

He glanced quickly over his shoulder without interrupting the compression cycle, his eyebrows rising with amazement at a sight unlike anything he'd ever seen: Lulu coming down in the middle of City Hall Park, alighting on a walkway no more than twenty feet wide. The downdraft of her rotors whipped the trees and shrubs bordering the walk.

But Musil could not be distracted. Pressing with his hands, he turned back to the boy and did his second mouth-to-mouth. He felt him relax, glanced at his chest, and saw it rise and fall on its own. He paused, looking down at the boy, praying quietly, waiting to see if he kept breathing...

His chest rose and fell again. *On its own.*

Musil's vision blurred. Even as tears began pouring from his eyes, he began laughing, giddily exultant as uniformed men swarmed over to him, facing the sky and thanking Almighty God for the honor of serving mankind.

Then he heard Cobb's voice again, but it wasn't in his earpiece now, it was coming from the crowd...

"We have the kid," he said. "Everything's gonna be all right."

Musil looked up at his broad, blue-eyed face. "Cobb?"

"You got it, man."

Musil realized fuzzily that the boy wasn't on the ground any-more. Angling his head, he saw men in EMT uniforms wheeling a stretcher off toward the park entrance. An instant later he heard another recognizable voice—SAC Harris's over the two-way.

"Nice, kid. Nice job. I'm proud of you."

Musil grinned.

"Thank you, sir," he said an instant before passing out on the hard, hot concrete flagstones.

28

New York City
July 27, 2023

I

The black Chevy Suburban rocked to a halt at an elevated steel delta barrier and was immediately approached by a pair of National Guardsmen in urban camo and body armor. Sliding down his window, the driver brandished his Secret Service credentials and waited. About half a minute later they lowered the hydraulic barrier and he was waved into the security zone outside One Police Plaza.

Day hopped out of the SUV even as it was easing to a halt. Hurrying around to the rear, he pulled open Harris's door and the SAC joined him in the hot sunlight. A few feet away, The Beast was parked behind a phalanx of uniformed troopers, mounted cops and Secret Service tactical operations agents.

"Come on." Day nodded at the blockish thirteen-story building. "We're expected at once."

Harris peered through the Suburban's tinted rear window. Julia had rolled onto her stomach and drowsily lifted her head.

"My driver will stay with her," Day said. "She'll be fine."

Harris nodded. "Okay, lead the way," he said.

Day sprinted up to the main entrance. "At first the triage was outside the building, but we have to protect our high-profile wounded from becoming targets of another assassination attempt," he told the SAC. "I ordered it moved into the auditorium."

"So that's where they brought the President and Professor Michaels."

"Affirmative for Michaels," Day said. "Artemis is on the second floor."

The NYPD's Real-Time Command Center, Harris thought. "That mean she's okay?"

"It means she's put herself in charge," Day said. "There's a difference. Though I won't advise you to try telling her."

Harris strode along beside him as they passed a group of sub-machine-toting police guards inside the entrance, then turned from the elevator banks toward the auditorium. He had visited 1PP often enough to find the hall blindfolded. He and Day showed their ID badges and went in.

The room was circular, the walls on either side paneled in wood, the one behind the stage done in brick. Harris's last trip here was for an obligatory appearance at an affair honoring the mayor. Now the stage was screened off like an examination area in a trauma ward, the chairs around the room replaced with rows of emergency fold-out beds—all occupied with people in need of urgent attention. Men and women in scrubs crowded the aisles, weaving between oxygen tents, IV stands, first aid kits, and islands of machines.

Day motioned at the stage at the opposite end of the hall.

"They're treating Michaels behind the curtain," he said. "Or they were when I left here half an hour ago."

They quickly went up the low stairs leading up to the stage

platform. Day hurried around the privacy screen and leaned into the opening.

Harris's eyes widened behind him. Bandages around his forehead and arms, Alex was on the bed with an oxygen tube in his nose and multiple intravenous lines running into him, the upper half of the mattress elevated so he was in a partial sitting position.

"Leo," Alex said, and mustered a weak smile. "Good...to see you. We...have been waiting."

Harris just nodded. He didn't know what to say—and it wasn't because of the professor, but the woman sitting on the edge of his mattress.

We.

"Madam President," he said.

"Hello, Agent Harris." She smiled. "I want to thank you for saving my life. Now let's the three of us talk."

II

"Well," Fucillo said. "Love is love."

Harris grinned from where he stood near the bed, watching Julia smother the professor with her tongue.

"Should I toss you a life preserver?" he asked. "After everything you've been through, I'd hate to see you drown in dog spit."

Alex turned his head toward him, a protective shell dressing over his right ear. His eye on the same side was swollen almost completely shut, its upper lid puffy and dark, the thin slit of white underneath it a flaring, bloodshot red.

"Sorry, Leo." He lifted a hand to the dressing. "*Minnnd* repeating that for me?"

Leo smiled thinly. The prof's eardrum had been ruptured by the blast. But his hearing wasn't the worst of his problems. Before Julia made her entrance, a doctor named McCutcheon had come over to examine him, trying to find the cause of his slurred speech.

"What's your mother's first name, Professor?" he asked, shining a flashlight in his eyes.

Alex had needed a second. "Irma."

"And her maiden name?"

"Hailey."

"Great," the doctor said. "How about telling me where you work?"

"Colmm... Columbia Universsity. School of... Computer Science."

"Perfect. Now...do you know what day it is?"

Alex had opened his mouth to answer, then closed it without a word.

"Can't remember?"

Alex shook his head.

"What about the month?"

Alex stared. "Don't...know."

"Do you know where you are now?"

"Of...*coursse*."

"And where would that be?"

Alex stared. "I... I suppose... I forgot."

The doctor patted his chest. "That's fine. You can relax," he said, slipping the flashlight into his pocket. "Let's take a closer look at your bumps and bruises." He had continued his examination, his eyes going to a swelling in Alex's lower abdomen, and another ugly bulge above his right knee.

"Tender?" he asked, lightly pressing three fingers into his midsection.

Alex had winced in pain.

McCutcheon nodded. "No further answer necessary... I'll wait to test the leg," he said. "We have a handheld scanner here someplace—it's called a retinal oximeter. Don't know who's using it right now, but I'll track it down."

"What's...it do?"

"It can help us find evidence of internal bleeding, and a few other things that could be related," the doctor said. "My guess is you have a fairly severe concussion. That's the best we can do without having MRI and CT machines for definitive imaging scans."

The exam left Alex dejected, and it did not escape Harris's notice. After the doctor hustled off, he had asked Day to check up on Julia, discovered her sedative had worn off, and then urged the triage nurse to let the dog in, thinking it might give the professor a lift.

The nurse wasn't thrilled. Triage rules prohibited it—even for a service dog.

That might have nixed Leo's idea if the President had not seconded him.

"The dog's trained in search and rescue," she said assertively. "I'll be responsible."

The nurse had turned back to her monitors, yielding. What could she say? This *was* the Commander in Chief.

"Executive privilege at its handiest," Fucillo whispered to Harris.

Now she was looking at him with something of that same authority in her eyes.

"We don't have much time," she said. "I'm being pressed to leave New York. Our country is under attack, all of it, and my aides insist I need to be at a national command center."

"Hard to argue," Harris said. "This whole thing started with somebody trying to take you out of the picture. You can't stay here in the dark zone."

"That's the logic," she said. "But what about the wisdom? It isn't coincidental that the cyberattack came during my Net Force speech. That was more than a challenge to me…" She paused. "I won't be a disappearing leader."

Alex slowly turned his head on his pillow, stroking Julia's neck with one hand.

"You…have a…point, Annemarie," he said. "But *sooo do* your people." He shook his head helplessly. "Damn. *Cn* hardly speak."

Fucillo shot a quick glance at Harris. Their worried expressions were almost mirror images.

"Alex, I can stay here. The second floor command center—"

"No." He took a long inhale. "*Thisisssn't* the place. HIVE…
Bryyan…"

Harris placed a hand on his arm.

"Relax," he said. And forced a grin. "Bet you never figured
on needing me for a mouthpiece."

Alex nodded slowly.

"According to Day, there's maybe a couple of days' juice down
here," Harris said, looking at the President. "But so far, so good
uptown at the prof's lab. And the HIVE…that's his—"

"Holographic Immersive Virtual Environment," Fucillo said.
"You'll never know what it took to get that project funded,
Agent."

Alex was looking straight at Harris now. "Bryan," he said.
"H-he…needs cllrrrnshss."

Harris didn't completely understand. "Rewind the second
part, Prof. Take it slow."

"Clear…an…*shh*…es."

Harris nodded, thinking.

"One of the prof's wirehead grad students…his name's Bryan
Ferago," he said to Fucillo. "The kid interns for us at Cyber
when he isn't camped out in the lab." He looked at Alex. "He
there now?"

"Was…last *nnnight*," the professor said. "Late."

"Meaning he probably pulled up his usual spot on the couch."

Alex gave a nod.

Harris furrowed his brow. "HIVE uses the same closed net
connections we do at the Bureau. That goes for most of the federal government," he said. "It's a combo of sat-based and PDS
fiber-optic."

"Protected distribution," Fucillo said.

"Yeah," Harris said. "But the RTCC internet uses civilian
fiber lines—the police didn't have the bucks for full PDS when
the center went online. It'd mean tearing down walls, hardening cables…not happening."

Fucillo nodded. "Whoever hit us could have fiber taps on the RTCC system," she said. "Fool me twice, shame on me."

The SAC looked at her. "If it's all about security, we should move you to the HIVE," he said. "Pull together a motorcade and—"

"Security is only part of the equation," she interrupted. "I told you, Agent... I plan to send a message."

Harris saw the determination on her face and stayed quiet.

"I'm going on your—and Alex's—say-so and giving your student genius Yankee White clearance. The same for any others you recommend. But I'm not leaving the dark zone. I *intend* to light it up," she said. "The RTCC in this building will be my command center. Period. That means I'll need a guaranteed flow of electricity, and a seamless link with the HIVE. Since laying cables isn't feasible, I'll also need access to a secure satellite network...or the ability to handshake with one. I hope to have Adrían Soto, the head of Cognizant Systems, put one up quickly."

Harris looked at her. Soto's name had occurred to him even before she mentioned it, coming to mind with such force he might have slapped his forehead if it didn't seem unbecoming in front of the President.

"Soto," he blurted. "Yeah, I know him!"

And then slapped his head anyway.

III

Adrían Soto walked through Central Park, heading toward the Columbus Circle exit. He had intended to make his way out along the less heavily walked foot trails, but a callback from Stan Freeman led to a necessary change of plans.

"Adrían, you have some kind of wallop. I got through to Secretary of Defense Waller."

"And?"

"He got through to the President of the United States...and she got you a lift."

That lift offered the straightest—and fastest—route toward his objective. But it also required him to stay on the drive among hundreds, if not thousands, of confused, jittery people. A trio of National Guard JLTVs rolled slowly northwest on its right shoulder, the prerecorded instructions coming from their PA systems ordering everyone indoors.

When he first saw them, Soto thought he might have found his ride, but the sensor pods on their roofs identified them as autonomous-capable vehicles. Driverless and crewless, they were on full autopilot.

He found room for a moment of pride. Cognizant had designed the GPS and IT components for the entire military fleet's robotic intervehicle and vehicle-to-communications-system's infrastructure, also launching the Block IIIF high-precision satellites that allowed the system to operate in dense urban areas. Soto felt the upgrades were essential, and especially valuable under contingencies like the present situation, sparing available manpower for wherever it was most needed.

But he was not about to stand there congratulating himself. He kept moving south, feeling pressed for time.

Soto was near the Columbus Circle exit when he finally saw the manned JLTV—it was the only one he'd seen since starting out—stopped on the road ahead of him, its front end turned toward the exit. A 69th Infantry Fighting Irish insignia was stenciled on its flank, and a crewcut young National Guardsman in uniform stood outside the driver's door.

Soto trotted up to him through the crowd, his Cognizant ID in hand.

"Sir," the trooper said, crisply saluting him. "I'm Sergeant Ramos. It's my great honor to meet you."

"A handshake's fine, Sergeant," he said. "How confident are you that we can get all the way downtown?"

"I think we can do it," Ramos said. "Broadway was already clear of traffic south of Times Square."

"Presidential security?"

"Exactly, sir. The pedestrian mall on 47th Street was the dividing line. We're in the process of towing stalled and abandoned vehicles between here and there."

Twelve city blocks, Soto thought. That would be no small task.

From his vantage near the park exit, he could see that the fountains out in Columbus Circle had stopped running. The stoplights around it were likewise inoperative. Trucks, cars, vans, and city busses jammed the plaza, many having swerved across traffic lanes to crash into each other with tremendous force. Troopers and police had cordoned off the area, while a fleet of large National Guard tows did its work.

The wail of police sirens filled the air. Though Soto had been vaguely aware of them in the park, their shrillness was muted by the foliage—either that, or he was too focused on reaching the exit to take notice. Now they seemed to be coming from every direction.

It occurred to him that Columbus Circle was miles north of the dark zone. If the power was out here, too, it could mean the blackouts were expanding outward from downtown, or that Con Edison was funneling available electricity from one part of the city to another to compensate for localized outages—or that the outside force that struck at Zuccotti was deliberately manipulating the network to cause increasing chaos.

Soto was no expert on smart grid technologies, but knew if the massive number of computers and other intelligent devices within the grid were used as entry points in a cyberattack, there was no telling which areas would be hit next. A widespread blackout was likely to be the tipping point that raised fear to a high level of panic—and not just in and around New York. With temperatures soaring, power consumption high, and the system under siege, the entire North Atlantic–Midwestern grid might collapse.

There was no time to lose, he thought.

"All right, Sergeant," he said. "We better get a move on."

Ramos nodded and opened the vehicle's rear door for him. Moments later, they were rolling.

BOOK IV

DUELING RAVENS

29

I

Carmody's left hand started to quiver about two miles north of the Baneasa Railway Station, after he had picked up the unmarked Tahoe they left there to board the train for Bucharest. Although the spasms were almost imperceptible, they unsettled him. He had been off the Coprox since Italy and felt optimistic about avoiding withdrawal symptoms.

Too optimistic, he supposed.

He tried to ignore the trembling and glanced at Kali. She had said little in the hour since they rushed from the café—remaining detached during the train ride—and was now staring out the windshield as they sped toward base.

"Not much to see but trees and fields," he said with a nod at the roadside. "The royal family owned a farm out here before the Communists. Eighty, ninety years ago, I suppose. The railroad station was built to bring them into the city."

She said nothing, her eyes on the foliage blurring past her window.

"End of history lesson," he said, and shrugged. "Might be good we talk."

Kali slowly turned her head to look at him but said nothing.

"Howard's going to know the laptop transceiver's kaput," he said. "He won't be thrilled."

She shrugged her shoulders. "I returned it to you in good working condition," she said. "Use it to bug someone else."

"Funny." He smiled. "Except Howard's no joke."

She fixed her eyes on him. "I don't fear your colonel."

"It isn't about fear. It's about seeing him for who he is. John Howard came up in a day when there was no playing nice. If he ever knew how to do that, he's forgotten. He's smart and capable and shouldn't be underestimated."

Kali was silent. After a moment she returned her attention to the unvarying greenery outside.

Carmody felt a fresh tremor run through his fingers and slid his hand down the rim of the wheel, hoping to place it out of her sight. Then he lowered his foot on the accelerator. There were no other vehicles on the road with them now. All he wanted to do was reach the compound before his shakes worsened.

"Those words that flashed on the television back at the café…"

"'God is not willing to do everything,'" Kali said, "'and thus take away our free will, and our share of the glory which belongs to us.'"

He flicked a glance over at her. "That the rest of it?"

"Yes."

"You know your Machiavelli."

She stared out the window in silence.

"It sounds like a boast," he said. "But I think it's also meant to send a message. Or maybe different messages to different people."

"Are you asking me a question?"

"Just wonder how you see it."

She turned to face him. "You were supposed to send me to the States. What changed it? Why bring me here with you?"

"Now who's asking the questions?"

She shrugged. "I appreciate your bread and water, Mike. But don't think it's all that will be necessary."

He drove on for a quarter mile without saying anything, then turned onto a narrow strip of blacktop cutting between the trees on either side. Kali looked up through the windshield at the intelligent cameras mounted beneath their crowns.

They were almost at the base. Carmody saw the perimeter fence up ahead, and not a moment too soon. The trembling in his hand was worse. If she noticed anything she gave no hint of it.

"Howard starts in, leave him to me," he said. "We clear?"

Kali seemed preoccupied with the robotic sentries at the gate as it slid open.

"Clear enough," she said.

II

Howard was waiting in the corridor past the guard station as they entered the compound's main building. He eyed Kali closely, his arms crossed over his uniform shirt, an unlit tobacco pipe cradled in one hand.

"Look who had a makeover in Bucharest," he said. "You hit the spa while hell broke loose in New York?"

"I always say nothing beats one of your welcomes," Carmody said.

Howard shifted his gaze to him. "The hipster renegade's in custody, 'case you forgot. Sorry I didn't hang no balloons."

For a moment neither spoke. Carmody could hear the air coming out of the vents up near the ceiling.

"You get what we needed?" Howard asked at length.

"Yeah. And more."

Howard snapped him a nod.

"We meet downstairs in fifteen," he said. Then he cocked his head slightly toward Kali. "She'll be restricted to quarters."

Carmody shook his head. "No," he said. "She's with me."

Howard ran his thumb around the rim of his pipe. "This is my command," he said. "I set the rules."

Carmody sighed. "Same old, same old."

"What's that supposed to mean?"

"Things accelerated a lot faster than anyone expected. We have somebody useful with us. And you're kicking up dirt."

Howard stared at him. "No," he said. "I am looking after the security of this base."

Another silence. Carmody met his gaze.

"Nobody questions your authority here," he said. "If you have a problem, you're free to contact Duchess."

Howard reached into his pants pocket, took out a worn leather pouch, and dropped a pinch of cherry tobacco into the pipe bowl.

"This ain't about posturing, cowboy," he said. "I won't have a fifty-cent showdown with you. We've got bigger worries right now."

Carmody remained still, saying nothing more. After a moment Howard raised the pipe to his mouth, looked briefly at Kali, then faced him again.

"We'll play it your way...for now," he said. "See you both at the conference."

Carmody watched the colonel turn and stalk off down the corridor. Angling his body away from the guards at the door, he looked at Kali.

"Told you it wouldn't be pleasant," he said in a low voice.

She looked at him. "Hipster renegade?" she said.

"If the shoe fits," he said, and grinned.

III

Drajan Petrovik ignored the tap on his shoulder. On his computer screen was an image of the incinerated police helicopter dangling from the Brooklyn Bridge, the arcing, high-pressure streams from the fireboats having finally doused its flames.

Another tap from behind, more urgent now, and he reluctantly turned to see Emil standing behind him. He removed his headset.

"Yes?" he said quickly. "What is it?"

"Zolcu phoned," he said. "He insists it's urgent."

Drajan had known Gustav Zolcu since college, and he was both an excellent forger and perpetual worrier. But this was no time to dismiss a call from him.

He rose from his chair. "Keep an eye on things here," he said, flexing his neck. "I'll be right back."

Emil nodded and turned to the screen.

Moments later, Drajan was out in the deep shade of the fir trees behind his mansion. The mountain air instantly refreshed him, and made him realize how badly he had needed to get out from behind the computer. It was vital to keep an eye on the present while looking ahead toward the future. He'd placed many things in motion, but still, the Wheel of wheels had not yet begun to spin. He was still short of the ultimate goal.

His encrypted satphone in hand, Drajan tapped Zolcu's name on his contact list. He did not have to wait a full ring for an answer.

"*Ce mai facie,* Gustav?" he said. "I'm told you want a word with me."

"Yes," Zolcu said. "I reviewed the phone log at the office this afternoon. It was my first chance since arriving in Bucharest."

"Is there a problem?"

"There could be. One particular call. A hangup, actually. It's date-stamped July 7. No message, or I would have known about it."

"Where did the call originate?"

"The unmasker reveals it to be a New York exchange."

Petrovik walked briskly, twigs crackling underfoot. His unmasking website utilized an American toll-free number that exploited a regulatory loophole in the country's caller ID system. Since calls to toll-free exchanges were paid for by the recipient, their IDs were never hidden. Thus, all lines used by SC Tomis were programmed to reroute incoming calls to one of the unmasker's toll-free exchanges. The unmasker in turn removed the block, logged the original. "Did you run the number back to its source?" he said.

"Yes. I asked Marko Kormasi to do it." A pause. "It traces back to the FBI. The New York field office."

Drajan stopped walking to stand under a tall fir. "And you're just informing me now?"

"Again, I just arrived here two days ago. If not for our meeting, I would still be at my summer home in Eforie."

Eforie, on the Black Sea coast, with its casinos, women, and endless so-called bliss cruises. Gustav Zolcu's appetite for gambling and carousing was insatiable.

Drajan stared into the woods, leaning more heavily against the fir tree. His thumb found the ring of skulls on his middle finger and turned it in repeated circles.

Koschei had warned him about the flare-up involving the Ilescu family and the cash mules. One of the white plastic cards could have been retrieved.

If the cards were tied to SC Tomis, where the plastic sheets used in manufacturing them were delivered to Bucharest, it was a problem.

Drajan paused for a long moment before he spoke.

"Has Werescu arrived yet?" he said at length.

"*Da.*"

"And Marko? He's with you?"

"Since yesterday. Came with what seems to be half the men in Sibiu."

"Tell them we're meeting tomorrow night."

"A full day early?" Zolcu sounded surprised. "But what of our guest?"

"That's my concern. Just see that the others are ready tomorrow. Until then, none of this is to be explicitly discussed. Not over the phone, through email, or by any other electronic means."

"All right," Zolcu said. "With Kormasi and Werescu present in the flesh, it will be quite the college reunion. If Emil accompanies you, I will be sure to send flowers to Stella."

Drajan was unamused.

"Gustav, you won't have time to fill your arms with roses," he said. "But enough words. *Cainii latra, ursju trece.*"

The dogs bark, the bear passes undisturbed.

Drajan ended the call. If the bank cards were stepping stones in an FBI probe, they had brought investigators dangerously close to his side of the stream. How did they come so far, and so quickly?

He could not afford to let the question dangle. But in the meantime, he would contact Quintessa Leonides, ask her to fly to Bucharest tomorrow. It would be well worth her while, and he doubted she would balk. Then, with their business concluded, he would contemplate how his enemies had found a path to him…and see that whoever walked the stones learned how slippery and treacherous they could be.

IV

"Duchess," Carmody said over his satphone. He knew Morse's ex had been at Zuccotti, and had wanted to check in. "Your man with the Feds okay?"

"Yes… I appreciate your concern," she said. "Anything to report?"

He sat down on his bed. Howard had given him and Kali adjacent billets on the main floor of headquarters, each barely large enough for a cot and a dresser. With plenty of spacious, available barracks laid out across the compound's back field, it was obvious the colonel wanted them close to him.

"I've done some scouting in the city," he said. "The wasps are stirring."

"Do you think it's connected to the attack on the President?"

"I'm not big on coincidences." Carmody paused. "We have to get inside the nest."

"And you want my endorsement."

"Since when can you read minds?"

"A trick of the trade," she said. "Look, I can't authorize a break-in."

"There might be records. Computer files—we can't risk them getting rid of anything."

"I understand. But I can't do it."

"Officially."

"No. I'm not playing semantics. The Romanians are very tolerant. They've opened their doors to our operations. It doesn't give us license to track mud across their carpet and raid the fridge."

He took a deep breath. "We'll clean up after ourselves."

"No one can promise that," Carol said. "Stuff happens."

"So, you're vetoing me? Even with what's gone down stateside?"

"I can't veto a plan I haven't heard. So far you've only shared your intent."

"I've got to work out the details. When that's done, you'll hear them. But it's a waste of time unless our options are open."

"Fair enough," she said. "I'll wait to decide. But understand that my head's on the line."

"Understood," he said. "And thanks."

"I stated my position. That's all. But there's one more thing."

"Yeah?"

"Outlier," she said. "Be careful with her."

He stood up from the bed, glancing at his watch.

"Always," he said, and ended the call.

V

When his encrypted smartphone rang on the end table, National Minister Ansari Kem was at his seaside condominium on the Birhanese coast, watching coverage of the events in America, and sipping cinnamon spiced wine as he awaited his dinner. With the sun beginning its descent, the breeze coming in over the Red Sea had grown cool, and he felt satisfied and relaxed.

Lowering the wineglass from his mouth now, he glanced at the phone's caller display, saw it was Massi, and quickly leaned forward in his chair to pick it up. He was hoping his cousin's report would add to his sense of accomplishment.

"Yes," he answered. "What do you have for me?"

"The United Nations inspectors. The two that were shot, and those in detention...it's a growing problem."

Kem noted the hesitation in Massi's voice. When they were boys, he had always fumbled the knockout drills as they played schoolyard football, lacking the confidence to keep his head up under pressure—and nothing ever changed. His promotion to captain in the NDF came only because of their shared blood. On his own merit, he would have remained at the lowliest ranks.

Kem eyed the flatscreen on the wall in front of him. With power and communications disrupted in downtown Manhattan—the dark zone, as a senator in Washington, DC, had referred to the area—the network was looping endless replays of Petrovik's animation, the explosions, and of course the Machiavelli.

"You're on a blackline phone, yes?" he asked.

"Yes."

"Then listen to me. You think I don't know the inspection team is a problem? Your men bungled the job, leaving me with no choice but to redirect the blame. To somehow turn that debacle to our advantage. But I do not want excuses for the inexcusable. Is that understood?"

"Yes."

"I hope so, cousin," Kem said. He sipped his wine to settle himself. "I'll make your mistake work for us. Meanwhile, you will do exactly as I instruct. Right now the American government is preoccupied. It gives us a window to finish what we started."

The captain was silent again, caught by surprise. "Excellency… I thought the mission accomplished. The protests have been snuffed out. The refineries are coming back online with my forces replacing the Satair laborers who called the work strike. I respectfully suggest there is nothing left to do but maintain order—"

"You are wrong," Kem interrupted. "The weeds have been killed. But their roots must be plucked from the ground."

"I do not know what more can be done…"

"Then I'll make it plain. You're to send every available tank and earthmover to Hagar and Bejatown. Demolitions teams as well. Give the barbarians still entrenched in those areas twenty-four hours to evacuate. In twelve hours move in. Raze every last building. Leave nothing and no one standing, understood?"

Massi was quiet. Staring at the television, Kem noticed the Machiavelli quotation was once again onscreen. The entire world had become obsessed with trying to infer its hidden significance. Would he have imagined such power and reach coming from Petrovik the student, while looking at his pale, thin face across an Oxford lecture hall?

He thought not. Although brilliant, Drajan was solitary and disengaged, even as his association with cybercriminals drew the close attention of university police. On campus he seemed like an apparition, almost dim to the eyes, as if he was migrating between worlds.

Kem heard the elevator arrive from the kitchen on the level below. He turned his head as the door slid open, saw Giraud and his sous chef wheel a silver dining cart into the room. It was time to finish up with Massi.

"Are you still there, cousin?"

"Yes…"

"I expect a thorough cleansing," he said. "Commit as many of your units as necessary. But see it is done."

"Yes, Excellency."

"Good," he said. "And remember…the inspection team is to get no further word out to the world. Keep the survivors alive. I will not tolerate further missteps."

VI

With its foot-thick blue steel walls, concrete floor, recessed LED ceiling lights, and softly humming NBC air filtration system, the underground room resembled a modern nuclear bomb shelter, a bunker meant to withstand disasters of the man-made and natural varieties…and Howard figured it could probably serve as one if Gabriel's horn ever blew to usher in Armageddon.

Truth was, though, it had not always been so clean and sterile. Seated at a black glass conference table, staring at the touchscreen display occupying almost an entire wall, he could picture how it looked once upon a time. Recall every detail that was scrubbed and sanitized with the facility's transition from counterterrorism to cyber-intelligence. The Pit, they called it in the bad old days…

The name had suited it perfectly.

His expression stony, he looked down the table at Carmody. The CIA man also remembered how it was.

Carmody had swaggered into Romania full of attitude, a twenty-seven-year-old Company man cherrypicked from AF-SOC's Twenty-Second Special Tacs—a Pathfinder. But when things got ugly, he walked. Like that gave him claim to the moral high ground. Like it wasn't just leaving the dirty work to someone else.

"Put up some fresh coffee, Julio," he said now, pointing his chin at the touchscreen. "Then let's run the video."

Fernandez nodded. As he went over to the coffee machine, Howard turned toward Outlier and watched her in silence a moment. She sat beside Carmody at the table, her face devoid of expression, a spiral notepad and pencils in front of her.

The colonel took a breath. He couldn't read her. Not one bit. And it made him uncomfortable.

He waited. Fernandez put the coffeepot and some cardboard cups on a tray, set it down in the middle of the table, and returned to the touchscreen.

"Okay," Howard said. "Roll it."

The recording ran about fifteen minutes, beginning with President Annemarie Fucillo stepping up to the podium, and ending soon after the takeover of the big screen...and the two explosions that blew apart the office tower and ripped through the stage.

Some damn kind of spectacle, Howard thought. And it was only the opening ceremony.

"My intel boys have been trawling for information," he said, looking around the table. "We got air traffic control systems knocked offline across the United States. Road collisions, train derailments...my gut tells me every major form of transportation's been compromised. But you know what? It's the little things going wonky that scare me the most. The Internet of Things," Howard said, reaching for his coffee. "It's a pretty term for the interconnectivity of devices. You ask me, we're better off just calling it a hot fucking mess."

He grinned without humor. "Everything from your car keys to your electric toothbrush to your watch is linked to a network, and every network's interacting with another goddamned network. A hundred billion things connected to each other...so they're really one big thing."

"A collective intelligence," Carmody said. "Like ants in a nest."

Howard nodded.

"Decent comparison, Slick. Probably better than you know," he said. "All those smart toys...you think about it, they're really pretty dumb. There's one, two, maybe three computer chips inside doing all their tasks. Cut them off from the internet, they're the dunces in the corner of the classroom. There's no space in their memories for firewalls. Or if there is, the people that build the gadgets don't think anybody'd want to hack into them. So they leave them unprotected...but guess what? You infect that dumbass toothbrush with a bug, you could have a major problem. 'Cause everything's part of the collective consciousness. The toothbrush is connecting with Mama's phone to let her know if little JoJo remembered to brush his back molars. Meanwhile, she's got a phone app to see if there's toothpaste in her smart medicine cabinet. The cabinet tells her it's almost time to buy a fresh tube, and links up with her drugstore's computer system to see if there's a sale. And the drugstore's linked to all kinds of other systems—homes and offices that do online ordering, pharmaceutical outfits, distributors, credit card companies, hospitals..."

"Hold up." Carmody looked at him. "What happened in New York was a precision strike. Perfectly timed and targeted. You're talking about something that's scattershot. Unpredictable."

"Maybe, maybe not," Howard said. "You already brought it up. Ants. And something guaranteed to turn your stomach called zombie fungus. But I'll let Julio explain, being he's our epidemic man."

Fernandez gave a thin smile. "I don't think I'd qualify as that. The colonel's referring to some undergrad courses I took at USC about a new area of cybersecurity...an interdisciplinary thing. Applies epidemiological models in nature to the spread of computer infections."

Kali glanced at him. "You studied under Dr. Frederick Elkael." It was not a question. The sergeant's face showed mild surprise. "You know him?"

"He is a brilliant man. A coauthor of the *Cybernation Manifesto*."

"With Rafael and Celeste Navarro and Dedalus Loran...they were one impressive group there in Paris," he said, nodding. "What happened to Navarro was real tragic. Both killed. And then their son...but I guess you know the story."

"Yes," she said. "I know."

Fernandez wasn't sure why he felt eager to move on to another subject.

"Back to that zombie fungus…it's a parasite that inhabits one species of carpenter ant in the Brazilian rainforest," he said. "*Ophiocordyceps camponoti-rufipedis*. This is a life-form that uses mind control to propagate."

Carmody turned to him. "Mind control."

"Believe it or not," Fernandez said. "The path it will take to infect an ant colony is close to how a computer virus or worm hits the Internet of Things, then vectors out through digital networks."

Howard rapped the table with his fingers. "Get to the fun part, Julio."

The sergeant glanced over at him. "First thing to know is that ants are good at protecting their nest from disease. When one of them dies in a tunnel, the workers drag the carcass out to a pile of other dead ants and leave it there. It's a clean, tight way of halting the spread of infection—"

"A natural firewall," Carmody said.

"You got it," Fernandez said. "Except the zombie fungus did exactly what hackers do and evolved a strategy for getting around it…and that's by luring the ants outside the nest to infect them." He paused to sip his coffee. "Once the spores land on an ant, it's brainjacked. Before they kill it, they take over its nervous system. Make it leave the nest and climb the underbrush outside. When it reaches a leaf, it'll attach to the bottom and die. The fungus grows a stalk from its body that reaches to the ground near the nest and sprinkles it with a carpet of new spores."

"So, the workers will crawl through them," Carmody said, following along. "Pick them up as they leave the tunnel."

Fernandez nodded. "One scientist called it a sniper's alley. An outbreak can kill off a whole colony and then spread to neighboring communities. Eradicate tens of millions of ants."

Carmody looked at him, feeling suddenly drained. He suddenly realized his hands were trembling.

No, damn it. Not now.

He dropped his arms to his sides, hoping Howard and Fernandez hadn't noticed.

"Bring this home for me," he said. "I need you to explain how it ties into Zuccotti and the rest."

"Easy enough," Fernandez said. "Those fake cash cards in New York—you know about them, right?"

Carmody nodded. "A little," he said. "Morse told me there was some kind of newfangled malware code in their smart chips."

"Same thing she told us," Fernandez said. "So, for argument's sake, let's say that's where this all started. If you're a hacker, and you want to penetrate a bank's internal system, attack its mainframes, the hard way is to link through your computer. There are alarms left and right, multiple layers of security. But the ATMs are susceptible. They have limited functions and pea brains. Their operating systems aren't hardened. And there are millions of them in every bank branch, shopping mall, ballpark—you name it. Turn them into zombies, and you're into the system." He paused. "But we should talk about the gadgets. The *things*."

Carmody felt his hands shake harder below the table. He took a deep breath, trying to will them to stop.

"I'm listening," he said.

"With airports going down like dominoes this past hour or so—I mean from JFK to LAX to Heathrow to Cairo International—we monitored chatter between air traffic control towers, checked in with NSA, touched base with our own contacts. The reason they've grounded their flights is they're picking up ghosts on their tracking systems. Inflight tracking's got the same problem. Aircrews are seeing bogies left and right. They can't tell what's real from what's fake."

"And remember...no big airport uses radar tracking anymore," Howard said. "Most went to satellite GPS a long time ago. The monitoring's software-based."

"Meaning someone's populating screens with the bogies,"

Fernandez said. "Or that an automated Trojan or worm in the network is injecting them. Fooling the computers."

Carmody inhaled, then let the air slowly out of his lungs. "These bogies...they can't be distinguished from real planes?"

"Not on the GPS displays," the sergeant said. "There's still usually radar backup in place, but nobody can afford to take chances. With all the confusion, they're keeping everything out of the air. And here's the deal... I can see a hacker getting into one airport's GPS system's firewall. Maybe a few. But infiltrating airports around the world? In this short a period? It isn't possible unless—"

"The toys," Howard said. "Everyone might as well be a walking, talking GPS transmitter these days. People have GPS in their phones, cars, boats, satellite radios, and jogging sneakers. Even the damn family cat's got a homing chip under its fur."

"Those unprotected devices...they're the ones I'd hijack if I wanted to screw with the airports and everything else," Fernandez said. "They're all over the place. And they're wide open to attack, like those zombie ants. You don't need a direct strike at the heart of any network. Why stress one area that's going to block your path when you can create and use infinite routes?"

"If you're right..." he said, and then abruptly lost track of the thought. The shaking was worse.

"I'm listening, Slick." Howard crossed his arms over his chest. "*What* if we're right?"

Carmody could feel heat creeping up his neck, feel himself sweating under his shirt in the air-conditioned room.

"Mike."

He turned toward Kali at the sound of her voice, saw her dark eyes on his face.

"I could use a break," she said. "It's been a long day."

Howard shifted in his chair to look at her. "A haircut in Bucharest, that's some rough treatment," he said. "I'll have one of the men escort you to your room, so you can sleep it off."

She ignored him, keeping her attention on Carmody.

"I only need fifteen minutes," she said. "Some fresh air."

He angled his head toward the colonel. "I want her in on the rest of it," he said. "We can all do with a breather."

His arms still folded, Howard continued to look across the table at them. "Go ahead," he said with a shrug. "I'll be here."

Carmody stood up and quickly slipped his hands into his trouser pockets. Rising from her chair, Kali fell in behind him, blocking Howard's line of sight.

The colonel waited until they stepped through the door before letting his hands drop from his chest to the conference table.

A haircut in Bucharest. And she left the violet streak in it, he thought.

Hating that he noticed.

VII

"You didn't have to do that," Carmody said, expelling a stream of cigarette smoke. "I was fine handling things on my own."

They were on the walkway outside the bleak army headquarters building. Kali looked out across the compound to its perimeter fence, where its robotic sentries were ceaselessly gliding along on patrol.

"I thought it a good time to step outside," she said. "That's all."

Carmody raised the cigarette halfway to his lips again. "Let's go," he said. "It's still hot enough so the mosquitos might be too dazed to eat us alive."

He turned on the walkway, Kali beside him. They rounded the corner of the main building, the pavement there becoming cracked and weedy before it ended in a field of dry, knee-high crabgrass.

After stepping about ten yards out into the middle of the field, Carmody halted in the westering sunlight and turned his back toward the building.

Beside him, Kali also stood facing away from it. Looking out across the field, she saw a thin row of trees screening what appeared to be a modular military barracks.

"The 'hogs have parabolic microphones," he said in a low voice. "There are two omnidirectionals on the rooftop—they look like black satellite dishes. As long as we keep our backs turned, and voices down, we're out of range. Nobody can hear us. Or take lipread videos."

She was silent.

"At its peak, there were maybe three hundred military and intelligence personnel at this base," Carmody said. "Howard used to call the troops to morning muster out here." He shrugged. "Times have changed."

She stood looking across the field. "How many men are on station now?"

"Maybe a hundred. They were set to pull out altogether two years ago. But the base is one of President Fucillo's rescues by executive order. Part of a plan she brought into office with her. She called it Cyber Shield during her campaign... I'm guessing the Net Force thing grew out of it."

Carmody was quiet then. The air was thick and breezeless and the grass didn't stir.

He was still standing in silence when a flapping sound caught his attention. He glanced upward to see a pair of large black birds pass overhead, their wings beating rhythmically as they flew toward the trees.

"Stone the crows," Carmody said.

"Ravens." Kali watched their shadows race across the tall, dry grass. "There is a difference."

Carmody stared off toward the trees. The birds reached them and alighted on a spindly branch.

"Coprox," he said. The word left his mouth with a long exhalation of smoke. "Ever hear of it?"

She nodded. "The sleep drug."

"When I was with Special Tactics, we just called it the Candy," he said. "You're on 'round-the-clock alert, time zone hopping, amped up for missions, flying in choppers...you need your shut-eye. The dose for insomnia is five milligrams. We'd get on a long flight and pop twenty mil like it was nothing." He paused. "I kept using it after I got out of the service."

"And became CIA?"

Carmody shrugged. "I'm not in the Boy Scouts."

She continued watching the ravens as they leaped from branch to branch.

"You use the Candy long enough, in heavy doses, it can make you confused," he said. "It messes with short-term memory. You look around for your phone and realize it's in your hand. Then you can't remember the code to unlock it. And that code's your mother's birthday." He finished his cigarette, flicked the stub into the grass, and ground it out with his toe. "When the side effects are really bad, they can make you see things that aren't there."

"Like headlights coming at you in the fog?"

"Yeah," he said. "But that's also a symptom of withdrawal. In my case, it was, anyway. Same with the shakes. And the sweats."

They kept looking straight ahead at the ravens. They stretched their wings gracefully as they bobbed and pranced across a branch, their low, throaty calls reaching across the field.

"A lovers' spat?" Carmody said.

"They're sparring," she said. "Developing their fighting skills."

"I would think that's instinctive."

"It's instinct to guard their territory against enemies," Kali said. "They practice the art of survival."

Carmody watched their back-and-forth dance. "Seems neither wants to give up the perch."

Kali nodded.

"It's part of their drill," she said. "If an enemy strikes, they have to be agile enough to shift between offense and defense."

He nodded. "Place too much emphasis on one and the other suffers," he said. "Basic Fujian kung fu."

Kali looked over at him.

"The drill is exactly like Fujian," she said. "They have to stay balanced. As individuals, and as a pair."

"And if one of them falls off the branch?"

"Both become more vulnerable to an aggressor," she said. "And both lose."

He nodded, watching the birds duel.

Kali turned to him, her face serious. "Our common goal is to find whoever used my scripts in the Hekate bug," she said. "You were right about it back in Italy, and nothing has changed. I never thought you were bringing me to a Scout meeting."

"Speaking of which… Howard resents you more than I thought," he said. "It's like he's just looking for ways to come at you."

She shrugged. "In his view, I don't belong here. It's that simple."

"Maybe," he said. "Maybe not."

Kali looked at him. "Howard's attitude doesn't concern me. But I do have concerns about you being compromised. That cannot happen, Mike."

"In other words, we're back to the Candy."

"There are no extra points for cutting out an addictive drug all at once," she said. "You might consider weaning yourself off it instead. Reducing the dosage."

He just shrugged. "I'm not sure I can trust myself with that."

"I can help," she said. "If you wish."

Carmody let her offer hang between them. When she didn't say anything else, he checked his chronograph and motioned toward headquarters. "Howard's theory about the bug spreading over the Internet of Things. What do you think about it?"

She waited to answer.

"I think," she said, "your colonel may have put his finger right on the dot."

Carmody nodded.

"Okay," he said. "We better get inside."

"Yes."

They were starting back when they heard the ravens squall

behind them—loud, high cries that sounded much closer than they were.

"Wonder if one of the birds slipped," Carmody said without looking around.

Kali did not slow her stride.

"If so, it's a lesson learned," she said as they reached the front steps.

30

I

"This is the Bulevardul Dacia in Bucharest," Carmody said. He was back at the conference table with the others, his tablet synched to the wall display using a VPN connection. "It's a pretty run-down part of town."

Howard, Fernandez, and Kali sat looking at the image. The street was a hodgepodge of nineteenth-century classical structures and Communist-era housing blocks. Shouldered together on small lots, the buildings stood in drab, unvarying disrepair.

"A slum's a slum," Howard said. "Show us the stim club."

Now, the tremors in his hands stilled, Carmody tapped his device, and one of the older buildings on the street enlarged to fill the screen; it was two stories of ornate Byzantine frameworks and casement windows beneath a stepped redbrick roof.

"'Club Energie.'" Fernandez was reading the LED-neon strip

light sign above the entrance. "The joint's a hot spot for cy-modders—especially ones with alien implants."

Carmody gave him a questioning glance.

"Illegal biohacks...enhancements you'll only find advertised on the Dark Web. A treaty with the Romanian government gives us license to go after hackers. But local authorities keep the nootropic drugs and outlaw biotech under their watch."

"Just as long as the payoffs flow," Howard said. "Got to keep the wives and mistresses happy."

Carmody dragged a finger down the screen of his tablet. On the wall monitor, the image slid to the building's second story. "I figure you know more about what's upstairs than I do," he said.

Fernandez nodded. "SC Tomis Industrial. It's one of three corporate offices in Romania. The others being in Constanta, Oradea...and Satu Mare."

"Hackertown," Howard said.

Carmody tapped on his device, and the image panned out from the Bucharest street to a terrain map of Romania—a pin marking the club's location in the southeastern part of the country, a roughly diagonal line running from there to a point six hundred miles to the north near the Hungarian and Ukrainian border.

"Satu Mare province is part of historical Transylvania... Dracula's home turf," he said. "That's where the *technologie vampiri* tag comes from. The hackers probably started it themselves, though they laid it on the law."

"Bullshit," Fernandez said. "It's a glamor thing. Dark, sexy, predatory. Some Goth styling mixed in. They see themselves as living outside society."

Carmody was pointing at the region on the map. "Seventy percent of the area's mountains, hills, and small villages. Farming and lumber country," he said. "Could be it gives them a sense of... I don't know. Separation."

"No." Kali shook her head. "The Space eliminates borders. Transcends them."

Everyone glanced in her direction. The words were the first she had spoken since returning to the table.

"An internet connection is a powerful gateway," she said. "It lets even children go as far as they wish, unbound by physical limitations."

Howard was staring at her. "Pretty language about a bunch of criminals," he said. "Sounds like you can relate to those princes and princesses of darkness."

"No one is absolutely good or evil," she said. "We are all human. We have choices."

"And from what I see, too many humans make the wrong ones." He gave Fernandez an impatient look. "All right, Julio. Talk about the *vampiri*."

Fernandez eyed the wall. "The *city* of Satu Mare is where the population's concentrated. It had about four hundred thousand residents at the last census." He paused. "Trade and banking built the town, but everything's changed with computer crime. It's the main homegrown industry thanks to the national colleges."

"Nothing like a good education to teach those kids to channel some of that internet power," Howard said, shooting Kali a glance.

She gave no sign that she noticed.

"Their tech students *could have* written a guidebook for hacking," Fernandez went on quickly. "They perfected the basic online scams like phishing, identity theft… Wire fraud was a talent. They would hack into somebody's webmail account, then message the person's contacts saying he was traveling somewhere, lost his wallet, and needed a transfer of emergency funds. That sort of thing. The mark would send it over, and the mules would pick it up and carry it back to Satu Mare." He paused. "When the dollars started flowing in, the city's banks and wire services looked the other way. In essence, they partnered with the eighteen-year-old scammers making money hand over fist. Those kids graduated, went on to higher universities in other countries, formed cybercrime rings in all of them, then came home to run the show."

"Driving Ferraris and Bugattis," Howard said.

Fernandez looked at Carmody. "We first got wind of SC Tomis up in Satu Mare a couple years ago. The Bucharest office has been there for just a few months. Its website lists a guy named Gustav Zolcu as the director of sales and marketing."

Carmody brought up a new image. It showed a thin, goateed man in a dark suit outside the building.

"Is this our boy?" he asked, enlarging his face on the screen.

Fernandez nodded. "He's an alum of Domna Stanca National College. And a professional counterfeiter—"

"Domna Stanca...that's in Satu Mare?"

"Right," Fernandez said. "Last year Zolcu got busted up there for producing fake IDs, credit cards, and other stuff based on stolen personal information."

"That stuff include ATM cards?"

"Not that we know. But it would be right up his alley."

Carmody nodded.

"His arrest never got past opening hearings," Fernandez went on, rubbing his thumb and forefingers together. "The hackers had the magistrate and prosecutors in their pockets."

"So Zolcu got a pass."

"And came to Bucharest to establish SC Tomis's regional office," Fernandez said. "Not long afterward, Energie opened downstairs. His name is on the club's ownership filings."

Carmody thought a minute. "The pictures of Zolcu were a bonus. When I went to scout the building, I saw him outside. My smart specs drew an F/R match—"

"What brought you there?" Kali asked.

He faced her. "I was informed that it had been used as a mail drop for a shipment of plastic sheets."

"Plastic for the American cash card forgeries?"

"Yes," he said, thinking he would not have divulged that even an hour ago.

She nodded silently, folding her hands on the table.

Howard frowned. "That's it? You gonna ask a question like that and *nod*?"

Carmody turned to him. "Lay off," he said.

"Uh-uh. Not this time, Slick." Howard was shaking his head. "The legendary Outlier. You chase her all around the world, bring her to my base, and she ain't giving up a single piece of information. You think that's okay?"

"She wasn't given conditions," Carmody said. "We'll talk about it later—"

Kali brought a hand up off the table, her eyes suddenly on Howard.

"I understand your feelings, Colonel," she said. "You have no reason to trust me. But we both know why your superiors wanted me here."

His scowl deepened. "Maybe," he said. "But nobody said I can't keep you under lock and key."

"Then why haven't you done so?"

Silence. He looked as if he might speak, hesitated, then leaned forward.

"There's a crisis back home, one like nothing before," he said. "I want to find out what the hell you can do."

Kali said nothing in response. They were quiet, their eyes locked. Then he settled back in his chair.

"Let's move on," he said, turning to Carmody. "What else you got?"

Carmody tapped his device. The image zoomed to a door behind Zolcu, then moved in closer to a square metal lockpad.

"This."

"It's a biochip scanner," Fernandez said. "That's the back door?"

"Yes."

"What about the club entrance out front?"

"Same thing," Carmody said. "I assume the front scanner's activated when the place closes... It wouldn't work for people

coming there to party." He shifted the view to the upper part
of the image and zeroed in on a surveillance camera above the
door. "There are cameras outside both entrances."

Fernandez grunted thoughtfully. "Okay," he said. "Next?"

"After he left the building, Zolcu headed over to a restaurant on the Strada Polona," Carmody said. "An Italian place."

Another photo appeared on the wall screen: Zolcu on the
sidewalk with two other men. The taller of them, wearing a
short-sleeved shirt with rolled-up sleeves, was either bald or had
completely shaved his head. There were heavy tattoos on his
brawny arms and on his neck above the shirt collar. The second man was of average height and wire-thin, his multi-toned
hair platinum on the close-cropped sides and almost reddish at
the longer top.

"Don't bother with the F/R," Fernandez said. "I know them.
The *vato* with the fancy hair is Filip Werescu, a card chip shimmer and cloner based in Hackertown. The big slab of muscle is
Cosmin Serban. He's Zolcu's manager at the stim club and his
overall facilitator."

Carmody looked at him. "Interesting that the shimmer's in
town right now," he said. "I'd like to know who besides Zolcu
was involved in transshipping the plastic."

"And its next stop on the line after Bucharest," Fernandez said.

"My people can't go inside the building, not without permission from the locals," Howard said to Carmody. "We're US
Army and that's stipulated in the Presence Agreement."

"But if we give them the lowdown, we might as well tell
Zolcu," Fernandez said. "He's in tight with the *peelay*...the con-
stabularies."

Carmody was thoughtful. "Say someone wanted to get in. *Not*
your people. How would they get hold of interior schematics?"

"Easy," Fernandez said. "A digital copy would be on file with
the city's architectural permits office."

"And if they wanted to avoid making an official request?"

"There might be an unofficial way to access the files," Fernandez said, waggling his fingers.

"Zolcu could've made changes to the inside of the place without reporting them," Howard said. "He ain't the type to worry about zoning regs."

"Agreed," Carmody said. "But we can't wait. There's no time. You said it yourself…we have to consider what's happening back home." He turned toward Fernandez. "Can you get us there and maintain deniability? Give us close support in case of surprises?"

The sergeant looked at Howard, who gave him a slow affirmative nod.

"One thing, Mike," Fernandez said. "Zolcu heads over to the club every night when he's in town. Eight, nine o'clock when the action heats up. So, you'll want to beat him there."

Carmody grunted, thinking. "I don't know what kind of security they've got inside the building. Dealing with it's a tall order, plus we need to get past the door readers."

Kali looked at him suddenly. "I'll need your biometric template. Can you provide it?"

Carmody met her eyes with his own.

"Sure," he said. "But I'm not in their database. How does that let us slide past the system defenses?"

Her face was intent.

"This is how…" she said, and explained.

II

Of the five gardens at the Royal Palace of Birhan, the one at its rear was Prince Negassie's favorite. With its white flagstone walks and courtyards shaded by palms, dates, sycamores, and mulberries, and its central pond stocked with rare Chinese goldfish, the grounds had a simplicity of design, an openness, that he found calming and restorative.

This afternoon he had summoned Ansari Kem to the palace, choosing this garden as the place to meet. He needed to walk in the brightness of the sun and feel its cleansing warmth. Kem, a friend and mentor since his youth, now awakened only shadows of doubt in his heart.

The use of sarin gas against rebellious Beja workers at the coastal oil refineries, the calamitous taking of the United Nations investigative team, and now the reported destruction of tribal villages on the Hagar Oasis...

"I will not waste time with preamble, Ansari," he said. They were moving toward a small decorative fountain, yards from the garden entrance. "You insist these things were done without your knowledge...but I ask how that is possible. And must caution against taking me for naive."

"I would never presume to do so," Kem said. "I am no teller of imaginative tales. If I were to spin them, I would seek to avoid stretching your credibility."

"Then explain it all to me." Negassie paused on the tiled path. "Are you truly so distracted, so unmindful of what transpires with the military services, that an insurrection could grow undetected? That someone could have ordered investigators arrested without your knowledge?"

Kem clasped his hands behind his back. He had prepared for this moment. The prince was, indeed, no fool. A complete untruth would only raise his suspicions.

"You are familiar with my relative, Captain Farai Massi."

"Of course. I assigned him to his post."

Kem counted off several seconds before affecting a sigh.

"On my recommendation," he said. "I have not forgotten that...to my shame."

The prince's head tilted with curiosity. "Massi commands the Civil Defense Force brigade outside the city. He is responsible for its defense."

"And the defense of the palace," Kem said. "This, too, is an assignment for which I am directly responsible. You can imagine my level of trust in him. Or my past level of trust, I should say."

"What are you suggesting?" Negassie asked.

"That I have been deceived by my own blood," Kem said. "That he and several others within and above his echelon have taken matters into their own hands...beginning with the raid on the home of Yunes Abrika."

"You tell me this now? At this late stage?"

"I never would have suspected him, Highness," Kem said. "It was only after I began to investigate that I received critical and verifiable evidence."

"From?"

"An eyewitness to the sarin launch," he said gravely. "Captain Massi's loyalists towed the missiles and tubes to a bluff overlooking the petroleum refinery. After they were fired, he had the entire unit eliminated. Their vehicles either hit hidden explosives or were sabotaged."

Negassie shook his head. "This is a horror," he said. "You speak of treason."

"Yes," Kem said. "I rode out to the bluff and saw the remains of the convoy with my own eyes."

"And your witness?"

"He is a survivor of the blast...someone who also has detailed, firsthand knowledge of the Abrika assassination," Kem said. "The guns found with the students killed with him were planted under Massi's orders."

The prince was silent for a long moment. "This individual's testimony has been recorded?" he said at last.

Kem nodded. "I have his full account, and will provide it to you at the soonest practical opportunity, Highness," he said.

Negassie stood in a bar of sunlight, a small bird catching the eye with a bright flash of color as it streaked from a hedge bordering the walk. He searched for cheer in the sight but found none.

"These are evil times," he said. "I see light and color around me, but feel surrounded by darkness."

Kem looked at the prince, satisfied. Poor Massi would be a necessary sacrifice to a larger cause.

"There will be better days."

It was the first outright lie he told that afternoon.

III

"This will pinch a little—I suggest you don't flex your hand for the next hour."

The base physician was a slight, thirtyish woman with dark brown skin named LaVonne Hughes. After dabbing Carmody's hand with alcohol, she leaned over the examining table, tented the flesh between his right thumb and forefinger, inserted the needle and depressed the plunger.

"How's that?" she said.

"Pinches a *lot*," he said, flexing his hand.

"I told you not to do that," Hughes said. She disposed of the needle, applied a Band-Aid, and peeled off her sterile gloves. "The NFC chip is biosafe epoxy resin, so it won't decompose or react to chemical changes under your skin."

"So, I'm officially a cyborg?" he asked.

"Not until I give you a robotic head," Hughes said. "In case you're wondering, the biochip has no internal power source, and remains inert until it comes within the magnetic field produced by a reader. You'll have a small scab, maybe some minor swelling and discomfort. But it should heal within a few days."

"And the transponder works immediately?"

She nodded yes.

Carmody stood, rolling his sleeve down over a triangular gray glyph tattoo on his wrist.

"Thanks, Doc."

"Don't mention it." She snapped on a fresh pair of gloves and reached for her kit. "You can send in my next victim."

He went out the door to where Long, Dixon, Wheeler, Schultz, and Kali sat in waiting room chairs.

"Ready or not," he said, cocking a thumb over his shoulder.

The men sat there giving each other hesitant glances. After

a moment, Kali stood up and strode past Carmody into the examining room.

"You guys make some posse," he said, looking around at them.

IV

Carmody had just stepped out of the shower when he heard a sharp rap on the door of his billet.

He grabbed a towel off a hook and wrapped it around his waist. As he passed the sink, the mirror above briefly became a moving mural reflecting the tattoos that covered most of his body. Turning out of the bathroom, dripping wet, he crossed the door in his bare feet and opened it without asking who knocked.

In the corridor outside, Howard eyed the artwork on his chest.

"Colorful," he said. "Your girl ain't hiding under the bed, is she?"

"Good thing I didn't hear that," Carmody said. "I'm tired... What do you want?"

"This ain't for public consumption."

Carmody stood facing him a long moment. Then he stepped aside to let him enter.

"Okay," he said. "Get to it."

Howard waited for the door to be closed. "Your friend tell you anything about Vulfoliac?"

"No."

"You even mention the name to her yet?"

Carmody looked at him. "I'll decide when the time's right."

Howard exhaled through his mouth.

"That the line you gave Duchess?" he said. "Don't know why she puts up with your shit, and don't care. But I'm a different person."

Carmody's face was dispassionate. "We finished, Colonel?"

Howard shook his head. "No," he said. "Outlier scragged the data tap on her computer. Julio says we lost the signal while you two were in Bucharest. Also told me it can't be disabled with software commands. You know what that means?"

Carmody said nothing.

"Means she removed the transceiver…jacked the little bugger right out of the cable," Howard said. "I'm thinking it would be pretty hard for you not to notice. Since an agent's responsible for the care and control of his prisoner, I figure you had her in sight at all times. Or am I wrong?"

Carmody looked straight at him. "You ought to be as concerned about chasing hackers as breaking my chops," he said. "I'm here, like it or not."

The colonel grunted. "Things go bad in Bucharest tomorrow, it's gonna rain on us *all*," he said. "I just want to make sure you realize what's at stake."

Carmody let that settle in a moment. Then he nodded, reached for the door handle, and pulled the door open.

"It's late," he said. "I'm about ready to hit the sack."

Howard nodded.

Carmody quietly watched him take several steps down the hall before he decided to call out after him.

"Howard."

The colonel stopped, turned, and then stood looking back at him under the cool white output of the LED ceiling panels.

"I know what I'm doing," Carmody said.

Howard slowly nodded his head.

"Tomorrow," he said, and walked off.

V

Kali set her laptop on the bedside table and went across the room to plug in its cord. She wore black gym shorts and a sleeveless T-shirt purchased in Bucharest, the tee the same shade of purple as the streak in her hair, and the orchids that once grew in Oma's garden.

She started to insert the plug…and hesitated. The razor-thin sliver of paper she had inserted between the upper edge of its back plate and the wall was gone. She looked around for it, her right eyebrow lifting by perhaps a millimeter.

After a moment she located it. About the size of a fingernail clipping, it was on the floor tiles a few inches from the box.

Rising from her crouch, Kali went to the corner of the room where her backpack sat on the floor, opened an outer pouch, and extracted the Swiss Army knife she had bought in the same little shop as her clothes. Then she returned to the outlet box, knelt back down, and flipped out the mini-screwdriver implement.

The box loosened from the wall with only a few twists. After disconnecting it completely, Kali turned it around in her hand and snapped the backplate off.

The micro-SD card was an immediate giveaway. She pulled it out of its slot, set it down on the floor, and then snapped its case from the outlet box. A quick inspection of the case revealed the tiny red lens of a motion sensor, and beneath it a tiny omnidirectional camera lens. They were on the side of the case facing outward from the wall.

Leaving the case and memory card on the floor, Kali reassembled the outlet box and screwed it back onto the wall. Then she picked up the card and camera, strode over to her door, opened it, and tossed them into the hall.

Kali returned to bed with the laptop, sat down, and looked around her square little billet. There were no other outlets. The colonel's men could have planted another surveillance camera in the ceiling or elsewhere, but she doubted it. One would have been enough in her cramped quarters.

Still, she would be on guard contacting Lucien Navarro. But she could no longer delay. Weeks had passed since they last interfaced via the cloud proxy. He would worry about her safety.

Dear, melancholy Lucien. He was overprotective, occasionally to her annoyance. But she understood him. Despite his genius in freeing people from physical boundaries, he was frustrated by his own limitations.

Of course, this time he had legitimate reason for concern. Her disappearance, the cyberstrike on America, the nature of the malware's attack...

Knowing Lucien, he would draw connections.

She crossed her legs lotus-style, angling the computer on her lap so its screen could not be seen from the ceiling. Her body would block it from behind.

Finally, she typed. Within moments she was no longer aware of the room around her. Back in her element, she reached out across the Space, seeking help from her oldest and dearest friend.

VI

His corncob pipe hanging unlit in his mouth, Howard dropped the micro-SD card and case into Abrams's open palm.

"This is getting old," he said. "That woman keeps tossing our equipment around like yesterday's trash, we're gonna have to bill her."

Abrams stood looking over the surveillance device in silence.

"I want it put back in the wall socket," Howard said. "Right where she found it."

The private did not answer. Across the room, Pierce sat at a small metal desk with headphones over his ears. In front of him on the desk was a flat black unit resembling a cell phone dock. The small LED screen in front displayed a horizontal bar graph.

Abrams cleared his throat, snapping the tiny memory card into its case.

"Respectfully, sir," he said, "why bother if she's just going to pull it out again?"

Howard produced a matchbook from his pants pocket. "Somebody bites me, I bite back," he said, turning quickly toward Pierce. "And how's *your* shit, soldier?"

Pierce slipped off the phones. "I can hear a lot of clicks through the headphones," he said. "The bar lines at the top are electromagnetic harmonics outside the audible range. See how strong they are on playback?"

Howard looked. The bars were jumping clear across the screen. "So, we got us a solid capture?"

"Better than solid," Pierce said. "When you don't have a previous recording of someone typing on the keyboard, you usually have to find a machine of the same make and model for comparison. But the CIA boys who geeked Outlier's laptop made one for us. And it's a goodie." He paused. "Want my best guess?"

Howard nodded.

"We do the comparison, run the whole results through predictive software, we'll reconstruct close to a hundred percent of whatever she typed into her computer tonight," Pierce said. "I don't think it'll take more than an hour."

Howard looked at him a moment. "You into Coltrane?" he said.

Pierce shrugged. "Can't say I know much about him."

"Well, you're in luck," Howard said. "We get even ninety percent of what that girl typed, I'm gonna pull out my sax and play you 'My Favorite Things.'"

"That's a new one," Pierce said.

Howard grinned "Only because you ain't done anything to deserve it before, Sergeant."

31

I

After an extended delay in Satu Mare, Drajan Petrovik, a whiskey tumbler in hand, gazed out his window on the chartered Learjet 75 and watched a long, jagged lightning bolt sketch its way through the cloud stack.

"There's bad weather from the Central Mountains to Bucharest," Emil said from the seat beside him. "Our asshole pilot lacks a healthy fear of the storm."

"So you want him flying afraid?"

Emil looked at him with his dark-ringed eyes. "Traveling through this system is madness. I see no reason why the meeting couldn't be postponed. As it is we're running an hour late."

Drajan gave a small smile.

"Relax, Emil. We would not be in the air if it wasn't safe," he said. "Never mind Gustav and the others…an alliance with the Leonides family is essential for us."

"Shall I believe your eagerness to make the trip has nothing to do with the beautiful Quintessa Leonides?"

Drajan saw lightning flicker across Emil's face. "I suspect there's more to her than beauty and heritage, although both hold some fascination." He raised his whiskey to his lips and took a sip. "Enough talk, Emil. I need to concentrate. And for that you will need to practice silence."

Emil nodded and said no more.

Stretching his legs out in front of him, Drajan turned back toward the window. Striking a deal with Bank Leonides was a vital component of his endgame, and he did not want any missteps.

The Learjet trembled in a crosswind, the turbulence so intense Drajan heard the ice cubes rattle in his glass.

After a moment the plane settled. Petrovik crossed his ankles and drank, the whiskey helping to relax him. It would be a while before he reached his destination, and he could best use the time to carefully review his plans.

II

Thunder shook heaven and earth as the unmarked Dacia Duster 4x4 and autonomous Citroen Picasso C4 minivan left the Piata Romana rotary, cruising south past the Libraria Bastilia and its gated shop fronts at the north end of Bulevardul Dacia. After ten o'clock at night, the traffic lanes were mostly clear, and the sidewalks empty.

"The longer I'm stationed in this burgh, the more I think it's haunted," Fernandez said. He was behind the Duster's steering wheel in civilian clothes. "Name another place that's famous for being infested with vampires, werewolves, and ghosts."

Carmody shrugged beside him. "Those folk stories tell you all kinds of things about people. If you pay attention."

Fernandez shot him a glance. "Sounds deep, bro," he said. "'Course, I'm only the driver."

Carmody looked out his window. In the Duster's back seat, Kali sat alongside Schultz and Dixon. The two men were Carmody's picks for delicate missions, Schultz former DEVGRU Black, Dixon handpicked from the 75th Rangers. Like them, Kali wore a stealth suit with soft armor—black track jacket, black trousers, black shoulder pouch, and black crepe-soled ankle boots. Smoothed back with gel, her hair gleamed darkly as they passed under the traffic lights.

After a few blocks, the boulevard narrowed to a one-way road. Fernandez slowed to let a graffiti-covered city bus pass him, the driverless Citroen keeping a steady distance at his rear.

Soon, Kali noticed a lighted storefront up ahead on the right. Beyond it a tree-covered campus. Fernandez had identified it as part of the technical college a half block west of Club Energie.

He nodded toward the storefront. "That café's one of the few places open for business at this hour," he said, pulling to the curb. His eyes went to the rearview mirror. "Okay, good luck all."

Carmody looked over his shoulder and nodded at the three in the back seat. Then he pushed his way out of the vehicle and slipped toward the shadows of the campus trees. Schultz and Dixon were next to exit, Kali reaching for the door handle a moment later and turning toward the café.

Fernandez watched them disappear in the rain as another loud peal of thunder cracked the night.

Delightful, he thought, and drove off along the boulevard, followed once again by the Honda minivan.

III

Fernandez checked his speedometer and dashboard clock and continued west past Energie. The clubbers outside were lined up in their stim web character costumes, neon lights flashing from the entrance onto the tops of their open umbrellas.

After swinging right off the boulevard onto a cobbled, northbound side street, he made another right onto the Strada Grigore Alexandrescu and headed on toward Piata Victoriei. The route was a deliberate zigzag along Bucharest's seemingly haphazard mix of one-and two-way streets.

A glance out the left side of his windshield and he noted the barred rear windows of the National Police Force's main head-quarters, an austere four-story gray stone building occupying an entire square block and fronting on the Strada Lascar Cat-argiu. Police cars, vans, and motorcycles were slotted headfirst into the parking spaces outside.

The sergeant coasted on past them, the Citroen trailing his 4x4 like a loyal hound. Up ahead, halide lights stood on tall poles to either side of a barricaded drive, the raindrops falling like slanted dashes in their high-intensity beams.

He drove past the mechanical barricades, noting the sentry house between the entrance and exit roads. The recessed fence opposite stretched on for another twenty yards or so, with ci-vilian vehicles parallel-parked outside it.

"Last stop on the Transylvania Express, Mr. Harker," he mut-tered. Then he looked at his dash display again.

His drive from the stim club had taken slightly over ten min-utes, while cruising along at fifteen or twenty-five miles an hour. The police vehicles would move a lot faster when they left the compound.

Double-parking alongside one of the cars, Fernandez cut his lights and ignition. Leaving the back wiper on to keep the tail-gate window clear, he slipped on his smart specs, adjusting the stems so he could hear the RoIP audio through their bone-con-duction microphones. Then he pulled down the keypad of his ruggedized dashboard multiple display control and typed out his commands to the minivan.

After a moment, he slid his seat back for some legroom, watching the autonomous vehicle go on its way.

In position now, he could only wait.

IV

Gustav Zolcu rose from behind his computer to meet his beautiful visitor. He was dressed tonight in exquisite *Goth Ro-mana* cosplay. The outfit was composed of a gray Edwardian suit jacket with a black lapel, a black shirt with a white collar and cuffs, a bicolor black-and-white metallic tie, and gray slim-fit trousers, all punctuated with silver skull cufflinks, a skull tie clip, a rhinestone-studded silver skull lapel pendant, and a stylized dragon head belt buckle.

And, of course, the shoes. Hand-tooled and burnished, with cleft leather heels, gothic broguing, and pointed toes, they were crafted for him in London at considerable expense.

Satisfied with his appearance, Zolcu went around the desk to his door, opened it, and watched Quintessa Leonides step from the elevator accompanied by his club manager, Cosmin Serban.

She was even more ravishing in person than she appeared online. Blonde and fair-skinned, with the long, delicate neck of a swan, she approached in a black lace dress, gold tassel drop earrings, and stiletto heels, moving a step ahead of Serban as she neared his door.

"Good evening, Madam Leonides." Zolcu stepped into the hall, smiled, and extended his hand, the diamond pentagram bonded to his right canine twinkling under dynamic LED ceiling panels. "It is my great pleasure to meet you."

She returned his smile with a flash of white teeth. Zolcu could smell her perfume as she came up close—poppies, with hints of citrus and spice.

"Tessa is fine," she said, her fingers slipping into his. "I realize my meeting with your organization has come up on short notice."

He tore his gaze from her eyes. "We'll be fine now, Cosmin," he said to the club manager.

Serban nodded. Almost seven feet tall, he was also in *Goth Romana* mode tonight, wearing a black-on-black checkered blazer, a silver skeleton key pendant on a chain necklace, a black leather vest, and leather pants. A tribal tattoo showed at the back of his bald head, its heavy, interlocked curves twisting down to his shirt collar.

"Thank you for escorting me upstairs," Quintessa said as he backed away. "Perhaps you can show me around the club later?"

"I would welcome the opportunity, madam."

The big man strode back to the elevator. Zolcu watched him enter it and then turned back to his guest.

"You've had a long flight," he said, the pentagram glittering as he showed his teeth. "Give me a minute to turn off my computer, and we can leave here."

"And what of Mr. Petrovik?"

"His flight is running late thanks to this unnatural weather," he said. "I took the liberty of making dinner reservations for two at my favorite restaurant."

She smiled. "If it's all the same, I would prefer to enjoy the club's stim web."

Zolcu tried not to look surprised, but she read his expression at a glance.

"You think bankers too unadventurous for such diversions?" she asked.

"Of course not. But in view of your pending business here…"

"I think it's perfect before such things, Mr. Zolcu—"

"Gustav, please."

"Certainly, Mr. Zolcu." She ignored his rebuffed frown, using her fingers to gather the long hair up from her temple. The tiny scar left by an endoscopic implant procedure was covered by a serpentine S-stud trending among cy-modders. "The stim energizes me—it's like being kissed by lightning. My next-gen BCI is cross-platform…compatible gaming across the stim web."

"How excellent." Zolcu looked at her stiffly. "You'll find our VIP suite unsurpassed."

Quintessa let her hair spill down again.

"I'm eager to visit it—in fact, I think I'll find my own way downstairs," she said. "Thank you again for your courtesy. I will be sure to mention it to Drajan."

He stopped himself from clenching his fists. "Enjoy your night," he said.

A slight smile.

"I will," she said, and got into the elevator, its door whispering shut behind her to leave him alone in the hall.

V

Kali entered the little cybercafé near the campus, brushing raindrops off her cheek. The place was mostly empty, with only a handful of young men at the table nearest the door. Probably students at the technical school, they reminded her of the kids at the café on Bulevardul Maghero, where she first learned of the strike on America.

"Ai grijă să mi se alăture?" the boy said in Romanian, asking if she cared to join him. Eighteen or nineteen, wearing a Greek fisherman's cap, he motioned to an unoccupied chair at the table. His guileless smile lightened Kali's mood.

"Nu vă mulţumesc, dar apreciez oferta," she said, politely declining.

He shrugged.

"Well, it's nice and dry in here anyway. A good place to wait out the storm."

"So it certainly appears."

"See? I may not be handsome, but I'm brainy," he said. "My name's Jon. In case you're interested."

A smile wisped across her lips.

"Enjoy your night, brainy Jon," she said before turning toward the barista.

At a rear table minutes later, Kali sipped at a latte and then opened her database of stim clubs listing Gustav Zolcu as owner or executive board member. They weren't difficult to obtain. In her quarters the night before, she conducted an online search of the Hoovers International business directory, using one of several hacked logins and passwords so it couldn't be traced back to her.

She found Zolcu's name attached to almost a dozen stim clubs besides Energie. One was in Satu Mare, another in Prague, a third in Belgrade. The fourth and fifth were in Moscow, and the sixth in Warsaw. There were also clubs in London, Berlin, and Amsterdam. The tenth—curiously the only club not on the European continent—was in Brisbane, Australia.

Springboarding off that information, Kali obtained the web domain and phone number for each club, then downloaded a caller ID spoofing application from the plethora of websites offering the shareware to unregistered users. If a diversion became necessary, she was more than prepared.

The next step would be cracking Energie's video security system.

Carmody's video grabs revealed two street-level closed-circuit IP surveillance cams outside the club—one above the front entrance, and a second over the back door. Using close-up image enhancements, Kali identified the model and manufacturer of the cameras, and fixed the building's geographic coordinates on a Google map. Then she input the data to a Dark Web search engine that she—with Navarro's aid—built to chart the IP addresses and authentication settings of millions of internet-enabled cameras around the world…along with information about an untold number of other devices.

It took under three minutes to harvest the addresses for eight security cameras at Energie's geographic location. She spent the next quarter hour canvassing the other six clubs on her list for security webcams, and came up with nearly a hundred additional cameras. All were the same brand, and connected to the same surveillance network.

None of that surprised her. In fact, she was counting on it. A shared, integrated CCTV security interface was easier to operate and administer than one that wasn't.

What Kali needed to decide was where to look for areas on the net that could be compromised, knowing a probe of the wrong area might trigger fatal alarms…while the *right* one might offer a pathway for her to traverse. Or hopefully, a series of pathways.

She ruled out any attempt to penetrate Energie's cameras directly. The webcam vulnerabilities she wanted to exploit relied on default configurations of their firmware—the operating data hardwired into their memory chips. And while it was possible Gustav Zolcu left the manufacturer's defaults, she knew his silent partner all too well—knew him better than anyone. *He* would have taken precautions and changed the passcodes.

The Brisbane location jumped out at her. It was six hours ahead of Bucharest.

Kali glanced at the world clock onscreen. It was 10:30 p.m. in her time zone, making it almost 4:30 the next morning in Australia—half a world away from the *technologie vampiri*'s physical oversight. She assumed the Brisbane stim club was closed at that hour, with even the managerial and cleanup staffs gone for the night. That drastically reduced the chance of anyone monitoring the club's security system.

Typing in the Australian camera's IP, she immediately got its authentication screen, opened her list of factory defaults, and entered the preset username/password combination.

And then she was in, feeling an almost mystical sense of elevation as she went riding through the Australian stim club's security network. From there it was child's play to infiltrate its remote access system as a confirmed user and connect to the local club networks around the world...including Club Energie's.

Kali checked the time again. 10:43. The next step was harder; Carmody and the others needed a way inside. She would need to crack the biometrics database for them to gain entry without detection.

Kali first noticed the blonde while exploring the interfaces between the club's security system and other areas of its local network. Her eyebrow lifting a bit, she immediately recognized her as Quintessa Leonides. She was upstairs on the office level with Gustav Zolcu.

What was she doing there? Her father a Solntsevskaya Bratva family head, her mother the daughter of Russian oligarchs, the Latvian cryptocurrency broker did not come all the way from Latvia merely to enjoy the stim.

Opening a window at the bottom right of the screen, Kali watched her turn from Zolcu toward the elevator, ride it down to the dance floor, and step over to the big, tattooed man Fernandez had identified as Cosmin Serban.

A key tap on her computer to switch webcams, a quick hop in perspective, and she was looking at her from an overhead corner mount.

What was she doing there...?

Kali reached for her latte and drank, thinking it would be important that she learn the answer.

VI

It was pouring rain as the Learjet landed at Otopeni International Airport's private charter terminal, about ten miles northwest of Bucharest. It eased to a halt yards from a pair of black Mercedes limousines waiting at the tarmac.

Drajan Petrovik, standing at the top of the aircraft's exit stairs, saw Werescu in the lead car's front passenger seat. As two other men approached the plane with large, open umbrellas, Drajan descended to the tarmac, Emil behind him.

They hurried toward the vehicle. Barely aware of the umbrella held over his head, Drajan felt the tingle of ozone in his nostrils. He was crackling with storm-heightened awareness and anticipation.

Standing outside the Mercedes in the downpour, a third man held a rear door open. Drajan and Emil slid in, the others following them, one of the men who met them at the plane climbing behind the steering wheel.

"*Bini ati venit la Bucaresti*...you look well, Drajan," Werescu said, shifting around to face him. "How was your flight through this miserable torrent?"

"We're here," Drajan said. "It was good enough."

Werescu glanced at Emil. Seated beside Drajan, he was pale and trembling from nerves. Some flew better than others. "Madam Leonides arrived a short while ago," he said.

"Then what are we waiting for? Let's move."

Filip nodded and turned back around without another word.

A moment later the car swung onto the access road, followed closely by the second, hissing off toward the motorway in the rain.

VII

The clubbers thrashed with ecstasy across the main room, many biohacked with stim web chips, some wearing wireless VR glasses. A few wore ultraviolet-reactive face and body paint, but that was throwback style.

The hall's open contours gave it an almost cavernous appearance, and Quintessa Leonides could hear moans of pleasure as she brushed past with Cosmin. She noticed a handsome young man with spiked dreads and an open tailcoat over his bare, muscular chest. Her eyes narrowing, she rolled her neck and shoulders in time to catch his movements, taking voyeuristic pleasure from seeing him when he could not see her.

After a moment she continued on. The stimmers' bodies moved rhythmically, some entwined. Dynamic headset sensors and software adjusted their virtual environments, generating surrogate imagery to prevent collisions.

The general scene was familiar to Quintessa. Energie was said to be world class, but a stim club could be located in a warehouse, a tent, or even a field. The creativity of its designers was poured into the virtual canvas, not physical décor.

She would see how the club's boutique cyberscapes compared to her best experiences.

"The Rift is through here...and downstairs," Cosmin said to her. He gestured toward a discreet entry door, its outlines barely visible in the wall. "Our Wizard of the Shape, Dimitri, is expecting us."

She followed him through the entry onto a flight of LED-illuminated glass stairs. At the bottom, a floor of reflective tiles. Opaque glass doors lined the entire space.

Dimitri stood outside one of the doors, wearing black pants and suspenders over a short-sleeved polo shirt, his straight black hair reaching almost to his waist.

"Madam Leonides," he said with a small bow. His purple nails were filed to sharp points.

She smiled briefly. "I'm eager to live your art," she said. "Would you mind if I saw your dashboard? My time is limited."

"Certainly. I have a unique list of options…single, partnered, and group play." He smiled back at her. "My templates may be adapted or combined to suit your wishes. You'll be impressed."

A throaty laugh. "You're sounding like Mr. Zolcu…but I admit you've piqued my excitement. Lead the way."

Dimitri gave a slight bow and turned toward the door behind him. Quintessa followed along, her heels on the tiles.

Above on the ceiling, a hidden webcam tilted noiselessly on its servos to track her progress.

VIII

Carmody ran across the campus lawn in the rain, ducked under a concrete awning over the tech school's main entrance, and removed his smart specs. After wiping them off with his sleeve, he put them back on and blinked his right eye twice.

Kali's video stream from Energie instantly cut from peripheral to high center view on the glass.

"Everyone with me?" he said, watching Quintessa Leonides enter a sublevel room inside the club.

"Beta Leader here," Schultz said, his voice clear over the RoIP. "Delta?"

"Check," said Dixon.

"Roadrunner, what's our window if someone calls the gendarmes?"

"I can buy you two or three minutes, tops. They'll be SIAS… the rapid intervention task force. They don't screw around."

Carmody stared out into the rain. "Outlier, let's do a visual run-through."

"One moment."

Carmody waited two or three seconds for her webcam tap. Ten long days had passed since Malta, and he was physically worn down. But so far adrenaline was taking care of that tonight. As a Pathfinder, fatigue had been par for the course, just another thing to deal with. He felt wired and heady, as he usually did before going into action…

Or was it really SOP?

The thought came unbidden, but it wasn't one he was prepared to dismiss. He couldn't take any chances.

Opening his shoulder pouch, he produced a small pillbox from inside, took out a Coprox tablet, and split it along the scored line in the middle. He dropped half into the pillbox, lifted the other half dose to his mouth…and abruptly brought his hand back down.

There were no good options. Any withdrawal symptoms—the shakes, nausea, the anvil headache—could be fatal at a critical moment. But the Coprox dulled his senses and reflexes. He couldn't afford that, not tonight.

Returning the pillbox to the pouch, he paid close attention as Kali streamed a night-vision infrared image of Energie's back door to his glass. Carefully and methodically, she hopped from one video feed to the next, working deep into the building, then cutting upstairs to Tomis's offices. There was nothing exceptional about them; each was furnished with a single desk and computer, metal wall shelves and some file cabinets.

"We hit Zolcu's machine first. The others if we have time," Carmody said. He thought a moment. "Someone has to be monitoring the security feed. Where?"

"Downstairs," Kali replied. "The front door."

Instantly, she went to a shot of an overhead split-screen monitor. Below was a large, thick-set man with eyebrow rings and wearing a black blazer, black T-shirt, and black trousers.

"I assume he doesn't keep a close watch on the monitors," Carmody said.

It would not have mattered. She had been discreetly changing angles. "He hasn't noticed anything," she said.

"Any other security stations?"

"No. But there are guards with mobile devices. Smartphones, tablets, handheld IP monitors."

"Can you knock them out?"

"Working on it."

A brief silence on the RoIP.

"Okay," Carmody said. "We all ready?"

"Affirmative." Schultz.

"Same." Dixon.

"Outlier?"

"Yes."

Carmody nodded to himself. "Let's do this," he said.

IX

Kali realized she needed to hurry. Mike and the others would be converging on the club and could not afford to stay out in the open.

She went to work, bringing up the login screen for the building's biometric access system. This time things would not be as simple as manipulating defaults. Entry to the database was restricted to its authorized operator—or operators—and they would have created individual user ID/passcode combinations.

Gustav Zolcu was certainly one of the operators. Perhaps the only one. He would want to control who had access to the building.

Kali needed his login information. *Fast.*

A last sip of her latte, and she opened her Access Mundi interface. Typing in her decryption key to enter the cloud vault, she scrolled down her cue of exploit tool kits.

Collectively, the kits were her greatest accomplishment as a code writer. Most often, an exploit's usefulness began the day a specific software flaw was discovered, and ended the day it was patched. Zero-day exploits slipped through holes not yet found by program designers and sold for tens or even hundreds of thousands of dollars on the Dark Web...

But her perpetual zero-day exploits had no expiration dates, no intrinsic timelines to obsolescence. They were not designed to target a single program, or a set of programs, but to overwhelm and infect random computer systems with a widely distributed blizzard of mutable exploits. When one exploit in the packet found a system vulnerability, the others rapidly learned to mimic its characteristics. Endlessly adaptive, they would continue transforming themselves within the system to avoid detection, spinning off codes, which allowed them to obfuscate their presence, or embed themselves in the computer's registry.

They were unique, highly coveted, very dangerous weapons, and she knew her responsibility as their creator.

Pulling a tool kit from the vault, she downloaded it to her computer and then sat watching her screen's digital timer, counting down the seconds as her exploits swarmed through the channel she opened into Club Energie's security system—unpacking their password stealers to scour network modules where logins were typically stored.

The hits started coming at ninety seconds in, the username/passcodes harvested and decrypted from a browser cache on one of the local network computers. By two minutes in, the onscreen list had been populated with a half-dozen combinations…and they all appeared to belong to Zolcu.

Kali looked at them a moment, thinking. There likely would be an automatic system lockout after several incorrect tries. It didn't matter that they were temporary. She couldn't afford a login freeze of any duration, not when every second counted. And the highest-security logins often didn't allow for more than three wrong entries before the lockout was enabled.

She typed in one and got an Incorrect Login notification.

She typed in another. Also wrong.

Inhaling, she typed in the third—GZS-ELRNG/LIZ3234-J— and the database's home screen suddenly opened in front of her.

Kali paused long enough to release her breath. Then she accessed her hard drive for Carmody's biometric data and uploaded it into the system with a rapid series of keystrokes and clicks.

X

Mike Carmody emerged from the campus trees, crossed the boulevard, and turned left toward Club Energie.

He reached the cross street east of the club, and saw two dark figures moving in his direction from a bus stop on the far corner. Stepping onto the near corner, they hooked to their left and vanished from sight on the west side of the building.

Without slowing his pace, he turned right on the building's opposite side, came up to the mouth of its cobbled back lane, and ducked into it.

"Outlier?"

"The back door and hallway are clear. I blanked the webcams."

"And my bio data?"

"Inserted. You have five minutes before it auto-deletes from the network."

"Great, stay with us."

He hurried to join Dixon and Schultz near the back entrance. Stepping up, he touched his thumb to the lock plate so it could read his fingerprint. Then he waved his hand in front of the near-field sensor below the plate and gently tried the door.

It opened slightly, unlocked.

Slipping on a pair of lightweight black gloves, he glanced around at his men. They assumed positions a half step behind him, Schultz to his right, Dixon to the left. Both were also wearing gloves now.

"Okay, ready and set," he said. "On my one."

Nods.

"Five, four, three, two..." Gripping the handle. *"One!"*

He shouldered the door all the way open, and they were in the entry hall. A rear entrance to the main dance hall straight ahead, the elevator to the left, a staircase to their immediate right.

They rushed toward the stairs in single file.

XI

They raced up two flights, then sprinted up the empty corridor. The doors along it were paneled hardwood, with old-fashioned crystal knobs, probably the originals. A quick twist of the knob to Zolcu's office and Carmody was in, Schultz entering behind him as Dixon rushed off toward another door.

The room was perhaps twelve feet square, even smaller than it looked on the webcams. A couple of tall multimedia storage cabinets stood side by side against the wall opposite the desk.

Schultz tried their drawers, found them locked, and got a pick set out of his carryall. "This shit's too easy."

Carmody smiled behind the desk. He must have heard those words a hundred times.

He reached into his own pack, producing a thin gumstick cloud drive transmitter. "Grab anything else that looks like anything."

"Gotcha."

Crouching to take the lowest drawer first, Schultz chose a pick from his kit, worked it into the keyhole, and listened for the click of its lockpins. After a half minute he pulled the drawer open on its tracks.

Behind the desk, meanwhile, Carmody pushed his cloud transmitter into one of the computer's USB ports, tapped the keyboard, and found himself looking at its network login screen.

"Outlier?" he said.

"Try username: 'Zolcu.' Password: '24689.'"

He typed the words into the dialogue boxes, and the main screen came up. With a relieved breath, he injected his transmitter's software into the terminal, and clicked the mouse to start cloning the machine. It would take several minutes for the drive to be duplicated in a dedicated CIA cloud locker even with the hyperfast link.

He glanced over at Schultz. "How we doing over there?"

"*I'm* doing fine," Schultz said. "Never—

"—dick around with the son of a master thief," Carmody said, finishing his sentence.

Amused glances between them.

"Stay humble," Carmody said.

XII

Urged by a professor of cognitive psychology at the University of Madrid, Kali once took a series of tests and neuroscans categorizing her as a supertasker.

Most of us like to think we can do two things at the same time, but we can't, he told her. *Only a tiny scattering of people have the ability to multitask. The rest can improve with practice, though not too much. The factor's genetic, how the brain's hardwired to absorb and process information. You're the exception to the norm. A true outlier.*

With lattices of open windows on her screen, Kali Alcazar the Outlier was now paying close attention to multiple webcam views of Club Energie and the offices above, simultaneously keeping an eye on the insertion team's livestreams. With the hard-drive cloning in progress, she needed to make certain they weren't caught by surprise.

While that was her primary focus, a window at the upper right-hand corner of the monitor was drawing her intense curiosity. Burrowing deep into the network, her exploit kits entered its stim web platform—the immersive cyberscape where clubbers interacted as role players in interactive games. The best Wizards of the Shape could merge their cyberscapes with one or more generated by colleagues, half a world away, porting gamers into real-time global collaborations.

For Kali, probing the interstices of the club's network presented another opportunistic opening. For all their sophistication, BCI implants were simply electronic devices, and like all such devices, they had IP addresses for the transfer of interactive data. When cy-modders entered the stim web, their IPs were automatically logged so the implants could communicate with gaming platforms—and with the neurotech carried by other cy-modders—using standard internet protocols.

Moments ago, Kali had come upon the club's stim web login page…a lingua franca English screen with three columns of data.

Kali glanced at the USER IP and LOGIN columns. She was most interested in the one who had logged in at 10:44:27 Eastern European Time. IP 10.635.473.739.

Kali stared at the screen. Now in the canvas titled Suite Arabai, the clubber was, without doubt, Leonides.

It offered an intriguing possibility. There were stigmas attached to neurotech use—and to frequenting stim clubs. High-end cy-mods often used multihop proxy servers to protect implantees from potentially uncomfortable social and professional attention.

She would archive this in her memory for the future. But right now she had other business.

Starting with the floor of offices above Club Energie, Kali checked that the hallway was still clear, then went room to room. Carmody remained in Zolcu's office, where the computer monitor showed its hard drive cloning was 63 percent complete. His team would need to stick around a little while longer.

Moving her left pointer finger over the laptop's touchpad, she shifted her view to the cameras downstairs.

XIII

Carmody checked the time stamp low in his smart specs' field of vision. Six minutes had elapsed since he started cloning Zolcu's machine, and the process was only 40 percent complete.

He waited, alone in the room now. Schultz, finished collecting digital media from the storage cabinets, moved down the hall to search through another one of the offices.

"Alpha?" It was Dixon over the RoIP. "Think I found a storeroom or something—there's a steel door and it's locked."

Carmody grunted.

"Better see what's inside," he said.

XIV

Dixon waved his hand over the near-field bioscanner, pushed through the unlocked door into a darkened room, and waved again for the lights, assuming the sensor would be right there in the wall. Overhead fluorescents came on, revealing a space about as large as the offices, with an industrial double-door storage cabinet on one wall, and an aisle of high warehouse shelves running down the middle. These were cluttered with ordinary office supplies: printer cartridges, copy paper, calculator rolls, stationery, envelopes of various types and sizes, mailing labels, binders, file folders, surge protectors...

Out the corner of his eye, he saw Schultz enter from the corridor and gestured at the storage cabinet.

Schultz tried its doors, but they didn't open. He noticed an old-fashioned cylinder lock alongside the handles, crouched, and brought out his tools—a small stainless steel Southord hook and tension wrench.

"Looks like a five-pin mechanism...four spool, one normal. All their high-tech bio shit and they have this fossil in here." Schultz pressed the wrench against the cylinder, turning it in increments as he raised the pins. "I'll need thirty seconds."

It took exactly eleven. Pulling the heavy steel doors open, he saw three shelves inside; each stacked with cartons—about twenty in all. Those on the upper shelves were unmarked, their flaps folded shut...but the half dozen or so on the bottom shelf instantly drew his attention. Sealed with tape, each box had a postal label on its side made out to SC Tomis in Bucharest, and bearing the shipper's printed address:

BOPLASI INT.
3673-A Uspens'ka St.
Odesa, Ukraine
65000-480

Exchanging a quick glance with Dixon, Schultz pulled one

of the larger boxes off the lower shelf and set it on the floor. Reaching into his pants pocket, he produced a small black tac knife and extended the stainless steel blade.

Carefully slitting the packing tape, he opened the carton and lifted out the first few plastic sheets at the top. They were gray, millimeters thin, and about twice the dimensions of ordinary letter-size typing paper.

"Bingo," Schultz said, looking down. "The stuff credit cards are made of."

Dixon measured one of the sheets against his shoulder bag. "Won't fit... Carrying it out's going to be awkward."

Following his own hunch, Schultz slid a carton forward on an upper shelf, opened the flaps and studied its contents. "Not when we have these nifty samplers," he said, reaching inside.

A moment later his hand appeared from the box holding a pack of about twenty credit card cores bound with rubber bands. Unstamped and unmarked, the chips not yet applied, they appeared to be made of the same type of plastic sheeting material in the labeled boxes.

Taking the cards from him without a word, Dixon dropped them into his bag and went over to inspect the machine at the end of the aisle. "This is a high end 3D laser printer," he said. "It could've been used to turn out the chip cards."

He snapped a series of photos with his specs, hurried back to the supply cabinet.

"Okay," Schultz said. "Let's put these cartons back where we found them."

They did and closed the cabinet doors.

"We done in here?" Dixon asked.

Schultz nodded and led the way out, pausing in the doorway.

"Thank you and good night," he said, waving off the lights as they left the room.

XV

Petrovik studied the youthful crowd outside the club through the lead Mercedes's passenger window. They stood in the rain, the glow of the multihued neon strip lights above the entrance bleeding over them like runny watercolors.

"We'll scatter the flock for you," Filip Werescu said up front, nodding toward the clubbers. He wagged his cell phone over the backrest. "Gustav knows we've arrived."

Drajan nodded. He loathed the stim, cy-mod, and drugs. They fed the lizard brain, distorting thoughts and emotions, making one a slave to the senses. He was his own master above all else.

He turned from the window now as the Mercedes pulled near the club entrance. Beside him, Emil was staring outside.

Drajan instantly read his expression and knew his friend craved a taste of the very distractions he abhorred. He clamped a hand around the back of Emil's neck instead.

"Listen to me," he said in a fierce whisper. "We're rising, Emil. *Rising.* And we must be ready." He tightened his grip, forcing him to angle his head toward the window. "What's out there can't be for you. Not anymore."

Emil's skin was cold under Drajan's fingers.

"Yes, of course," he replied. "Aren't we here on business?"

Drajan heard his unconvincing tone, looked at him almost sadly, and dropped his hand to his side. There were other matters that needed his attention.

Preparation. It meant leaving nothing to chance. Zolcu was a schemer, and one with a wide streak of jealousy running through his dissolute soul. His thoroughness—not to mention his loyalty—were hardly to be trusted.

"Filip," he said, turning from the window. "The men in the car behind us…have them check out the rear entrance and offices to make sure they're clear. I want no surprises."

Werescu nodded, then raised his cell to his ear again.

The two Mercedes eased to the curb and halted, Werescu's men exiting them at once. Drajan watched the group from the follow car hurry around back, while those from his vehicle opened a path for him out front, parting the crowd around them with their thick bodies and arms. After a minute or two they snapped open their umbrellas and returned to his door.

Drajan slid across the seat, preparing to step out into the rain.

XVI

At her table in the campus café, Kali saw the black Mercedes S560 sedans pull up to Club Energie, watched the four men exit the second car to hurry around back, and instantly registered what was happening.

"Alpha Leader," she said into her headset. Quietly, her lips barely moving. "We have a situation. Men heading upstairs."

"How many?"

"Four. And they aren't alone. There is another car. Its passengers have not yet exited."

A beat of silence.

"Cloning's at seventy percent," he said. "We have to wait."

Kali thought about the arrival of the SUVs. Every cell in her body was vibrating.

She took a deep breath to calm her mind, her nervous system, her*self.*

"Leader…these men are a threat."

"We can't leave," Carmody said. "Not without what's on that drive."

Kali was unsurprised. She would have made the same decision.

"I'll buy you some time," she said.

XVII

In the lane behind the club, Drajan's bodyguards moved quickly toward the back entrance. Under their jackets were Skorpion submachine pistols, short-barreled M84 variants with synthetic rear grips.

Outside the door, one of the guards raised his hand to the bioscanner and waited for the green light.

It did not flash.

A huge slab of a man in a gray blazer with a dagger-and-serpent tattoo on his cheek, he frowned and waved his hand again.

The door stayed locked.

His frown deepened. His biometrics were in the system—what was wrong?

He reached for his smartphone, calling inside. "Lucas? It's Raul. We've arrived from the airport. Come let us in the back door."

"What are you doing out there?"

"Never mind," Raul grunted. He was getting soaked. "It won't open."

"Are you certain? The scanner—"

"Screw the scanner, Lucas. Do you think I'm stupid?"

"Okay, calm down. If the system's hanging, I have a manual override."

"Whatever," Raul said. "Just hurry."

"Right, right, give me half a minute."

Raul silently pocketed his cell and waited in the downpour, thinking a solid kick to the door might get him in faster than any override…

But Lucas was swift. Opening the door in thirty seconds sharp, he made good on his promise as Raul, dripping wet, led the men inside.

XVIII

Drajan emerged from the car onto the street. Werescu and Emil close behind, the rain pounding hard on the umbrella over his head.

As he moved toward the entrance, several drops of rain splashed onto his shoulder.

He did not notice.

XIX

"Alpha Leader?"

"With you."

"The men are inside. I jammed the biometric lock. But it was manually reset."

"Okay, got it. We'll deal with them."

Kali checked the front camera feed. Gustav Zolcu, in his elaborate cosplay, was emerging from the club to meet the lead Mercedes' passengers. He waited under the awning as they stepped out onto the sidewalk, flanked by several bodyguards with umbrellas.

She pointed and clicked to change the camera angle, zooming in on the new arrivals—

And then saw him. Dressed in a black raincoat. Tall, slim, dark-haired, his posture perfectly straight as he swept through the crowd.

Her fingertips cold as ice, she moved the camera closer...

Closer. Onto his face. His eyes.

I love you. I pledge. I'll take whatever road you choose.

She could still hear his voice, see the solemn look on his face in the moonlight. Standing at the crossroads near the Temple of Hekate, in Turkey, where he made a promise he never intended to keep.

Drajan.

Kali inhaled to quiet her inner turbulence.

"Leader, do you read?" she said.

"Yes."

"It's the Wolf. *Vulfoliac.* He's walking toward the club. Five others with him."

She waited. But Carmody asked no questions.

"Okay," he said. "You know what to do."

Her posture straight, Kali looked at her monitor. Inhaling, exhaling, clearing her mind and emotions.

You know what to do.

Yes. She knew. And there could be no wavering.

Focused, controlled, she went to work.

32

Romania
July 27, 2023

I

It being a quiet night at North Bucharest's 112 Emergency Services Center, Madalina Bratianu was putting the downtime to good use, making up a shopping list for her husband's surprise fortieth birthday party on her tablet.

But all things in the world were temporary, and the quiet was not to last.

Madalina had just plotted out their dessert menu when the call logged onto her console's main screen at 10:55:54 p.m.—a ringtone simultaneously sounding in her headset.

"Unu-uno-doi, care e urgenta?" she said, snapping her attention from the tablet to her monitor. The call was registered to a Club Energie on the Bulevardul Dacia.

A female's voice on the other end: *"Ajuta-ne!* Help us. There's a man with a gun. He has hostages!"

Madalina was already typing on her keyboard, bringing up a GPS city map for the club's exact location.

"Madam, stay calm. Are there injuries?"

"*Da.* I don't know how many. He was firing into the crowd. I think it's a machine gun."

"Are you in danger at this time?"

"*Spune că ne va ucide pe toți.* He says he'll kill us all."

"And your name?"

"Please, listen to me! We need you to send help right away!"

"We will," Madalina said. "But tell me—who am I talking to, madam…"

"My name is Lorie. I saw a phone behind the bar and called—"

"Lorie, I need you to follow my instructions, *da*?"

"Yes."

"I am contacting the *polizei*," Madalina said. "Stay on the line"

"I can't. He'll kill me!"

"Madam Lorie—"

"I can't."

The connection died in Madalina's ear, but she had all the information she really needed. Falling back on her training, staying collected, she rapidly typed in the code for the main police station on Strada Lascar Catargiu.

II

Waiting under the club awning, Gustav Zolcu saw Drajan and Emil approach. In close escort around them, Filip Werescu and his bodyguards motioned the crowd back as they neared the door.

"*Bine eti venit,*" Zolcu said, stepping forward. He thrust his right hand out to Petrovik, clasping his arm with his other hand. "*Ce faci*…how are you?"

"Well enough." Drajan glanced past him into the club. "Where is our Latvian guest?"

"Downstairs," Zolcu said. "She wished to try the stim."

Drajan's dark eyes reflected the neon. "Have someone bring her upstairs," he said. "With all due respect to her wishes, we have business to conduct."

Zolcu nodded. "My office is ready," he said. "I'll send up coffee."

Drajan looked at him. "Don't bother. We'll be leaving here shortly."

Another nod. Zolcu hoped his jealousy had remained out of sight. "Come, then," he said. "I'll take you to the elevator."

Petrovik freed his hand from the club owner's grasp.

"I know my way," he said, and strode inside ahead of him.

III

Fernandez watched a small fleet of black armored vehicles speed from the gated area behind police headquarters and turn in his direction, tongues of rainwater lapping up at their tires. His eyes fixed on the rearview mirror, he saw a pair of tactical trucks with body-armored SIAS police riding the boards, followed by a laddered medevac vehicle and a huge BearCat personnel carrier.

As they shot past his parked SUV, a troop of regular national cops came rushing from the headquarters building into cruisers parked out back. Within moments they joined the elite squad, their sirens blaring in the night.

"Cavalry's on the way, Leader," he said into his microphone. "Six SpecOps plus regs, copy?"

"Read you," Carmody said. "ETA?"

"Two and zero seconds. Ghost Rider's ready, I'm heading over to— Wait, wait. Stand by..."

The sergeant looked over his shoulder, his attention drawn toward the unmistakable throb of aerial power plants in the sky to his right. An upward glance through his specs, and he saw the running lights of a helicopter making its ascent above the SIAS compound's treetops. Leveling off at a few hundred feet, the aircraft wheeled in the air to set its course and head east toward the Boulevard Dacia.

"You see my stream?"

"Yeah," Carmody said. "They don't screw around."

Fernandez started up the Duster.

"Me neither, dude," he said, and stepped hard on the gas.

IV

Cleaning his pipe with a reamer, Howard looked at the video wall in front of him. After a moment he swore, not too quietly, under his breath.

There were three other men in the room with him. Bathed in its ambient blue light, Privates Geoff Ryder and Chris Berra sat at consoles below the high-res wall display with headsets over their ears, computer keyboards at their fingertips, and smaller widescreen monitors directly in front of them. Abrams stood behind them with Howard, intently keeping tabs on the insertion team in Bucharest.

Looped into their video and RoIP streams, the two privates could monitor their console displays and see and listen in on everything Fernandez, Carmody, and the rest of the group saw and heard almost a hundred fifty miles away, even while skillfully fusing each of their remote feeds into a real-time operating picture on the video wall.

Right now that picture did not please Howard in the least. His comprehensive OpPic of the club's surveillance cam feed had gone black, cutting him off from whatever was happening inside.

"This is some kind of shit," he said to Abrams. "I mean serious, serious shit."

Abrams was watching the Romanian Special Forces vehicles speed through the compound's gate. "That's one hell of a diversion," he said. "Give Outlier props. She's good."

Howard played restlessly with his pipe. She was also someone every international law-enforcement agency he could name had been chasing for years. Someone in CIA custody, whose identity and background were a total unknown to him.

How did she wind up pulling the strings tonight?

There was the real question. Why in the name of *God* did he let Carmody have his way?

He reached into a trouser pocket for his tobacco pouch.

"I'm stepping out," he told Abrams, thinking a quick walk through the halls would clear his mind. "Keep an eye on that screen."

The corporal nodded. "Got things covered, sir."

Howard glanced up at the wall and saw an image of a chopper rising above the SIAS compound's treetops.

"Sure," he said.

In the hallway a moment later, he filled his pipe, packed the tobacco with a tamper, loosely added some short flakes to the top, and lit up.

Puffing, he turned down the corridor.

Give Outlier props. She's good.

Good? No, that didn't come close to describing her abilities as a cyber. She had used those surveillance cams to take control of the club's computer network with ease, and did more than impose her will over the system. It sounded crazy, absolutely crazy, but it almost seemed as if she *immersed* her consciousness into it, slipped into the Space, and made it part of her...and if that was true, even to a degree, it made Outlier one powerful force to reckon with. One powerful *weapon.*

Howard puffed on his pipe as he rounded a bend in the corridor, tasting the sweet flavor of cherry tobacco. The truth was, they needed a weapon like her in Bucharest tonight. Despite his misgivings, he couldn't deny it, and that was why she was there. But he didn't trust her. There was no *reason* to trust her. Nothing Carol Morse and her pet op Carmody could say would change that for him. A weapon that couldn't be trusted was one that could blow up in your face at any time.

No way would he let that happen on his watch. No goddamn way.

Once the dust settled, he would have to figure out what he was going to do about the mighty Outlier. And when he did, he would take decisive action...

Morse and Carmody be damned.

V

"Leader...tangos coming upstairs," Schultz said over the RoIP. "I can hear them."

Carmody looked at the computer screen. The drive copying was at 94 percent. His bespoke software took its sweet time scanning for hidden and encrypted nonsystem partitions with sensitive information, but it was imperative to finish cloning Zolcu's machine.

"I need a few more minutes."

"You have seconds at most." This from Kali. "They're on the first landing."

"And the gendarmes?"

"The sirens are close."

"Roadrunner—"

"Bulevardul Dacia. Circling back toward the campus."

Which left Schultz and Dixon inside the storeroom.

Carmody glanced at the monitor again. The cloning had reached 96 percent.

"Outlier—can you cut the lights up here?"

"Yes, they're on motion sensors." A pause. "The schematics also show a manual control box. Top of the stairs."

Carmody guessed it was left over from before the sensors were installed. He was hoping not to find out whether it was still active.

"Turn them off," he said. "On the stairs too. We need to be quick."

VI

The SIAS vehicles and police cars came racing onto Bulevardul Dacia to stop in a cluster opposite Club Energie's neon lights. Pouring onto the street, the special forces troopers hurried to establish a perimeter in the rain, throwing up sawhorses to divert traffic in both directions.

Their sirens were loud inside the club. Moving through the

dim space between the elevators and dance floor, Werescu's men all around him, Drajan whirled toward the entrance.

Gustav Zolcu was rushing inside, a phone to his ear.

"What's happening?" Drajan snapped.

"It's the special police." Zolcu waved the smartphone. "I'm on with a contact in emergency services. They believe there's a gunman in the club…a hostage situation. I don't understand—"

"Just tell them it's a mistake."

Zolcu shook his head.

"Procedures," he said. "They're coming in for a look."

Drajan stared at him. "How do you account for this?"

"I don't know. The call was from one of our telephone lines."

"Are you sure?"

"Yes," Zolcu said. "It's in their computers."

A beat of silence. Drajan noticed a webcam on the ceiling above him. He raised his head.

"Check the security system for an unfamiliar user," he said.

Zolcu looked at him. "You think we've been spoofed? That this is a prank?"

His chin angled upward at the camera, Petrovik stood there in his raincoat like the wolf that was his avatar, hunting the wind for a scent. *No, not a prank.* He returned his gaze to Zolcu.

"Kill the cameras," he said. "Throughout the entire building. Understood?"

"Yes. But why—?"

Drajan ignored him and returned his attention to the camera lens.

"Come with me," he said to Werescu, and swept around toward the elevator.

VII

"Shit, what the hell's this about?" The guard with the dagger tattoo on his face paused just below the second floor landing. The lights had suddenly cut off, pitching the staircase into darkness.

"Should we head back downstairs, Raul?" said the guard immediately below him. "I can't see a damn thing."

Raul muttered another curse. He was thinking the outage was probably due to the storm, and that the lights might not come on for a while...but they had their orders.

"Fuck it, this will do." He got out his phone and turned on its flash. "Be ready—you never know."

Drawing their firearms, they started to climb again.

VIII

Drajan was a step or two from the elevator when he abruptly realized Emil was no longer with him. He glanced past Werescu's bodyguards and saw him drifting off toward the dance floor, where some of the clubbers remained lost in their stim zones, oblivious to the arrival of the police.

He held a hand up to the guards and strode over to him.

"Have you lost your mind? Why are you lagging here?" he said. "We must be quick."

Emil turned from the dancers, looking at him in silence. His eyes had the peculiar glassy stare associated with a peaking nootropic high. He must have taken the drug during the long wait at the airport, or possibly even in flight.

"*Fratele meu,*" Emil said after a moment. "You are my brother. And are we not both brothers to Stella? Me through flesh, you through the blood oath we three took as children."

Drajan regarded him darkly. "There is no time for this now."

"No. Of course not. When *has* there been time since her disappearance?"

Drajan stood perfectly still. He would give no physical prompts, but let him make his own decision.

"Emil," he said, "stay or be with me."

Emil looked at him, his eyes too bright. His head jerked—a tic Drajan associated with the drug's effects on his autonomic nervous system.

"Do you remember when all we did seemed a game?" he

said. "It doesn't now. I mean, *Stella*...where is she? Everything is complicated—"

"No," Drajan said. "It's simple. We cut what weighs us down and move on."

"Even if it is part of us?"

"The strong do it," Drajan said. "A leg, an arm...the heart, Emil. It's the art of survival."

Emil snapped his head back and forth between him and the dance floor, as if pulled by opposing gravities. But his legs did not budge.

Drajan could stand there no longer. Being too weak to choose was in itself a choice.

He started back toward the elevator, where Zolcu and his personal bodyguards stood waiting for him. One more step toward it, and he might not have heard Emil behind him.

"Wait," he said, rushing to catch up. "I intend to meet Madam Leonides tonight, and see if she walks as she talks."

Drajan continued without slowing.

"We'll find out together," he said.

IX

Kali had seen Drajan turn his head up at the camera.

That fixed expression on his face. It was the look that came over him when his intelligence was working at its highest level, his brain synapses making rapid-fire connections. She could almost hear the faint click of his tongue against his teeth.

He knew, she thought. *He knew.* And knowing, he would act. But how?

It did not surprise her to see Zolcu's administrative command appear in an open browser window. He was taking the security cameras offline.

Her fingers danced across the keyboard.

"Alpha Leader?"

"Here."

"Vulfoliac ordered the cameras cut."

"You sure? We're in the dark, but I still have a vidstream—"

"I blocked his command, input my own," Kali said. It had blanked the club's monitors, while continuing to give the insertion team the video feed.

"I'm pulling you out," Carmody said.

"No. You need my eyes. I can't jump off the grid."

Another instant's pause.

"You won't," Carmody said.

X

Inside the storage room, Dixon and Schultz stood on opposite sides of the open door, Mini-Uzis pulled from under their windbreakers. They could see men approaching from the stairs, four of them, their weapons also drawn, brightly shining phones held out in front of them.

Dixon clipped his Uzi's sound suppressor over its muzzle. His smart specs gave nowhere near the light amplification of the best NVGs, but they would be adequate.

He glanced across at Schultz, then peered around the door frame. They were not about to let the guards come too close. This wasn't the movies, where you conveniently placed your gun within an opponent's grabbing range. Guns were distance weapons, and in the real world, you got the drop while you had the chance.

"Leader," he radioed in a near whisper. "Tangos heading toward you."

"Roger," Carmody said. "Hold them."

Dixon brought up his left hand. The guards were approaching in pairs, the first two walking shoulder to shoulder—the one at the far side of the hall a big, broad figure with a dagger tattoo on his face, the guy on his side slightly shorter. Both carried sound suppressed semiautos… Czech guns from the looks of them.

He inhaled and started a silent countdown, bending his fourth finger, his middle, his forefinger, *three, two, ONE…*

Schultz took the lead, scrambling through the door in a shooter's crouch, crossing the hallway, and squatting against the opposite wall. Dixon followed a beat later, pivoting around the door frame with his gun extended, one hand clenching its forestock, the other wrapped around its rear grip.

As the shorter guy turned his phone flash toward the storeroom, his weapon starting to come up behind it, Dixon fired a three-round burst to his chest, taking him out before he could fully raise his gun.

The guard reeled around in a loose-legged circle before he collapsed, momentarily blocking Dixon's line of sight. At that same instant, Dagger Tattoo spotted Schultz on the opposite side of the hall, angled his flash in his direction, and fired a hurried burst.

But Schultz was already on the move. Crouched low, he pushed away from the wall, heard rounds whine past his ear, and turned his own gun toward the bulking guard. He could hardly see with the brilliant light in his eyes, though, and that gave Dagger Tattoo the edge as he triggered another burst.

Schultz felt bullets wallop into his right shoulder with bone-shattering impact, blood exploding through his shirtsleeve, his Uzi flying from his grasp. He swayed weakly as he sank to his knees, and saw Dagger Tattoo whip his light back around at him.

The snubby barrel of his gun following its trajectory, the guard was poised for the kill.

XI

Carmody heard gunfire out in the hall, pulled the cloud transmitter from Zolcu's computer, and drew his Uzi. He was successfully finished with the cloning—and not a moment too soon.

Sprinting toward the office door in the darkness, he took in the situation down the hall at a glance—Schultz kneeling on the floor, a guard sprawled between him and a huge figure with a dagger tattoo on his face, the big man rounding to fire on him. The other two guards were coming from the stairway landing...

And Dixon. Outside the storeroom, he braced for a shot at the big man.

Carmody thought Dix had him nailed, but wasn't taking any chances.

He brought up his weapon with a fluid motion, firing a tight automatic burst from the open bolt, hitting the big guard left of his breastbone. At the same instant, Dixon caught him high on the right side of his chest.

His blazer puffing out around him like a curtain in the wind, Dagger Tattoo did a grotesque little shuffle and then reeled. His phone slipped from his hand and skidded across the floor, its beam shining upward to throw bands of light and shadow across the ceiling.

But he did not drop the machine pistol. It tilted upward in his hand, his finger spasming over its trigger to release a wildly uncontrolled salvo that drilled holes in the wall inches above Schultz's head.

Carmody knew they had to finish him. Taking quick aim, he put three into the area of his heart, *pop-pop-pop*.

This time he fell like a log, blood sheeting from his mouth... but Carmody was not about to exhale. Farther down the hall, the remaining two guards had been momentarily chased back by the gunfire ahead of them. But now they were splitting off toward the opposite walls, their weapons raised.

Carmody saw the guard on his left—the side closest to where Schultz was sagging in a pool of blood—swing his machine pistol around at him even while discharging a long burst of ammunition. Bullets chewing into the door frame near his shoulder, he pointed and returned fire. The guard fell in a heap.

One left, he thought.

Pivoting on his heel, Carmody snapped his weapon to the right. A second, maybe less, and he registered Dixon near the storeroom door. His Uzi extended toward the guard, he was standing very still, not firing, his finger frozen on the trigger...

Carmody instantly understood why.

The guard had leveled his gun on Schultz, gripping it in one hand, his flash steadied on him with his opposite hand.

"Muta ci il amor," he said in Romanian.

Carmody spoke enough of the language to understand him. But his threat would have been clear whether or not he knew a single word.

Move and I'll kill him.

Carmody exchanged quick glances with Dixon.

They were at a standoff.

XII

The girl with the purple streak in her hair went rushing out of the café, her computer bag over her shoulder.

Back up front with his friends, Jon moved toward the window to look outside, drawn by the sirens and whirling lights. Just a few yards to the west, SIAS troops were setting up roadblocks.

"Where do you think she's going?" he asked one of his friends. "I hope she isn't in danger."

The other boy regarded him. "Danger? What sort?"

"I don't know. She picked an odd time to leave," Jon said. "Have you ever seen her before?"

"No," his friend said. And shrugged. "I wonder what's going on over at the club."

Jon frowned. "You worry about the club... *I'm* in love," he said. "Seriously, she's the woman of my dreams."

The other boy gave him a bemused glance and turned back toward the street, where people were filtering out of their apartment buildings into the rain, wanting to check out the commotion. Meanwhile, an SUV had pulled over to the curb outside the café, its front passenger door opening for the object of Jon's affection.

After a moment she slid in next to the driver and rode off, the truck veering off the noisy boulevard onto a side street.

Jon's friend looked at him again, cocking a thumb toward its vanishing tail lights.

"Blow Dream Girl a kiss goodbye," he said.

XIII

Drajan watched the elevator's door slide open but did not board it.

"Have you heard from the men upstairs?" he said, turning to Zolcu.

Zolcu shook his head. "I'll radio them—"

"Don't bother, they won't answer. You stay here and deal with the police."

Zolcu cast a tense glance toward the front of the club, where Serban was attempting to stall the helmeted SIAS troops at the door.

"And if they want to see the offices?"

"Alert me at once."

Reaching into the elevator, Petrovik felt for the control panel and pushed the Up button. Then he turned toward the men around him.

"Emil, Werescu, I want you with me." His eyes went to the guards. Assigned to Zolcu from his own security organization, they were two of the club owner's best. "Matei, take the rear entrance. Stelios, the front. See that no one enters or leaves."

They nodded.

Drajan heard the door close on the empty elevator behind him, and then the faint whir of its hoist mechanism.

A moment later, he turned toward the back staircase, Emil and Werescu falling in at his heels.

XIV

Fernandez turned sharply off the Bulevardul Dacia, pulled the Duster to a halt at the curb, and reached under the dash.

"I installed a tail light kill switch," he told Kali. "Makes it harder to follow us."

She sat with her computer on her lap, scanning multiple video streams from the target building. Upstairs on the office level, Schultz was down, and Carmody and Dixon—

Her eyes jumped to a feed from the club below.

"Alpha. The Wolf is coming up. With more men."

"How many?"

"Two. They're taking the stairs."

"Roger."

She took a breath. "He suspects I'm involved in what's happening tonight," she said. "And he'll want to kill you."

A heartbeat of silence.

"His problem," Carmody said.

XV

His weapon still on the guard, Dixon noticed the elevator's lighted indicator arrow. It was coming up.

"Shit," he said into the RoIP. "Orders?"

Carmody knew they had bare seconds. "Outlier."

"It's empty," she said. "A distraction."

Carmody kept his submachine gun out in front of him, ready to shift his aim between the guard and stairs.

"Hang fire, Delta," he said.

And suddenly realized his fist was trembling around the Uzi's grip.

XVI

Drajan reached the stairwell to find it in darkness.

He stopped at the bottom, Emil and Werescu close behind him. It wasn't just the stairs. The second floor also appeared to be without lights.

He pulled his Skorpion from under his raincoat, got his phone out, and turned on the flash. The office level's LED overheads were on motion sensors, and should have activated when the guards went upstairs. Someone must have deliberately cut the lights...the same network intruder who breached the building's security system with skillful manipulations of the biometrics and cameras.

It seemed to bear *her* shrewd mark, Drajan thought. But he could not afford to dwell on his hunch.

He peered upstairs. Back when he purchased the building, he had instructed Zolcu to install manual backups in case of a hack, ordering a switchbox at the stairway's middle landing.

Signaling the others to follow, he raced up to the landing, aimed his light at the wall panel, and opened it—but then hesitated before flipping the switch. He could hear a loud commotion downstairs. *The police.* Their arrival was no coincidence, but an orchestrated distraction...

His teeth clicked together. *Shrewd.*

Turning, looking downstairs. Werescu and Emil were a step or two below him, hugging the walls.

"Get your driver ready to pick us up out back," he told Werescu. "And find Madam Leonides."

Werescu nodded, brushing past Emil as he raced down to the club.

Drajan looked at his old friend in the glow of his flash. He needed to trust him. There was no other choice.

"Listen carefully, *fratele meu*," he whispered, and gave his hurried instructions.

"Drajan—"

Petrovik silenced him with a wave of his hand. "Do as I tell you," he said.

An instant later, he went bounding up toward the second floor, his long, thin legs taking the stairs two at a time.

XVII

"Captain Florea, rest assured, nothing is wrong here."

"That is for me to decide, sir."

"Yes, certainly. I meant no disrespect." Gustav Zolcu faced the tall, lean SIAS officer standing inside the entrance. "I was just pointing out that my patrons haven't been harmed or threatened. I see no good reason to tie up your manpower..."

"Don't you think a hostage call good reason?"

"Normally, yes." Zolcu's gaze passed over the close formation of helmeted troopers behind the captain outside the club. "However, we're clearly victims of a malicious prankster."

"Again, sir. I will make that determination."

Zolcu smoothed his goatee. Only his political influence had thus far kept the captain's men from pouring through the door, turning the club inside out, and lining the dancers up against the wall for body searches. Searches that would surely turn up large quantities of nootropics, MDMA-4, and perhaps other contraband, opening him to criminal charges.

It would also be difficult to explain away the white plastics in the upstairs storeroom.

Zolcu frowned. The SIAS troopers would insist on taking a look around regardless of whether they saw signs of a gunman. It was standard operational procedure. He could, however, manage the situation with a calm head.

"Captain, I am a great friend and supporter of the *Commissar de Politei*," Zolcu said. He did not add that it was a costly friendship won by stuffing his bank account and arranging frequent cruises with high-priced female escorts. "Did you know?"

Florea lowered his voice. "Yes. I'm aware of your relationship with him."

Zolcu pounced. "We obviously see things from different angles," he said. "It must frustrate an honest agent of the law like yourself to have such a low opinion of the men in charge…and know they have the power to make or break your career."

The captain stared at him, his eyes flaring with anger. For a moment Zolcu wondered if he'd overplayed his hand, but then Florea visibly calmed down.

"I'll need to do a walkaround," he said. "A walkaround at the minimum."

"Yes, Captain."

"My troopers will have a look inside the club without disturbing your patrons. And I'll need you to bring me, and another of my officers, up to your offices."

Zolcu was thinking he could live with that if necessary. Drajan was, for all the world, someone with legitimate businesses and a silent stake in the club. There was nothing wrong with him being upstairs. Still, he would not be pleased to see Florea.

"That's very gracious of you, Captain," he said. "But I prefer we skip the offices. One of my partners arrived for a late business meeting and—"

The captain frowned, waving one of his troopers over to his side. "Listen carefully," he said. "Sergeant Maisar and I are going up. You'll escort us, we'll have our look, and then we shall leave. That's the compromise." He glared angrily "Push me any further and I'll tear this place down around your head... your friends in high places be damned. *Intelegi?*"

Zolcu sighed, and nodded.

"We'll take the elevator," he said.

XVIII

Fernandez sped through the heavy downpour, Kali beside him, her computer still balanced on her knees. In a minute or two he would pull up behind Club Energie, but the Romanian chopper overhead was a major concern. Even if its crew missed him, he was certain the bird would have thermal and infrared sensor mounts...although the rain might help him avoid detection. As long as it kept falling, the Duster's IR signal would be scattered off the raindrops, and possibly degrade enough to mask the heat emissions.

In a world where his wishes came true, anyway.

He drove on over the flooded cobblestones, his headlamps off to match his extinguished tail lights.

"There it is—Club Energie," he said, nodding his head toward the back door.

Kali was silent as they passed. Slowing to a halt about three or four yards up the street. Fernandez turned off the wiper blades, cut the front lights, and looked over at her.

She was rapidly typing on her keyboard.

"What's happening?" he asked.

Her eyes did not leave the computer screen.

"Zolcu is on his way up in the elevator. With one of the troopers."

"Goddamn," Fernandez said. "Anything you can do?"

Kali shot him a look.

"They're going to find out," she said.

XIX

His Mini-Uzi pointed toward the landing, Carmody took a deep breath, trying to stop his hand from shaking around the weapon's trigger. Meanwhile, Dixon continued to hold his weapon on the guard. He had him dead to rights, but wouldn't be able to get off a volley fast enough to stop him from taking out Schultz.

They were at an impasse, all of them understanding that a hasty move would leave Schultz a goner. And he probably wouldn't be alone...

The LED lights came on suddenly. Kali had warned Carmody about the two men coming upstairs—and the manual switchbox. He was expecting the lights. But the transition from total darkness to cool white brightness still physically startled him as the man in the trenchcoat appeared in the stairwell entrance, a submachine gun in his left hand.

"Stop right there." Carmody peered at him over his front sight. He did not think his tremor was visible. But he felt it. "Don't move."

The man halted, his own weapon extended, staring at him from the far end of the hall.

Vulfoliac, Carmody thought. One more for the party.

They stood motionless in the light, their eyes locking, the three or four yards between them seeming to shrink to inches.

A second passed.

Two.

"Now we can see," the man said. He was tall, lean, black-haired. His British English crisp and clear. "We can see each other."

Yes, Carmody thought. They could.

"Alpha. He sent one man downstairs. There is another right below him."

It was Kali over the RoIP, her tone low and modulated in his ear. Carmody also heard sirens out on the boulevard, and the loud chop of the helicopter circling overhead...

"That's the *polizei* outside," he said over his outthrust weapon. "How long before they join us? A minute? Two?"

The man did not move.

"Return what you took from me," he said. "Then I'll let you scrape your wounded off the floor and leave."

Carmody held the Uzi level with his chest, gazing at him over his front sight. "Neither of us is in a position to bargain," he said. "We've got the same options."

The Wolf looked at him...and then shook his head.

"No," he said.

And bringing his gun hand up from his side, he feinted to one side with a swift, almost balletic movement, as the man on the stairs sprang into the stairwell entrance with his machine pistol spitting fire.

XX

Emil Vasile learned to shoot a twenty-two-caliber rifle as a teenager, hunting small game with his father in the Satu Mare countryside. At sixteen, he fired his first round using a 9mm Russian Makarov that Drajan obtained from a black marketer in the city, trading stolen website passwords for the pistol.

Emil was an average shot on the target range they set up in a meadow near their homes. Practice improved his aim, but he lacked arm and shoulder strength, and a tense trigger finger undermined his control.

Drajan's targets consistently showed tight groups of shots over the ten ring. Emil was too often wild and never approached his blood-brother's innate calm and sureness of hand. The gun would shift in his palm during recoil. He could not hold it still.

Lately he had practiced point shooting with the Skorpion machine pistol, Drajan insisting he train in the state-of-the art target range beneath his mansion. But turning targets made his hand jump. He got ahead of the movement and pulled too soon. Time accelerated rather than slowed for him.

Bounding up to the landing now, Emil felt it running out too quickly to even think. He never before imagined killing a man with a gun, did not even know if he could do it, but knew he must for Drajan.

Afraid...so afraid. His senses hyperacute from a nootropic cocktail, his nerves trembling like spider silk, he stepped onto the landing, raised the weapon in his sweat-slick fist, and squeezed its trigger. He was aiming for the man down the hall, the one outside Zolcu's office. But the automatic would not stay under control, and he very nearly hit the bodyguard standing between them, his gun on the wounded intruder.

The wayward shots made the bodyguard flinch a little—and Dixon noticed. He was a professional, and this was his chance. His weapon steady in his grip, he fired three clean, expertly placed rounds into the man's head.

At the same instant, Carmody saw Emil with his weapon stuttering away near the stairs, and triggered a quick burst in his direction—but then his own gun jerked in his hand, an involuntary twinge that sent his salvo high and wide, spraying the walls to Emil's left and right with ammunition.

Carmody swore under his breath, registering the brutal absurdity of his situation. It was the Coprox. Suddenly he was as wild a shot as the man on the landing.

"Alpha! Shooter, left!"

Kali.

Her voice in his ear.

Warning him.

He dove on her word, trusting it, no hesitation, hitting the floor just as a volley sizzled over him from the left. It barely missed taking his head off, tearing chunks of masonry out of the wall behind him. A split second later, Carmody sprang onto his knees in a shooter's crouch, pivoted on the balls of his feet, left, and came up to see the Wolf tracking him with his weapon.

The Mini still shaking in his grip, Carmody focused his concentration on getting off a volley, managed to catch the Wolf in his arm or shoulder, then saw him lurch sideways against the wall.

"*Drajan, no no no...*"

Screaming, almost shrieking, the shooter in the stairwell entry swept his gun toward Carmody, but Dix had the drop from outside the storeroom. He caught him in the chest with a continuous burst, punching him out, knocking him off his feet in a red cloud of blood.

Carmody instantly sprang from his crouch, his weapon extended in front of him, his tremors seeming to subside. The Wolf was standing against the wall—

No. Not standing. Leaning.

He was propped against it, his legs bent and rubbery, his trench coat soaked with blood above the elbow, blood dripping from his sleeve to slick his fingers. His Skorpion machine pistol lay near his feet in a dark red puddle.

Carmody held his fire, Dixon retrieving the weapon, then hurrying over to Schultz to check him out. Sprinting past them at once, Carmody stepped up close to Vulfoliac and patted him down. There was nothing hidden beneath his coat.

"Your friend was a lousy shot," he said, pushing his weapon into his throat. "You should have listened to me."

The Wolf looked at him with cold, undiluted hatred. Only once before had Carmody seen eyes filled with similar malevolence, and they belonged to someone more monster than man.

"Alpha, guards front and rear." Kali was speaking quickly over the RoIP. "The elevator is mine—I'm buying you time. But the troopers will take the stairs."

The gun under the Wolf's chin, Carmody tilted its snout upward, forcing his head back against the wall, while grabbing his arm with his free hand and digging his fingers into the blood-soaked sleeve of his coat.

"Call off your men," he said. "Tell them to leave the entrances. Or I'll kill you."

Vulfoliac remained silent.

Carmody clenched his bloody forearm and twisted. He felt his blood squeeze up between his fingers, heard it pattering to the floor...

And then heard another sound. New but recognizable.

Cables.

Cables moving in the wall.

He glanced over at the elevator and saw that the indicator light blinked on. The car was rising.

I'm buying you time.

"Time's run out," Carmody bluffed. He nodded toward the lighted floor indicator. "The gendarmes are on their way up here."

Vulfoliac's eyes went to his and locked on them. "How do you know?" he said. "How *can* you know about the entrances? Or be sure my men would clear them?"

Carmody pushed the gun into his throat.

"Never mind," he said. "I told you to call off your dogs."

There was a ripple of expression on the Wolf's face, a tightening of his lips and jaw.

"Is she here?" he said. The words scraped out of his throat as if they were tearing soft tissue.

Carmody kept the gun pressed to his neck.

"I don't know what the hell you're talking about," he said. He was thinking he could take him out, finish him right there on the spot. One to the head, and it might be for the best, avoid a lot of pain and trouble in the long run.

But he was not a stone killer, and there were important questions in his mind. Letting him live might be the only way to get answers.

Carmody stood there another moment, matching his stare. Then he heard a faint, thready breath from the man Dixon shot over by the stairs.

"If I was on my game, he wouldn't have a breath left in him," he said. "You make your decision?"

The Wolf seemed to be listening to the sound of the elevator.

"Yes…and the future will tell which of us it favors," he said. "My phone is in my left coat pocket."

XXI

Crammed into the car with the SIAS troopers, rising from the ground floor, Zolcu was hoping there would be no trouble upstairs. He had suffered more than his share tonight.

They had nearly reached the second floor when the car abruptly jolted to a halt, Florea lurching so hard he stumbled against Zolcu's arm.

He caught his balance and glowered at the club owner. "What sort of unsafe rattletrap have I stepped into?"

Zolcu looked at him. "Everything at this club is top-notch," he said. "There's no need for insults—"

They started moving with another shudder and were crawling up the shaft at a snail's pace…which he found as confusing as their unexpected stop. He did not lie to Florea. The elevator was brand-new and normally very speedy.

The captain stared at him. "Mr. Zolcu, if this is a stall…"

Suddenly furious, Zolcu spread his hands in the air. "Was that a joke? How can I be *stalling*?"

"I don't know. But I find this delay suspicious."

"That's absurd," Zolcu said. "May I remind you that I am a victim? The object of a criminal stunt?"

The captain fumed. "That is to be determined."

Zolcu swallowed a retort, thinking he did not want to provoke more trouble with the bastard. Let Drajan negotiate with him.

The elevator crept up the shaft. To Zolcu's great relief it had almost reached the next floor…

And that was when it suddenly shook hard enough to make his stomach lurch, coming to a halt again, sending Florea and Sergeant Maisar crashing against the sides of the car.

A moment later it reversed direction, going down fast.

XXII

Carmody pulled his gun away from Vulfoliac's throat, keeping it trained on him, and slowly backed down the hall toward the landing. Schultz would need his help. It was either leave him or the hacker behind.

No real choice.

"Let's get him up," he told Dixon, nodding toward their teammate. "We have to move."

Dixon draped Schultz's good arm over his shoulders, Carmody went around his other side, and they hefted him to his feet. His legs buckled twice before he managed to walk at all, leaning heavily on the other men.

"Leader, I'm dead weight," he said. "This'll slow you down—"

Carmody cut him off. "We're getting the hell out of here together," he said.

He shot a last glance at Vulfoliac over his extended gun, their eyes holding briefly. A moment later the three Americans were on the stairs, Carmody and Dixon half carrying Schultz down between them.

Carmody did not fully take his eyes, or his weapon, off the upstairs landing until they reached the bottom.

XXIII

As a member of Drajan Petrovik's armed security team, Matei dealt with all sorts of volatile situations, but none came close to tonight's for sheer craziness. The special forces police, the armored vehicles, the helicopter...craziness.

Matei had worked many dangerous jobs in his time. As a freelancer with Blackwater and CACI, he'd seen action in more shithole countries than he could count. Dangerous and crazy were not always one and the same, however.

His present concern was the club's back door. Werescu would pull up in his Mercedes any minute, arriving for Petrovik and the haughty Latvian blonde. That was his understanding anyway.

Matei tried to check on their status over his comm, but there was dead silence in his earpiece. He frowned, quickly examining the receiver clipped to his belt, switching channels to be on the safe side. The result was the same. How could that be? It was working fine earlier.

He told himself to forget it. Its malfunction perfectly suited this odd, unpredictable night. But no matter. His job was to watch the back door, very simple. As he waited at the bottom of the stairs, he patted the Beretta 93R concealed under his blazer.

He opened the door and looked outside. Rain crackled on the cobblestones beyond the sidewalk, so loud he could hear little else. Stepping through the entryway, he saw a vehicle parked with its lights off down the street. At first he thought it was the Mercedes, but after an instant he realized it was an SUV with tinted windows.

He didn't like it being out there. Not at all. But he was reluctant to leave his post without notifying anyone. And of course the damn comm was out.

Thinking he could at least contact Zolcu, Matei reached into his pocket for his cell and tapped the Home button.

A frown crossed his features. The phone was frozen on the lockscreen. *What the hell was going on?*

He tried the phone one final time, got no result, and put it away in frustration. It was pointless to stand there fidgeting with it. The SUV was only a few yards down the block; he would have a look at it while keeping the back door in sight.

His hand hovering over his Beretta, he started toward the vehicle in the rain.

XXIV

"We're coming down," Carmody said over the RoIP. "Copy, Roadrunner?"

"Roger," Fernandez said, and suddenly heard Kali snap her computer shut.

He watched the rearview mirror. A figure was moving toward them from the building's doorway.

"Last thing we need," he said. "He's packing."

Kali said nothing, her eyes on the wing mirror. She had already seen the man's hand reach under his jacket. Pushing the computer off her lap, she slid against her door as the bouncer came up through the rain.

Fernandez looked at her. "What are you doing?"

"Wait, Julio," she said, grabbing her door handle. "Wait."

XXV

Crouched over Emil in the hallway, Drajan reached down to touch his face, but his hand stopped an inch above it and went no farther.

He looked him over quickly and saw the blood pooling in the middle of his chest. A large, tattered swatch of his shirt had been sucked down into it.

His face tightened. A droplet of his own blood spilled from his wrist onto Emil's sallow cheek, running down the line of his jaw.

"Emil," he said in a low voice. "Can you hear me?"

Emil stared vacantly up at him, his eyes glazed, pupils dilated. His mouth moved but shaped no words.

Drajan inhaled. He could not afford to be slowed by a dying man. *We cut what weighs us down.*

He leaned closer to him, his lips almost brushing his ear.

"We were a tale of three," he said. "You, me, Stella. Magicians…young magicians learning our arts. Like in those stories you would read us over the campfire."

The thinnest of breaths escaped Emil's mouth. Drajan leaned closer to him, a hand over his own wounded arm to staunch the bleeding.

"I loved you as a brother," he said quietly, remembering the children they once were. *And now, because I must, I will forget you.*

Rising to his feet, he took one last look at Emil. Then he turned away and hastened toward the stairs.

XXVI

The guard was nearly up to the Duster.

Her fingers around the door handle, Kali watched him approach through the wing mirror, getting closer to the vehicle. Coming within a foot or two of its cargo door.

He paused, inspected the back of the SUV, resumed walking toward the front end, his hand still under his blazer. Loose, ready, Kali waited. He took another step forward, another, reaching her door...

She pushed it open, pushed *hard*, slamming it into him, sending him stumbling backward even as she sprang out into the night.

As he tried to regain his balance on the rain-slicked pavement, his weapon appeared from under the jacket, a compact semiautomatic, its barrel coming up in his fist.

She needed to disarm him—and quickly.

Her eyes on the weapon, precisely aware of its position in front of her, Kali struck out at the underside of his wrist with the outer edge of her right hand, going for the radial nerve and its branches to loosen his grip. Then she hooked her fingers down over the artery to compress it and numb his fingers, the basic palm-and-hook of wushu kung fu.

Quickly.

With her right hand still pressing into the nerve bundle under his wrist, Kali stepped in on him, moving in what her sensei called *slow time*, seeing his hand and gun clearly in front of her, raindrops hanging around it as if suspended in midfall. Her left hand open, fingers straight but relaxed, she brought her left arm up from her waist, the flat of her palm striking the bottom of his wrist.

His weapon flew to the sidewalk, splashing into a puddle. But he was quick to recover. Bringing his arms up, his legs planted apart, he took a stance she recognized at once as Systema Spetnaz—the Russian military fighting art.

His left fist jabbed at her twice, the first blow missing wide as she feinted sideways, the second grazing her cheekbone, while bringing him forward slightly off balance.

Kali would not miss her opening. Coming up underneath him, she drove her elbow into his throat, hitting him precisely at the point of the Adam's apple, feeling the small tracheal bones give way where they were nested inside the cartilage. He sank to his knees gasping for air, hands going to his neck. Taking no chances, she kicked him in the face as he went down, driving her boot heel into his nose to shatter his septum. Then she hurried over to his fallen pistol and snatched it up.

As she shoved it under the waistband of her slacks, Kali heard the club's back door open again. She spun around to face it as she shifted from her attack posture to a defensive one—her legs bowed as if she was riding a horse, her back straight, her hands raised to block and parry.

But this time it was Carmody and Dixon, Schultz between them, his arms slung over their shoulders. Already out of the SUV, Fernandez came splashing onto the sidewalk, tore the rear passenger door open, and helped them ease Schultz into the back seat.

"My upholstery's gonna be fucked," he said.

Schultz managed a grin. "Send me the cleaning bill."

Fernandez waited for Dixon to get in, glanced over at Kali. "You ready?"

She nodded.

Silently noting the puffiness above her cheek, Carmody looked down at the man gagging on the pavement and turned to Fernandez.

"We're done," he said. *"Vámonos."*

XXVII

Fernandez shifted into Reverse and started backing toward the mouth of the lane, wanting to avoid Boulevard Dacia and the front of the club.

He was almost halfway there when he saw headlights lancing through the rear window, with their twin beams dazzlingly bright in his rearview. Another vehicle was turning in to the lane behind them.

He expelled a breath. "This is *so* not what we need."

Carmody leaned forward in the rear seat. "What if you take us straight out of here?"

"It puts us inside the police cordon," Fernandez said. "We'll be caught between their barricades." He paused. "Hang on tight. I'm backing out. Then it's Percy's show."

Carmody looked at him. "Percy?"

"What, bro, autonomous cars don't deserve names?"

Carmody sat back. "Hit it," he said.

XXVIII

The Mercedes's driver did not immediately see the SUV as he turned into the lane. It had no tail lights and was backing up at an insane speed, surging toward him in the rain and darkness.

His headlights glanced off its rear reflectors, illuminating the rainwater spraying up from its tires. There was no time for him to reverse direction.

"What the hell is this?" he exclaimed to the limousine's empty interior, cutting the wheel sharply to the right to avoid a collision.

An instant later he jumped the curb and bounced onto the narrow sidewalk, banging his head on the roof of the car. His foot slamming on the brakes, he crashed into a row of trash cans before coming to stop.

"Fucking asshole!" he shouted angrily. *"Futu ti mortii!"*

He twisted halfway around and shook his fist over his backrest, but knew the gesture would be lost on the maniac that drove him off the road.

The SUV had already screeched out of the lane, bearing east toward the outbound highway.

XXIX

Drajan, rushing out of the club's rear entrance, took in the scene with two rapid glances: Matei on his knees and elbows, crawling along the sidewalk toward the door. And the Mercedes backing off the sidewalk into the street.

He swept over to the bodyguard.

"What happened here?"

Matei raised himself onto one knee. He tried to speak, but could barely get a sound out of this throat.

Drajan stepped closer. "I asked you what happened," he said. "Tell me."

The guard coughed violently, hacking blood onto the wet pavement. "It was...*un...demon*."

Drajan stared down at him, the muscles above his jaw tensing slightly.

"What did this demon look like?"

Matei looked up. His nose was smashed.

"Dark hair," he croaked. "Black...eyes."

"Man or woman?" Petrovik did not say it to mock.

Matei spit more blood. "Never saw...a woman fight like that," he said, and gave a weak shake of the head. "I...don't know."

As the Mercedes finally pulled up, Drajan heard its back door open, turned, and glimpsed Quintessa Leonides standing with Filip Werescu at the bottom of the stairs—blonde hair, a black lace dress.

He gestured at the limousine.

"We have to go," he told her.

Stepping out the door ahead of Werescu and his open umbrella, she crossed the sidewalk through the downpour and paused in front of him.

"Drajan Petrovik," she said. She looked at his bloodied coat sleeve. "You're hurt."

His eyes went to hers, feeling their cold pull. "It will heal," he said. "Pain never lasts."

"Is that a medical assessment?"

Petrovik shook his head. "The practice of forgetting," he said, sliding into the car behind her.

33

I

Shaken, dizzy, and nauseous, Captain Florea stepped from the elevator onto the building's second floor. The car had shot up and gone down several times before one of Zolcu's security people overrode its electronic control system to stop it. On its third downward plunge, Florea found himself reciting an impassioned Ave Maria, certain the cables would snap and send the car, and everyone in it, crashing to the bottom of the shaft.

Florea took a moment to let his stomach settle, holding on to the wall, breathing hard as Zolcu and Sergeant Maisar exited.

Then he registered the grotesque scene in the hallway. There was blood *everywhere*—pooled on the floor, splattered on the walls and doors, its sharp, metallic smell working its way from his nostrils to the back of his throat.

Blood—and bodies.

"What in God's name is this?" He looked at Zolcu. "Do you know these people?"

Zolcu's face drained of color. "Yes...well... I suppose it would depend on your definition of 'know.' They're acquaintances."

Florea pulled his hand off the wall and discovered his legs were still wobbly. "Acquaintances? What sort?"

"Professional acquaintances."

The captain eyed him warily and then turned toward Maisar. "We need some men up here right away—they're to take the *stairs*," he said. "Tell them to be on the utmost guard."

Maisar began speaking over his comm. Meanwhile, Florea snapped his eyes back to Zolcu. "Do you have knowledge of what happened here?"

The club owner shook his hood. "None."

"You're certain?"

"Captain Florea, I'm as horrified as you are," he said truthfully.

Florea was studying his face in silence as a voice came over his communicator. It was Azcan, another of his sergeants.

"Sir...we have aerial pursuit of a suspicious vehicle. A Citroen van."

"Where?"

"Bulevardul Dacia. Bearing west toward the 1-A Motorway at high speed."

The captain's face tightened. That was a main highway. Unfortunately, the Colibri surveillance-and-pursuit helicopter's tracking equipment had been hampered by the rain until now.

"Get our cars on it immediately," he said. "They'll want SIAS tac support."

"*Da*, Captain."

He stood thinking a moment.

"What is it?" Zolcu asked, his eyes bright with tension.

Florea was in no mood to answer him. "These premises are now a major crime scene," he said. "The club will be closed until further notice. You, your entire staff, and all your patrons will remain here for questioning. No one goes home. That includes any other...professional acquaintance. Understood?"

Zolcu looked as if he might pose another question, then seemed to reconsider.

"Yes," he said. "Fully."

II

His eyes on the dash display, Fernandez shifted the Duster into Park and left the engine idling. He swung into a dead-end alley midway between Club Energie and the Motorway on-ramp, a quarter mile to the east.

"The chopper's hauled off after Percy," he said, listening to the fading rotors overhead. He pointed to the display. "Score one for us. They think she's our getaway wagon."

Looking at the screen from the back seat, Carmody saw bird's-eye GPS images of four vehicles racing in the opposite direction on Bulevardul Dacia—eastbound toward Motorway 1-A North-South.

"We're inside the *polizei*'s fleet tracking network—I hacked their telemetrics a while ago," Fernandez said, sliding a finger over his keyboard's touchpad. Information balloons opened above each vehicle to mark its precise speed and direction. "Three are regular cruisers. But you see the one tagged Camion 2?"

"An SIAS tac truck," Carmody said. "Weren't there two out of police HQ?"

Nodding, Fernandez dragged and zoomed the map. "Looks like the other one's still outside the club," he said. "Hang on, I'm switching to my AI." He paused. "Pickles...give me Percy's live feed. Rear cam."

"Certainly, Jules." A silky female voice.

Kali looked over from beside him. "Pickles," she said. "And Jules."

Fernandez shrugged. "Things tend to get personal for me," he said.

After a second, the overhead street view was replaced by a ground-level HD video stream—the front end of an armored SIAS car speeding over a multilane road in night-vision gray-scale.

"You synched your system with the *polizei*'s," she said.

He nodded. "Full integration—I can cut back and forth like they're one and the same." He glanced at his rearview mirror. "How's Schultzie? We'll need a minute."

Carmody turned toward the wounded man leaning back between him and Dixon. He'd given him the old Pathfinder drug cocktail used to treat injuries in the field: a fentanyl lozenge between his gum and cheek for the pain, a modafinil tablet to keep him as alert as possible. But the drugs were not going to stem his blood loss. He required medical attention—and soon.

"I'm okay," Schultz said weakly, answering for himself. "Just get it on."

Fernandez nodded again. "Pickles," he said. "Code S for Stopper."

III

Percy the driverless minivan bumped onto the 1-A in the rain, veering north at almost eighty-five miles per hour, well in excess of the national speed limit. But the trio of police cruisers in pursuit rapidly gained on her, terse orders blaring out over their public address systems, clearing the lanes of civilian traffic.

Their high-performance engines throbbing, tires splashing through puddles to eat up the blacktop, the chase cars soon came up on their quarry, slicing the two-hundred-yard gap between them in half…then down to seventy-five, fifty, and forty yards. The SIAS tac truck lagged slightly behind, its heavily armed and armored troopers on the boards.

When the cruisers were within thirty yards of the autonomous vehicle, Fernandez, watching at a distance, almost punched his palm in exultation. The Romanian badges were getting close—right where he wanted them.

Concealed under the storage panel of the minivan's cargo section, its microwave pulse jammer was about the size and shape of a large briefcase. Tiny distance sensors in the rear hatch, ranging the lead police car at one hundred fifty feet, actuated a process that first generated, then modulated, and finally transmitted a series of high-energy electromagnetic pulses from the less-than-lethal vehicle stopper's parabolic antenna—each ten-kilowatt pulse two thousand times more powerful than the energy radiated from a cell tower to a phone.

Directed squarely at the cruiser, the pulses penetrated and attacked the electronic control unit that sequenced its engine and fuel lines.

The consequences were instantaneous. The ECU was the police car's electronic brain. Scrambled by the pulses, its electronic system kicked into an automatic reboot sequence, then rebooted again, again and again, killing the engine to stop the car dead in its tracks. Behind it, the second police vehicle skidded wildly into the next lane and sideswiped the third cruiser, which was screaming along parallel to it.

Around them, the smattering of nearby drivers swerved left and right, trying to avoid collisions with the police cars, each other, and the guard rails. Some were unsuccessful. Horns honked and metal crunched.

Bringing up the rear in the rumbling SIAS tac truck, Captain Eduard Stoica remained calm and composed behind the wheel. Behind him in the cab's jump seat, his second-in-command, Sergeant Luca, stared perplexedly out at the messy accident scene ahead.

"What's happened here?" he said. "I don't understand."

Stoica did not answer, but glanced at the helmeted trooper riding shotgun.

"Tell the men to hang on to the rails, Vali," he said to his radioman, who was in the passenger seat beside him. "I'm opening up wide."

Vali nodded. As he communicated with the crew on his headset, Stoica tightened his lips and swung around the jam-up. He did not know what caused the cruisers to suddenly lose their traction, but it was doubtless associated with the miserable road conditions. His own vehicle, however, would not spin out and be so easily shaken off.

More tank than truck, it would stay on course, he told himself, his foot putting pressure on the accelerator.

IV

Howard reentered the operations room, having stepped out to pace the corridor for the third time in less than an hour.

"Somebody tell me we heard from Fernandez," he declared. "No, strike that. I *better* hear it."

Still standing behind Ryder and Ferraro, Abrams turned toward the door. None of them had budged from their positions at the console.

"Sir, I'm sorry," Abrams said. "He's in silent running mode. Our tracker last put him east of the target."

Howard frowned. "How about the autonomous?"

Abrams shook his head. "He's firewalled her. Level-5 stealth."

"So the Romanians can't tap his machine-to-machine."

"That's my guess, sir."

"Meaning we're fucking blocked too."

"Yes, sir."

Howard glanced at the screens. "That souped-up bumper car's loaded with black tech. Gonna be a very bad thing if the Romanians get hold of it."

"Agreed, sir."

"Also won't be good if SAIS learns we're behind tonight's house party," Howard said. "Romanian government intelligence…they'll know or figure it out. Maybe keep a lid on if we stroke 'em. But the *polizei* can be owned."

"I wouldn't argue the contrary, sir."

Howard pulled the pipe from his mouth. "Those bastards pick up Carmody and his boys with the plastic—it's a serious prob-

lem," he went on. "Fernandez being with them takes us way
out of bounds. There are treaties. We're United States Army
and official guests in this country."

"Yes, sir."

The colonel stared at him. "You're full of agreement tonight,"
he said.

"I would say our assessments are in line, sir."

A moment passed. It occurred to Howard that the worst
problem of all would be the Romanians detaining Outlier for
any length of time. Like it or not, she was essential for the res-
toration of sanity back home. *Indispensable.* Morse couldn't have
been clearer about that.

"When I report what happened to Washington and tell them
I authorized it—"

A loud, sharp rap on wall beside the entryway interrupted
him. Turning, he saw Pierce lean into the room. "Colonel? Can
we speak privately?"

Howard noticed he was holding a clipboard with a small
stack of papers, and glanced back around at Abrams. "Keep me
posted," he said.

Once in the corridor, he waited for the door to slide shut behind him. "Okay, what is it?"

"Outlier, sir. The key click captures were perfectly clear. Sub-
audibles and inaudibles," Pierce told him. "It took a little longer
than we expected, but our predictives gave us every word she
typed into her laptop."

Howard motioned to the clipboard. "That a transposition
you got there?"

"Yes, sir. One thing you should know—"

"I'll check it out for myself," the colonel said, snatching the
clipboard from him.

He looked down at the top sheet in the stack for a long moment, reading. Frowned. Flipped to the next sheet, then the one
beneath it, and the one beneath that.

And finally looked back up at Pierce's face.

"What the hell is this?" he said.

"Sir, I was about to tell you…"

"*This* is what she typed?" Howard said. "You sure it's no mistake?"

"Yes," Pierce said. "I'm sure."

Howard returned his eyes to the clipboard. "'And I had done a hellish thing, and it would work 'em woe: For all averred, I had killed the bird, that made the breeze to blow,'" he read slowly, then looked back up at Pierce. "You know what you got here?"

"We didn't at first, sir. But we searched the web…"

"'The Rime of the Ancient Mariner,'" Howard cut in. "That's what you fucking brought me to read."

Pierce exhaled. "Sir," he said, spreading his hands slightly in front of him. "It's what she input."

"'Instead of the cross, the Albatross, about my neck was hung,'" Howard growled. He wasn't reading from the pages this time, but reciting the line from memory. "God*damn* it. She's playing us again."

Pierce stood there at a loss. Howard pushed the clipboard back into his hands, turned toward the operations room…and halted, his shoulders coming up straight.

"It's code," he said, looking around at the sergeant. "You SIGINT geniuses should've figured it out for yourselves."

"Sir, we've barely started our analysis. I wanted to get you the hard copy right away—"

"Well, you can go ahead and give it back to your boys," Howard barked. "Have 'em go over every period, colon, and semicolon. Every word and space. Every *spelling*. And then match what they find against the original poem."

"That's our plan—"

"There's a message in there someplace, Pierce. I want it figured out. And I want to know who it was meant for…catch me?"

Pierce nodded without another word.

"Albatross for shit sure," Howard muttered, and pushed back through the door into ops.

V

"Those tacs are getting too close for comfort," Fernandez said. Watching Percy's video feed on his dash screen, he could see them hot on her tail. "Their truck's gotta be EMP-hardened."

Carmody was thinking the same thing. Microwave pulses needed seams to penetrate a vehicle's body, and the tactical truck's armor shielding would have very few compared to a police car. He doubted the stopper would affect its onboard computer.

"They bag the van, it's trouble, Julio," he said. "Can you give her some separation?"

Fernandez nodded. Where the vehicle's guts weren't vulnerable, its human passengers would be.

"Pickles," he said. "Code L for LIPE. On my command."

"LIPE activated," the AI said. "Powering five seconds, four, three, two...laser fully charged."

The sergeant shifted into Reverse.

"Pickles, acquire target and fire," he said. "Hang tight, everyone."

And, backing out of the alley, he turned toward the eastbound highway leading toward the city's outskirts.

VI

The laser-induced plasma effect weapon, or LIPE, developed to suppress unfriendly parties in otherwise friendly nations, was one of the sweetest plums of the United States military's less-than-lethal arsenal.

Stowed in Percy's rear, it used a fifteen-second burst from a powerful femtosecond laser—the individual pulses of which would last a quadrillionth of a second—to create a ball of plasma, or ionized gas, in the air, and then play around with it.

Plasma did interesting things when subjected to electromagnetic effects. It put the glow into fluorescent and neon lights, and sometimes caused the luminous discharge known as St. Elmo's fire after lightning strikes. Plasma fields also bent and shaped soundwaves passing through them, with measurable, calibrated acoustic frequencies resulting in highly specific tonal oscillations. For that reason, astronomers studying faraway stars and galaxies—which expelled vast amounts of plasma—were able to gain knowledge of their size, density, and life cycles by listening to their songs across the reaches of outer space.

Additionally, charged plasma could have a wide range of effects on living creatures depending on its gaseous concentration, its chemical composition, and the bandwidths of the electrical charge firing through it. In humans, it could raise body temperature, irritate skin, and even make blood vessels contract or dilate.

Creating a plasma ball by zapping the air with a femtosecond laser, then, was the first part of a LIPE's job as a nonlethal contraption. The second part was inducing specific effects by hitting that ball with a *second* finely calibrated nanolaser that could be tuned to one or more wavelengths.

Fernandez thought the LIPE's capacity for manipulating sound and vision was a uniquely imaginative, versatile way to give people fits without killing them, a freaky ray gun set to stun.

As a Trekkie since age twelve, he liked that idea a lot.

VII

"What's that up ahead?" Vali glanced over at Stoica. "My God, what *is* it?"

A huge, strangely glowing blue cloud had appeared fifty or sixty yards in front of them, hovering in midair between the troop truck and the Citroen.

The cloud was like nothing Stoica had seen before in his life. Ten or fifteen feet high, it was strangely bell-shaped, the bottom flat, curving on top, with a central core of intense white light. Swirling snaps of brilliance throughout its misty form reminded him of fireflies or camera flashes…but they were brighter than either. *Blindingly* bright. Despite the rain slashing into it, the cloud held its integrity, hovering motionless above the blacktop like a huge radioactive jellyfish.

Stoica tried to steer around it, but it abruptly grew and expanded, its size doubling in under a second, becoming too large for him to bypass—

"We have to get around that thing!" It was Luca in the jump seat, his tone scaling upward toward panic. "I don't— *Wait!* Do you hear those *sounds*?"

Stoica could indeed hear them as he plowed into the glowing blue mist. High-pitched, overlapping, alternately whining and buzzing, they seemed to come from everywhere at once, sounding like sped-up human voices, but talking in a language he did not speak. He thought them almost, but not quite, intelligible as they spooled around the cab's interior.

Vali clapped his hands over his ears. But they only seemed to grow higher and shriller to him. *"God!"* he cried, unable to block them out. *"They're in my head!"*

"And mine!" Luca howled behind him. *"What are they saying? Can either of you tell what they're saying?"*

Focused on controlling the vehicle, Stoica silently imagined people chattering through heavy static. Not with actual words, but with garbled vocalizations *suggestive* of words.

And then he heard an entirely different noise…men shouting and screaming outside the cab. Caught in the swirling blueness, the dazzled troopers on the platforms had been overcome with fear and bewilderment. Stoica didn't know how long they would last out there.

Stoica felt his cheeks prickle with heat, as if a rash was spreading over his face. He didn't understand what was happening. He didn't understand any of it. But he could no longer command the wheel or himself.

"Warn the men, Vali—I'm stopping!" he exclaimed. But the sergeant sat there gagging and unable to speak, doubled over with nausea, his hands on his stomach.

Stoica could not wait for him to call the alert. He wrenched the wheel to his right, pulled onto the service lane, and braked to a lurching halt.

A moment passed. Vali was still retching violently. Then Luca gestured out the windshield, his arm shooting forward.

"Look!" he exclaimed. "Look around!"

Stoica dragged a sleeve across his eyes to clear them of moisture. The blue cloud was gone, along with the voices…and the damned Citroen. The murdering criminals from Club Energie had slipped the net.

The captain sat staring out the window into the stormswept darkness. He heard Luca breathing hard behind him, heard rain battering the roof of the cab, heard his men scrambling off the platforms, their boots splashing down onto the wet service lane. A car swooshed slowly by, a civilian vehicle, and he let it pass out of his field of vision. He did not care about civilians too idiotic and reckless to stay indoors tonight. He cared only about the escaped fugitives.

Then it struck him. Though he still heard the police chopper, the sound was no longer coming from directly overhead. Nor were its running lights visible above the highway, as a glance out the windshield revealed to him.

He turned to Vali, abruptly restarting the truck. "Wipe the puke off your lap and get me an uplink to the helicopter," he said. "It's still on top of the bastards in that van."

VIII

As Percy swung east off the 1-A onto a gradually curving exit ramp, the SIAS's Hummingbird surveillance-and-pursuit helicopter stayed on her, even in the pouring rain.

A few hundred feet from the motorway, the ramp fed into a large parking area fronting the Cladiu Magazin de Materiale de Constructii—a major supplier of construction materials. It was well past business hours, and the lot was dark, as was the prefab concrete structure housing the store, sawmill, and warehouse at its north end.

After slowly leaving the ramp, Percy coasted to a halt in the approximate middle of the lot. The chopper buzzed low over-head in a standard holding pattern as police sirens and flashing lights converged on the lot from all directions.

First to reach it were eight patrol cars from the Sector 4 Po-lice Station, covering the Vacaresti and Bercini suburbs east of town. Captain Stoica and his tac team arrived next, followed by a light armored personnel carrier also detached from the cordon outside Club Energie.

Within minutes, Percy was encircled by a squadron of over fifty officers and troopers, the latter springing from their ve-hicles to assemble in a tight phalanx. Crouched behind ballistic shields, bearing assault rifles and shotguns, they waited a cautious distance from the minivan, the Hummingbird illuminating the scene from above with its high-intensity spotlights.

As ranking officer, Captain Stoica was quick to take charge. Exiting the cab of the truck, he pushed to the front of his troops, then studied the motionless Citroen through one of the shields.

The van's lights were out, its engine silent. Stoica could see no one and nothing through its tinted windows.

Water streaming down his helmet, his uniform already soaked, he raised a bullhorn to his lips.

"Esti inconjurata—iesiti cu mainile sus!" he hailed. Telling the minivan's passengers they were surrounded, and instructing them to exit with their hands above their heads.

Nothing.

"Iesiti din vehicul!" His voice firm, he gave no hint that his face still crawled from the effects of passing through the inex-plicable blue cloud.

Nothing again.

"You are to exit peacefully or face severe action," he said. *"Extra viti vii.* This is your last chance."

Stoica was not a man who threatened or bluffed. He motioned to a trooper with a shotgun.

"Blast the tires out from under it," he said.

The man nodded. He was perhaps a half second from squeezing the trigger when Percy self-destructed with a thunderous boom heard for miles around, making the issue of shooting out her tires moot.

IX

On the opposite side of Bucharest, Fernandez was driving south on Motorway 1-B aboard the Duster when the minivan blew. While mindful of Schultz's condition, he was trying not to push too far past the speed limit and draw the highway patrol's attention.

He glanced at the hacked night vision image on his dash panel. Flames were rising around the van's blasted wreckage like the petals of a huge flower.

"That's all, folks—she's flushed," he said. "The C-4 charges lit her up good."

Kali nodded in the shotgun seat. "They will have very little of Percy to inspect," she said.

Fernandez glanced over at her.

"They got pieces of a van," he said, winking. "Percy's another thi—"

He broke off, hands on the steering wheel as they rode on through the slashing wind and rain.

"Is something wrong?"

He shrugged. "Nothing," he said. "It just occurred to me that I still don't know your name."

She sat quietly.

"Kali," she said after a moment, raising her voice so everyone in back could hear her clearly. "My name is Kali."

Behind her, Carmody grinned. "Seems we always make these announcements when we're in motion."

She sat back without answering him. But when he lifted his eyes to the rearview mirror, it was right in time to see her smile.

34

I

"First question: Who brought the deck of cards?" said President Annemarie Fucillo. A cup of tea and mobile satphone in front of her, she was at the head of a conference table in the Real Time Crime Center on the second floor of One Police Plaza. "Since there are too many of us for bridge, I think we should stick to poker."

SAC Leo Harris grinned in his chair. "A few beers, I'm good to go," he said.

The President's eyes were tired above her smile. "Sadly, Leo, the best I can offer is Earl Grey or coffee."

A moment passed. Fucillo's gaze moved from her Homeland Security chief, Cliff Parsons, to Harris, briefly came to rest on Vince Dunn, the FBI liaison to the White House, and next went to New York Police Commissioner David Cowans at the far end of the table. Finally, it landed on Adrían Soto to her immediate left.

Farther off on that side of the room were rows of computer workstations, half of them manned by critical NYPD operations techs, the others deserted, cleared of personnel for the meeting. An enormous multipanel wall screen showed the faces and upper bodies of several of its remote participants at hardened communications centers in New York and Washington, DC: New York Mayor Bill Devries at his OEM command post in Brooklyn, and Vice President Stokes, Secretary of Defense Evangeline Waller, and CJCS Bernard Fowler in the White House Situation Room. Professor Alex Michaels was linked in from the triage area two floors below, as were Bryan Ferago and Natasha Mori at the Columbia University HIVE ten miles uptown. Stan Freeman, Soto's Vice President of Operations, was also feeding in remotely from Cognizant's corporate headquarters on Broome Street.

"Before we proceed—and I promise to make this meeting brief—I want to formally introduce Mr. Adrían Soto, the founder and Chief Executive Officer of Cognizant Systems, to the entire group." POTUS nodded in his direction. "Everyone here has surely heard of Adrían and his accomplishments. But I don't know how many of you have had the pleasure of interacting with him." She gave another smile. "I'll reiterate what I told him privately yesterday. He has been an inspiration to me for many years. His innovative IT and tireless public service are a blessing for this country. Moreover, Adrían is as humble and solid a human being as you will ever meet. I knew at once that he would be integral to our recovery efforts after the cyber attack. What I didn't know was that he would immediately make his way downtown, trying to reach his business headquarters through the heat, chaos, and security barricades. Going contrary to the evacuation. He was determined to see that his employees were safe and assist in getting the cellnet operational." She began lightly clapping her hands together. "Thank you, Adrían, for your dedication."

He gave a slight bow of his head as applause spread around the table and rippled from computer speakers.

"Madam President, you're too kind," he said. "It's an honor to be in your great company."

Fucillo sipped her tea as she collected her thoughts.

"Friends, we have a boatload of problems right now. As SAC Harris, Professor Michaels, and Mr. Soto know from a prior huddle, I intend to target one at a time." She checked her wristwatch. "It's now a quarter past ten in the morning EDT. I'm going to repeat here what I told our smaller group yesterday at Alex's bedside. I want secure mobile communications and internet restored to lower Manhattan within forty-eight hours. And I want the lights turned on by *tonight*. At six o'clock this evening, I plan to address the nation from this very room and make it known that New York and America are not only back on their feet, but standing tall. I will also finish the message I was sending out at Zuccotti Park." She paused. "Consider those deadlines fixed—that sound you may hear is me cracking my whip."

Harris looked at her a moment. She had been injured when the stage exploded—he could see the cuts on her face, see how stiffly she was moving, and knew she was in pain. He figured she was also tired, pushed to her mental and physical limit. But for all that, she was a formidable presence.

"Annemarie, I'm smart enough not to argue with you when your mind's set," Parsons said. "But it's a tall order. The reality's that the telecom network and energy grid are full of infection. Far as I know, we still haven't figured out how to decontaminate and lock down those systems. We don't even know what else might be hatching inside them. And say we're able to clean out every trace of the bug. How do we undo the existing damage? Prevent reinfection from other systems that interface with it? This is all just off the top of my head."

Soto flicked his hand up in the air. "I think I can answer some of your questions." He glanced at POTUS. "If I may interject."

She nodded. "Please."

"Madam President mentioned my trip downtown yesterday—
it spanned half the length of Manhattan Island," he said. "I can't
describe the devastation. There were smashed vehicles everywhere. Injured people..." He let the sentence trail. "The 69th
Infantry Regiment had mobilized, of course. That's how I got
here from the park—on a JLTV. There they were, two or three
miles uptown, rolling around just fine. On the way from Central
Park, I noticed my company's sensor pods on the roofs of different vehicles. Some were manned, some weren't. But they're
all upgraded for autonomous robotic driving."

"This might be the time to mention that the Fighting 69th is
the first National Guard unit to trial the drone fleet," said Secretary of Defense Waller on the flatscreen. "We didn't count
on it being field-tested in quite this manner...but so far it's performed up to our highest expectations."

"And there's a reason," Soto said. "Just over a decade ago,
my assignment in Baghdad was to work with them on Route
Irish...our name for the main highway linking the Green Zone
to the international airport."

"The most dangerous stretch of road in Iraq," Waller said.

Soto was nodding. "My CECOM unit was laying communications infrastructure while the 69th ran cover. They were
our pipeline to Baghdad and caught hell from suicide bombers,
IEDs, drive-bys, snipers...those attacks came day and night. The
men took heavy casualties, but they never stopped protecting
us—and delivering equipment and supplies." He tented his hands
on the table. "I never forgot. I kept thinking that some of their
supply runs, *maybe most of them*, could have been unmanned. It
would have cut their losses by sixty percent. So, when I returned
to the States and started up Cognizant, I got my R&D people
working on autonomous fleet technology. One of the basic design requirements was that the system be secured against hostile
takeover, if you will. A cyberattack." Soto looked at Parsons.
"We applied that hardening throughout the system's architec-

ture. Every physical component, all the software, was embedded with Argos."

"Hera's…guardian," Professor Michaels said. "The herdsman with a hundred eyes…"

"Who never sleeps," Soto said. "The system was designed to safeguard against insider and outsider strikes at all times. I probably don't have to explain why we chose the 69th to field the robotic vehicle prototypes. They took good care of my team, and I was glad to return the favor." He turned to Parsons. "We say Argos is system aware, Mr. Secretary. In other words, it monitors the normal processes aboard a vehicle and responds with a battery of self-tests and countermeasures when they deviate from logical operating patterns. And it learns as it goes along. In cases where an attack is merely suspected, Argos will alert the human operator. In extreme cases, it can independently reconfigure the entire system."

"And you think this system can be applied to the telnet?" Parsons said.

"Yes," Soto said. "The 69th's autonomous vehicles have a constant exchange of data with Cognizant's navigational and communication satellites. That's how they orient themselves, adjust to changing road conditions and obstacles, and subsequently find their destinations. We've seen for ourselves that they're completely functional."

"As opposed to almost everything else on the ground," Fucillo said. "And in the air."

"Uh… Mr. Soto, sir? Can I ask a question?"

This came over the speakers from Bryan Ferago. Soto turned toward the multidisplay.

"Yes," he said. "Please."

"I read about Argos. I mean, I understand how it works— you're one of my gurus."

"Thank you," Soto said, smiling. "Compliment taken."

Ferago tugged at the wisp of beard on his chin. "Tasha and I…we think what makes the Frankenbug so tough is that it acts exactly like Argos, except on the *dark side* of the Force. It can't outsmart the system, and isn't even exactly an artificial intelligence. But it has coded survival tactics that can fool whatever we throw at it."

"We don't know where the bug came from, where it's hiding, or how it's capable of mutating," said Mori. "The fact is, we really don't know all that much about it. But we have to assume it will shapeshift even as Argos adapts. Then Argos will have to readapt. And on and on." A pause. "Mr. Soto, I'm guessing the robot trucks and Jeeps avoided infection because they're part of a closed system. That's part of your security protocol, correct?"

Soto nodded. "Right," he said. "There's no charging cell phones or music and video streaming in autonomous-capable vehicles. We worked with the army on giving their operators a full education on internet security and put strict guidelines in place to reinforce what they learn. Argos is a powerful immune system. But if it's constantly exposed to unprotected gadgets and files, it's going to be compromised."

"So, let's say Argos purges the Frankenbug from the cellnet, the electrical grid, or both," Mori said. "Unless we figure out how to isolate the bug in other systems...inoculate the digital infrastructure against it...someone with a dirty phone or robot vacuum cleaner's gonna contaminate it all over again. And the truth is we're really talking thousands of somebodies. Maybe hundreds of thousands."

"All valid points," Soto said. "But there are two things to keep in mind. First, we're broadcasting right from this room, and its systems appear clean precisely because of the hardening and safe practices I mentioned. Second, I'm making sure we get the electrical substations to the area online in a matter of hours... and that will give us light." He paused. "Will it be it possible to rid the cellular phone network of the bug in a day or two? No, I don't think so. But Mr. Freeman and I have a plan for restoring mobile communications *without* the cellnet. One I'm certain will fall within Madam President's deadline."

Fucillo's eyes went quickly around the table. "Adrían already shared his idea with me, and I think it's brilliant," she said. "He—"

Her satphone's ringtone interrupted the sentence. She silenced it by answering.

"Hello…yes…can it wait? I—" Her eyebrows arched. "Okay, hold on," she said after a moment. "I have to take this right now."

Moving slowly, Fucillo pushed herself up from her seat and turned toward the workstations across the room.

II

"All right, I'm alone," she said, lowering herself into one of the empty cubicles. "I was in a meeting. With your ex in attendance."

"You've told him?"

"Not yet." Fucillo adjusted herself in the chair with a slight grimace. Her burned leg was throbbing miserably, and she'd made a conscious effort not to let anyone see her limp. "Back to what you told me a minute ago. I want to confirm I heard it correctly."

Carol Morse took an audible breath. "Our coverts ran into trouble," she said. "Base just informed me. They were able to break away. But there were fireworks. The local authorities became involved."

Fucillo frowned. She had approved the Bucharest operation on Carol's endorsement. She was not about to second-guess herself—or her top operations officer—but certainly this was not what she wanted to hear.

"How did it happen?"

"I don't have the details."

"Janus didn't inform you?"

"Our conversation lasted roughly thirty seconds," Carol said.

Fucillo sighed. "If there's more bad news, you better share it."

"An army regular participated in the op. He likely wasn't discovered. But we lost a vehicle loaded with black tech."

"Did the locals get hold of it?"

"Negative. I'm told it was scuttled."

Fucillo took a moment to digest all that. Morse's people had conducted an operation of highly questionable legality, and the army's participation was an outright breach of faith with the Romanians.

"We use that country as a transit hub, refuel our aircraft at their bases for missions in Central Asia, even train our expeditionary forces there. They give us a tremendous level of cooperation that this can seriously jeopardize."

"Yes, I understand."

"And the regular...why even send one on the mission?"

"I don't know the answer. But I will."

POTUS frowned, thinking. A break-in involving an American soldier, along with a fugitive from international law enforcement...it was a sticky affair. She could only be grateful they weren't caught. "Was the operation successful?" she asked.

"Also TBD," Carol said. "I expect to have more for you very soon."

Fucillo thought some more. Birhan, Zuccotti, and now this latest plateful of trouble. The dominoes kept falling.

"Your people will have to be pulled out. Returned stateside. I don't want our Romanian friends sniffing them out as ours."

A pause.

"It's a whopping ask...but I would urge they be given more rope," Morse said. "There's still work to be done in-country."

"*An ask?* Is that how you characterize it?"

"I think I used the word *whopping*."

Fucillo sighed, looking across the room at the conference table. She wanted to conclude her meeting before the painkillers wore off.

"I'll consider it," she said. "No guarantees."

"Thank you."

Fucillo thought a moment.

"On the subject of our ex, I like him," she said. "He's tough. No-nonsense. I get a good feeling."

"Yes."

"That's exactly the kind of man I want."

A brief silence on the line.

"I can relate," Carol said.

III

"Agent Harris, if you please," President Fucillo said. "I'd like to discuss something before you go."

Harris and Adrían Soto were walking toward the RTCC's elevator bank when she called out to Leo from the conference table. He had started to bring Soto up to snuff on the Bureau's probe into the Unity Foundation theft. Although the Zuccotti attack appeared to have pushed it off the board—and *only* something of that magnitude could ever sideline an investigation into a fifty-million-dollar online heist—he increasingly thought the crime linked to the party or parties behind the strike.

"Paged by the Pres," Leo said, pausing halfway to the elevators. He hesitated. "Mr. Soto?"

"Adrían. Please."

"We'll get whoever robbed you, Adrían," Harris said. "I promise."

Soto looked at him.

"Thank you," he said. "But hundreds died yesterday, and I'm blessed with my life. A chance to help...that's my priority right now."

And that was that. Seconds later, Harris was back in his chair next to the President, only the two of them left in the room.

"I'll make this brief," Fucillo said. "You have a lot on your plate."

Harris looked at her. "You're the Commander in Chief," he said. "Kind of puts my plate on your table."

She smiled. He could faintly discern a dark row of stitches through the adhesive bandage above her left eyebrow, a jagged scab at one corner of her lip, smaller nicks and scratches on her

cheeks and forehead. She was pretty badly knocked around…
but not knocked out.

"So," she said. "What do you think of Mr. Soto's plan?"

"I'll say he's a genius. Besides being a saint."

Fucillo nodded.

"Agent, I haven't properly expressed my gratitude for your
actions yesterday," she said. "Your quick actions saved my life.
As if that wasn't enough, you pursued the bomber for a number
of blocks without concern for yourself. I don't know how others define heroism. But I think the shoe fits."

He looked uncomfortable. "I was doing my job," he said.
"That's it."

Fucillo began reaching out for the teakettle and abruptly
stopped, her arm falling to her side. Harris did not let on that
he'd noticed her repressing a wince. He reached for the kettle,
poured, moved the cup and saucer closer to her.

She took a sip. "Cold," she said. "But it's something."

He gave a small smile.

"Agent Harris, I'll get to the point," she said. "About your
job… I want you to consider a new position. Titles aren't my
forte, but for now we'll label it Director of Cyber Investigations,
Net Force. You will head an organizational branch with global
reach and resources and answer only to Professor Michaels. I'll
give you discretion to hire whoever you want. That's without
exception, up and down the ladder. What do you think?"

He looked at her, momentarily at a loss.

"Agent Harris?"

"Sorry, I'm trying to convince myself this is for real," he said.
"Carol…my ex…well, you *know* her…she's been pushing me to
consider a move to Net Force. But it's always been *when* there's
a Net Force. And I never thought it would happen for sure, or
be this *kind* of move." He paused. "What makes you think I'm
your man? I mean, I don't even use email if I can avoid it. Carol
must've told you. And yesterday was a wild day, but it doesn't
qualify me for—"

"I would not base my offer on yesterday alone, Agent." Fucillo's eyes were sharp. "I've done my due diligence. You're my first choice. And I'm hoping I won't have to go to a fallback."

Leo inhaled. He released his breath slowly, letting the moment sink in.

"Madam President," he said, not quite feeling the chair underneath him. "You got yourself a top cyber dog."

IV

The Hagar petroleum refinery at Port Birhan was quiet at midnight. It was the stillness after a storm.

Quiet, *quieter* than it had been for weeks. A silence punctuated only by the rhythmic hum of the facility's half-dozen multiacre pumping stations, all with three pumps, each of them a huge cylindrical tube driven by a five-thousand-horsepower motor the size of a pickup truck.

Connecting the unmanned stations were the pipelines. These ran aboveground; the corrosive saline aquifer ran too near the surface along the coast to allow for any subterranean pipes.

Around the pumping stations and pipelines were a galaxy of support structures: electrical substations, prefabricated storage buildings. At a somewhat greater distance, concrete operations centers housed computer banks that monitored and remotely controlled the pumps.

Designed and installed by civilian engineers, the operations centers were now manned by Ansari Kem's elite Red Berets. Although the troopers lacked the training and experience of the slaughtered workers, Kem viewed this as a trifle in the short term. Since the vast majority of the refinery's processes were automated, the guards were primarily tasked with patrolling the facilities until permanent replacements could be hired and trained from among his own Ja'alin tribal majority. In the interim, the Foreign Minister saw no reason to expect that the refinery's production would be slowed or interrupted. Barring an unprecedented catastrophe, he expected the machines would handle themselves.

It was something he later came to view as his greatest miscalculation.

V

The takeover began at two minutes past midnight, with an undetected failure of the air-cooled heat exchangers inside all three motors at the pumping station PS-1.

Slowly, the motors overheated, their internal temperatures soaring until their rubber hoses and drive belts melted. It all led to their rapid shutdown.

As the powered pumps went offline, the monitoring system designed to alert the operations center personnel remained silent. There were no audible signals through what should have been mounting alert levels, no visual warnings on the computer displays...nothing to suggest that the station had crashed. The Red Berets on overnight shift at the OC neither saw nor heard anything out of the ordinary.

Within seconds, a second station, PS-2, went down after the pump motors succumbed to blistering internal temperatures. At nearly the same moment, station PS-3 was lost, again without any of the routine indicators. Inside the affected pipelines, thousands upon thousands of gallons of heavy crude ceased to flow, blocking and backing up oil that continued to be routed toward the pumps from working stations.

By 1:00 a.m., this backflow began to create a highly dangerous pressure buildup within the pipelines. Meanwhile, the three pumping stations still in operation maintained their steady output, boosting oil through the lines at a rate of almost three million gallons an hour.

The pressure in the pipes mounted. Exponentially.

It was shortly after two in the morning when the quiet over the refinery was shattered by the roar of crumpled steel, a segment of pipeline near PS-1 bursting at its seams to spray a geyser of crude tarry oil hundreds of feet into the darkened sky.

A quarter of a mile away at the nearest operations center, the overnight watch detail of twenty-five Red Berets was jolted by the sound of the blast. Drawn outside the facility by the thundering noise, the troopers were sickened by a wave of rancid, sulfurous air from the violently released bitumen.

The second pipeline burst within seconds approximately a hundred yards from PS-3, where one of the disabled pump motors caught fire. As the spill pooled around the burning motor, it quickly ignited, spreading flames from the ruptured pipes to the jetting oil. Moments later, the fuel turned into a tower of flame that lit up the night sky for miles around.

Captain Faaris Abdo, the ranking officer and commander of the Hagar Guard, was in a restroom at PS-3's operations center when the two pipe explosions sent tremors throughout the refinery grounds. Whistling a favorite tune at the urinal, he jumped in startled surprise, the melody on his lips abruptly cut short.

Abdo raced over to the primary monitoring room to find the men on guard staring at the banks of computer displays with stunned incomprehension. Their backs to the door, the troopers were too baffled by what they saw to notice him.

Moving toward their consoles, he shot a glance at the screens...

And that was when the music boomed from the computer speakers, stopping him halfway and shocking the troopers off their chairs and running heedlessly toward the entrance.

The captain stood gaping at the screens for a long moment, his bones seeming to pulsate from the music's terrific volume.

Then he spun back toward the door, fleeing the room as if Satan's very fanfare had sounded within.

VI

Leo Harris snapped his eyes open. It took a second or two before he realized he was on his office couch at 26 Federal Plaza.

Then the rest came back to him in a rush. Blue Suit, Zuccotti...and his private conversation with the President of the United States.

Director of Cyber Operations, Net Force.

The title seemed almost unbelievable. And made him unbelievably *proud.*

He sat up, and ran his fingers through his hair. He must have walked over from One Police Plaza at—what time? One, one thirty, he guessed. He'd gone to his office for a fifteen-minute siesta, feeling at once exhausted and overwhelmed.

A glance at his wristwatch, and Harris realized it was almost four o'clock. How did fifteen minutes turn into almost *three hours?*

He stood up and got a spare blazer from his closet. *Coffee,* he thought. He would go into the kitchen, drop a pod into the brewer, and have a badly needed cup. Then hurry back to 1PP so he could be there for Fucillo's address to the nation.

Shrugging into the blazer, he went over to the door and opened it.

Ki Marton was standing out in the hall, a file folder in one hand, the other raised to knock.

"Ki?"

"Sir."

"What the hell are you doing here?"

The ASAC cleared his throat. "Working," he said.

Leo looked at him through the doorway. "You could have stayed home," he said. "In case you need to take care of things."

Ki took a deep breath. "There's nothing for me at home, sir. This is where I can be useful."

Harris was quiet. He hadn't seen Ki since before his partner's death, and only got the news from his sub.

"I'm sorry about what happened to Mark," he said, shutting the door.

"Thank you, sir."

"It stinks."

"Yes, sir. It does."

Harris looked at him a second or two. "You holding up okay?"

"I suppose," Ki said. Then shrugged. "I only wish I'd been at the hospital."

Harris was quiet again, thinking about how to answer. "He lived with an FBI agent," he said. "Trust me, he understood."

Ki swallowed.

"Yes, sir," he said. "And thanks."

Harris nodded, pointed to the file folder. "What've you got for me?"

Ki glanced at the folder as if he forgot he was holding it. "I decided to check into something," he said. "Those laminates you recovered from the bomber...they actually came from two separate places. The John Rainey StageWorks tag is a forgery. A very good one, but a counterfeit nevertheless. The VIP credential's different. Authentic."

Harris raised an eyebrow. "Wait a sec," he said. "It can't be real. Rainey's a strawman. He doesn't exist."

"Except in the Office of the Police Commissioner's database," Ki said. "It went offline yesterday when the power failed, but they were able to get it back up about an hour ago. At least, long enough for me to get into it."

"So, who put Rainey in the system?" he said.

"The database was obviously hacked," he said. "That credential is loaded with security features. It has a 3D seal, microprinting, and other design elements that make it almost impossible to fake."

Harris's forehead creased in thought. "The tag got him past the checkpoints," he said. "And into the parking areas."

Ki nodded. "It's SOP for guests to submit their names in advance. If they're okayed, they're placed on a list from which the laminates are made up and distributed well beforehand." He paused. "There's an accompanying tag that goes on their vehicles. With bar codes that are scanned on arrival."

"What else?"

"The official parking facility for the Zuccotti event was an indoor garage on Worth and Hanover," Ki said. "There were some other street side parking areas, primarily for technical and security vehicles. But everyone else who arrived by car had to leave it in that garage."

Leo's eyes widened. "You found Rainey's *car*?"

Ki nodded. "A Tesla Model Y."

"And you're telling me it's still there."

"Yes," Ki said. "Ironically, it's the cars with high-end onboard computer systems that have been knocked out of commission. And even if they're roadworthy, the area's almost completely cordoned off to traffic."

"There's nowhere for them to go."

"Exactly, sir." Ki held out his folder. "I have all the information hard-copied here. I also sent it to you via email. But without data service, I'm positive you didn't receive it."

Harris took the folder from his hand. "Good work," he said.

Ki nodded.

"Damn good."

Ki nodded again.

Harris looked at him.

"Now stop fucking around and get back to it," he said.

VII

President Annemarie Fucillo stood waiting in the wings as the TV technicians finished setting up their lights, cameras, and boom mikes for her broadcast. She had written her speech herself and it wasn't difficult...well, aside from her inability to settle on an opening line, which was nothing new. But she wanted to communicate a clear and straightforward declaration that she, the United States of America, and all those representing a civilized world would not be intimidated or overwhelmed. That they would bear their losses in their minds and hearts, pull together, and stand tall.

In the end, her message was that simple.

They would stand tall.

Fucillo looked across the room at her selected backdrop—the mosaic wall of flatscreen displays.

It was ideal.

"Madam President?"

She turned to the tech standing beside her. "Yes?"

"We're set for a run-through," he said. "We'll need to get you miked and do some checks."

Fucillo looked at him quietly. "That's fine." She noticed the name on his laminates. "Your name is John Kennedy?"

The tech nodded. "He was my grandparents' favorite."

"Mine too," Fucillo said. "'Let us explore what problems unite us…'"

"'…instead of belaboring those problems which divide us.'"

They smiled at each other a moment.

"I can hardly believe we just did that," he said.

Fucillo's smile broadened.

"John, you've inspired me," she said, and strode toward the television lights.

VIII

In the rear cockpit of his Kazan Mil-Mi-17 helicopter, National Minister Ansari Kem stared down at the blazing refinery fields. He'd left his residence on the Red Sea after being awakened with news of the pandemonium, compelled to view the evidence with his own eyes.

Over the past three hours, the vast Hagar complex had gone into a complete shutdown, its automated pump systems crashing, its pipelines opening to release their flow of crude. Three of its stations were on fire.

It was a far worse disaster than anything caused by the protests, and Kem was convinced it would take months, if not years, to recover. The cost of repairs and new equipment, the vanished oil revenues…the total loss was incalculable.

He closed his eyes, massaging them with his palm. The music blasting from the refinery's computers…the French national anthem, "La Marseillaise"…

What did it all mean? Who could have struck at the refinery with an attack of such tremendous sophistication?

There must be something that would hint at an answer. Some sort of *clue*…

Kem breathed. His hand dropping from his eyes, he abruptly leaned forward to speak to his pilot. "Make for the capitol," he said. "I've seen everything I need to see here."

The pilot nodded and banked eastward.

As the helicopter left the burning fields, Kem took a final look out his window and then reclined in his bucket seat, turning his gaze from the fires below.

His face tensed.

Reflected in the windscreen's glass, the flames seemed to spin round and round in the night up ahead with a fury that would not be outdistanced.

IX

The moment he heard about the abandoned Tesla, Leo Harris knew he wouldn't be waiting till after President Fucillo's address to check it out. Nor would he delegate the task to any of his agents. But he wanted to hear the speech, and asked Ki to set him up with a dedicated audio channel so he could listen in.

Reaching the garage around a quarter to six, he found a contingent of black-clad and body-armored NYPD SpecOps police guarding its entrance—the scene having somehow fallen under their bailiwick after all the jurisdictional issues were sorted out.

"Okay if I look at one of the vehicles?" Harris said, showing his creds to the officer in command. "If I gotta take anything out of it, I'll let you know."

The cop looked up at him. "No problem," he said. "All the keys are in the parking booth."

"The attendant around?"

"Nope," the cop said. "We cleared the guy to leave this morning."

Leo nodded, walked up the ramp, and entered the vacant

booth. There was a large metal key cabinet on the wall, a clock above it, a desk holding a computer, and a rolling office chair. The computer was either off or idling, and he tapped its keyboard. It awakened at once, the words GOD IS NOT WILLING TO DO EVERYTHING floating on the monitor.

Up but not running, he thought.

He turned to the cabinet, opened the door, and saw three partitions of fobs—most of them keyless—hanging from strips of numbered hooks. Most weekdays the garage would have been filled to capacity, with five or six hundred cars pulled into it. Now Harris guessed there were no more than a hundred, hundred fifty, all left here since the day of the Zuccotti event, when the spots were reserved for politicians and other notables...including the top-level StageWorks people.

That would make things more manageable for him.

He scanned the first partition, didn't see any Tesla fobs, and then flipped it to look at the other side.

"All right," he said under his breath.

He was looking at the fobs to two different Teslas, one on hook 15 and other on 68. Leo glanced through the booth's window and saw that the spaces marked with the lowest numerals were on the ground level.

He slipped on his evidence gloves, took both fobs off the hooks, shut the cabinet, and then suddenly noticed the clock above it. It was 6:00 p.m. on the dot...he'd lost track of time.

Reaching for his comm control, he tuned to the dedicated frequency Ki set for POTUS's address.

"—fellow citizens of America and the world, if I may borrow a phrase from John F. Kennedy...'let us begin anew,'" Fucillo was saying. "Less than forty-eight hours ago, I stood in this great city of New York...a short distance from my present location...expressing my awe at being able to communicate with so many over the global computer network we call the internet. And while some sought to shatter our unity, they have only reminded us that the Space must be protected for all..."

Leo strode between rows of vehicles. The first Tesla was nosed into a spot on his left about ten yards from the entrance ramp. But he could tell at a glance it was one of the older models... made before Blue Suit's Model Y went into production.

Just to be on the safe side, he checked out its license plates, comparing them to the plate numbers he'd entered into his smartphone's notepad. When they didn't match, he moved on, walking up the ramp to the next level.

"...I speak of internet security, not only for Americans, but for people everywhere in the world. I speak of cyberspace as a tool for peace and understanding even as we too often see it used as the new face of war. This is not about opposing governments, and drawing territorial lines. It's about the growing connection of humanity across the planet..."

Leo found spot 68 toward the rear on the second level, and immediately identified the car occupying it. Parked between a Mercedes and a huge Cadillac SUV, the sleek silver Tesla's plate numbers corresponded to Ki's info.

He felt something inside him. It didn't have a name, or at least a name he knew. Other agents talked about the thrill of the hunt. He got what they meant, but that wasn't part of his makeup. Not a big part anyway. For him it was the work. Figuring out where to look for clues, and then finding them...and knowing that when he found them, it would bring him a step closer to taking down the bad guys.

"The lives lost in the cyberattack haven't yet been counted. But we draw hope from the fact that just two days later, we have already begun to recover through the combined efforts of many good, selfless men and women..."

Still wearing his evidence gloves, Leo pressed the fob button to unlock the driver's door, opened it, and leaned over the front seat to inspect the interior of the car.

He saw nothing distinctive except that it looked very new. The upholstery was immaculate and in perfect condition. The same was true for the dash, door handles, and other surfaces. There were none of the items people would sometimes leave inside their vehicles—no phone chargers, empty coffee cups, nothing.

Could be it was a high-end lease or rental, he thought. Or maybe its owner was just neat. Or just didn't drive it around a lot.

"…over the past twenty-four hours, Adrían Soto, chief officer of Cognizant IT Systems, has worked with regional electricity providers to restore power to lower Manhattan—and we expect to have it back at seventy-five percent capacity by sundown. Tomorrow morning, Cognizant will be distributing fifty thousand pristine satellite phones, originally earmarked for the military, to New Yorkers without terrestrial cellular service. These phones will be free and unblocked until the cellnet is back online…"

"Way to go," Leo said to himself. Pulling his head from inside the car, he straightened and went around back. The Tesla's rear bumper was almost flush against the garage's concrete wall guards, so he moved between it and the adjacent SUV, popped the trunk, and lifted it open.

He saw the body at once—and then was nearly overcome by the sickening odor. The man's head was half gone, his arms and legs folded at haphazard angles. There was blood all over his face and clothes, soaking the trunk liner underneath him.

His eyes wide, Leo noticed the corpse was dressed in some kind of uniform…and then saw the embroidery on his breast pocket:

HANOVER STREET PARKING

The attendant around?
Nope. We cleared the guy to leave this morning. Haven't seen him since.
"Shit," Leo husked.
And tilted his head intently.
He'd heard something. A faint click somewhere inside the Tesla.
His pulse quickening, he let go of the trunk lid and turned to get the hell out of there.
Ten seconds later, the car bomb detonated with a roar that fractured the evening.

X

"These phones will be free and unblocked until the cellnet is back online," President Fucillo said, barely needing to read from the 'prompter. The rest of what she had to say was nothing fancy—yet from the heart. "Soon I will again speak to you about my Net Force initiative. Our freedom is inseparable from our cybersecurity, and creative new approaches are needed to ensure that the internet stays open and safe...a tool for our knowledge and enlightenment, not a weapon for those who would threaten freedom and peace.

"To my fellow citizens, and our friends around the world... thank you, good night, and may God bless America."

With a firm smile into the camera, she stood waiting for a cue from the young female technician serving as her floor manager. The tech's hand cut across her throat, and there it was—her signal the telecast had ended.

Fucillo expelled a breath. Her leg had been hurting badly for the last couple of minutes, and she was eager to find a chair.

She was moving toward one when the small crew broke into unexpected applause, all of them standing up, adding cheers to the mix as they clapped their hands. The ovation instantly spread around the room to her detachment of Secret Service agents—including Agent Day, who joined the group while the cameras were on.

Surprised and pleased, Fucillo paused there behind the lights and equipment, her eyes moving around the room.

"Well," she said. "This is quite a lovely sigh—"

The explosion killed the sentence before it finished leaving her lips. Coming from outside the building, somewhere out in the night, it shocked everyone in the room into silence.

Fucillo turned to Day with a terrible feeling of déjà vu.

"What was that?" she said.

The Secret Serviceman looked at her in mute silence, the stunned expression on his face his only answer.

EPILOGUE

New York/Paris
August 19, 2023

I

"I still don't get why we needed to buy two fucking twelve-packs of water," Cris Walek said to his brother, puffing sweatily as he dropped his on the table. "We got forty bucks left to our names, we spend ten on water at a ripoff bodega. What's the sense?"

Tony set his pack down beside it and wiped his brow with his arm. "I told you already," he said. "How many times you want me to repeat myself?" He glanced across the room. "And by the way, weren't you supposed to leave a window open in here?"

Cris nodded. "Right," he said. "I did."

"Oh yeah?" Tony nodded his chin at the windows. "Take a look around."

Cris turned toward the wall facing the alley. Their room at Carla's Short-term Rentals in East Harlem—where they had been lying low since that mess with the Ilescus at the Romanian restaurant—only offered a pair of fire-escape windows, and both were, in fact, shut.

"I don't get it," he said. "I swear to God I left one open."

"I'd cut the swearing, if I were you," Tony said. "Bad enough *I* know you're full of shit. Now God knows too."

Cris stared at him a moment, and flapped a hand in the air.

"Look…what's the difference anyway?" he said. "I still want to hear why we actually paid money for water when it's free from the sink."

Tony produced a monumental exhalation.

"We paid, Cris, because it's like an oven in here and I don't want to roast to death," he said. "And because the water from that sink tastes like it's piped in straight from a toilet bowl. And because we're stuck in this dump until all the heat dies down over the white plastic. Which might be *never*, considering what we know about the Ilescus, and how they're connected to Koschei the fucking Russian-who-never-dies—"

Cris made a slicing gesture. "I don't wanna talk about him," he said.

"You're the one who changed the subject from the window," Tony said. "In case you forgot, *I just* wanted to know why you left it shut."

Cris frowned. "We're back to that, fine," he said. "I'm tellin' you, man, I opened it before we left for the bodega to…"

He let the sentence fade. There had been noise outside the door. A faint scuffling of feet in the hallway…or so he thought.

"You hear something?" he said.

Cris looked at him. "I dunno," he said. "Maybe."

"Maybe? Whattya mean *maybe*?"

Cris's eyes were enormous. "I mean…maybe."

Tony stared at the door and listened, saying nothing. The *downstairs* door weighed a ton and had a big metal guard plate around the lock. In this neighborhood, with all the crime, you needed that kind of heavy-duty protection; nobody was getting through that front entrance without making a loud racket.

Their door, though, was another story. The door, and their windows. Anybody wanting to get into their room could have climbed the fire escape from downstairs, come in through the open window…and closed it.

Which, he thought, would make the room a trap… Chris turned to his brother.

"Tony," he said. "I feel really cold."

Tony looked at him.

"Me too," he said.

He heard the sound again now. Just out in the hallway. Then another noise, a low spitting *hiss*. The door rattled slightly on its hinges…and opened a crack, its lock shot out.

And then the door opened wider, and the silenced gun fired again, twice, into the room.

II

"Par ici! J'ai un taxi!"

Stella Vasile was outside the dance/stim club Porte Écarlate amid the row of scorching-hot nightspots on Rue de la Roquette when she heard Gabriel—or was it Delmar?—calling from a few yards to her right. A glance in his direction, and she saw him pull open the door of a taxi with a flashing green LED sign on its roof.

Stella turned to join him, but took only a single hurried step before her stilettos got caught on the pavement. She might have taken a hard stumble if not for a strong hand grabbing hold of her arm.

"Facil le fait, belle." It was her second handsome boy from the club… Delmar. Or was it Gabriel? His hands encircled her waist, bracing her. "Easy does it. You might want to take off that other shoe too."

Other? What was he talking about?

Confused, Stella looked down at herself and realized she was wearing only a single pump. It was on her left foot; her right was bare on the sidewalk.

She frowned. Where was the absent shoe?

She remembered through the fog in her head. It was moments ago, when someone stole a taxi from her. She was stepping out of the club with her two boys, her arm outstretched to hail it.

But as the cab pulled over, a couple raced in front of her and scrambled inside. The driver was already angling back into the street when she angrily hurled her shoe at his vehicle.

Her boy was absolutely right. She could not walk in one high-heeled shoe.

Clinging to his muscular shoulder now, Stella slid her foot out of the remaining pump, and once again almost took a spill onto the sidewalk. Perhaps she'd gone a bit hard on the vodkas tonight. But thankfully, he was as gallant as he was good-looking.

"Authorize moi," he said. "Come on—let's hurry before more taxi thieves steal our ride."

Seconds later, Stella was sliding into the cab between Gabriel and Delmar—their order still uncertain. Was Gabriel the bearded one? Or the one with the diamond hoops in his ears? She wasn't sure. Nor was she certain that she had given them her name, or even *a* name...or that either of them asked for it. But what did it matter? She only wanted to know their bodies. Both of them, together. It would be something new for her, a fantasy indulged.

Excited about the prospect, she gave their driver the address of her Airbnb in the Seventh Arrondissement, and snuggled in between her new friends as the cab swept east through the city.

"We should pick up some champagne on the way," she said, fishing her smartphone out of her purse. "I know a twenty-four-hour liquor shop on the Rue Noilet—Le Vin C'est la Vie."

The boy on her right glanced over her shoulder, watching her place the order on her app.

"An entire case of Krug Grande Cuve?" he said, surprised.

"Relax!" Stella laughed. "The lady is treating tonight!"

III

Her head swimming, Stella stared vacantly at the taxi's backseat television as it halted in front of the liquor shop and her two handsome boys—Gabriel and whomever, she forgot right now—jumped out. Though August was far from over, autumn weather had made an early arrival across the continent, and the cabbie was not even running its air-conditioner. Instead, the driver kept his windows halfway down to admit the breeze.

Stella felt its cool on her cheeks and sat up a little. She wanted no part of the neurotech at Porte Écarlate, and could have happily done without *any* reminders of cy-modding, though they were impossible to escape these days. Nevertheless, she sampled many other great things, legal and illegal, in the club's backrooms tonight. If pressed to reveal the substances floating through her bloodstream, she would have found it impossible to list them…and it was funny, very funny, because she was never like that in New York. In all her nightclubbing there, she set her limit at a few drinks, and never popped or snorted anything. What made Paris so different? Or was it Paris that made her feel different? Or that something might be different about *her*?

A sigh escaped her lips. As far as New York…the television in front of her was tuned to *France Vingt-quatre*, the state news station, and of course most of it was centered around the business at Zuccotti Park with the American President. Nearly a month later and it still dominated the headlines. If it wasn't that, it was Net Force, and Cybernation, and Birhan…and suddenly, this past week, as if things weren't gloomy enough, the Russians entering the mix.

Stella had done her best to block it all out since coming to Paris, and part of it was to avoid watching the news. All she wanted was to forget about her old city, forget the rest of the world. Just show the boys her bed, and spend the rest of the weekend rocking it off its posts.

Eager for them to return to the cab, she reached forward to change the channel—and paused with her finger hovering over the channel button. The chyron at the bottom of the screen read:

ROMANIE: NOUVEAUX DÉTAILS EMERGE
À PROPOS DE TIRS DE CLUB DE DANSE

The video showed Club Energie—Gustave Zolcu's place in Bucharest. Her eyes widened. Zolcu, a glorified pimp, was one of her least favorite people…but *what* shootings?

Her fingertip went from the channel button to the volume control. Turning it up, she listened to the French broadcaster give a bare summary of a July shooting at the club, a multiple homicide, and the highly secretive police investigation surrounding it. New information about the victims' identities was being disseminated by officials in the hopes of finding the perpetrators, he explained.

"...suspected members of a northern Romanian cybercrime network commonly known as the *technologie vampiri*...based in Satu Mare," the broadcaster was saying.

The rest of his words did not register with her. Her ears seemed dead.

The television was flashing what appeared to be a driver's license photo of her brother.

"Emil," she mouthed silently. Her voice, too, refused to work. "Emil."

Feeling a claw slice through the center of her heart, Stella snatched at her door handle with trembling fingers.

IV

"She didn't say a word," the cabbie told the woman's two companions. He was standing outside his car moments after she fled into the darkness. "She just opened her door and ran out."

The bearded man stood on the sidewalk holding the case of champagne. He looked up and down the rows of terraced buildings along the darkened street. "Where did she go?"

"I have no idea." The driver shrugged and held up her shoe. "She left this on the floor in back."

"Like Cinderella," said the one with the earrings.

The bearded man looked at him. The carton was getting heavy. "Is that how the story goes?"

"Yes," he said. "Her chariot turns into a pumpkin, and the horses change into mice. The driver too."

"*Merde,*" the driver said. "Don't either of you think *I'll* be a goddamned mouse about collecting my fare."

The man with the beard ignored him. "And the girl?" he asked his friend. "What does she become?"

"Maybe something good," he said. "Or something terrible." A shrug. "Sorry, I forget, I'm stoned as hell."

The men stood silently a moment. Then the bearded man hefted the carton in his hands. "So," he said. "What will we do with all this bought-and-paid-for bubbly?"

The one with the earrings shrugged again.

"Find some other girl to share it with us—and hope *her* magic can outlast the night," he said.

V

Launched from deep in the Birhanese desert, the two Spirit III microdrones glided over the Hagar fields, dipping up and down between altitudes of three and five hundred feet. Each little crab-shaped VTOL flew silently on four brushless rotors, its omnidirectional nighttime video camera gathering high-definition images of the refinery's flaming pumps—and of the Red Beret troopers pouring from OCs around the complex.

Embedded with time and date stamps, as well as precise geographic coordinates for their targets, the digital video was transmitted to their remote operators in the desert and routed to a complex network of VPN servers for storage in a secure cloud vault...

For storage, and for real-time observation.

Some forty-five hundred miles away, in Paris, a pair of eyes watched the Hagar shutdown from behind lightweight Bluetooth smartglasses. Deep in his immersive reality environment, the wearer of the glasses felt as if he was flying with the Spirits—and in a sense, he was.

Liberté pour l'humanité, he thought. Liberty for humanity.

This was a night to be marked, a night to remember. On the eve of its emergence, Cybernation—the world's first *virtual* nation—had struck a blow to the enemies of that liberty...

One that would change everything for all time to come.

★ ★ ★ ★ ★